EDGE OF
RESURRECTION

James Sullivan

TOTAL
PUBLISHING
AMERICA

www.TotalPublishingAndMedia.com

ISBN: 978-1-63302-296-6

TABLE OF CONTENTS

CHAPTER 1

FAREWELL, SANDRA

Junior Senior's "Move Your Feet" is playing in the enormous dining room at the mansion of Logan Brodie, the 34-year-old CEO of Horizon and son of logistics tycoon Jack Brodie. Horizon is one of the largest logistics companies in the country, based in Seattle.

Tonight is the retirement party for Sandra Mathis, the head maid for the Brodie family for thirty-four years, who eventually became the nanny for Logan's two young daughters, McKenna and Madison. Two months ago, Sandra's husband, Daniel, passed away from a long battle with Dementia, and she wanted to move close to her grown-up children in Minneapolis. Logan watches Sandra dancing with his daughters while nursing a scotch and soda.

Logan never dressed like your typical billionaire. With jeans, sneakers, and a buttoned dress shirt, Logan Brodie was all about comfort instead of style. A little too comfortable, to say the least. He looked like he crawled out of bed wearing the same wrinkled dress shirt for three days straight. He walked toward Clinton Thomas, his butler/Godfather, or some would say his "Alfred" to Logan's "Bruce Wayne."

"So, how's the nanny hunt?" Logan asks.

"It's coming along," Clinton says as he stabs the roast beef with the serving fork onto his plate.

"I'm hoping by the time you get back from Atlanta, I'll have someone permanent. Son, don't worry about it. I'll take care of it. Let's just worry about giving Sandy the send-off she deserves." Logan lifts his hands.

"Hey, you're the expert; I just own the joint."

Clinton notices the dark circles under Logan's eyes.

"Logan, you need sleep, for God's sake. Your raccoon eyes are out of control."

"Trust me, I'm trying, but I've got a lot going on. I'm not looking forward to Atlanta with Christmas on its way." Logan tried to convince Clinton, but he knew this kid too well.

"Madison told me at breakfast that you were talking to Mommy. What were you talking to Renee about?" He concernedly asked. Logan nervously brushed his hair.

"Just about Sandra leaving. You know Renee loved her. I'm going to get a beer. Do you want one?"

"Sure, thanks." Clinton was waiting for Logan to slither out of their conversation, which always happened when Renee was the subject. He looks at his employer and godson in fear. Tony Devanzo, the Brodie's chef, approaches Clinton.

"Dude, what was that all about?" Tony questions Clinton.

"Madison caught Logan talking to Renee again."

Tony looks up at the ceiling with concern. "Ah, shit. Hey, I've got suggestions for the next nanny. Big rack, killer legs, hot ass."

"That's amazing. The girls suggested the same thing." Clinton slaps Tony in the back of the head. "Boy, you're out of your mind."

"Think about it. Hey, I'm just looking out for my boy. Something to help him move on."

Clinton shakes his head as they both look at Logan. Soon after, Clinton's wife, Maggie, approached with a bottle of Corona. "Here, Ebony, Logan asked me to give you this."

"Thanks, Ivory." Clinton softly kisses his wife's cheek.

"What are you guys talking about?" Maggie asks.

"The new nanny." Tony remarks

"Tony wants me to hire a big, breasted young chippy with a perfect body." Clinton says sarcastically.

Maggie shrugs her shoulders, looking at her husband wonderfully, "Why not?" Clinton's brows creased, shocked at his wife's reaction.

"Even my wife has gone insane?"

"I don't think it's a bad idea. The priority is the kids, of course, but having someone young will boost him up because when will it be enough?"

"Madison caught him talking to Renee," Tony informs Maggie.

"You see. How long is Logan going to talk to his dead wife?"

After Logan's wife Renee died of cancer, Sandra became McKenna and Madison's nanny three years ago.

For three years, Logan Brodie was living in a shell. It was nothing but work, spending time with his daughters, and repeat. He always showed his daughters and Crew a brave front, but they knew he was dying inside.

Cortez Jackson, Logan's bodyguard, chauffeur, and best friend, approaches the group.

"Alright, Sandy is all packed up; I'm going to take her to the airport in the morning." Clinton nods.

"Very good. She wants one last staff meeting before she leaves, so I appreciate you guys coming in on your day off."

"Of course, anything for Sandy," Tony responds.

Clinton, Maggie, Tony, and Cortez watch Logan put a massive crown on Sandra's head, saying, "Happy Retirement, Your Majesty." Sandra hugs Angie and Rosa, her fellow maids she trained twenty years ago. Clinton looks at Tony.

"Big rack, huh?"

Tony nods. "Young, too."

"What did I miss???" Cortez looks in confusion.

"I'll fill you in later, big guy." Tony grins broadly, thinking of his master plan.

The four of them look on at Logan, hugging Sandra, knowing that she's known him all his life and this would be another crushing blow to him.

The following day, Sandra picked up her bag and looked at her pool house one last time before heading towards the mansion. She covers her mouth, trying to hold back the tears, thinking of her first day being the Brodie's maid. The thirty-four beautiful years of memories flew through her head while closing the door for the last time.

She walks through the backyard taking in one final look around. She opens the backdoor that leads to the kitchen to see Clinton, Tony, Angie, and Rosa, or what the Brodie's called "The Crew," waiting for her with huge smiles on their faces. Even though they dreaded saying goodbye.

"Well, thank you for making it here on this beautiful Sunday morning," Sandra says, taking a deep breath and fighting her emotions. "I know it's your day off, and I thank you so much, but I needed to see you all together one last time. You all have a job to do." She looks at all of them. "It's not to clean, drive, cook, or supervise." Sandra chokes up, not being able to stop the tears. "It's to watch over that boy and those two little darlings." She sniffs while Clinton holds a box of tissues, waiting for this moment. She grabs a couple, wiping her tears. "I'm sorry. We owe it to Jack, Katie, and mostly Renee. We promised to help him move on, and I still need you all to keep that promise. It's going to happen. One day. I have faith in that boy, and I have faith in all of you." Sandra cries harder. They all embrace each other for a group hug.

"Crew for Life," Angie says aloud, tears trickling down her cheeks.

"Amen." Clinton softly says

They break apart. Sandra looks at the Lopez sisters, Angie and Rosa, who started working for the Brodie's twenty years ago, and to them, Sandra was their second mother.

"Girls. I don't need to tell you to keep this place looking like the palace it already is. You two do it every day." Sandra caresses both their cheeks. The sisters look at each other.

"We learned from the greatest." Rosa barely gets the words out.

They both kiss and hug Sandra. She goes to Tony, taking his hands.

"These are the hands of a genius in this kitchen. Remember that. Keep feeding those girls the best because they are growing like weeds."

"Will do. I love you, Bella." Tony wipes a tear away as he holds her.

"I love you too, sweetheart." She takes two steps and looks up at Clinton. Her tears were uncontrollable at that point. She shakes her head as Clinton takes her and hugs her hard.

"We've gone through a lot with them." Her cracked voice muffled, being buried in his embrace.

"I know, I miss them too. You enjoy Minnesota, Okay? We'll take good care of them." He pulls

Sandra away to look down at her glassy eyes. "I promise. He'll find someone." McKenna and Madison run down to see Sandra one last time.

"Wait, Sandy. We want one last hug!" McKenna yells out. They both hug Sandra tight.

"I'll miss you, Sandy," Madison says with little tears coming down her four-year-old face.

"Oh, you beautiful angels. You need to come to see me in Minneapolis one day. Tell your daddy you need to see the Mall of America." Sandra tries to perk them up

"Please, that's McKenna's top five places she wants to go. Of course, we'll come to see you." Logan says as he enters the kitchen.

"Come walk me to the limo." Logan grabs her bag. She turns to look at the Crew one last time with a slight smile on her face. "Until next time. I love you, all."

Logan walks out with Sandra as the Crew, and the girls watch her leave. They go outside as Cortez waits outside the limo.

"Thank you for letting me use the limo and the jet."

"Of course, I was not letting you use an Uber and fly commercial," Logan says, putting her luggage in the trunk.

"I'm going to miss those beautiful blue eyes. Are you happy, young man?" Sandra smirks.

Logan took a while to come up with an answer. "Yeah. I am."

Sandra shakes her head before putting it down. "Don't you dare lie to me. Not before I leave." Sandra says in an angry, hushed tone. "I can't allow you to disappoint me, Logan." He looks at her with disheartedly since she is the closest thing he has to a grandmother. "I'm scared, Logan. I'm moving halfway across the country. I've lost your parents, Renee, and my Daniel. Now I'm saying goodbye to my other family. I know I will be in Minnesota every day, worrying about you. Please let Renee go."

Logan pulls Sandra into his chest and holds her while she sobs.

"I'm trying, Sandy," Logan says, trying to convince her. Sandra brushes her hand across his rough face, which hasn't been shaved in over a week.

"It's going to happen. You are not meant to be lonely, Logan. She's out there, and she will wake you up. I promise, sweetheart." Logan holds her hand against his cheek. Cortez opens the door, and Logan helps her in. Sandra rolls down the window to look at Logan one last time. "She's out there, honey." Sandra reminds him. Logan just nods as he watches the limo drive off. He runs his fingers through his brown hair, looks up in the sky, and closes his eyes, feeling increasingly lost. In a ten-year span, he lost his parents and his wife. Emotionally, he felt his life spiraling out of control.

It took a half hour for them to reach Sea-Tac to Logan's private jet. After Cortez gives her bags to the handlers, he approaches Sandra. She reaches out her hands to him. He lightly held him while she looked up to see a tear coming down from under his sunglasses.

"You continue to protect him and be that teddy bear for those little angels." She says as she squeezes both of his enormous hands.

"Yes, ma'am." Cortez agrees in his deep, broken voice.

"You remember what Renee told you on that day."

"That he's not going to take this well."

Sandra nods as she looks at him with his Ray-Bans still on his.

"Honey, please take off your glasses." Cortez takes his shades off to look into Sandra's eyes.

"Two and a half years. Help him get out of that prison he put himself in."

"Yes, ma'am." Sandra hugs Cortez. He lowered down so she could kiss him on the cheek. "You take care, Sandy."

Sandra walks into Logan's private jet. The jet took off ten minutes later; Sandra looked out the window, taking one last look at the Seattle skyline. She closes her eyes and whispers. "I promise, Logan."

Later that night, after putting the kids to sleep, Logan went to his movie theater. He was scrolling through the menu on the giant screen with a remote in his left hand and his third tequila sunrise on the right. There was nothing on Netflix, Hulu, or Prime that interested him. He then saw home videos on the menu. He turned on an old video Cortez recorded of Logan, Renee, and the entire Crew with their families in the same theater for a Seahawks/Broncos Super Bowl party. Cortez turned the camera to himself.

"43 to 8, baby!!!! We're doing it!!! We are one minute away from being Super Bowl champs, baby!!!" He pans the camera on Logan and Renee, who are both wearing Seahawks jerseys with neon green and silver painted on their faces.

Logan was sitting in the same spot he was in the video. He turns to look at the empty lounge chair that was Renee's where a golf ball-sized lump hits his throat when he looks back at the screen. Everybody started counting down the last seconds of the game. Once the clock hit zero, pandemonium went out in the theater. Logan jumped up and down when Renee slipped Logan a long white stick with two blue strips on it into his hand.

"No!!!" His voice was husky from yelling all night, but his eyes blew up in happiness.

"Yes!!!" Renee cries and nods. She hugs Logan tight.

Logan breaks their hug and turns to everybody in the theater with the biggest glow on his face. He screams out.

"CREW!!!!! WE'RE SUPER BOWL CHAMPIONS!!!!"

"AND WE'RE PREGNANT!!!!!" Renee yells out, holding the pregnancy test.

An eruption of happiness came, and everybody swarmed to Logan and Renee, congratulating the soon-to-be parents when Logan paused the video at the glow on Renee's painted face. The stabbing pain of grief struck him hard. He closed his eyes, feeling the pain of loss as his soul pierced through his heart. He looks again at her empty chair when he breaks down and collapses. Tears stream down his face, screaming in agony. He jumps out of the same Lazy Boy he climbed on six years earlier in pure happiness and heads to his backyard.

He ran to the dock paced back and forth, trying to compose himself. He leaned onto his speedboat, trying to catch his breath. He sees the chair where Renee sat to paint. The dock was her favorite spot in the compound. He sees little drips of dried paint on the wooden planks overlooking Lake Washington. He looked out at the lake when a tremendous wind hit Logan in the face. Deep inside, he thought it was Renee telling him she was right there. He jumped into his speedboat and sat in the driver's seat. He leaned back, looked up into the heavens, took advantage of the rare clear Seattle sky, and talked to Renee all night through the brightest star he could find.

CHAPTER 2

DRIVE CAREFULLY, COME BACK SOON

"Steal my Sunshine" by Len was blasting in Jade Murphy's eardrums. She was lip-synching down the stairs, carrying a tote full of designer shoes outside her Las Vegas apartment,, packing up her 2016 Toyota Camry. Tomorrow morning, she heads up to Seattle, where she'll move in with her roommate from Cal State Fullerton, Tonya Thomas. She starts to dance up the stairs to get another load of clothes when she gets a call from Tonya. She presses her left ear pod to answer.

"You've got Jade, lucky you."

"Oh, my God!!! Oh my God!! I can't wait for you to get here. What time are you planning on arriving?" Tonya squeals

Jade grabs an arm full of clothes to throw into her car. "I can't wait, too!!! Tonight's my last night at Topaz, and then I leave early in the morning, hangover pending, of course, and start my nineteen-hour….. Ah, hell, I'm staying in Vegas. Nevermind." She shakes her head, not looking forward to the nearly whole-day drive.

"Oh, no, you don't!!!! You're Seattle property now. I need my girl here."

"I'm just messing with you. I want everything new, such as no sun, constant rain, and moody, depressing surroundings like any normal person wants. Also, I'm all yours with your sweet deal with the apartment. Plus, getting a job will be easy. I'm cute, and I have a killer body." She tries to push the trunk down, but it's stuffed to the max. "Dammit, I may have to leave some things behind."

"Hey, I will take care of anything you need, my CSF sister." They both pound their chest and raise their fists, screaming together. "Go, Titans!!!"

"Also, my parents are downsizing in Spokane, and my uncle Clinton lives here, so they said if you need anything, just ask. You have family here."

"Yeah, your mom and dad are my redemption parents since those other two were a complete bust. Listen, girl. I got to get ready for work. See you tomorrow."

"Ciao darling, love you." Tonya hangs up.

Jade shakes her head, trying hard to get rid of the image of her parents. Once she turned her music back on, Jade returned to her bubbly self. Her ultra-religious parents raised Jade until she was sixteen when she was officially emancipated from them. Jade was an invincible fire that couldn't be contained. Her mother knew it after she came out of her womb. There was no connection between Jade and her mother, Robin, when she was swaddled for the first time and placed in her arms. There was nothing between them literally from day one.

She headed back upstairs when she ran into her next-door neighbor, Athena, and her five-year-old son, Cody. They were living on their own when Cody's father left them six months ago because he couldn't deal with the fact that his son had Down Syndrome.

"Hi, Jade," Cody says with a massive smile.

"Cody Maxwell Cameron, you handsome ladykiller." He runs to hug Jade. Jade looks up at his exhausted mother. "Hey, supermom. How's she doing?"

Looking at Jade with her darkened, raccoon eyes from lack of sleep.

"On to job number two, here I go. Are you ready for your last Vegas ride?"

"Sure am. I'm going to miss you two so much." She tussles Cody's hair. "Especially you, cutie."

"Believe me; this place won't be the same without you. If I don't get to see you tomorrow, good luck in Seattle." Athena says with disappointment in her voice.

"Thanks, love." Jade hugs both Athena and Cody. "Hey, keep fighting, survivor."

"That's all I can do. Love you too, Jade."

Athena takes Cody's hand and heads down the stairs. Jade would sometimes help watch him for free while his mother worked two jobs as a craps dealer at the Bellagio and waitressing at an Italian restaurant on Fremont Street. A stabbing pain went through Jade, realizing she couldn't help them anymore.

Around seven O'clock, Jade and her roommate, Carly, got ready for Jade's last day of work. She was the head bartender at Topaz, the most prominent gentleman's club in Vegas. Carly was taking over Jade's position after tonight.

She puts on a tight red mini dress with black over-the-knee suede boots with a two-inch heel. Being 5'3, she usually wore four-inch heels, but working in them would be murder. She hears a car honk outside her apartment. It was their friends Chelsea and Laura, who were waitresses at Topaz.

"Girls!!!!! Get your hot asses down here for the last time!!!" Chelsea yells out. Jade and Carly go downstairs and enter Chelsea's jeep.

"I'm going to cry. This is it." Laura gets emotional in the back seat. Jade turns from the passenger seat to look into her glassy eyes, which fill with tears.

"Oh honey, stop!!!" Jade reaches for Laura's hand.

"Well, you're giving me an excuse to go to Seattle," Laura says, wiping a tear.

"Uh, you girls better come see me up there, by God," Jade demands the three of them.

"Promise." All three girls yell out simultaneously.

"OK, listen up. Let's do this for the last time." Chelsea turns on "Dani California" by the Red Hot Chili Peppers, which was Jade's stripper name. The girls scream at the top of their lungs.

Jade closes her eyes, feeling the love from her friends. "I love you girls so much!!! If I had the capability or the certain emotional aspect to cry, I would."

The song blares through the lit-up Las Vegas Strip. While listening, Jade reminisces about her three years in Vegas while watching the neon lights go by. She thought of the nightclubs, the pool parties, and cheering on her favorite hockey team, the Vegas Golden Knights. Still, Jade wanted a fresh start in the Pacific Northwest and a familiar face in Tonya by her side. After the song ends, she asks her friends.

"OK, girls, I just need one huge favor. Don't let me go nuts after work with the hooch."

"The hooch?" Chelsea laughs. "That's what my grandpa called liquor."

"Well, I feel it deserves a comeback." Jade sarcastically responds.

"I still can't believe you're leaving, Jade," Carly says, still in denial.

"I know, sweetheart, but I have to figure something out. I just turned twenty-five, and I've had so much fun since college, but I know I won't get anywhere here."

"Is that why you chose Seattle because the suicide rate is so high? You're going to put your degree to good use?" Chelsea asks

"Shit, Chelsea, a little morbid, huh? Also, maybe." Jade majored in Psychology at Cal State Fullerton with a double master degree. "Right now, I want to enjoy this night, make gas money, then make stupid decisions with you girls and not see the sun nine months out of the year. Thank God Seattle has a good selection of tanning salons."

"Well, let's give you the last epic Vegas night and do this shit!!!!" Carly yells out.

When they arrive at Topaz, the girls scream out the windows. It would only be a five-hour shift for Jade and the girls. She just wanted one last night to do something she loved doing: slinging drinks on a packed Saturday night with guys flirting with her and getting evil looks from their girlfriends. Around nine, Eric, the owner of Topaz, went to the DJ booth to turn off the music.

"Everyone, tonight is Jade's last hour with us as she will bring some sunshine to Seattle. So, everyone, raise your glasses to Jade. Good luck at the Emerald City. Salute!!!" The whole club lets out a "Salute!!! Jade blows a kiss to Eric as the music plays on.

"One more hour!!! Where are we going first?" Carly asks Jade.

"Wait, last hour?" Jade takes her phone to take a selfie with Carly and posts it to Facebook and

Instagram with the caption "Topaz's final hour with Jade."

The hour goes by, and Jade collects the $540 in tips. After hugging and saying goodbye to her fellow bartenders, she approaches Eric and gets on one knee, bowing to hand over her dishrag. Eric laughs and hugs Jade.

"I'm losing my best bartender." He informs Jade.

"I know. I say this place will fold and implode by February." She jokes with him. Eric then hands Jade an envelope with $1,500 in cash. "Whoa, what the hell, Eric?" Jade yells out in shock.

"A parting gift. You deserve it." He said, giving her a sincere look. She hugs Eric one last time. "I hope you find what you're looking for in Seattle." Jade pulls away from him and gives him a parting wink.

She started heading towards the entrance where Chelsea, Laura, and Carly were waiting for her, but there was one last person she needed to say goodbye to. Jade enters one of the private booths to find Brandy or her customer name, "Tara," while on the clock. Tara gave Hank, a regular at Topaz, a lap dance.

"Sorry to interrupt, Hank. I just want to say goodbye to Tara."

"No problem, Jade." Hank says being understanding.

Brandy was the lead stripper and Jade's mentor when she filled in for her occasionally while taking night classes at nursing school. Brandy continues to grind on Hank.

"Oh my God, I will miss you so much." She sincerely tells Jade.

"Oh, don't start with me. I'll miss my Jedi master."

"You were such an easy student. Your future husband is going to soak himself the way you move." Jade rolled her eyes when Brandy mentioned her getting married, which was something Jade was not fond of or not planning on doing ever. "Oh hey, I got my results last week.

Ninety-six percent!!!"

"BOOOM!!!!" Jade screams out

"Yeah, I will be leaving here soon, just like you. So Hank, enjoy this because you'll be one of my last."

"I'm truly honored," Hank says

"Hey, the girls are waiting for me, so I gotta go. Love you, sweetness." Jade kisses Brandy's cheek. "Bye, Hank. You take care."

"Bye, Jade. good luck in Seattle."

The girls wait for Jade. Before getting into the jeep, she turns and takes one last look at Topaz, blowing it a kiss. Chelsea drives off while Jade unzips her boots.

"Laura, please, for the love of everything holy, tell me you brought my Steve Maddens you borrowed last week, or I will be forced to disembowel you."

"Yeah, here you go." Laura hands Jade her red buckle strap sandals.

"Thank you, sweet angel. I'm not spending my last night in Vegas wearing comfortable two inches. I need four painful inches the way God intended." Jade says in relief as she puts on her heels and admires them when she puts her beautiful, tanned left leg on the dashboard. "I mean, look at these delicious gams."

The girls scream out, "Woo!!!!" at Jade. They head down Las Vegas Boulevard for Jade's last night in Vegas. She unbuckles her seat belt and stands, feeling the cold November air hitting her face and her blonde hair whipping in the wind.

"Vegas, I'll always love you!!! Seattle, Jade is coming for you, bitch!!!" Jade screams out at the Vegas strip.

The girls scream, determined to give their good friend one last great Vegas night. They started with a ride on the High Roller, the giant Ferris Wheel on the Strip, eating sushi at Nobu in Caesars Palace, selfies in front of the giant fountains at the Bellagio, and finally, a little craps playing at the Cosmopolitan.

Their last stop was drinking at the Skyfall Lounge at the Delano. Jade was tipsy coming out of the bathroom with her fifth Mai Tei in her hand when the beam from the top of the Luxor caught her eye. She went outside to the patio, which was pretty empty since the temperature dipped into the low forties that night, but the cold never bothered Jade. She stands behind the protected glass, taking in the view on top of the 64th floor. She raises her Mai Tei and yells out to the city.

"Thank you for taking care of me for these past three years. Don't listen to what anyone says!!!

Sin City, my ass. You are beautiful. Don't change a thing!!! Vegas Strong!!!" Jade takes a drink. She then looks up into the sky, where the beam shined to the heavens. "Hey yo, J.C.!!! Wait, I'll put my drink down to be respectful." She puts her drink on a small table and sits on one of the lounge chairs. She looks back up at the night sky. "I just gotta level with you. Everyone keeps asking me why I'm moving to Seattle, and the truth is, I DON'T KNOW, but You know what a nutball I am. I mean, You made me!!!! Just do me three favors, please. One, watch over Athena & Cody next door. I know this is a long shot because you could care less about sports, but I'll ask anyway." She points to T-Mobile Arena. "Get my Golden Knights a Stanley Cup!!! GO, KNIGHTS, BABY!!! Three, take care of those three beautiful girls inside. They mean so much to me, and I love my Topaz sisters. If you could do that for me, that would be mega awesome." Jade exhaled a breath of happiness, knowing she could always count on God at any time.

She turns around to see Laura, Chelsea, and Carly standing outside, freezing with tears strolling down their cheeks. They walk towards Jade and embrace her. All four hold each other, looking up at the beam.

"Lord, watch over our Jade. We love her so much. We all know she will start trouble in Seattle; just don't be mad at her too much." Laura prays.

Chelsea and Carly shout, "Amen!!!!"

"Okay, are we done talking with Jesus? I'm freezing." Carly asks while chattering her teeth.

"Yeah, I'm done. Let's go inside," Jade says as all four rush towards the warm bar inside. They get about halfway through when Jade realizes she forgot her Mai Tai and returns to the table. Right when she was about to grab it, "Ready to Go" by Republica was playing in the bar. In Jade's mind, she took it as a sign from God, like a last dance for her time in Vegas.

She started bobbing her head, hopping to the music, lip-syncing the words to all of Vegas when the girls noticed her. Even though it was cold, they wanted one last dance with their soon-to-be departing friend. The girls started singing and dancing with Jade as it was an appropriate farewell song.

The following day, around eight, Jade wakes up in a spinning haze. She sees Chelsea with her in bed, still in her purple dress. She stumbles out of bed, walking like a newborn fawn. Jade closes her eyes and steadies herself, heading towards Carly's room and past out in bed with Laura. Jade is impressed—no random naked guy in Carly's bed for once.

"Alright, Carly. Way to show willpower." She says, relieved she didn't have to make breakfast for some stranger again. She goes to the kitchen and puts a coffee pod into her Keurig as she opens a bottle of Ibuprofen and pops four pills into her mouth. She sighs as she swallows the pills until the moment hits her. She runs to the bathroom, throwing up everything from the night before. She opens up the cabinet under the sink and grabs an emergency bottle of water they left under the sink. Jade and Carly were always prepared since this was a regular occurrence every other week-end. After gargling and spitting out the mixture of Mai-Tai, sushi, tequila, and double-double cheeseburgers from "In-N-Out," she gets off the floor and sees the bedhead on her blonde hair from the mirror.

"Okay, let's start moving this life over." She starts waking up the girls, clapping her hands. "Alrighty, time to get up and kill each other for my couch and bed." Jade takes her dress off and puts on a pair of jeans and a Meghan Trainor tour shirt. "I want to get these goodbyes over with and as painless as possible," Jade says, knowing she was lying to herself. Especially when Chelsea, Carly, and Laura come together disheveled looking from the night before. "Oh my God, impossible. I'm going to miss you three so much." She whined when they came together for a group hug. The girls have a long pause, hating to say goodbye. Laura is the first to break down and cry.

"Good luck, babe." She says, wiping a tear, not wanting to let go of Jade.

"All right, that's enough. We got to be strong, my sisters. Jade needs to go." Chelsea tries to reason with the girls.

The girls walk Jade to her car. Carly opens the door for her. Jade looks at the girls.

"Topaz bitches for life!!!"

"For life!!!!" The three yell out. Jade starts the car when she hears a voice yelling for her. It was Cody.

"Jade!!!" he screams out for her, running down the stairs. Jade gets out of the car to comfort him.

"Cody, what are you doing out of your apartment?" she yells, worried. Cody looks down, unable to look Jade in the eye.

"Mommy fell asleep, and I just wanted to say goodbye again. I'll miss you, Jade." She lifts his chin.

"Honey, I'm going to miss you too." She hugs Cody tight. After a few seconds without thinking twice, Jade pulls out the envelope of cash she got last night.

"Sweetheart, I need you to give this to your mommy."

She hands him the envelope while the girls smile, unsurprised by Jade's generosity.

"We'll make sure Athena gets it." Carly assures Jade. "You get out of here, girl."

Carly and Chelsea take Cody's hand and walk him back to his apartment. Jade stares at the four of them as they walk away. A smile grows, knowing that this will never be a forever goodbye. She then returns to her stuffed Camry and peels out of the complex.

"CODY!!!" His mother screams frantically, running out of her apartment.

"We got him, Athena!!! He's okay!!!" Carly comforts her worries.

"Thank you so much, girls. Don't ever scare me like that." She squeezes Cody tight.

"I just wanted to say goodbye to Jade. Look, Mommy, she left a letter." He hands his mother the envelope. It didn't feel like a letter to her. She opens it and goes stoned-eyed, looking at the wad of cash. She looks up at the girls.

"Oh my God, Jade left this for us?"

"Of course she did. It's Jade we're talking about." Chelsea says.

A tear ran down Athena's face, astonished at Jade's selfless act. She felt a gentle pat from all three girls, letting her and Cody know that they were never going to be alone.

Before Jade's nineteen-hour trek to Seattle, she stopped at the famous "Welcome to Las Vegas" sign. On the other side, it says, "Drive carefully, come back soon." She sees a newlywed couple standing in front of the sign, taking selfies of each other.

"Excuse me. First of all, Mazel Tov, can you take my picture on the other side after I take a picture of you two kids?"

"Sure." The bride says, handing over her phone.

Jade takes a picture of the newlyweds and then poses, hugging the sign to send to the girls and Instagram with the caption, "I'll be back, real soon!!! I will always love you three and LV!!!!"

CHAPTER 3

UNEXPECTED CAREER OPPORTUNITY

A week passed since Jade moved in with Tonya, and it was like college again.

Binge-watching old "Hart of Dixie" episodes while drinking tequila and eating cookie dough. The difference was Tonya had a career as a psychologist, and Jade was still trying to figure out her life after college. She had a good four months of savings, which she brought along with her. One Friday afternoon, Tonya was on her laptop working from home when she heard a knock at the door.

"Hey, Uncle!!!" She hugs Clinton, surprised to see him since he usually calls ahead.

"Hi, sweetheart. I was in the neighborhood and haven't seen you in a while." Tonya closes the door behind him and heads towards the living room. "How's the new roommate?"

"Well, to be technical, returning roommate." Tonya closes her laptop and lies on the couch. "It's like times haven't changed since Fullerton. I've missed her so much. She's clean, an amazing cook, and she's helped me with some of my cases. Right now, Jade is out looking for a job."

Clinton sits on the recliner when the name Jade jogs his memory. "Wait a minute. Jade? That cute little blonde girl your auntie and I had dinner with in Huntington Beach about five years ago."

"The one you said looks like Grace Kelly with the mouth of Richard Pryor. One and the same." She nods.

"What is she doing here?" He asks.

"Well, she missed her best friend, naturally, and she wanted a fresh start and to go somewhere completely different than she's used to. She lived in L.A. her entire life, with a short stint in Vegas before coming here. Right now, she's being interviewed for a bartending position at Shorty's."

"Good for her."

Tonya mirrors her uncle's body language. His shoulders are tightened, and he crosses his leg with his foot, fidgeting. She knows he is stressing about Logan.

"So, how are Logan and the kids doing?" She asks.

"Oh, they're fine. They're still not grasping Sandra moving away. We're still looking for her replacement. Maggie and I take turns caring for them while Logan is in Atlanta. I've interviewed over a dozen candidates, and I didn't feel anything about them. Would you mind quitting neuropsychology and watching over those two??? You would be making a hell of a lot more." He tries to entice his niece.

"I do love those girls, and what a cush job that would be, but I've gone this far, and the hell I went through to get my Master's for it. What about Logan? Is he doing better?" She asks nervously; he looked like a complete mess since she last saw him three months ago. Clinton slowly nods.

"He has his days. It's just one day at a time for him. He refuses to give in and see somebody or talk about Renee." Clinton gets up off the couch and takes a few steps. "He never sleeps; he stays in his loft in his office at least twice a week. I think he does it so he doesn't let the girls see him talk to their mother. He's still trying to connect with her somehow. I cannot believe it will be three years since she died, and that poor kid refuses to let her go."

"And he hasn't seen anyone or dated since?" Tonya asks. Clinton shakes his head.

"No. I don't know if he feels he's betraying her or punishing himself, but I just know it will get so much better once he meets someone. He just puts on that happy mask in front of those girls and the Crew, but when he's alone. That mask comes right off."

"It sounds like he has Complicated Grief. He's losing his mental control. He needs to see somebody."

"That boy is so damn stubborn when it comes to that." Clinton slowly shakes his head and scoffs. Tonya leans and grabs his hands to ease him.

"You got to think about this, Uncle. The love and devotion he has in himself—for Renee, the girls, and the five of you. The second he gets to that edge of reason and finally agrees to be with someone, that girl is not going to know what hit her. The problem is, the longer this goes, it will only worsen for him."

Clinton ponders hard at what Tonya said when he hears the front door open with a familiar voice entering the apartment.

"Ahhhh, what a day!!! I need a beer and my dinner, angel tits!!!" Jade yells like a husband who just got off a twelve-hour shift in the coal mines. She walks into the living room to see Tonya & Clinton standing together. She covers her mouth. "Oh God, you have company!!! I'm so sorry." Clinton laughs while Tonya covers her face in embarrassment.

"Uncle Clinton, you remember Jade N.F. Murphy, my best friend in the entire world." Clinton steps to shake her hands.

"N.F.?" He asks.

"No filter. You know how they nicknamed Deadpool "The merc with the mouth." Well I'm "The Murph with the mouth." Jade answers while Clinton bursts into laughter again. He couldn't get enough of her sense of humor.

"How did the interview go?" Tonya asks

"Good. I think they want me. Of course, I flashed some boobage, so I earned points there. So I'll bartend Friday & Saturday nights and find something for the day, too."

Clinton was gobsmacked at the sight of Jade. She was funny, bubbly, and stunningly beautiful. The light bulb over his head lit up. He didn't think of killing two birds with one stone but three. He needed a nanny, she needed a job, and Logan needed a new life.

"Jade, have you ever babysat or taken care of children?" Tonya's eyes went wide when Clinton asked Jade, who had a confused glance on her face

"Well, I occasionally helped babysit a friend's son with special needs while living in Vegas and the typical babysitting gigs in high school. Why do you ask?"

"Maybe we can help each other out," he says with a big smile. "Do you know the name Logan Brodie?" Jade squints her eyes.

"Nope, it doesn't ring a bell."

"Oh my God, J!!! I've told you about him and how Uncle Clinton was his butler." Tonya says bluntly, while Jade shrugs her shoulders. "The billionaire!!!"

"Ohhh. That Logan Brodie. Ok, I still don't know who he is."

"I'll explain. He has two daughters, and their nanny just retired, so I'm wondering how you get along with children?"

"I love kids. I love being around them, and we…" Jade interrupts herself. "Wait a minute. Billionaire kids? They're not the "rich spoiled little shits" type because I would be forced to kill them."

"Jade, McKenna, and Madison are complete angels. They are not spoiled whatsoever. They are grounded. Logan and their mother taught them well." Tonya assures her.

"No kidding?" She asks Clinton.

"No kidding, Jade. Logan has taught them that money is not the basis of life. He ensured they wouldn't grow up, as you would say, "rich spoiled little shits". So, when Logan is there, you'll have your own poolhouse, but he requests that you stay in the mansion in the guest room next to their room when he's out of town on business. You'll have full use of the Escalade. You're there six days a week. Saturdays are yours free unless you want to stay there full time, which you'll more than likely want to do because the poolhouse is stunning."

"That sounds amazing, but what about you, Tonya? I just moved in." Jade asks, worried about this affecting her.

"You don't worry about me. I'll be fine. Jade, this will be perfect for you."

Clinton folds his arms. "So, I'm sure you're wondering about salary. What do you think would be a good monthly number for you?"

Jade paces with her arms behind her back. "Hmmm, well, since L.A. and Seattle are no different from each other with living expenses. I think $5,000 a month would be survivable." Clinton and Tonya look at each other with a sinister smile.

"Ohhh. That would be way out of Logan's price range." Jade shrugged her shoulders, thinking it didn't hurt to try. "He pays $9,500 a month." Clinton said point blank. Suddenly, Jade couldn't even comprehend a thought from the shock. Her mouth immediately went dry, and her eyes lit up. "Plus medical, dental, and three weeks paid vacation."

Clinton and Tonya walk towards a frozen Jade who turns into a statue. "Logan Brodie will be one of the rarest people you will ever meet. He doesn't refer to us as his employees but as his "Crew." That consists of me, his butler, his cook, two sister maids, his chauffeur slash bodyguard, and you, his daughter's nanny. We are his family. We do family functions together, go to his daughters' soccer games and dance recitals, and go to Seahawks games. We do it all. I have been the Brodie's butler for almost thirty years. I've known Logan since he was five and I am also his godfather. He pays us all an overwhelmingly generous salary because he is grateful for our help. So Jade, would you like to be part of our "Crew" and take care of his two biggest investments that mean the world to him and all of us?"

Jade stares at Clinton with her glossy, hazel eyes, overwhelmed and unable to utter a word. Tonya walks toward Jade, wrapping her arms around her waist. "Uncle, you're witnessing a historical first. For the first time in her life, Jade Murphy is completely speechless. So, I will speak on her behalf. She will happily take the position."

"What, what she just said." Jade nods like a bobblehead doll and whispers, barely getting the words out. Clinton claps his hands.

"Excellent. Oh, there is one more perk, Jade."

"Dear sweet Jesus, there's more." She turns to look at Tonya. "Tonya, there's more."

"Just breathe, sweetie."

"Have you ever been to Barbados?"

"If memory serves, no."

"Well, he owns an island there, and every December 26th, he takes the Crew and our families there until New Year's Day. Would you like to join us in Barbados?"

Tonya had to turn away because she was about to explode from laughter, while Jade felt like she would pass out.

"Sure, why not?"

"Fantastic!!! Well, I better go, honey, and call Logan and tell him about the new hire." Clinton kisses Tonya on the cheek. "And Jade, I'll see you tomorrow." Clinton extends his arm for a handshake, but Jade looks at it, runs in for a hug, and buries herself into Clinton's arms.

"Tomorrow!!!!" She yells out. Clinton pats her back.

"Good, good. Well, you girls have fun today. See you tomorrow." Tonya closes the door behind him. She sees Jade about to explode. Clinton is halfway to the elevator when he hears Jade's screams.

"WHAT THE FUCK JUST HAPPENED TO ME????"

Clinton busts up laughing as he enters the elevator, hearing her joyous yell.

"Breath, Jade, Breath." Tonya pleads. Jade grabs her head, pacing back and forth in the living room. "Oh my God, $9,500 times twelve." Jade tried to do the math, but her head was clouded. "Uh, uh, a shit ton of money, T!!!" Jade collapses on the couch, still in shock, grabbing a pillow to smother herself. "I can't believe this."

"It's called the right place at the right time. Girl, let me tell you something about Logan. He is the last of a dying breed. He's a multi-billionaire, but he hardly shows up on TV, doesn't nail every girl in sight, and he throws money to charity like it's water. Oh, and his parents were the most amazing people ever." Tonya gives Jade a crash course on the Brodie family. Jade turns to look at Tonya, noticing she used the past tense. "Wait, were?"

"Yeah, they both died ten years ago."

"Oh no."

"That's not all. He lost his wife three years ago." Tonya adds while Jade's mouth goes wide.

"Lord, give the guy a break, will you? WOW!!!"

"I know, and Renee was the biggest sweetheart on the planet." Tonya waves her hands, returning to Jade's new job. "Seriously, J, you will fall in love with those girls and the crew; let's just say my uncle handed you the golden ticket himself to Willy Wonka's factory." Jade pulls back her blonde hair, trying desperately to stay on planet Earth.

"God, this is nuts!!! I need to see a picture of this guy." Tonya gets her phone and Googles Logan Brodie. Pictures start popping up, and Jade is instantly infatuated. "He's hot as hell. He can go anywhere and throw a rock at any girl and take her home."

I know, but like I said, he's not that kind. Uncle Clinton told me he hasn't been with any girl since Renee. He was that devoted to her. Logan has been in mourning for three years and is really damaged. Jade, I think you are with you being there and how you are. You're going to bring life to that place."

"Oh, I'll blow the shit out of that place with sunshine and rainbows." Tonya covers her face.

"Oh dear God, this was a mistake."

"NO!!! NO!!! I'll behave." Tonya gives her a "Seriously" look. "To a degree, at least. I've got to pack, AGAIN!!!!"

Tonya was so happy seeing Jade excited as she jumped up and down the loveseat while whistling "Beautiful Life" by Ace of Base. She smiles, imagining her being around Logan's daughters and knowing how they would hit it off instantly. More importantly, she hoped Jade and Logan would click themselves, knowing her painful history with her parents and her bad luck with men. Tonya thought of it as not just a career opportunity but a life opportunity for her because there was someone who deserved to be in love; it was Jade.

CHAPTER 4

MEETING PRINCESS JADE

After repacking her car the next day, Jade followed the GPS, passing one giant mansion after another. The nerves and anticipation drove her crazy when she turned into a giant brass gate. She presses her personal code, which Clinton gave her, to open the gate. They slowly open, and she drives up a long, curvy hill. Her mouth was filled with awe at the sight of the giant fortress that is Brodie mansion. Jade slowly slips off her aviators.

"You can't be serious." She whispers to herself.

She drives to a long driveway to see a breathtaking three-story, 10,600 sq ft modern mansion overlooking the skyline in the background. She sees Clinton in front, waiting for her with his arms behind him. He opens her door for her.

"Welcome, Jade. What do you think?" She looks around at the giant palace.

"No moat? I thought this guy was rich." She says sarcastically while Clinton chuckles.

"He insisted, but I talked him out of it."

They both chuckle when they see Cortez approach the driveway after dropping the kids off at school. Once he gets out, Jade gasps at his enormous, intimidating frame wearing all black.

"Jade, this is…" Clinton tries to introduce each other when Jade suddenly starts screaming.

"OH, MY GOD!!!! Notorious B.I.G. IS still alive and living in Seattle!!!" She points at Cortez, shocked at his resemblance to the late rapper.

"Everyone thought I was nuts, but my conspiracy theory was right!!!"

Clinton laughs uncontrollably while Cortez just stands motionless, standing like a statue.

"No, Jade, this is Cortez Jackson. He is Logan's bodyguard and chauffeur." He leans to whisper in her ear. "Trust me, people confuse him for Biggie many times. Madison & McKenna refer to him as their "Teddy." Cortez, this is Jade, the new nanny."

Jade strolled towards Cortez, who towered over her. "I beg of you, please sing "Going back to Cali" for me. I would just die." Jade looks up waiting for a response. He kept his Ray-Bans on while he checked out her off-the-shoulder gray sweater with tight white jeggings and black boots.

"Hi!!! My eyes are right here, pumpkin, not down here." As she points to her breasts. Cortez stays quiet and unresponsive. Jade looks at Clinton. "Apparently, we're having a staring contest. Well, I'm game." Jade puts on her Aviators. After ten seconds of silence. "I can do this all day, big guy." Cortez doesn't change his serious demeanor. He says with a deep, serious voice.

"White, blonde, spunky." He turns to look at Clinton. "Oh, I like her, C. See ya soon, honey bunny." Cortez walks towards the garage.

Jade gasps. "He's seen "Pulp Fiction." His stock just skyrocketed. I love you already, Cortez!!!" She yells out at him while he turns to blow Jade a kiss.

Clinton couldn't hold back his laughter. He was enthralled at how this little blonde girl broke the ice when meeting someone for the first time. He looked at Jade like a revelation.

"My God, girl. You're going to fit in great. Well, before we meet the rest of the Crew. Let's check out your poolhouse."

Jade gives him a goofy two thumbs up before walking towards the massive pool. A large grin forms when she sees the steam coming from the pool, knowing they keep it heated. Jade noticed the exterior of the poolhouse was two stories. Clinton opens the door, and Jade's shoulders collapse. She sees the marble flooring with a fully furnished living room, a massive LED TV, a full kitchen, a dining room, and a spiral staircase leading to her massive bedroom.

"If this is a dream, destroy my phone so my alarm doesn't go off." Jade says in shock at her new place.

"I was wondering how many trips back to the apartment you need to make to get everything. I can get my truck and help you out."

"Actually, I got everything in the Camry. Just two suitcases and a couple of boxes. It'll take me minutes to settle in."

"Speaking of your Toyota, you might as well sell it. Cortez mainly drives Logan in the limo, and on his days off, he'll drive his Mustang only, so you get full range of the Escalade when you take the kids to and from school. We all take Uber from home to here."

"Really??? Awesomeness!!!"

Clinton claps his hands. "Well, ready to see the compound and meet your fellow Crew."

Jade extends her elbow. "Ready when you are."

Clinton hooked his arm with hers, and they walked through the enormous backyard like they were going to meet the Wizard of Oz. They walk into the kitchen, where they run into Tony. Tony was a Queens native in his late thirties. His mouth dropped when he first saw Jade. He thought to himself, "Tits, ass, legs. Clinton got everything off my checklist."

"Jade, this is Tony Devanzo. He has been the Brodie's personal chef for the past twelve years."

Tony extends his hand. "Jade, pleased to meet you."

"Likewise. Twelve years, huh."

"Yup, the Brodie's are pretty simple to cook for."

"Well, I'm not. Can you whip me up a baked Alaska?" Jade says, wanting to know how good he is.

"Ohhh, a challenge."

"This man is one of the best chefs in all of Seattle." Clinton boosts Tony's ego.

"No, no, no. Nah, it's true."

Jade lets out a snort as Angie and Rosa run in.

"Is she here yet???" Angie yells in excitement. Jade yells back.

"Why, yes, she is!!! Hi, I'm Jade."

"These are the Lopez sisters, Angie & Rosa. They're our maids." Clinton introduces them to Jade, who lifts her finger at him.

"Ah, excuse me, you mean the household sanitation technicians." She turns to Angie & Rosa. "I got your back, sisters."

Rosa laughs while she looks her up and down, admiring her attire. "I love your outfit!!!!"

"Thank you!!!!" She checks out Angie & Rosa's attire, noticing they weren't in dresses with aprons and a headpiece like typical maids to a billionaire. Except they were wearing jeans with a blouse. In contrast, Tony wore a red polo shirt with a New York Mets cap. "I happen to notice nobody wears uniforms."

"No, this isn't like "Dynasty." The Brodies wanted everyone to relax and enjoy themselves while working here."

"So, this would be my uniform." She says, showing off her attire.

Cortez enters the kitchen and grabs a bottle of water from the refrigerator.

"I'm all for it, Shorty."

"Jade, you have no idea what you're in store for here. You're never going to have a better job in your life." Angie informs her. Clinton then gives her a rundown of her duties.

"So, this is going to be your routine. You are to take the girls to school at 7:30 a.m. and pick them up at 3:30. Except on Fridays when Logan usually gets them if he's not out of town. He usually takes them out to dinner on Friday nights. He'll let you know when he comes home, but sometimes he crashes in his loft at the office."

"Do I get to meet Daddy Warbucks today?" Jade wonders.

"No, he's in Atlanta for the next four days on business. One rule, it's Logan, not Mr. Brodie. He hates being called mister. So, the game plan for today is for you to settle in and get used to the place. Cortez will get the girls today so we can all have dinner together and introduce you to them. How's that sound?" Clinton sees the glow in her eyes.

"That sounds amazing. Thank you so much, you guys. I'm going to unload the car and get everything together," Jade says, feeling so welcome. She is already heading to her poolhouse with the Crew looking on.

"What do you think, guys?" Clinton asks for his fellow Crew's opinions. Tony points at Jade.

"I think if I wasn't married to Bridget, I was twenty pounds thinner and ten years younger, that girl would be in a lot of trouble with me. What do you think, Rosa?"

"In a normal world, I would be thinking, "How dare she walk into this house with that perfect body wearing a size negative two with those huge breasts and perfect ass in front of me," but I like her."

"I like her too. The bitch." Angie spits out her jealousy. "What do you think, Clinton?"

Clinton had his arms folded, feeling increasingly optimistic. He felt her vibe explode the second he met her, and now, that vibe came into the house. The air felt fresher somehow.

"I have a feeling this girl is going to light this place and every-thing around it on fire."

"Hey, sis, why don't we help her unpack?" Angie asks her sister, wanting to hang out with Jade.

"Sure, let's do it."

Rosa and Angie go to help Jade unpack her Camry. Tony walks behind Clinton, wrapping his arm around his neck.

"Uh, C. Is there something you want to…"

"Tony, it was your idea. You called it." Clinton interrupts.

"Thank you, that's all I wanted to hear."

Tony smacks Clinton's back before heading to Jade's car. Clinton looks at one of Renee's paintings hanging over the breakfast table.

"Renee, sweetheart, the ball is rolling."

It was around four o'clock when the girls got home from school. They see Clinton waiting for them.

"Hi, Clinton!!!!" They run to hug him.

"Hi girls, how was school???

"Good," Madison says

"Girls, I've got a surprise for you."

"What, what???"

"Well, I found someone to watch over you girls when Daddy is busy," Clinton says as the girls' eyes light up.

"Does she look like Sandy?" Madison asks when Clinton chuckles.

"Not with this one. Her name is Jade. She's very nice, very pretty and a lot of fun and we're all going to have dinner together so you can meet her. So, why don't you go upstairs and play."

"OK!!!" They yell out, running upstairs to their room.

Clinton was relieved to see their excited expressions, especially since they missed Sandra so much. A couple of hours later, dinner was ready. Tony made chicken carbonara with a Caesar salad and homemade breadsticks.

"Girls, dinner is ready!!!!" Tony tells the girls through the intercom.

Angie, Rosa, and Jade set up the dining room table. When they run down the stairs, Clinton and Tony prepare the girls' plates.

"Are you excited to meet them?" Rosa asks Jade.

"Yeah, this will be easy. I know how to speak to kids. I've been stuck at twelve for the past fourteen years." She says confidently, but deep down, Jade was a little nervous. Clinton waits for them at the bottom of the stairs, taking their hands and walking them to the dining room. "Ladies, this is your new nanny, Jade."

Jade turns around with her long blonde hair whipped and a massive beam on her face. The girls were bowled over, thinking she was a life-sized Barbie doll. Madison squeals and runs to her, hugging her waist. Jade turns to Rosa.

"Okay, maybe this will be tougher than I thought." She sarcastically says to Rosa. McKenna slowly walks to Jade, completely hypnotized by her presence.

"You look like a princess?"

Jade gives McKenna a smile from ear to ear with a twinkle in her eye. Without skipping a beat, she looks down at the both of them. "That's because I am. I come from a majestic land of Excaliburs, Luxors, and Stratospheres!!!! I can raise my arms and let water fly into the desert sky. I've lived in a land filled with Raiders, Golden Knights, and Thunder from Down Under!!!!!"

"WOW!!!!!!" McKenna's eyes glowed.

Rosa and Angie bite their lips, trying so hard not to laugh. Cortez and Tony had to walk away because they had lost control. On the other hand, Clinton held it together, watching the three of them click instantly. First impression, check.

It was a big family dinner, even without the patriarch. As they ate, The Crew watched the girls and Jade interact with each other, chatting her ear off about their day at school, riding on Daddy's boat, and their love for Disney princesses. Jade told the girls about all the times she'd been to Disneyland and met all the Disney princesses. She took out her phone to show the girls pictures.

"Check this out. I've met Ariel, Jasmine, Snow White, Cinderella, and my favorite, Princess Merida."

"Why is Merida your favorite?" Madison asks with her eyes hypnotized by Jade's.

"Because Maddi, she didn't care what anybody thought of her. She knew who she was when she was born. She didn't change her way to please everyone, not even her mother. Her mother wanted her to be a certain way, and Merida said, "I don't think so!!!" That's why she was "Brave"; she dared to do what she felt was right for her. She always knew deep in her head and deeper in her heart.

Rosa looks at Clinton and mouths, "THIS GIRL IS GOOD!!!!". Clinton nods and smiles.

"OK, girls. Did you have enough to eat?" Clinton asks the kids who simply nod.

"Why don't you two go upstairs, show Jade your rooms, and pick a pair of PJs you want to wear tonight."

McKenna and Madison jump out of their seats and go to Jade. "C'mon, Jade!!!!"

The girls reach out each hand for Jade to take. Jade grins as she takes both hands and runs upstairs.

"Geez, girls, how many stairs are there!!!!" Jade yells in the distance upstairs while the girls giggle.

The Crew looks at each other, gobsmacked at how well they got along. This girl was a revelation. McKenna and Madison showed Jade the massive bedroom they shared with princess castles, their endless stuffed animals collection, and McKenna's Barbie Malibu dream house that was as tall as Jade. Around eight o'clock, Rosa & Angie come upstairs to get the girls ready for bed. They walk in and see all three girls in princess costumes. Except Jade's is very snug.

"Having fun, girls?" Angie asks, trying not to laugh.

"Yes!!!" The three of them say at the same time.

"Well, it's time for bed."

"No!!!!!!!!" The three of them yell out.

"Five more minutes?" Jade begs Rosa

"No, sleepy time," Rosa says with a stern response.

Jade stomps her feet, throwing a fit while taking off her pink dress. The girls climb into bed.

"Well, girls, this was way too much fun, but I will see you two in the morning," Jade says while walking out of their room when Madison stopped her.

"Wait, Jade. Can you sing us to sleep?"

Jade felt a sudden emotional pain when Madison asked her to sing to them. Jade had a beautiful singing voice at one point in her life, but an incident when she was fifteen made her stop. While looking at their sweet faces tucked in bed, Jade knew how to push back the pain. "It would be my honor." She tells them with a gleam in her eye.

"Looks like you're on the clock now. We'll leave you, girls, alone. Goodnight, girls." Angie grins at Jade.

"Goodnight, Rosa and Angie."

Jade goes in between both their beds, sitting on her knees.

"What are you going to sing to us?" Madison asks.

During dinner, Jade heard stories about Sandra and how she was the grandmotherly type. More than likely singing "You are my Sunshine" to the girls every night. Jade had a different choice of songs.

"Hmmm. What would be a good one?"

"Itsy bitsy, spider," Madison shouts out.

"Yeah, I don't know that one."

"Star light, star bright," McKenna suggested. Jade taps her chin, looking up at the ceiling.

"Star light, star bright? Nope, doesn't ring a bell."

"Well, what are you going to sing to us?" McKenna wondered

"I know one that suits us girls. Pay close attention because I want you two to always play this song in your head when you start your day."

In a very soft tone, she starts singing "Unstoppable" by Sia to them. Not only did Jade look like an angel to them, but she also had the voice of one. The girl smiled, hearing her soothing singing voice. It took very little time for the girls to fall asleep. Jade gets up and pats both their stomachs. She walks to the door and looks at them with their night light glowing. She whispers to them before closing their door.

"This is the start of a beautiful friendship, M&M."

CHAPTER 5

MEETING AT THE PIT

After leaving the girl's room, Jade heads downstairs when Rosa & Angie wait for her at the bottom. Rosa takes Jade's hand.

"Now, it's adulting time. Come with us."

Rosa and Angie take Jade to the five-car garage where the wine cooler is. All three look when Jade grabs a bottle of Chateau Lafite-Rothschild.

"Oooh, this is a good one for either meeting the new nanny or binge-watching "The Real Housewives of Orange County" with a box of Twinkies and Ho-Ho's." Jade jokes around.

"Sweet. Let's take it. By the way, Jade, I heard you sing to the girls. You have an amazing voice. Have you ever thought about singing professionally?" Angie wonders. Jade goes frozen, trying to explain why she didn't become a singer.

"I don't like to sing in front of people because…" Jade turns and sees the white Cadillac Escalade trying to deflect the subject. "God, that is a beauty?" She sees another car sticking out behind the SUV. "What's next to the Escalade, girls?" Angie & Rosa smile at each other.

"Oh, that's the other woman of the house," Rosa says.

They walk Jade to see Logan's black 1967 GT Mustang Shelby.

"SHE'S EXQUISITE!!!!" Jade yells out, grabbing her chest.

"Yeah, this is Logan's pride and joy. It was his dad's. They are the only two who've driven this baby. You'll have better odds of winning the lottery before Logan will let anyone drive this thing."

Jade grins and nods her head, saying to herself. "Challenge accepted!!!!"

"C'mon, let's get boozing." Rosa cheerfully says.

The girls head to the conversation pit of the enormous living room as the guys wait.

"Well, it's about time." Tony impatiently reacts.

"We just wanted to get a good bottle and show Jade the Shelby." Rosa responds

"Isn't she stunning?" Clinton says to Jade.

"Let's just say that car and Kid Rock are the two things that came out of Detroit I would love to ride."

Cortez choked on his beer, coughing hard. The whole Crew laughs hysterically. Clinton shakes his head, trying to control his laughter.

"My niece was right. No filter."

"And proud of it." Jade raises her fist before grabbing a corkscrew and quickly opens the bottle like a pro. She pours glasses for the Crew and serves them their wine, except Cortez is nursing his beer. She hands Rosa her glass.

"Thanks. Have you always been carefree?"

Jade sits on one of the armless vanity chairs with her feet tucked under her legs.

"No, I grew into it. My parents were kinda conservative." She chuckles. "I'm messing with you all. They were lunatic religious fanatics. Enough to a degree where Mother Teresa would call them assholes."

"So it's safe to say that you're rebelling," Tony says, figuring Jade out.

"My dear Anthony, I am a rebel without a care in the world." Jade takes a big drink of her wine. "I grew up being raised that I had to be liked by everyone, but you finally realize you don't have that power, and I didn't feel beautiful inside because of it. I had to create my own beauty, attitude, and behavior and forget everyone else because it's all up to you. Luckily, I found that on my own."

Angie nods her head. "Good for you, Jade."

"Thanks, Ang. I live by this quote, a famous rebel said, "Don't mistake my kindness for weakness. I am kind to everyone, but when someone is unkind to me, weak is not what you will remember about me.""

"Who said that?" Clinton asks.

"Al Capone." Jade, Angie, and Rosa respond at once. Jade gives the girls a strange stare.

"We're from Chicago." Rosa explains. Jade raises her chin in understanding.

"Ok, note to self. Never piss you off ever." Tony is warned. Everybody chuckles as Jade gives Tony a warning wag with her index finger.

Angie raises his glass. "Crew, a toast to princess Jade!!!" They all raise their glasses, and Cortez holds up his Heineken. "You hooked those two, girl!!" Angie points upstairs. Jade takes what Tony said earlier.

"No, no, no, no. No, it's true." They all laugh. "I just can't believe I'm here. I was in Vegas stripping at Topaz two months ago, and now I live at the Taj Mahal."

The Crew's eyes perked up, not believing Jade would say that revelation so freely.

"Whoa!!! You stripped at Topaz. I love that place." Cortez says excitedly.

"Wait a minute, you were a stripper?" Angie is in shock.

"Just a fill-in occasionally, but I was mainly the head bartender. You don't think less of me, do you, Angie?"

"To tell you the truth, can you show me some moves to do for my husband."

"Absolutely, you hot little whore!!!" Jade yells out, making the bond stronger.

"Jade, we don't judge anybody here. I mean, we all have a story to tell." Clinton says, which catches Jade by surprise because all her life, judgment was something she constantly faced.

"Did you know anything about the Brodie family?" Tony asks Jade.

"Not at all until Clinton hired me. I went on Wikipedia and researched the family later on. I learned how the grandfather found Horizon, and it was passed along to his dad and eventually Logan. I checked out pictures of him. OH MY GOD!!! He has the bluest eyes I've ever seen on a person."

Clinton and Tony raised their eyebrows at each other as if they were telepathically saying, "She's smitten."

"Honey, wait until you see them in person. He looks like a young Paul Newman." Rosa tries to sell Logan to Jade, who notices her fawning over him.

"So, how long have you been the Brodie's crew?" Clinton started since he was the leader.

"I was a center for the Seattle Supersonics in the mid-eighties. I was making excellent money, beating the lottery-type odds of being drafted into the NBA. I then took a giant shit on it by meeting cocaine. I got suspended numerous times, and the Sonics released me. No team would sign me, and I was finished. I only got to play for four years, and I had no idea what was next for me.

Then I met Jack. He went to every home game with his five-year-old son. When I was playing, every now and then, I would look at him, and he would give me a wink. I found it strange until later on in life. A few years after my last game, my bank account went bone dry, and I got a job at a coffee shop." Clinton drinks his wine, staring at his glass, grinning. "One day, Jack came in with his son. He ordered a black coffee and said, "Thank you, Clinton." He glances at Jade. "He remembered me. Instead of putting his change in the tip jar, he put a white piece of paper in it.

As they walked out, that little boy turned around and said, "Bye, bye!" and waved." Jade smiled.

"I opened the paper, and it said, "Want a second chance? Call me."

"So I called Jack a couple of days later, and he said he needed someone to be his assistant or his "Alfred." Someone to watch over when we have to travel on business and watch over his place. Take care of the family's affairs. He had a poolhouse I could stay in, the place you dwell now, Jade. Also, I had the same reaction you gave me when he told me how much my salary was." Jade chuckles. "Jack told me his only condition was to go to rehab, which he'd take care of. I asked him one simple question, "Why me, Jack?" I'll never forget his response. "Why not, you?" and he hung up.

Clinton gets up from the couch and hands Rosa his glass. He pulls out his wallet, removes that little piece of paper Jack gave him, and hands it to Jade.

"You still have it." She looks at Clinton, aghast.

"Thirty years, my dear. I met my Maggie. We didn't have kids, but on Logan's thirteenth birthday, he opened one of his presents, which were legal papers. Jack & Katie made me his godfather. That boy fell into my arms, and I did not let go. I still haven't, and I never will." A somber pause went out until Rosa spoke.

"I was eighteen, and Angie was sixteen, living in the projects on the Southside of Chicago. Hearing gunshots was a normal occurrence. It seemed like the Fourth of July every day. We didn't know our dad, who left after Angie was born. So, it was just the three of us until our mom died of a stroke. She worked two full-time jobs and took care of her two girls. Then it was just us." Rosa grabs her sister's hand. Angie dropped out of school, and we just worked. I was a waitress from 5 a.m. to noon and a maid at the Blackstone Hotel from 1 to 8 p.m.

One day, I was working on the top floor when I must've slept standing up in front of my cart. What woke me up was a soft voice that said, "Sweetie, are you OK?" I turned and saw this beautiful face with gorgeous flowing brown hair, and next to her was this handsome young man with those Paul Newman eyes I was telling you about. Katie and Logan were visiting relatives in town and heading to Soldier Field for a Seahawks/Bears game. I told her I was tired from caring for my sister while she was sick. I could tell she knew it was just the two of us. Katie asked me, "How long have you been up?" I told her, "Thirty-one hours and still going."

"You need help, sweetheart?" she said. I didn't answer. I was tongue-tied because of my stupid pride. Without thinking twice, she said, "Stay here; we'll be right back." She and Logan went back to their Presidential suite.

Three minutes later, she hands me an envelope and says, "Open it when your pride isn't in the way." She patted my shoulder, and they were on their way. Logan turned around, and Rosa started choking up, her eyes glassy. "He said with those blue eyes, "Have a good day!" God, he was such a sweet, polite boy. I looked at that envelope for days until a bullet grazed through our wall one night, just missing Angie's head by three inches. I tackled her to the ground and stayed down for a few minutes. The second I stood up, I tore into that envelope, and there was a check for $1,000 with a phone number and address." Tears ran down Angie's face. "Seeing the check being from Seattle, I thought, "Time to move.""

We packed up, got bus tickets, and headed here the following day. Once we got to that gate, I asked, "Is this the Brodie residence?" We then heard this guy's voice?" Angie grabbed his hand and kissed it. 'He said, "Are you the Chicago sisters?" I nodded with tears coming down. The gates opened, and he said, "C'mon in. We've been expecting you."

"Now, we have condos in Belltown, both married with a couple of kids and not a day goes by that I don't thank God for this family," Angie adds, wiping her tears.

Jade sees so much aberration coming from this group, overcoming so much. Knowing the pattern with them, she looks at Cortez.

"Well, what about you, chatty Cathy? What's your story?"

"I bullied Logan in high school."

Jade looks at him with confusion: "You bullied him?"

Cortez nods. "You would think a rich kid would attend a rich, swanked private school. Not Logan, though. He wanted to be normal." Cortez shrugged his shoulders. "I was being ignorant to the rich, white boy. The thing was, he never flaunted his wealth. He never wore Gucci or anything, but everybody knew who he was. I wanted to be the guy who beat the shit out of Richie Rich and make a name for myself. Yet, he took it and never told anyone.

One day, Spencer Baldwin, this Neo-Nazi skinhead motherfucker brought a semi-automatic to school. He was ready to mow down everybody who wasn't white. I was his first target because it was known I was beating up a white boy. That gun was pointed in my face when Logan tackled the piece of shit out of nowhere. Gun went off, hitting the ceiling. Logan knocked the gun out of his hand and started pounding him to a bloody pulp. I went right behind him, protecting him from anyone pulling him off Spencer. I wanted Logan to have all the time in the world with that swastika-wearing son of a bitch. He was a bloody mess after Logan was done with him. I asked why he saved my life after what I did to him. He said the same thing his daddy said, "Why not you"?

From that day on, I've always got his back. I ensured I got a football scholarship at Washington U and became a Huskie like him, so I was right there to protect him. He's my best friend. He's my brother."

Jade takes a deep breath, soaking in all their stories. She could not believe the heart this family had.

"Ok, why hasn't the Pope turned these people into saints? It's so sickening watching the news, and you're bombarded with how horrible people are, but then you hear this, and your faith is restored instantly." She wondered. The whole Crew nodded in agreement. She stares at Tony. "What about you, Ant?"

"I was on "Throwdown with Bobby Flay." They said my grilled eggplant lacked flair and I got eliminated. Jack and Katie thought I lost unjustifiably, so they offered me a job and I took it." He shrugs his shoulders. "That's it." Jade just stares and slowly breaks into uncontrollable laughter, which starts a chain reaction with everyone else. Tony nods, knowing why everyone is laughing. "I know, I get it. I am a giant bore."

Jade finally composes herself. "Tony, that Carbonara was extraordinary, so Jack and Katie had a reason to hire you."

"Thank you." Tony bows to Jade. Rosa looks at her phone.

"Well, guys, we better get home. God knows what my husband made for dinner for the kids."

"Yeah, it's getting late." Clinton checks his watch. They all get up and order their Ubers for the night. Oh, Jade. I just remembered another perk for you. Give me your phone."

Jade, puzzled, hands Clinton her phone. He downloads an app called Brodie Stereo. She opens it and notices all her favorite songs and a list of every room in the house.

"What is this?" Jade asks

"Did you notice all the speakers all over the house? Logan has the stereo system of stereo systems. I'll show you." Angie runs to the kitchen. "I Cry" by Flo Rida starts blasting. Angie pauses it and comes out. Jade's eyes light up.

"Are you trying to tell me that all of our music is connected to every room in the house?" Jade asks excitedly.

"Try it," Clinton suggests. Jade presses for the living room and plays "Butterfly" by Crazytown. The song blasts throughout the room. Her mouth drops in amazement.

"No way!!!" she screams. "And this guy is paying us almost six figures?"

"Welcome to your dream job." Clinton grins and winks. Rosa gets a notification on her phone.

"Angie, our Uber is here; well, Jade, we'll see you bright and early." Everybody starts to head towards the front door when Jade stops them.

"Hey, guys." The Crew turned around to look at their new member. Never in her life did she feel so welcomed. "Thanks for all of this and for embracing me. I'm so happy to be here."

Clinton smiles. "We're very happy you're here, Jade. We'll see you in the morning."

Everyone leaves at the same time, leaving Jade all alone in the mansion. She takes a deep breath, looking at her surroundings, not believing for a second that she's here. In just a week and a half, Jade Murphy served Jameson shots at a Gentlemen's Club in Vegas to become the nanny of a billionaire's children in Seattle. She closed her eyes and focused deep inside of her. Jade wasn't going to ask herself how life got her here. She was going to focus on the job at hand. She started walking up to the first set of stairs to the landing where one of the six Christmas trees was placed. She sees a nativity ornament, smiling at the baby Jesus.

"Thanks for guiding me here, J. Please don't let me screw this up."

Jade kisses her finger and puts it on the forehead of the Jesus figurine.

CHAPTER 6

WHEN LOGAN MET JADE

Logan returned from his Atlanta trip to an unseasonably warm December Seattle day. For three years, his business trips were a routine. Go to meetings, stay in his hotel, talk with Renee, and repeat. There was no R&R for him. He would usually get something for the kids at the airport before coming home. This time, though, he was clean-shaven, his clothes weren't wrinkled, and his hair was straightened, knowing he would meet the new nanny. Logan yells from the front.

"Hey guys, I'm home." From a distance, Angie yells from the girls' room upstairs, folding laundry.

"Hey Logan, welcome home." Tony walks from the kitchen and gives Logan a shoulder-to-shoulder bro hug.

"Hey, chief, how was Atlanta?"

"Oh, it was PEACHY," Logan says painfully sarcastically.

"Ewww. That was terrible." Tony groans after that lousy pun.

"I know. I heard that a lot down there." Tony notices Logan looking damper, which is a rarity.

"Dude, you look good."

"I knew I would meet the girl's new nanny, so I wanted to look semi-presentable. Where are the kids?" He asks while picking up his mail and heading towards the kitchen.

"They're in the backyard with Jade. They're enjoying this strange, warm weather and doing yoga outside."

Logan thumbed through his mail.

"I know, it was like thirty degrees in Georgia." He wrinkled his brow when it donned on Logan what Tony just said. "Wait, the girls are doing yoga?"

"Yeah. They have clicked instantly. I didn't think they would get along at first because she's very soft-spoken, kind of a wall-flower, plain Jane type, but she's great. Very conservative, though." Tony grins with anticipation to see Logan's face.

"Really? Jade, is it?" He questions.

Tony nods as Logan continues looking at his mail. He momentarily looks up and sees Jade in the backyard with the girls practicing yoga together. He went into complete shutdown mode, dropping the mail to the floor, when he saw Jade in the tightest pink sports bra a woman could ever wear. Tony walks behind Logan, biting his lip, trying to hold his laughter. He pats Logan's shoulder, laughing.

"I'm just messing with you, bro. She's the hottest girl I've ever seen in my life. Next to Bridget, of course."

Logan sees Jade and the girls on their stomachs with their heads up. Logan only looks at Jade, not his daughters, whom he hasn't seen for almost a week. He watches Jade's breast practically spill out, breathing in deeply while her blonde hair beamed in the sun, which was pulled into a ponytail. So many thoughts rapidly were flying through his scrambled head. Within seconds, he imagined what Jade would look like naked. He quickly shook his head. "What the hell am I thinking? Most of all, what the hell was Clinton thinking?" He sees Jade stand up and turn, facing the lake. He gasps when he sees her bend down in her white yoga pants. Her body was perfectly toned, and her skin was beautifully bronzed, and he admired the most perfect ass he ever saw on a woman. Logan got a feeling back that he lost a long time ago. The feeling of lust. He closes his eyes and shakes his head again when reality slaps him.

"Hold it, that's the new nanny?" Logan's voice goes up, asking Tony.

"Yup. She's Tonya's best friend from college."

"Where the hell is Clinton?"

"He went to the store to get some things for dinner. He should be home any minute." Angie and Rosa come downstairs to hug Logan. They hug Logan together.

"Hey Logan, how was Atlan…"

Logan interrupts with his mind on Jade. "It was wonderful; the traffic was great. Anyway, um…" Logan was tongue-tied. Angie and Rosa look at each other, smiling with a "He's blown away" look. "Um, the nanny."

"Jade? Oh my God, Logan. She is wonderful. She preps the girls' clothes for the week, and started teaching them self-defense and meditation. I can't believe how hands-on she is with them." Angie informs him.

"M&M are in love with her." Rosa retorts.

"M&M?" Logan shakes his head.

"She calls them M&M. It's adorable. After she picks them up from school, they do thirty minutes of yoga daily to clear their heads from negative vibes."

Logan stares at Jade's heaving chest, going in and out while she breathes heavily. He quickly looks away, erasing any dirty thoughts, and concentrates on his kids practicing with her.

"Well, that's important. They're hitting it off?" He wonders.

"Right off the bat." Angie snaps her fingers. "Why don't you go out there and meet her."

Logan takes a deep breath, brushing his hair. "Well, they're meditating. I don't want to disturb…."

"Logan, go introduce yourself now." Rosa cuts him off and says sternly, like he was twelve.

"Ok, I'm going." Logan says in a defeated tone heading outside.

"Did you see that?" Tony asks both sisters. The three of them watch Logan approaching Jade and the kids.

"What, the look on his face, the sweat coming down his brow, or the erection he had in his pants?" Angie asks bluntly.

Logan approaches the girls, who have their eyes closed, legs crossed, arms out, meditating. Every day, all three girls practice heavy yoga, learning to remove any negative aura in themselves. Jade teaches them in the most soothing voice. The girls lift their heads to the sky.

"Ladies, your mind is free. Embrace your inner self, your inner soul, your inner serenity. You are..." Logan clears his throat. The girls open their eyes and scream, "Daddy!!!" Jade's eyes remain closed. "Not just yet, ladies!!! Just a few more seconds." McKenna and Madison quickly go back to close their eyes, and all three lower their heads and exhale. "What are you, ladies?" All three speak at the same time. "We are one... We are beautiful... We are us."

The girls open their eyes and run to Logan. Jade opens her eyes and sees Logan for the first time. In a few seconds, Jade goes from being one with the earth to thanking God she wore panties. Jade sees this man wearing a tight red sweater vest over a black shirt, showing off his built chest, tight jeans, wavy brown hair, and the bluest eyes imaginable.

"Oh, hi." Jade gets off her yoga mat without taking her eyes off him. Logan stares her down as he towered over her.

"Hi, um, Jade?" He reaches out his hand. Those blues still hypnotized her.

"Uh, yes."

Once they shook hands, they immediately felt the connection. The electricity went through both of them, making it difficult for them to say anything. Jade then looked at the tree trunk, which was Logan's arms.

"So, how have they been for you? The girls, I mean?" He nervously asks.

The girls run to stand by Jade. She grabs them from behind, playfully holding them.

"They are amazing. You raised them well."

"I do the best I can. I want them grounded even when they're living here. I love what you're doing with them with the yoga."

"Well, kindergarten and preschool are trying times. I say take advantage early and manage their stress early."

Jade's gaze was still glued to his eyes. Much like Logan, she got a feeling she hadn't experienced in a long time—the feeling of lost control. Logan was the first man in so long that she felt any sense of attraction. Realizing there was a long pause between them, Logan quickly excused himself.

"Well, it's great to meet you. I'm assuming you're settled in the poolhouse." His mouth goes drier with every word.

"Poolhouse? You mean that little five-star resort. Oh my God, you know how to treat your staff."

"Well. You're part of the Crew now. I want to take care of you."

Jade shivered when he said that, but he wanted to kick himself for saying it. Both of them were desperate to come up with anything to say to each other, but their minds were clouded by the instant chemistry they had for each other.

"Alright, girls, you two have fun with your daddy. He hasn't seen you for days. I'll see you both tomorrow."

"Bye, Jade." The girls both give Jade a big hug.

"Wow, four days, and you three are in hug status. I'm impressed."

"Hey, I'm awesome. What can I tell you?" she says with a playful, smug response. Jade looks at

Logan as she walks by. "Bye, Logan."

"See ya."

As she walked past Logan, he smelled her perfume. He watched her walk to her guest house and noticed her large angel wing tattoo on her back. It was not possible, but he was turned on even more. He always had a thing for women with tattoos. His mind was in a complete fog when Madison pulled him out of it.

"C'mon, Daddy!!!!"

Logan holds both girls' hands as they walk back into the house. Jade looks back and then starts sprinting to the pool house. She quickly grabs her phone to call Tonya at work.

"Hey J- girl. What's up?" She answers

"OH, MY GOD!!! Google images have nothing on this guy!!! LOGAN IS GORGEOUS!!!!! It took every ounce of my well-being not to jump into Lake Washington and cool my body down. I'm so fucked here, Tonya!!!!"

Tonya couldn't keep the smile off her face hearing Jade's infatuation with Logan.

"OK, sweetie, sweetie. Listen to me very carefully. Your priority is McKenna and Madison, and that's it!!! You've got an amazing paying job to do. You're welcome, by the way."

This was the first time she'd heard Jade go insane over a man since they were sophomores in college.

"You're right, but he is so tall, his arms. He could throw me across the room onto my bed and…

What am I saying? I'm losing my mind over here!!!"

"The hell you say?"

"Well, I'm going to try and calm down, so I'll be in the shower for an hour or three. I'll talk to you later. Bye."

Jade hung up quickly, collapsing on her couch and covering her face with a pillow in disbelief at Logan's attractiveness. Meanwhile, at the same time, Logan heads back to the house and sees Clinton back from the store.

"Girls, take those bags to Tony and help him with dinner. I got to talk to your Uncle Clinton." His eyes locked deep into his god-father's, who was waiting for this talk.

"OK, Daddy!!!"

They grab the plastic bags from Clinton and run to the kitchen. A slight grin creeps on Clinton's face.

"So Logan, how was...?" Logan quickly interrupts. "Screw Atlanta, we need to talk, NOW!!!" They walk into his office. Clinton sits back on one of the chairs, knowing the topic will be Jade.

"What's up?" Clinton asks. Logan shakes his head, leaning on his desk.

"No, no, no. Don't give me that condescending "What's up?". Where did she come from?"

"First, her name is Jade, and she just moved here from Vegas. She's Tonya's best friend from college, and she needed a job, and YOU needed a nanny. So, here you go, and you're welcome because I assume a thank you was coming up very soon." Logan jumps on top of his desk, looking completely flustered.

"You said you wanted me to take care of the new hire, and I did. You said all you cared about was how well she took care of the children, and Jade is amazing at it. So your criteria has been ful-filled." Clinton shoots Logan the truth between the eyes. He grabs his temple, not getting the image of her out of his head.

"She is....stunning."

"She is at that. Your point is what, son?" Logan shrugs his shoulders.

"Hell, I don't know. I just didn't expect her. I was expecting another Sandy or at least a Mrs. Doubtfire. An old, grandmotherly type, someone who doesn't walk around in tight yoga pants, with hot pink toenails, and who has that glowing bronze Vegas skin." Clinton exits his chair and leans on Logan's desk beside him.

"Listen to me, boy. Would I hire anyone who didn't treat McKenna and Madison like gold? She's got a gift. She's funny, strong-willed, independent. I will warn you. Jade has kind of a liberal side."

"Example?" Logan asked, intrigued.

"Let's just say the Seattle weather doesn't bother her. I mean, she lived in Vegas. I can't tell her what she can or cannot wear. There's no dress code here, and she is her own woman. Also, she does have a mouth on her." Logan gives Clinton a questionable glance. "Let's just say she would make a marine gasp." She knows how to turn it off in front of the children. I know those are small potatoes to you because, like you said, as long as the kids love her."

At that point, Logan imagined what else Jade would be wearing next and the image of the girls giving her a big hug before they left. That was his main priority.

"I have to say. I haven't seen them brighten up like that in a long time. It's just..." Clinton stops Logan from going on.

"Go play with your daughters before dinner. They haven't seen their father in almost a week." Logan nods in agreement.

"You're right. Listen, you guys go home. I'm thinking of dinner and a movie date night with them."

"Very good. Hug your godfather."

They both hug as Clinton leaves. Logan looks out the window at the lake, still thinking at the sight of Jade.

Logan and the girls were in their PJs in the kitchen, cleaning up the lasagna plates Tony made for them. They were heating some popcorn in the microwave, discussing their week. They talked about school and what they did while he was away. Logan wanted to pick their brains and tell him everything they knew about Jade.

"So tell me, what does Jade do with you two?"

"Every day, she wakes us up, gets us dressed, and makes us look so pretty. She does our hair, and she lets us wear makeup. She said every day, we must look in the mirror and say, "You are beautiful, and never let anyone say you're not." McKenna tells her daddy.

"That's nice of her."

"It's called self-esteem," Madison added. Logan gets the pop-corn out of the microwave.

"That's right, sweetheart. That's very important for a young girl. It's great that she teaches you that. I hear she taught you girls what to do when a stranger approaches you."

They start walking to the theater with a bowl of popcorn, a bag of M&M's, and bottled water.

"Yeah, Jade says, never stop screaming. "Stranger, stranger." If they get us, spit, bite, and kick.

She said the best place is the gentles."

Logan stops looking straight ahead, realizing they meant gen-itals. They sit on the long couch facing the giant screen. Logan grabs the remote.

"Hey, Daddy, do you like Jade?" Madison asks.

"Umm, I think she's great."

He takes a handful of popcorn and throws it in his mouth.

"Like a girlfriend?" Madison asks, which causes Logan to choke on his popcorn.

"Girls!!! I just met her today." He shook his head, realizing what he said. "I mean, she's your nanny, girls. I can't be with your nanny."

"Becca from school, her daddy is with her nanny, and she is her new mommy," McKenna tells Logan.

McKenna doesn't know that Becca's daddy LEFT Becca's mommy for Becca's nanny. Logan covers his face and says under his breath.

"Oh, good God. Well, that's different, girls. Marriages have problems."

"Did you and Mommy have problems?"

Logan thought about if he had fights with Renee.

"No, we didn't. I wanted to do everything for her and give your mommy everything."

"Like us," Madison says with a glow. Logan grins, holding Madison's wrist.

"Especially you two." Logan smiles as he sees Renee in both of them. "So what are we going to watch?"

McKenna and Madison smile at each other and say at the same time. "Brave!!!"

"Sure, but you never showed interest in seeing it," Logan asks, surprised.

"I know, but now we do."

The girls laugh while giving them a puzzling look. He turns on Disney Plus on the giant screen and puts on the movie.

At that time, Jade heated some old leftover Chinese and was preparing to read "The Poor Man and the Lady" by Thomas Hardy on the couch when she got a text from Tony.

Tony's text: "Hey, I saved you some lasagna in the refrigerator. Hopefully, Logan and the girls didn't ravage it."

Jade text: "Thanks a bunch."

An excited Jade slams her book, quickly puts on a pair of jeans, and heads to the mansion. She punches in the security code and deactivates the alarm. Upon entering, she hears familiar noises coming from the movie theater. She tiptoes to the entrance and sees the back of Logan with McKenna and Madison side by side on the couch, watching her favorite Pixar movie. Her face lights up, growing warm, thinking they're watching it because of her. She walks back to the kitchen with a prideful smile, grabs her plate of lasagna, snatches a beer out of the refrigerator, and heads back to the poolhouse, knowing that she is in with everybody.

CHAPTER 7

No Press for Christmas

The Saturday morning before Christmas was one of Logan's favorite days. He built the Jack & Katie Brodie Children's Memorial Hospital eight years ago. Every year, Jack Brodie would throw the mother of all toy drives. On every floor at Brodie Tower, the headquarters of Horizon, trash cans and totes were left for employees to donate throughout the year. Then, they were distributed to a warehouse on the Brodie property. Along with Logan and the Crew's donations, the warehouse gets emptied. The Saturday morning before Christmas, the Crew would come over and volunteer to help ship and deliver the toys.

"What time are the U-Hauls getting here?" Angie asks while filling up her coffee.

"They'll deliver them in a half hour, and we'll take them back when we're done." Says Logan while pouring syrup on the kids' pancakes that Tony made for everybody.

"How many trucks are we getting?" Tony asks as he flips a pancake into the pan.

"Six. One more than last year. We had more donations come in." Clinton states when Jade walks into the mansion wearing tight jeans and an off-the-shoulder Christmas sweater that reads, "Dear Santa, Define good."

"Morning, y'all."

"Ok, you won the best Christmas sweater this year." Rosa applauses.

"Wait a minute; you haven't seen mine yet." Tony disputes.

"The lady said the contest is over, and I am the champion of Christmas!!!!!" She playfully responds while pouring herself a cup of coffee. Logan lowers his head, chuckling. He gets a text from the hospital's director.

"Alright, listen up soldiers. The hospital is ready for us, and they're ready to unload, so we've got two hours to load up the trucks and haul it over there." He informs the Crew when a familiar voice emerges from the front door.

"Merry Noel, everybody."

Sasha Turner, Logan's assistant, and her husband, Rick, entered the kitchen. She was one of Renee's best friends from Washington U, and Rick was head of Horizon's accounting department. They were the poster couple of opposites attracted. Sasha was once a supermodel with flowing brown hair, green eyes, and a perfectly shaped body. Rick had a skinny figure with glasses who looked like an accountant.

"Awesome, you guys made it," Logan says aesthetically.

"Of course, we'd never miss your favorite day, Logan," Rick tells Logan. He then turns his eyes to Jade.

"Sasha, Rick, this is McKenna and Madison's new nanny, Jade. Jade, my assistant Sasha, and her husband, Rick." Rick shakes Jade's hand.

"How are you? I've heard a lot of rave reviews about you from this guy."

"And they're all true." She jokes with Rick as he cracks up laughing.

Jade goes to shake Sasha's hand, giving her a crooked smile and a soft handshake. It wasn't that Sasha was jealous; there was another beautiful woman near Logan, but she was very overprotective of him. Jade could feel the tension out of the handshake, but she would be cool about it. Under her smile, though, she thought, "I've seen that look, and I can read your mind, so bitch if you start something, I sure as hell will finish it!!!" She gives Sasha her brightest smile.

"Nice to meet you, Sasha."

"Likewise." Just then, Cortez walks into the mansion after scoping out the warehouse.

"Hey guys, let's get moving. We need to start unloading the warehouse now. Logan went nuts this year."

"Compared to which year, Cortez?" Rosa shrugs her shoulders.

"Wait a minute. Let me get this straight: that warehouse is filled with just toys? You don't put your boat in there."

"Nope, my boat is winterized. The warehouse is strictly for this day alone. Come on, I'll show you."

Jade puts her cup down and walks with Logan toward the warehouse. Jade was a step behind Logan when she couldn't help but look at the back of his body. He wore a light, long-sleeved hoodie perfectly aligned to his massive back. Her eyes scrolled down to his Adonis-like ass which his jeans perfectly hugged. Jade's head was going into a place she shouldn't be in. She scrambled her head desperately, trying to escape that dirty place. She took an extra step to match with him.

"Let me ask you something. Sasha and Rick. I mean this with no offense, but what's the story of those two, and when did he give his soul to Satan?" Logan laughs while walking on.

"I know. Rick looks like he auditioned for "Big Bang Theory," and Sasha walked out of a Victoria's Secret catalog."

"Yes!!! The cheerleader married the geek." She says with glee.

"You nailed it. When I hired him, he came from M.I.T., and they hit it off."

"Wow. Good for him because Sasha is beautiful."

"She is at that, and he's a great guy. They deserve each other."

Jade glares at Logan's kindness. She suspects him to be the old-fashioned romantic who goes out of his way for his girl. She thought about how well he treated his help and the woman of his life. They reach the front entrance to the warehouse.

"You really need six U-Hauls for this?" Jade asks.

"Not normally. Six is the new record, so you're here to witness history."

Logan dials the code to the lock. The door opens, and Jade's mouth drops. As far as she could see, there were endless toys. Jade walks in and takes it all in. She sees thousands of dolls, remote-controlled cars, board games, and action figures. It was endless. Her heart was filled with his generosity.

"Mother of God!!! Logan, this is amazing."

"This is the one place in the house where I really feel rich. I have this tradition where I'll play one certain video game, and I'll donate the highest score I get. Super Mario Brothers, Donkey Kong, Burgertime. This year, it was Ms. Pac-Man."

"What was your score?"

"538,000 points"

"So you don't pledge but donate $538,000 in toys?" She asks while scanning Logan's toyland.

"Plus, whatever people privately donate, the Crew takes a piece out of their paychecks. So, you're looking at over a million dollars worth of toys here."

"Oh, the break you get from the IRS."

"True, but I don't do this for the tax breaks or the P.R. I just want to give those kids something since they're stuck in a hospital and not at home sitting under the Christmas tree."

So many thoughts are going through Jade's head, but one thought stands out. "This man is not only beautiful on the outside, he's stunningly beautiful on the inside."

"You are something else, Logan Brodie."

"You're too kind, Jade, but I'm as flawed as possible."

What did he mean by that?" She thought. "Was he trying to get right with God for something he did, or is he that modest?" She folded her arms, looking out at the never-ending view of toys.

"How long have you been doing this?

"Eighteen years. The game thing was my dad's idea. He was playing Centipede one day, and it popped into his head. So, I continued the tradition."

Logan looked away from Jade and gazed at all the toys, feeling his father's presence. From his look, she could feel his connection with his dad.

"Logan, the trucks will be here in five minutes!!!!" Sasha yells from the outside.

"Alright!!!!!" He yells back.

Jade couldn't stop looking at Logan. Everything about him tugged at her heart, and she saw him genuinely excited to wipe out this enormous warehouse, donate it all, and fill it up again.

"So, what are your plans for Christmas?" Logan asks, hoping she has no plans so he could invite her to spend Christmas with him and the girls. "Oh, Tonya and I will spend it at Clinton & Maggie's place."

"Oh, nice." He hid his disappointment well.

"I've been meaning to ask, what do I get the girls for Christmas?"

"Well, McKenna loves female comic book characters, Wonder Woman, Harley Quinn, and Captain Marvel, and Madison loves anything "Minions and Despicable Me". I'm going to be perfectly honest, they'll love anything coming from you." Jade felt a warmth going through her when his eyes locked on her.

"OK, cool. What about you? What does Logan want for Christmas?" She asks while Logan laughs.

"Oh, for God's sake, NOTHING!!!! Just come to Barbados with all of us."

"Gee Logan, I don't know," Jade says, playing fully sarcastic. Of course, I'm coming. Let's get to the bottom line: you own an island? You have a place big enough for." Jade tries to count when Logan stops her.

"Twenty-Five. The mansion there is twice the size as this place." He says casually.

"It's a 19,000-square-foot mansion?"

"21,000 to be exact. Fifteen bedrooms, ten baths, and three swimming pools, all with waterfalls. I'll show you."

Logan gets closer to Jade and whips out his phone. Jade inhales softly at Logan's cologne. Really bad thoughts were crossing her mind at that point. That was until she saw the wallpaper on his phone of a wedding photo of him and Renee. He finds the picture folder of Barbados. Jade's mouth falls when she doesn't see a mansion but a fortress. She hands Logan back his phone after she is done scrolling.

"So, what do you think?" He asks.

"It's going to be a happening time, as the kids say nowadays." They both crack up laughing.

"You are a crack-up." Logan shakes his head.

"What can I say? I am a gift from God."

A horn honks as Rick drives the first truck right to the front of the warehouse. Logan enthusiastically claps his hands.

"Let's do it!!!"

Jade smiles, watching Logan walk out of the warehouse pumped up. She repeatedly looks at the collection of toys, shaking her head.

"This guy is unfuckinbelievable."

They all emptied the warehouse and filled all six trucks in just under two hours. They then headed to the children's hospital. Jade was riding in one of the trucks with Angie while they both lip-synched to "Last Christmas" by WHAM.

"God, I love Christmas" Jade yells out, getting amped up to deliver toys.

"Are you going to see your parents in California?" Angie asks.

"Nope, I haven't talked to them in years."

"Oh, I'm sorry."

"Don't sweat it, I'm not."

"Hey, you're welcome to spend Christmas at our place." Angie extended an invitation.

"Ahh, thanks, Ang, but Tonya and I are going to Clinton and Maggie's place."

"Thank God. I didn't want you alone," Angie says relieved.

"Aww, you're a jewel." Angie smiles at Jade. She was dying to know how her alone time with Logan went.

"So, what did you think of Logan's toy shop?"

"OH, MY GOD!!!! Is that guy for real? His generosity is astounding. "

"That man is no bullshit, Jade. He is the most caring person alive. I just wish he learned to care about himself."

"I don't follow," Jade stated, confused at what Angie meant. She took a deep breath before telling Jade a horrible chapter in Logan's and the Crews'.

"He's never recovered since Renee died. I know you don't see it because it's all an act. He tries to show a brave persona to everybody, but we know him too well. The only thing that keeps him going is McKenna and Madison. They are the center of his existence. Thank God for them because I don't think he'd make it."

"What did she die of?"

"Ovarian Cancer."

"Jesus, wasn't she only in her 30s?" Jade says in shock.

"Yeah. I think that's what eats him alive the most. They never caught it because she was pregnant with Madison when she got it."

"Oh, my loving God!!!"

"Yeah. It kills me to watch him suffer. Well, it kills all of us."

"He's never tried dating and moving on," Jade asks curiously. Angie shakes her head.

"Nope. I know women try to throw themselves at him because he's rich and drop-dead handsome, but he wants no part of them. His will to move on died with Renee. He's never shown interest in other women."

Jade was trying to come up with anything to say and mostly trying to understand how this genuine man of the people was just an empty shell inside.

"My heart is getting torn apart here."

"I know, but we've been torn apart for over three years. Today, though, you'll see who Logan Brodie really is."

Angie looks at Jade and sees the sincere pain on her face for him, yet she is smiling inside because Jade is the only woman Logan has paid attention to since Renee's death. They reach the children's hospital, with volunteers already unloading the toys out of the other trucks. Jade gets out of the cab and notices Logan is nowhere to be found.

"Ant, where's Logan?" Jade asks Tony.

"He had to talk to the administrator about the toy handouts and meeting with some parents."

"Alright, guys, It's showtime!!!!" Clinton declares.

The Crew goes inside the front entrance. The floors are crystalized marble with pictures of Jack and Katie Brodie. They walk into the Renee Brodie Memorial wing of the hospital. Jade looks around in amazement at how beautiful this hospital is. She recognizes the artwork lined up through the halls. They are similar to the ones at the house. She looks closely and sees "RB" on the bottom of the canvas.

"Are all these Renee's? They're stunning." Jade asks Clinton.

"Yeah, she was very gifted. Logan isn't one of those billionaires who spend on priceless Monets and Picassos. He'll blow up pictures the kids drew and hang them around Brodie Tower."

"This guy does not know how to stop outdoing himself."

"You ain't seen nothing yet, sweetheart."

Clinton and Jade turn the corner to see children lined up in the wing, waiting to see Santa Claus. As she walks past the line, Jade sees children dragging respirators, having bald heads from chemo, and in wheelchairs. Jade got slapped with the ultimate dose of reality. Being blessed for twenty-five years, having a healthy life, living in paradise while witnessing these young lives suffering with their parents, and wondering if this was their last Christmas.

"Here's your headset, you two." Sasha hands Clinton and Jade a headset with a tiny microphone.

"What's this for?" Jade asks.

"So we can communicate and get advanced warning about which toy each child wants. Rick and Tony are three floors down with every toy category based on gender, and they will find that specific toy as it shoots up behind that certain Santa bag. So we eavesdrop, talk to the parents, and understand what they want."

Jade puts her headset on with a heavy lump in her throat. She turned to look around for Logan, who still wasn't around. All of a sudden, sleigh bells start ringing.

"Ho, Ho, Ho!!!!!!!!"

The children start cheering. Santa walks in, and he is decked out to perfection. Jade was impressed with how Santa looked because he didn't look like he came from the mall. Logan went all out to get the best one.

"Hello, boys and girls, and Merry Christmas to you all," Santa tells the children.

Jade looked around for Logan. This was his essential day. It hit her when Santa came close, and those Pacific blue eyes under those glasses walked past her. She covered her mouth while Clinton looked at her and grinned.

"Logan." Clinton shakes his head.

"No, Jade, Santa."

"As I said, you'll see who Logan Brodie really is," Angie whispers in Jade's ear.

Logan was utterly unrecognizable, dressed as St. Nick. Wearing a fat suit, make-up that excels age, and a spot-on beard, it was a perfect incognito. Jade watches Logan hand out toys for over two hours. He was not looking tired, but he looked like he was born to do this. She looks around in disbelief that there's no media coverage. Even though Logan was a huge public figure, he refused to have any recognition it that this was all him. One boy named David, who looked to be Madison's age, gripped onto a respirator, pale white with a large scar over the top of his head. He goes to Santa with a smile ear to ear.

"Hi, Santa!!!." The boy said with so much happiness in his voice.

"Hello, David; what can I get you for Christmas?"

"Can I have a remote control Batmobile?"

"Well, let me see what we have…" Santa begins to hum, looking into his giant bag. He gasps and pulls out the Batmobile. "Would you look at that?"

David's eyes light up. Before Santa hands it to him, David goes into Santa's arms. "I love you, Santa." Santa gently hugs and pats his back. Logan accidentally loses his Santa voice and tells him in his natural voice. "I love you too, son." Jade turns to look at David's parents. She sees his mother sobbing on her husband's shoulder, holding her tight, sobbing along with her. All the signs were right there. She goes to Rosa, whose eyes are glossy, holding back the tears.

"Uhh, how long…" Jade had difficulty asking when Rosa cut her off with a heavy voice.

"Two months. Inoperable brain tumor."

The helplessness was eating inside Jade. She looks around at one sick child after the next. It was getting too much for her.

"Hey, I have to run to the bathroom. I'll be right back," Jade tells Rosa.

"Okay"

Once out of the area, Jade runs to the bathroom. She whips the headset off and stands in front of the mirror, looking deep into her eyes. Jade Murphy was never a cryer. To her, it was a sign of weakness. From childhood, she developed the ability to block any emotion and prevent tears from coming down her cheek. Today, though, she almost reached her breaking point. She never imagined being at a hospital full of sick children fighting for their lives. She took deep breaths but could not stop thinking of Logan with little David getting to play with his Batmobile for only three months. She starts to talk about her reflection.

"Not one tear, Jade. Don't you dare. You will be as strong as they are. You will be as brave as they are. You will look at those kids with every ounce of hope because that's all they've got. You will not pity them because they don't deserve it. They deserve a wonderful Christmas, and you will help them."

She exhales hard before heading back, returning with the group. Sasha sees Jade, suspecting she had a breakdown since they all had one their first year.

"You OK, Jade?"

"Yeah, I've been holding it in for a long time. I just don't want to miss this." She tells Sasha.

"I don't blame you. It is a beautiful sight, isn't it?"

Jade stares right at Santa's smile at the children. "It sure is."

They watch the parents taking selfies with Santa, not realizing that the man in the red suit is Logan Brodie. The man responsible for giving their kids a day to smile. A little girl in line holding a teddy bear with second-degree burn scars on the right side of her face from a house fire stands in front of Jade. She looks up at her and smiles.

"You're beautiful." The little girl tells Jade. She looks down at the little girl and smiles.

"You're so sweet, angel."

The little girl had a glowing smile when Jade said that. She went down to one knee and brushed the hair out of the little girl's face.

"What's your name, honey?"

"Aurora. What's your name?"

"I'm Jade."

Angie sees Jade talking to Aurora and taps on Rosa's shoulder. Each member of the Crew grinned, watching Jade interact with her.

"Do you know Santa?" Aurora asks.

"I sure do. We're good buds. Are you excited to meet him?"

"I'm a little nervous. That's why I brought Sadie with me." Aurora shows Jade her teddy bear. Jade shakes her head.

"There's nothing to be nervous about, Aurora. Do you want me to go with you so I can introduce him to you and Sadie?" Aurora's face glows.

"Really?"

Jade takes Aurora's hand, and they wait in line together.

"I heard you were on the super, mega nice list, and that's a hard list to make, so what are you wanting for Christmas?"

"I want a makeup kit so I can be as pretty as you," Aurora tells Jade. Knowing Aurora would undergo many skin grafts and plastic surgery in her childhood, Jade knows she has a long mental road ahead.

"Are you sure you need makeup because you are so pretty already? Santa will get you a makeup kit." Jade says it loud enough for Tony to hear.

"Ricky, make up kit. Little girl with the teddy holding Jade's hand."

Rick looks at the surveillance camera while Cortez scrambles around the girls' section of the toy room.

"We're on it. Logan, did you catch that?"

"There you are, young man. Merry Christmas!!" Logan whispers, switching voices. "Yeah, there are four kids ahead of her. Hurry, boys." He switches back to his Santa voice. Why hello, my dear. What can Santa get you?"

"GOT IT!!!" Cortez yells out. He tosses it to Rick, who slips the makeup kit into the shute and sucked it up to Santa's bag. Aurora looks bashful as it's her turn to meet Santa.

"Why hello, Jade dear, and who is this beautiful enchantment?" Santa asks Jade.

"What's up, Santa? There's someone I want you to meet. This is my friend, Aurora." Santa gasps.

"Just like Sleeping Beauty. Now, I have a feeling I know what you want for Christmas."

"What?" Aurora wonders excitedly.

"You want a makeup kit?"

"That's right!!!! How did you know?"

"Oh, I've been doing this for so long, sweetheart. It's one of the tricks of the trade.

Santa goes through his bag and pulls out a Disney princess makeup kit. Aurora covers her mouth. Her parents watched from a distance, crying at how excited their little girl was.

"Thank you, Santa." Aurora hugs Santa tight.

"You are more than welcome, my dear." Aurora runs and hugs Jade.

"Thank you, Jade!!!"

"Of course, Princess Aurora." Aurora runs to her parents to show them what Santa has got her.

"Mommy!!! Daddy!!! Look!!!"

She jumps into her father's arms; tears welled in her mother's eyes. She stares right at Jade and mouths to her. "Thank you so much." Jade mouths back, "Merry Christmas." Jade turns to see Logan, who is with another boy; he looks up at her and gives her a wink.

"You think you can get used to this every year?" Clinton asks her through the headset. Jade turns to look at Aurora's glowing face, going through a huge adrenaline rush.

"Absolutely."

After the toy drive ended, the Crew was ready to return the U-Hauls. Jade sits in the driver's seat, waiting for Angie, staring into space, thinking about the past four hours that grabbed her soul. She couldn't get the images of all those happy children, and she had an inkling of responsibility for it. Logan's wink was another thing she couldn't get out of her head. Angie then gets in the cab, all excited.

"God, what a great day!!!! Alright, let's take this bad boy back."

"Not just yet," Jade tells Angie with a sinister grin. Angie looks at her confusedly.

"Jade, why do you look like you're up to something?" She asked. Jade's grin grew as she turned on the engine and slipped on her Aviators.

"Don't worry, Angie, you'll get used to this look."

A couple of hours after the U-Hauls were returned, there was still no sign of Jade and Angie.

Rosa tries again to reach her sister, but it goes right to voice-mail. Rosa paces back and forth.

"Logan, I'm freaking out; what if something happened?" Rosa asks frantically.

"Hang on, let's all calm down. There are no reports of accidents, and I just don't see them joyriding in a U-Haul. There's got to be a reason for this." All of a sudden, McKenna yells through the intercom.

"Daddy!!! Jade and Angie are here."

Everybody runs to the backyard. "Little St. Nick" by the Beach Boys blares inside the truck's cab with the windows down. Jade drives by, looking right at Logan, giving him a cool, slow chin nod as she drives past him. Confusion, anger, and worry are going through his head.

"What the hell are those two doing?" Clinton asks.

"They're heading to the warehouse," Tony answers.

The truck stops right at the entrance. Everyone starts walking towards the warehouse.

"Voy a mater a mi hermana" Translation: "I'm going to kill my sister," Rosa yells.

"Will you calm down with the Spanish? They're back, and they're fine." Logan tells Rosa.

Jade and Angie leave the truck and head towards the rear, waiting for everybody to catch up.

"My sister looks pissed." Angie nervously tells Jade, who shrugs her shoulders.

"Relax, she'll get over it. Just fold your arms and look cool."

Angie folds her arms with Jade standing on opposite sides of the truck. Logan stretches out his arms.

"Girls, what the hell?" he asks while Jade looks at him cool as ice.

"Well, we had to do a little shopping," Jade responds.

Angie unlocks the backdoor of the U-Haul and slides up the door. Everyone is in a state of shock at what they see. Inside are brand-new toys—roughly $2,500 of Jade's money came from selling her Camry.

"I had money to burn since Clinton suggested I sell my car. At first, I considered using the money to buy a new pair of Louis Vuitton boots that I was eyeing online, but this was a better alternative. So, let's fill her up again!!!"

Logan and Clinton look at each other in amazement while Cortez orders everyone.

"Guys, you heard Shorty. Let's go."

The whole crew started unloading all the toys into the newly empty warehouse to be filled up again. Logan just stood with his arms folded with a slight grin, staring at Jade. Not only was this girl beautiful and full of fire, but she had a heart of gold. Jade carried two tricycles, one in each hand to the warehouse. She could feel Logan's stare. She turned slightly at him and gave him a wink back as he did to her as Santa. When she went inside, she closed her eyes and exhaled. She knew willing herself was going to be damn near impossible. The more she saw Logan, the more she was falling for him. Jade was about to go to war with her temptations towards her new employer. Logan looked out at the lake, conflicted because he was fighting the same battle.

"She's your daughters' nanny, stupid. She's your daughters' nanny. Don't even think about it." He commands himself.

CHAPTER 8

TWAS THE TWO NIGHTS
BEFORE BARBADOS

It was Christmas Eve. Logan and Clinton are in the kitchen on their laptops, finalizing preparations for their annual trip to Barbados. The Brodies charter a second jet every year just for the Crew's families.

"OK, if everything goes perfectly, our flight plan should all arrive in Bridgetown simultaneously, even with the layovers. Maggie and I have our jet cards, so we're ready." Clinton tells Logan.

Awesome!!!! Jade, does Tonya have her card? Logan asks Jade.

"Yup, she's ready."

"Great!!! Rosa and Angie told me their families are good; Tony and Bridget are set." Logan gets a text from Sasha. Sasha's text: "We're set."

"Beautiful, we're all good."

"Daddy, will Jade fly on the jet with us?" McKenna asks her daddy, hoping Jade gets to fly with them.

"Honey, of course, the whole Crew flies with us."

McKenna and Madison jump and down, screaming, then Jade joins them.

"Yay!!!! I get to fly on the first jet!!!" She continues jumping up and down with the girls.

Logan starts to laugh and shakes his head. He still can't get over the chemistry those three made on each other. An hour later, Jade was in the kids' room going through a basket of clean laundry, getting the girl's clothes ready for the trip, when she found one of Logan's shirts mixed in. She sees Logan's bedroom door open a crack. She walks in and sees Logan's wet backside coming out of the shower. For a split second, her brain froze, framed by Logan's perfectly toned ass glistening against the light. She quickly hides on the other side of the door, squirming at the thought of what's on the other side.

"Oh, my God. He's soaking wet, and so am I. Breathe, Jade, breathe." She whispers to herself.

She slowly went towards the stairway to see if anybody was coming. The coast was clear, and she quickly returned to the door's crack. Logan is covered from the waist down with a towel. He walks toward his bed, and Jade completely melts, seeing his rock-solid chest. She was in utter disbelief at how perfect one man's body could be. With that body, those eyes, and an ass, Michaelangelo could only sculpture. The heat rapidly went through her body until Logan disappeared into his closet.

"NO, COME BACK!!!! COME BACK'" She silently screams to herself.

Logan walks back in tight boxer briefs, holding a white T-shirt, when Madison yells, "Jade!!!!" from the intercom. She quickly tip-toes to the girls' room and calmly goes to the intercom.

"I'm in your room, honey!!!! I'm getting your bathing suits packed up." She lets go of the button and says to herself. "I'm not visualizing drying off your father with my tongue."

There's a knock on the door, and Jade holds her breath. Logan opens the door wearing a tight white T-shirt jersey with cargo shorts, standing and gripping the sides of the door frame. Jade turns around to acknowledge him. "Hey!!" She quickly returns to the laundry basket, getting enough time to see his solid muscles flexing. She closes her eyes and bites her lips, trying to play it cool. Except she looked so flushed.

"How's the packing going?" Logan asks while Jade can barely look at him in the face.

"Good. I'm almost done. What do you think? Three bathing suits each, perhaps?"

"Yeah, I think so." He stood next to Jade, going through the clean laundry. Madison loves that one." They reached for Madison's polka-dot suit and brushed each other's forearms. Jade could feel the heat of his body, smelling his cologne.

"Oh, sorry." Logan nervously apologizes. Jade laughs it off.

"Oh no…problem." Her eyes were deadlocked on his biceps, filled with goosebumps. "Are you stacked up? I mean, packed up."

"Yes. I've got clothes down there, too, that I leave there throughout the year."

"Good thing you stay in shape. God forbid you gain weight, and nothing fits there." She yells at herself in her head. "Oh, please shut up, Jade, and dear Jesus, could a man smell any better?"

"No kidding. I hit the punching bag at least two hours a day." Logan then yells in his head,

"Could you sound more of a bigger douchebag?"

Jade rapidly changed the subject. "So, how long have you been doing this tradition?"

"Going on twenty-two years. My parents honeymooned in Barbados and fell in love with the people there. My mom said it was the closest thing to heaven she could imagine. So, my dad bought a place for her. Her idea was to invite everyone over to thank them for caring for us every year."

"And you continued the tradition."

"That's right." Jade grins and shakes her head.

"I swear, how in God's name can you keep greed from your way of thinking?"

"It's because everything can be taken from you. Just like that." He snaps his finger. After hearing that, Jade got a glimpse of his logic. Remembering that in his mid-thirties, he lost his parents and a wife.

"You have got to look around your surroundings. What would I rather do? Spend the money on another car, a Rolex, or a yacht I don't need, or pay you a good salary for helping me and my kids. It's not that hard of a decision for me. Having all this is a major league blessing for me."

Was this the mask people said Logan wore? Even with all he'd lost, she just couldn't grasp the fact that this man with so much care in his heart would be so sad inside.

"Well, let me tell you something. I feel blessed being here, and I'll be looking forward to Barbados every year."

"Well, now that you're here, I'm looking forward to it more."

Jade thought, "Did he just say that? This guy is flirting with me; he's good at it." Jade noticed their interactions with each other more and more—the goosebumps, the stares that lasted a little too long. It was apparent what she needed to do and what she did best. Play with one's mind.

Jade puts the girls' bathing suits in their luggage.

"What time are we meeting at Sea-Tac?"

"Six a.m. Dress warm because we're expecting snow in the morning. Are you packed and ready?"

"Please, I started packing the day Clinton hired me and told me about this. What's the weight capacity the jet can hold?" Logan grabs the girls' luggage to take downstairs.

"Ahh, you're one of those women?" He says as they walk down the stairs.

"You mean one of those women who buy twelve different bikinis and will wear all twelve on a six-day trip. Damn right, I am? I love fashion; what can I tell you?" She playfully messes with his mind. It worked because he came to a screeching halt.

"Wait, you have twelve different bikinis?" He asks.

Jade slowly nods playfully, her eyes squinted and a grin on her face. Logan's face immediately goes red, and his imagination goes to a place that is becoming normal for him. It usually involves him and a very naked Jade. Throughout the day, members of the Crew left to spend Christmas Eve with their families. It was around four when Clinton and Jade were the last to leave.

"You almost ready, Jade?" Clinton asks while putting on his scarf. Jade runs with a couple of presents in hand.

"Just need two minutes. I want to give the girls their Christmas gifts. Girls!!!!!" She yells out.

McKenna and Madison run from the kitchen, making Christmas cookies with their daddy. Their faces glow, seeing Jade with two presents reach out for them.

"Merry Christmas, M&M!!!!!"

The girls open their boxes and inside are customized Jade-made T-shirts. Madison's was a shirt with three Wonder Woman's with Jade and the girls' faces, and McKenna got one with Minions with their faces."

"I'm freaking out. I love it!!!!!" McKenna screams out

"I love mine. Thank you, Jade." Madison says when they both run and hug Jade tight.

"Merry Christmas, gals."

Logan whistles while holding a small box.

"Forgetting something, girls."

"We got you something." McKenna takes the box from their daddy's hand and hands it to Jade. She opens it to see green and red M&M earrings, symbolizing the girls' favorite color.

Jade gasps. "NO WAY!!! Girls!!! This is too awesome." Jade takes out the earrings she had on. "Well, these are out of here." She puts on the M&M earrings and pulls out her phone to see. "I look beautiful."

"And Italian." Logan jokes. Jade rolls her eyes.

"Your daddy is a dork. Wait a second." She takes a selfie to post on Instagram and Facebook with the quote. "I got M&M earrings for Christmas. Let the envy sink in". "OK, girls. Come here. It's selfie time for my personal album." Jade never posted any pictures of the girls in any social media format. She snaps a photo with their tongues sticking out. Logan and Clinton look at each other, smiling. "God, the three of us are so cute."

"No argument here." Logan agrees while smiling at the three of them. Jade smiles at Logan. "Now, I want you two to have a great Christmas with your daddy." Clinton clears his throat.

"Save some love for me." The girls run to Clinton to hug him. "Merry Christmas, Clinton!!!!!!" They say at the same time.

"Merry Christmas, angels. Well, let's get going, Jade. Tonya texted and said dinner will be ready in a half hour." Clinton goes to hug Logan. "Merry Christmas, Master Bruce."

Logan chuckles. "Merry Christmas, Alfred." Jade gives them an annoyed stare.

"Wait, he can't be Alfred. He looks like Morgan Freeman and doesn't sound anything like Michael Caine. You are insulting me and the entire Batman universe." Jade crosses her arms in pretend anger. Clinton looks at Logan, confused.

"Is this girl for real?" Logan shrugs his shoulders. "To be fair, you could try to sound like Michael Caine or Jeremy Irons." He says, trying to control his laughter.

"Ok, we're leaving." He says irritatedly while Logan and Jade start to laugh. "We'll see you three on the 26th."

When Madison yelled out, Clinton and Jade were about to head out the door.

"Wait, Daddy. You didn't hug Jade and wish her Merry Christmas." Logan and Jade look at each other with awkward smiles.

"Merry Christmas." They say at the same time while they both awkwardly laugh. They embraced for a hug, and the heat radiated between them. Jade cupped Logan's shoulders down and gently held her petite back when she whispered in his ears.

"Merry Christmas, Logan. Remember twelve." She tells him in a seductive tone.

Logan went frozen and unable to respond, visualizing her twelve bikinis. Jade pulls away with her eyebrows up and a smirk on her face. Not realizing it, she gave Logan a Christmas present for when the kids go to bed.

CHAPTER 9

BEER PONG WIZARD

Christmas morning is a challenging day for Logan Brodie. It was the fourth morning opening presents without his wife snuggled under his arms with a cup of coffee in hand. What's helping him get through it is what Jade whispered in his ear. Twelve bikinis. He kept looking at her suitcase by the front door, screaming at him to open it.

"DADDY!!!! DADDY!!!!" McKenna yells at her dad. Logan snaps out of his daydream.

"Sorry, baby. What's up?"

"Open our present." The girls were excited when Logan looked down at his partially opened present. He finishes unwrapping it. "Wow, a monocular."

"Jade found it," Madison said.

"She said it will be great to see dolphins in Barbados," McKenna exclaimed.

"Oh, she did, huh? Wasn't that nice of her?"

"Yeah, she said yesterday there are twelve special ways to see them." McKenna retorts.

Logan's eyes open wide. Jade is playing mind games with him and using his daughters. After they opened the last presents, the girls played with their new toys. Logan texts Jade, thanking her for his present.

Logan text: "Thank you. I just love the present you and the girls got me. I will definitely put them to good use to look for dolphins."

Jade text: "You're more than welcome. There are so many amazing things to see in the morning along the beach. See you tomorrow."

Logan text: "Bright and early."

Logan was wondering what she implied by that. He just had to wait and see. The girls passed out on his bed while watching "The Santa Clause II." Logan snuck out of bed and headed to his balcony. He noticed something different was happening this Christmas. He felt more alive. He tried to garner a conversation with Renee, but he had nothing.

"Merry Christmas, Renee. I love you." He said, looking out at the lake.

He then walked back into his bedroom, feeling confused. It was the shortest conversation he had with her in years. He heads to bed when he sees the monocular on his end table. He grabs it and puts it in his duffle bag. Logan heads back into bed with a strange feeling inside of him.

The last time he felt it was when he first met Renee. The feeling grew stronger thinking of what Jade was going to wear on the flight. It was at that moment he realized that feeling was anticipation. The following day, it was only thirty-one degrees with snow flurries. Logan sent a group text to dress warm and change in the jet. It was a ten-hour flight to Bridgetown, Barbados, with a slight layover to refuel in Tampa. Around five a.m., Logan, Cortez, and the girls arrived at Sea-Tac, where his personal pilot Captain Jacobs greets him.

"We're on schedule, Logan. There's no heavy snow coming, and we should be smooth once we get to Tampa." Captain Jacobs tells Logan. "Phenomenal. Who's here already?"

"Everyone except Clinton and Maggie."

Logan looks at his Fitbit. "They also have Jade and Tonya, I'll text to see their status."

Clinton's Dodge Ram was heading their way before he could get his phone out of his pocket.

Clinton, Maggie, and Tonya come onto the tarmac wearing Parkas, skull caps, and sweaters. Then there was Jade. She opens her passenger door and comes out in a tropical print sarong with a right leg slit to her thigh, a pair of four-inch wedges, and a sun hat. Logan couldn't keep his eyes off Jade as her bare left leg was exposed to the bitter cold, totally unfazed. Tonya climbs up the steps and approaches Logan.

"I love what a brave front your friend is showing. Just giving a middle finger to double pneumonia." He says to Tonya, who turns to look at Jade.

"Well, that's just Jade. It wouldn't be her if she wasn't giving the middle finger to someone or something."

Jade climbs the steps with Logan extending his hand. Jade takes it, and they stand face to face.

"Thank you, kind sir."

Logan notices her erect nipples on her dress.

"Little cold?" He asks. She looks down at her chest.

"Nope, just excited as hell." She then looks down at his pants. "Looks like you are too."

Logan closes his eyes and looks down at his stoned erection. He then looks at Captain Jacobs, who looks away, biting his lip, trying not to laugh. Logan shrugs off the embarrassment. "Let's jet, Dave!!!"

Logan lets out a huge exhale, looking up at the sky, knowing that the next six days and five nights would be pure torture with Jade around. Logan enters the bathroom twenty minutes after take-off and removes his winter clothes. He walks out in a short-sleeved white shirt, black pants, and black loafers. Angie and Rosa whistle when he approaches them.

"Damn, Logan, looking good," Rosa says

"Yeah, who are you trying to impress?" Angie asks.

"Well, Prime Minister Mosley and I will meet when we arrive." He tells them loud enough for Jade to hear.

Jade looks at him and returns to her phone, keeping a straight face because she was turned on immediately seeing Logan. As he walks by her, she turns on the camera to purposely snap a picture of Logan so she can use it later when she's alone. Jade sees McKenna and Madison catching her in the act.

"Oops, it wasn't in selfie mode. Girls, get together with me."

McKenna and Madison sit with Jade in the middle and take a selfie. Jade pulls her hair back, modeling off her M&M earrings.

"You're wearing our earrings," McKenna says, elated.

"Duh!!! I'm never taking these off. These are priceless."

Logan overheard and looked back at the girls together and smiled until a flashback of Renee entered his head from her final trip to Barbados. He remembered Renee taking a selfie with McKenna holding her pregnant stomach. Her pale skin and her darkened eyes when the cancer was attacking her hard. Throughout the years, Renee would fill herself with Xanax so she could sleep through the long flights. Her final trip, she was at piece knowing the end was coming. He swallowed as his heart sank. Logan sat in his office in the back of the jet. He covered his face, trying not to get sucked into the dark rabbit hole of desolation. Thankfully, she was able to sleep for a few hours.

Once he got up, he headed towards the bathroom to see everyone was asleep. He walks to see both girls sleeping with their heads on Jade's shoulders. She was also asleep, with her neck awkwardly positioned. He gets a small pillow to prevent her from getting a stiff neck. He headed to the bathroom when he heard a soft moan coming from her. She crossed her leg in her sleep, and the slit from her sundress brought her beautiful tanned, toned leg out in the open. Logan closed his eyes, not believing a woman could have a more stunning body than Jade's. He slapped himself, trying desperately to knock the lust out of his head. After a brief stop in Tampa to refuel, they make their approach to Bridgetown.

"I've never seen the ocean that blue," Jade tells Tonya, looking out the window while descending.

"I know. I can't believe I'm here." Jade had a confused look on her. "Wait, I thought you came here every year."

"No. This is for the immediate family. This is the first time Logan invited me because I'm your best friend, and that was immediate enough. He said he didn't want you to feel alone."

Jade grinned, feeling so touched Logan did that for her even though it took no effort for her to make friends. She was already close with the Crew, but that gesture made Jade want Logan more. She knew what she had to do. Step up the mind games with him. Once they landed in Bridgetown, Logan was greeted by Prime Minister Mosley and her staff.

"My dear Logan, get over here." P.M. Mosley embraces him.

"Prime Minister, it's so good to see you." Logan hugs her tight. Jade emerges from the jet and sees Logan talking to the P.M. like a sister.

"Wow. Logan is talking to the head honcho of Barbados." She tells Tony, thoroughly impressed.

"You have no idea, Jade. The Brodie family is royalty here. They've built schools, hospitals, and soccer fields. They have pumped millions into this country." Tony explains. At first, Jade wondered why the Brodies weren't considered saints. Now she was convinced they had their own wing in heaven. She walks along until Logan calls for her.

"Jade, wait. I'd like you to meet somebody. Jade, this is Prime Minister Janet Mosely. Prime

Minister, this is McKenna and Madison's new nanny, Jade Murphy."

The Prime Minister extends her hand. "Welcome, my dear."

Jade went completely frozen from starstruck. Logan couldn't help but smile because it was reminiscent of when he met Ken Griffey Jr. for the first time when he was six. Jade could barely raise her voice. "Hi."

"So, how are you enjoying working for the best boss you can ever have and looking over those two beautiful dolls?" The P.M. asks Jade. She clears her throat, trying to compose herself.

"So far, it's been a thrill."

"Well, I cannot wait to meet you for many years."

"Thank you so much, Madame Prime Minister."

The P.M. waves Jade off. "Please, sweetheart, call me Janet."

*Okay, thank you, Janet."

She walks off with her mouth open while Logan and Janet continue talking. Tonya has the same expression as she waits for her.

"You just met the country's leader," Tonya whispers to Jade.

"I know, I KNOW!!!" She squeals through her gritted teeth.

Ten minutes later, four Chevy Suburbans wait to take everybody through Bridgetown, heading towards the port. The townspeople come out to say hello to Logan and the Crew, blowing kisses and waving to them as they drive by. Jade takes off her sunglasses as she takes it all in. It was like the Beatles landing in America. While stopping at a red light, a little boy runs towards the Suburban Jade is in and hands her a lily.

"Thank you so much, sweetie."

"Welcome." The little boy tells Jade before running back to his mother.

Jade looked at the lily and thought about the wild and crazy journey of the past month. She closes her eyes and thanks God for everything at this point. She put the lily in her hair, looking at the crystal blue ocean, thinking she could get used to this every year.

They reached the port with two cruise boats waiting for them. It was a ten-minute boat ride to the island. Jade lets out a gasp when she sees the mansion in the distance.

Twenty-nine acres, three swimming pools with swim-up bars, a lazy river, basketball and beach volleyball courts, fifteen bedrooms, and a Wi-Fi tower. Jade and Tonya couldn't do anything but look at each other in disbelief.

"Have I thanked you again for being Clinton's niece yet?" Jade asks.

"Not today. Now, let's get our drinking on." Tonya looks at the monstrosity that was the compound referred to as Chateau Katie.

"Hells to the fuckin yes!!!" Jade nods in agreement.

"Island in the Sun" by Weezer starts playing on the giant speakers planted throughout the island. Jade looks up at an enormous balcony with Logan and the girls standing together, watching everybody coming off the boat. The girls wave down at Jade, and Logan gives her a wink. Jade turns to see the Crew's families getting off their boats, gathering all together looking up at Logan in his balcony.

"Smiles, everyone, smiles!!!" Logan quotes Mr. Roark from "Fantasy Island."

"You all know the routine. Enjoy and relax while we close up this year. Some dream of visiting Times Square and watching the ball drop in sub-zero temperatures. Do you?" Everyone yells out a loud "NO!!!"

"I thought not. So, all of you kids, get your trunks on and let's swim. Adults, let's start adulting and hit the giggle juice."

All the adults cheer while Logan and the girls return inside; they run to their room to get ready to swim. Logan lets out a relaxing sigh when he collapses on his couch, exhausted from the traveling. Knowing how excited the girls were, he had no time to relax. He springs off the couch, and in the corner of his eye, Logan sees an old photo of him and Renee. He reaches for it when he hears

Jade and Tonya laughing, coming out of their room. The sound of Jade's laughter woke something inside of him. He gently tucks the picture into his nightstand. Fifteen minutes later, Logan heads to the main pool. He sees a crowd screaming and cheering while Moby's "Bodyrock" blasts through the speakers. Within the cracks of everybody at the bar, he sees Jade mixing drinks at the pool bar wearing a snakeskin bikini with a cowboy hat and her aviator sunglasses, flipping whiskey bottles in the air and pouring, shaking her body. Everybody chanted, "Go!! Jade!! Go!!" while she legitimately body rocked to the music. Logan quickly gets into the pool to cover up his enormous erection that was about to lance through the fabric of his swim shorts. Clinton and Maggie wave to Logan.

"Logan, come here!!! You have to check out the nanny. She's a pro and has seen "Cocktail" one too many times." Clinton yells out.

Logan swims up to the bar and sits on one of the stools.

"What's your best drink?" Logan asks.

"Oh, I'm good at "Fucking on the Beach." Tony spits out his mojito, laughing his head off.

"Bridget, your man needs a bib."

"Excuse me?"

"It's my version of "Sex on the Beach" except 98% booze. First, can you do me a favor, be my waitress, and send these to the cute ones over there?"

Jade hands Logan four Oreo cookie blizzards for McKenna and Madison who are playing with Rosa and Angie's young sons.

"Here you go, kids."

Logan hands all the kids their blizzards.

"Thanks, Daddy!!!"

"Thanks, Logan!!!" Rosa and Angie's boys say.

"No tip? Cheapskates." Logan jokes.

The kids laugh when Logan swims back to the bar.

"All right, here you go." Jade hands Logan his drink.

"Superb." He gasps, sucking down all the alcohol on the bottom of the straw.

"Awesomeness." She puts a towel over her shoulder, leaning on the bar. Her breasts are in perfect view of Logan's sight. "So, does this place just sit here 360 days out of the year?"

"No, we donate it as an AirBnB for families with sick kids throughout the year, so the money goes back to the country. My parents paid $110,000 for this place, and right now, it's worth $70 million." Jade's mouth drops.

"No wonder you meet up with the Prime Minister."

"Yeah, I just need five days here out of the year. Enjoy this time with my extended family."

Jade couldn't help but focus on how hot Logan looked with his Ray-Bans and wet hair. Jade goes to the bar and pulls out a bottle of Patron and two shot glasses. Logan goes warm inside when he sees the large, black angel wings on Jade's back.

"Well then, we must toast to the family." Jade pours the glasses and raises hers. "To all of us."

Logan raises his glass. "To you."

Jade took a shot while Logan hesitated because he was fixated on Jade's tits when she lifted her head up. "Thank God for sunglasses," he thought to himself. He takes his shot, exhaling the deep burn from the Patron.

"Nice wings you got back there. What's the story on those?" He asks while Jade leans onto the bar, pouring another shot.

"They're just a reminder to myself that there's good in me even though I can be really bad. No matter what, no one can ever take my wings away. That's why I got them inked on me." She quickly downs her shot like a pro without feeling any effect. Logan's mind was conflicted on what was giving him more of a buzz, Jade or the liquor. "I'll tell you one thing. Of all people who should have these wings, it's you. You are an endangered species, Logan Brodie."

Logan slightly grins, even though he is very uncomfortable with anyone complimenting him.

"You're too nice." He says while Jade scoffs.

"I work for you." She points to Clinton. "He works for you. We're all related to the fact that we're your hired help, and you treat us to a yearly vacation on a majestic island. Seriously, who does that? Unless you were Stalin in a past life and trying to redeem something, you're kicking ass at the good person persona."

Hearing it from Jade, Logan wasn't feeling so uncomfortable this time. He has a crooked grin when he sucks down the rest of his drink.

"It's not just being a good person. You have to crave it. Making an impact in someone's life. I desire that." Logan pours his heart when Jade sees Cortez and Rick slithering behind Logan, pulling him off his stool into the water. Everybody cracks up into laughter.

"You two are dicks!!!" He playfully yells at Cortez and Rick.

"Bro, three on three beer pong at the Cabana?" Cortez tells Logan,

"Oh, I'm in!!!!"

Back at Washington U, Logan and Cortez were an unstoppable force at beer pong. Their hand and eye coordination was perfect no matter how drunk they were. They went undefeated in all four years. Yet, right behind the bar, there was an unstoppable force in her own right.

"I'll play. Guys vs. girls." Jade quips. Logan, Cortez, and Rick nod in agreement; telekinetically, Logan and Cortez look at each other like this girl has no idea who she's up against.

"Tonya!!! Sasha!!! Beer pong!!! Ladies vs. tools!!!"

"Oh hell yeah, girl!!!" Tonya yells.

"Are you kidding? To have the chance to beat my boss and my husband at the same time? Of course."

"Let's do it!!!" Logan screams out, getting pumped.

Jade hops over the bar, with Logan reaching out to help Jade. He grabs her waist, helping her down off the counter. They come face to face with each other when she hits the water. He slowly lets go of her waist. They give each other an awkward smile when they walk out of the pool.

"That's sweet of you, even though you'll be my bitch very soon."

"You chicks are so cute. After we kick your ass, you can go to the kitchen, rattle some pans and make us a pie, broad."

"Ohhh, after I'm done with you, all you'll drink are Cosmopolitans."

"Oh yeah, I will fuck you up and down." Jade stops to turn at Logan and lowers her sunglasses to the bridge of her nose to glare at him. Logan's face goes an instant scarlet, realizing what he just said. "I mean, we're going to fuck you, I mean." Logan groans while looking at his glass, trying to calm himself down. "How much booze did you put in this thing?"

Jade giggles at a nervous Logan, giving him mercy. She walks into his personal space. "It's OK, Logan. Up and down, huh? That's naughty." Jade spanks herself hard in the ass. "Very naughty." She spanks herself again as she walks on. "Bad Logan." Then again. "Bad".

Jade smiles as she pushes back her glasses and walks off. Logan just stares as she walks on. He couldn't believe what came out of his mouth. He also couldn't believe how soft Jade's body felt when he picked her up from the bar. He took a breath, putting on his game face because, to Logan, there was one rule in beer pong. Kill or be killed. They reach the table which is set up. A crowd formed wanting to watch the battle of the sexes. Women on one side, guys on the other.

"Alright, let's shoot to go first," Rick says.

"No, it should be ladies first," Sasha interjects to her husband.

"Good point, Sasha, so go ahead, Logan." Jade disses Logan in front of everyone, which starts a loud "Ohhh" through the crowd.

Cortez and Tony start singing their own version of "Pinball Wizard" by the Who called "Beer Pong Wizard."

Cortez and Tony sing together. "Since he was a young boy, he played that ping pong ball. He must have played them all from Portland down to Pullman, but I haven't seen anything like him in any college hall. That tall, rich, white boy sure plays a mean beer pong."

Jade rolls her eyes, disgusted at the notion they would destroy a classic hit from The Who. Logan shoots and makes his first shot. The guys cheer. Tonya chugs a cup of beer. Rick and Cortez miss their shots. Now, it's the girls' turn. Sasha is about to take a shot.

"Wait, Sasha. I should take the first shot," Jade says.

"No, I want to go first."

"I'm a pro at this game, trust me."

"Jade, you're new here."

"Wait, what does that suppose to mean?" Jade snaps back.

"It means that you shouldn't say who goes first."

"Sash, you want me to be a bitch because I promise I'm better at it than you." They glanced at each other, which meant it was going to be catfight time.

"Girls, don't fight." Tonya tries to ease the tension. Everybody around started to get uncomfortable. Logan tries to calm everything down.

"Seriously, this is supposed to be a fun game."

Jade takes the ball from Sasha, and both say to Logan simultaneously: "It is."

It was all a diversion as Jade quickly bounced the ball and went into one of the cups, which meant the guys had to chug two cups. Sasha, Jade, and Tonya high-fived each other laughing. Sasha points to the ball in the cup.

"Do we have your attention now?" Jade says with a total game face on. Logan takes both cups and chugs down, staring down at Jade.

"I'll be watching you." He tells Jade.

"What have you not done?" She sneers back at him.

Logan's jaw clenched when Jade said that because she wasn't lying. Sasha goes next and makes her shot. Rick pounds one down, and Tonya goes next and misses. The guys are up. Cortez gets one, and Rick then puts it in Cortez's cup. Logan looks directly at Jade as he also puts it in Cortez's cup. That's four cups the girls have to drink. Jade drinks while her eyes beamed at Logan; she then grabs another and chugs that one down. Tonya tries to grab a cup, but Jade snatches it from her hand and chugs that one; she then grabs the last cup and chugs the last one. Everyone cheers for Jade's drinking ability while she licks her lips slowly while staring at Logan. Logan's heart was beating nonstop as he watched.

Tony goes to Cortez and Rick and whispers to them: "Seriously, that was the hottest thing I've ever seen in my life."

Rick whispers, shaking his head. "Totally."

"She's got a gift," Cortez says, impressed.

Tonya goes for her shot and sinks one. Sasha then puts it in the same cup. Jade then looks out to the ocean.

"McKenna, Madison look, is that a dolphin out there?" Everyone, including Logan, looks out. Jade bounces the ball, but Logan swipes the ball from going in. Logan shakes his head and wags his finger. Cortez drinks both cups.

"Pretty pathetic to use my children to help you win," Logan says.

"It's beer pong, sugar." Jade hits back.

They go back and forth, with the guys down four cups to one. It was the guy's turn to shoot. Rick shoots and makes a shot; Cortez then hits the same cup. It is down to one cup; if Logan made it, the guys would win. The guys cheer him on. Logan was as cool as ice lining up for his shot. His eyes were locked on that last cup. That was until Jade stood right in his point of view behind the last cup with her hands on her hips. His concentration was gone. That pose was the hottest tease she could do. He imagined having the island to themselves and fucking her right on that table with her legs wrapped around him like a vice. He shakes his head. He shoots, and the ball circles in the cup, but Jade lowers and blows into the cup for the ball to pop right out. All the guys groan as the girls cheer.

"Is that legal?" Clinton asks, not knowing the rules.

"Yes, it is," Logan says to Clinton as he keeps his stare at Jade.

The girls needed to make two shots in the same cup to win. Tonya misses her shot. Sasha then made hers. It was up to Jade. Jade looks at the cup and then at Logan. She kisses him as she shoots and hits nothing but the bottom of the cup. All the girls jump up and down as all the guys look dejected. Logan, on the other hand, had no emotion. His eyes never left Jade, completely fixated. All he was thinking was that this girl was making him feel something he hadn't felt in years. Sasha consoles Rick with a kiss, and Cortez shakes Tonya's hand with a curtsey. Everyone leaves the cabana; the only ones there are Logan and Jade. They both grin at each other. "I know we didn't bet, but I deserve some kind of reward."

"Granted." He agrees.

"Quote the last line from "Robocop." She requests.

At first, Logan was taken aback at Jade's request. He looks away, trying to remember the last line. Especially since he's seen it dozens of times, he chuckles when he remembers it knowing where Jade was going with this. After Robocop saves the Chairman's life, he says to Robocop, "Nice shooting, son; what's your name?" Of course, he had to tweak the line a little for Jade.

"Nice shooting, dear; what's your name?"

"Murphy." She says in a gruff voice like Robocop did.

They both laugh together. "Logan, you were a noble and worthy opponent. You have nothing to be embarrassed about. Put her there."

She extends her hand. Logan grins and shakes her hand.

"Well played, Jade." Logan pulled her closer to him as she was about to let go. She gasps and inhales his cologne. He slowly whispers in her ear. "Very well played." Logan then gives her a hard, swift smack on her ass. She jolts with a stunned look. "Bad Jade."

He lets go of her hand and walks out of the cabana with a slight grin and a small strut. Jade stood there with her mind racing out of control. There was only one thing she badly needed to do, and do it immediately. She hears Rosa's voice in the distance.

"Hey Jade, us girls are going jet skiing; you wanna come?" Rosa yells. Jade, trying to compose herself, yells back.

"Sure. Um, can you give me ten minutes?"

"No problem, we won't make a move without you," Sasha tells Jade.

Jade power walks back to the mansion. She starts to run up the stairs as she passes Maggie and Bridget.

"Jade, are you OK?" Bridget was concerned since Jade was flying up the stairs. "I'm cool; I just need to get something out of my room. I'll see you girls in a minute."

"Alrighty," Maggie says.

Jade says under her breath. "I probably won't need a minute."

Jade makes it to her room, locks the door, heads to her suitcase, and pulls out her vibrator. She takes it, runs to her bed, and starts going through Google images on her phone. Jade knew she was in a time crunch, so she pulled her bikini bottoms down and inserted the vibrator inside her. The humming charge goes through her, biting the top of her lip when she pulls her vibrator in and out. She keeps scrolling and scrolling when she finds an image of Logan standing next to Steve Ballmer in a tuxedo at a charity function at the Four Seasons. Her eyes were locked on his photo.

She paints a picture in her head of being Logan's date at that same function, wearing a tiny red dress with black four-inch strappy gladiator heels, standing four feet away while he and Steve Ballmer were getting their pictures taken together. Except, he couldn't take more than one second off of her. The last thing on his mind was those photographers and the founder of Microsoft. Logan was locked on Jade, looking as beautiful as a rose. He excuses himself and marches with intensity toward her. He leans down to her level and whispers. "Dinner is in a half hour, but I'm starving. I need something to eat." Logan gets a firm grip and walks Jade with him without knowing where he's going. He takes her into one of the conference rooms, slamming the door behind them. Logan pulls his bow tie off while she walks backwards with Logan's promiscuous scowl following her. The back of her legs hit one of the long conference tables. He just stood there for a few seconds, looking down at her. Out of nowhere, he grabbed the side of her waist and planted her on the table. He leaned down and spread her legs wide, licking his lips, knowing she wasn't wearing any panties. Logan gets on his knees…

Jade throws her phone down and smothers herself with a pillow, screaming in pleasure while riding an intense orgasm. After coming down, she takes the pillow off her face, gasping for air.

"Son of a bitch!!!! I've only been here for five hours. What is happening here?" She says to herself out loud, sounding completely horse. Jade was losing her mind from temptation and dying to avoid any risky situation with Logan. Jade realized she had to avoid Logan as much as possible to survive this trip. Easier said than done staying on an island.

CHAPTER 10

ALL IS QUIET ON
NEW YEAR'S DAY

Logan bounces out of bed when his alarm goes off at 5:30 on New Year's Eve. He gets his ear pods and starts playing from a mixed playlist of Pantera and Metallica. He puts a Dunkin Donuts French vanilla K-cup in his Keurig machine and starts brewing coffee. While it brewed, he did his daily routine of a hundred sit-ups and push-ups. His heart was pumping faster once six o'clock hit. He grabs his coffee and the monocular he got for Christmas and heads to the balcony. He sits down, puts the cup on the table, and turns off his heavy metal playlist. The ocean had a golden glow with the sun slowly rising.

Right at that time, he saw another glow. It was Jade walking onto the beach with a yoga mat under her arm and her phone on the other hand. A smirk hits his face as he turns on "Who's That Lady" by the Isley Brothers. Jade lays out her mat and stares at the ocean for a few minutes, wearing a white sports bra and the tightest low-rise pink tights you could wear. Logan took a deep breath, seeing her toned abs and bronzed, smooth skin.

Jade pulls her blonde hair into a ponytail and kneels on the mat. She slowly lowers the top half of her body with her ass still up in the air. Logan quickly pulled his monocular away since he could only look at Jade in small doses. Especially when he saw a hint of crack coming out of her pants and shook his head in amazement at her flawless figure; his heart was pounding, and his face was blushing. He grabbed his phone and shot her a text.

Logan text: You're right; your Christmas gift works best in the morning.

Jade was listening to calm meditation music from her ear pods. With her legs crossed and her neck up, a notification goes off that she received a text. Jade's concentration was interrupted as she wondered who would text her so early. She reads Logan's text, realizing he's watching her. She doesn't respond and throws her phone down at the mat. Logan swallows hard, thinking she is upset. He looks down at his phone and notices it is the third consecutive text he has sent her without a response.

"What the hell? Is she pissed at me?" Logan mutters to himself.

Logan noticed she was distant and wasn't playing her usual mind games. He gets his coffee and heads back to his room. He plops on his couch but thinks that is part of her game. Granted, there was a lot to do on the island with all the jet skiing, para-sailing, going into the town, and shopping. Also, Jade was having quality time with the kids and getting to know the Crew and their families.

Logan didn't know that he was constantly in Jade's mind from watching him fish with the guys without his shirt on, teaching Madison how to swim, and seeing him do one of Jade's favorite things, lip-syncing. It took every ounce of her impulse not to text him back. "Don't do it, Jade. Don't text him back." she thought while she returned to meditate. The damage was already done, though.

Visions of Logan slamming her in the shower from behind, riding on him while jet skiing, bouncing on top of Logan on the giant water trampoline in the middle of the ocean. Every dirty thought she could imagine crossed her mind. She was starting to sweat as she could not be in one with serenity because all she could think of was Logan inside of her. "SHIT!!!" she yells out in frustration, snapping out of her sexual haze. Jade gets up quickly, grabs her phone, and returns to the mansion. Logan was loading another coffee pod when he heard a door slam that sounded like it came from Jade's room. He went out his front door and walked towards Jade's door when he heard a muffled buzzing sound, and then suddenly, her T.V. came on. Logan had no idea what was going on. He just shrugged his shoulders and headed back to his room. After the girls woke up minutes later, the three of them went downstairs and had breakfast together on the kitchen island.

"So, what are we going to do today?" Logan asks, pouring Reese's Puffs into McKenna's bowl.

"We're going swimming with Jade. Then go fishing, and then she will do our hair tonight." McKenna tells Logan about her planned day.

"Oh my gosh, you girls are going to look stunning." He looks at the girls, hoping they have inside information about Jade's behavior. "Speaking of Jade, does she seem mad to you?"

"No. Did you do something wrong, Daddy?" Madison asked while Logan quickly responded.

"No, I was just wondering if she was OK. I don't know; she just seems upset to me. She hasn't said much since we played bee…apple juice pong." Logan didn't want to make too much fuss in front of the girls. "You know, forget it. Just please don't say anything to her, alright." He sits down with his granola

"Ok, Daddy. Remember, don't say anything, Maddi!!!" McKenna commands her sister.

"I won't."

Later that afternoon, Logan and the guys were on his balcony drinking beers, chatting, and watching their wives while lounging in one of the pools.

"I swear, I'm not ready to let this go tomorrow." Clinton sadly says, dreading leaving.

"Keep drinking; it eases the pain." Cortez advice

"Look at the women down there. Do you think they're talking about us?" Rick asks.

"Of course they are. They're probably comparing who's better in bed." Tony answers with wishful thinking.

Clinton notices Logan just staring out at the pool with the girls. Mainly Jade. "Logan!!!"

"What's up? Sorry, just thinking of work." He says, coming up with any excuse.

"Bullshit, you're thinking of Jade," Rick replies.

"What are you talking about?" Logan says

"Son, do you think we're that stupid? Beer pong. You could not be more obvious. It's okay to be attracted to her. She's a beautiful woman." Clinton explains. Logan gets out of his chair. "How? She's my kids' nanny. Isn't that kind of a stereotype? Falling for the hot nanny."

"Yeah, but you're not married anymore," Tony says but realizes what she said when Rick, Clinton, and Cortez give an awkward stare with silence. "Logan, I'm sorry. I didn't mean anything by that."

"Tony, I know what you meant. Don't sweat it." Logan stares at Jade, laughing, wearing a neon pink bikini.

He was starting to miss the feelings a man had attracted to a woman. "Guys, the fact of the matter is that I can't stop thinking about her. I'm conflicted here." Logan breaks down, telling the guys the truth. Rick gets out of his lounge chair to confront him.

"Logan, this is the first time I've seen you interested in a woman in a long time. Jade is beautiful, full of fire, fun, and…"

Logan interrupts, looking out at the pool. "She's twerking with your wife/my assistant."

Rick's eyes bulge, and quickly turns around to look at the pool. Then, the other guys leave their chairs to look out at the pool. Jade is showing Sasha her stripper moves. Rick was frozen solid with his eyes beamed right on his wife.

"The things you learn in Vegas." Cortez chuckles. Rick was glued entirely on his wife's twerk.

"She is gifted at moving that body." Tony agrees

"Wait, what did she do in Vegas?" He asks. Clinton knew he would probably freak, but he shot at Logan point blank.

"She was a stripper there."

Logan whipped his head to look at Clinton. "A WHAT??????"

"She was just a fill-in, but she was bartending there mostly. Hence the moves she showed at the pool bar." Logan thought his head was about to explode.

"My children's nanny was a stripper!" His voice rises as the guys sush him. "Can we grasp what is wrong with that sentence?" Logan questions, which makes Clinton snap.

"Oh, Logan, that is enough!!! I'll repeat this: she just moved here and needed a job. I did something your mom and dad would have done. It's not like I hired a Satanist." Even though he didn't say much, Cortez wanted to throw his two cents.

"Why are we even thinking about this, Logan? She was a stripper. So what? The most important thing is that the girls love her, and she loves them. She's doing the job Clinton hired her for. As Ricky said, I haven't seen you look interested in any piece of ass for so long."

Tony interrupts. "Speaking of Rick." The guys see Rick taking his wife out of the pool and heading toward the mansion. He looked like he needed his wife's help to find something. "Wow, how did he get down there so fast?" Tony asks

"Logan, listen to me. I wouldn't hire just anyone. You know that. I just had this feeling about this girl. Jade is a strong, vibrant, independent woman. Someone McKenna and Madison can look up to, and you know that. She's teaching them yoga, self-defense, and to be beautiful in their inner self. This past month, I haven't seen them look so happy. It's all because of her." Clinton assured Logan. Suddenly, "Lonely Boy" by the Black Keys came on. He couldn't stop glancing at Jade while she lip-synched and danced with the girls.

"It's a leap of faith, Logan. She's the total package any guy would kill for. She's hot, funny, and the girl can throw a beer like anyone's business." Cortez is trying to be the voice of reason while Logan looks at him. Tony then tries to get the guys' attention.

"Guys, come here quick." Logan, Clinton, and Cortez walk fast to Tony. "Follow me."

They walk down to Tony and Bridget's room next door to Rick and Sasha's room. They hear pounding and yelling. They can hear Sasha's muffled screams through the walls.

"Baby, what has gotten into you!!! Oh, fuck me harder. Oh my God!!!! Oh my God!!!" Sasha moans while the guys are trying hard not to laugh.

"God, we don't even have to put our ears to the wall. I never thought of Sasha being a loud one. Atta boy, Rick," Clinton whispers while Sasha's screams get louder.

"My God, are you sure he's not killing her in there?" Logan asks as the guys snicker. While the guys were listening, they didn't know that Tonya was standing in the hallway peeping by Tony's door. She runs back to the pool.

"Well?" Bridget asks.

"Two things: oh, they're going at it, and yes, the boys are eavesdropping. You called it, Jade," The girls yell and cheer. The guys didn't know that Jade noticed them watching all this time.

Again, thank God for sunglasses and for having excellent peripheral vision.

"Our husbands are such pervs," Maggie said.

"Maggie, they're boys. They always will be. Fuck them, and I mean that literally." She tells them while they burst into laughter.

"Jade, how are you single? I mean, any guy would murder to be with you. You're hot, have a guy's sense of humor, and don't put up with anything." Angie asks, being stupefied; she's not involved with anyone.

"Right there, Angie, you answered your own question. I know this sounds egotistical, and I apologize in advance, but they can't handle me for all three reasons. I don't need to get laid. I WANT to get laid. That line is very thin to me. So, I just keep looking. I'm just the "better be safe than sorry girl." That probably stemmed from my childhood. My parents were the two prime examples of people who couldn't handle me."

"Why is that? I mean, what was the deal with them." Bridget asks curiously.

"They were the model ultra; everything is a sin, Jesus is a hit man, I will go to hell for this, and that stuck in the 16th century burned at the stake Christians. Believe me; they wouldn't know what Christianity was if it bit them on the ass."

'How did you deal with that?" Rosa questioned. Jade took a big swig of her Margarita.

"For sixteen years, they tried to put fear and guilt and pound it into me. I was eleven when my grandmother passed away; God rest her soul. I loved that woman. She left me a plot of land and $20,000 on my sixteenth birthday, which my parents knew nothing about. That next year, I divorced them." The girls had a gloomy look for Jade. "July 8th. That is my personal Liberation Day. I took that money and put myself through college. Met my T-girl there." Jade grabs Tonya's hand and holds her. "After graduating, I was clueless about what I wanted. Tonya left for Seattle.

I hung around Vegas for a few years when I decided to follow Tonya. Then I met your husband,

Maggie, who introduced me to those amazing darlings there." They watch McKenna and Madison play with Rosa's sons in the water playground. "Now I'm here in paradise drinking margaritas with you all."

All the girls give Jade a collective "Ahhhh!!!"

"When I hear the stories of Jack and Katie, I ask myself "Why couldn't Steve and Robin be a tenth of Logan's parents? It's just the cards I got dealt, but the fact of the matter is I'm just Jade Nicole Murphy. I'm beautiful; I'm strong; I'm responsible for myself. From then on, I looked at that mirror and said, "Nobody is going to fuck with you today or tomorrow or ever. That man you want will be right behind you, saying, "I always got your back, baby." So I'll let God pick him out and play the waiting game. He just won't know what's going to hit him. It took a very long time to find myself. Before I moved out, I got a job at Abercrombie and Fitch, which Steve and Robin were dead set against. When I got my first paycheck, I bought my first mini skirt. I put it on, looked in the mirror, and nodded. I found my first puzzle piece. I drove back to the mall and got my first pair of heels, a makeup kit, and a tube top. I put those on, looked back at that mirror, and found a big piece. I said, "Hello, Jade. We finally meet." I vowed not to hold back a fucking thing and grab life by the jugular. That's the moral of today's lesson, ladies. Don't let doubt, insecurity, or anybody mess with your mind. Look into that mirror, raise both middle fingers, and say, "My guns are locked and loaded, and they'll always be ready."

The girls go silent. They're captivated by Jade's words. They were envious of her self-esteem and will. Angie raised her glass proudly.

"I bow down to you, Jade."

The rest of the girls raise their glasses and bow. Jade raises her glass to the girls.

"No, ladies, I bow to all of us."

Around six o'clock, everybody is getting ready for the New York Eve party. Every year, the Brodies would throw a different themed New Year's party. This year was the 80s. Logan walks into McKenna and Madison's room dressed as Sonny Crockett from "Miami Vice" to the girls' room. He sees Jade with her hair French braided, giving the girls the same treatment giving Logan a quick glance.

"Hey, gals!!!"

"Hi, Dad. Jade made me into Madonna." McKenna started singing. "Like a virgin, touched for the...."

"Whoa, whoa, whoa!!!! Logan stops McKenna from going any further while Jade cracks up laughing. "Honey, why don't you learn "Lucky Star." I beg of you." He stares at Jade. "Seriously, of all of Madonna's songs, you could teach her."

"It's the song that made her, you can't fault me on that. At least it's not "Like a Prayer." Madison, here is Buttercup from "Princess Bride." Jade kisses Madison's nose.

"My God, they're beautiful, Jade," Logan says in awe at his daughters.

"I know, I'm awesome. Look at you, Crockett. Nice five o'clock shadow and everything. Is Cortez playing Tubbs?"

"I wish, but he's going as Prince." He says as Jade lowers his head, imagining a 270-pound Cortez dressed as Prince.

"Remind me to thank Clinton for hiring me so I can have that image with me forever," Jade tells Logan while he laughs. This was the most they'd talked to each other in three days. Logan's mind was racing, wondering if she was over his spanking or hiding it because the kids were around.

"So, who are you going to be?" He nervously asks.

"It's a surprise. Tonya and I had to do much research since I'm a child of the nineties, but we remembered many of the eighties in history class." Jade jokes to make Logan feel old.

"Ok, I'm out of here before you make me feel ancient."

"Seriously, I just learned about Miami Vice an hour ago from Google. I've never heard of Crockett and Tubbs before."

"Alright, STOP!!!!" He begs Jade as she laughs. His mind started feeling at ease since she was goofing with him.

"I picked something cool. You'll see."

"Tubular." He says, giving her an 80s compliment. She pushes out the door.

"OK, get out of here. Now I have to Google "Tubular." Jade closes the door and looks at the girls. "Your daddy is funny."

"Do you like him?" McKenna asks. Jade's eyes go big.

"Uh, no. I mean, I like your father, but not how you asked." Jade staggers her words.

"Are you still mad at him?" Madison asks.

Madison!!!! Daddy said not to say anything. McKenna yells at her sister. Jade folds her arms, leaning towards the door.

"Alright, what's up, girls?"

"Daddy thinks you're mad at him because you haven't talked to him after you played apple juice pong?" McKenna explains.

"Wait a minute. He thinks I'm mad at him?" She asks, mortified. The girls just nod. Jade closed her eyes, feeling horrible because she was avoiding Logan but not realizing she was coming on too strong. She remembers the texts she didn't return, the one-word sentences, and not making eye contact with him for the past two days. She thought, "How can you ever be mad at Logan? He's the sweetest, most caring person alive, and you're on a tropical private island in Barbados because of him. Also, he's ripped to shreds, drop-dead handsome, and those blue eyes. I can't imagine what he's got down…"

"Jade!!!!" Madison yells, breaking Jade's train of thought, which is about to get dirtier.

"Oh, sorry, Mads. No, I'm not mad at your daddy, girls, and I'll show him. Now run off and go get your shoes." The girls run off as Jade bangs her head against the door out of frustration. "God, Jade. Why is this guy making you so stupid?"

An hour later, guests started filing into the cabana. Logan hired a DJ to play 80s music playing throughout the island. Clinton walks out in his full Supersonics uniform he wore during his playing days, and Maggie is dressed as a Sonics cheerleader.

"I can't believe it still fits." He says in disbelief.

"Hey, my physique hasn't stopped. Neither has the clock, though."

They see Tony and Bridget walk in as Bill S. Preston and Theodore Logan, Esq. from "Bill & Ted's Excellent Adventure."

"Excellent!!!!" Logan and Clinton tell out simultaneously.

"What the hell? That's our line." Bridget yells back.

Rick and Sasha soon after enter the cabana as Beetlejuice and Lydia.

"Ironically, we heard her call his name three times earlier," Tony whispers while Logan and Clinton start snickering.

The DJ puts on "Send Me An Angel" by Real Life when McKenna and Madison walk in. Just behind them was Tonya dressed as one of Robert Palmer's background dancers. Then, there was Jade. She wore the iconic collarless gray sweatshirt and red pumps Jennifer Beals wore in "Flashdance." Logan couldn't focus on anything but the song that was playing "She looked like an angel." Her beautiful blonde hair was curled, her sweater went down just to her upper thigh so her legs were at full force, and most of all, those red stiletto pumps were doing a number on Logan's psyche. He was under a spell at the sight of her. Her hips swayed with every step. She walks past him with the tiniest look from the corner of her eye.

"Would you look at my beautiful niece?" Clinton says, kissing Tonya's cheek.

"I know; I'm simply irresistible." She responds using one of Robert Palmer's famous songs.

"Ok, how many 80s puns can we cram in tonight." Tony wonders.

"$20 says we can hit a hundred," Jade tells Tony. She could feel Logan's stare, who was in a different world at that point, fantasizing about the scene from "Flashdance" of Jade pulling a lever with water falling on her.

"You look…nice." Logan tried to spew out any word from his tongue-tied mouth. Jade could quickly tell Logan was trying to pull any word out of thin air. One of the cooks hired for the party tells everyone dinner is served on the beach. Jade whispers as she walks past him.

"I think your pants have a better response than "Nice," Jade says, grinning as she walks past him. Logan smiles to himself, relieved. "There's the Jade I've been missing." They head to the beach, where Sasha visits Jade, admiring her costume.

"Wow, I hope you shaved?" Sasha asked

"Sure did," Jade responds but suddenly winces, snapping her fingers. "I forgot to do my legs, though." Sasha and Rick laugh hysterically. "Look at you; the virgin bride looks like she got laid." Rick and Sasha stare at each other with grins.

Everyone sits down to a long table of twenty. Lobster and crab are shipped from Maine, the best cut prime rib from Texas, and UFO-sized pizza from New York City for the children. Every now and then, Logan took small glances at Jade to see if she was enjoying herself. She laughed a lot and would be in conversation with everybody. After dinner, he got up and clanged his glass.

"Everyone, I just want to say thanks for another great year. I know it won't be the same without Sandy, but Jade…" She looks up at Logan with a surprised look. "Thank you for taking Clinton's offer and coming into these girls' lives." McKenna and Madison both look at Jade and smile. "Mostly our lives, hopefully for years to come. Cheers, Jade." He raises his glass along with everyone else.

"Jade!!!" Everyone yells out while clinking their glasses. Jade just stares at Logan and mouths "Thank you" to him. Rosa then gets up from her chair.

"I have something to say. Logan, you serve us prime rib and lobster, invite us to your private island, and give Angie & me your suite when our White Sox play the Mariners, but mostly, you give us all of you." Rosa's voice starts to crack as tears come down her face. "Your parents took us all in because we needed help, and you continue their legacy as being the kindest, most giving human beings I've ever heard of because you don't have to do this for any of us. I know you don't think of us as your employees or crew but as your family because I can tell everybody you're a part of our family. We love you so much, Logan!!!" Everyone raises their glass and yells out, "Logan!!!!"

Logan gets out of his chair, heads to Rosa, and hugs her tight as she continues crying. Angie then gets up crying and hugs them both. Right at that point, Logan was missing his parents but mostly Renee. Jade couldn't help but keep her eyes on him throughout dinner. She could tell from his body language that he was not in a good place, and she was increasingly feeling guilty for avoiding him because of her impulses. She was getting a glimpse of the mask Logan was wearing that everybody was talking about.

An hour later, they headed back to the cabana and electric slided to the new year. People would write down requests for their favorite 80s songs. A little after ten, Madison passed out in her daddy's arms.

"Well, she almost made it," Angie says, brushing her hair from her sleeping face.

"We'll let her take a power nap and wake her before midnight," Rosa says.

"Let's put her on one of the lounge chairs," Jade suggests, holding a blanket.

What Jade said triggered something in Logan's head. Those were the exact words Renee said the last time she was in Barbados when McKenna was three and fell asleep before midnight.

"Logan!!!" Jade yells at Logan, who snaps out of it. "Do you want to put her down, and I'll cover her up?"

"Yeah," Logan replies.

Throughout the night, his past was getting to him. Visions of his parents and Renee start to plague him as he sees them everywhere he looks from past years. The depression overtook him until he saw McKenna still filled with energy, dancing with Cortez and Tonya. His heart ached when she and her sister didn't have a mother. Logan was dying for any connection he could have with Renee. He couldn't do anything but go to the DJ booth and talk to the DJ. He then approaches his oldest daughter. He reaches for her hand.

"May I have this next dance?"

McKenna takes her daddy's hand as "She's Like the Wind" by Patrick Swayze starts playing. Everyone stops at once and leaves the dancefloor to have it all to themselves. Logan lifts her up and sways her around. Seeing so much of Renee on his daughter's face, he felt peace. Especially since she had her mother's smile. Like everyone else, Jade was frozen, still watching a beautiful father/daughter moment.

"Isn't that an amazing site?" Sasha whispers to Jade.

"It sure is."

"This was Logan and Renee's wedding song," Sasha informs her. Jade looked at Sasha, whose eyes were glassy, trying to hold back tears.

"Do they dance to this every year?" She asks

"No, this is a complete surprise. He really must be missing her right now." Sasha says with a cracked voice.

Jade's heart sank as she watched Logan stare into his daughter's eyes. It was tearing her apart more, thinking Logan felt she was upset with him. She looked at her phone, and it was 11:48.

After the song was over, he hugged McKenna tight and said, "I love you, angel!!!" The DJ plays

"Heart and Soul" by Huey Lewis and the News to boost the party up again. Logan puts McKenna down as Jade keeps an eye on him, who goes to a sleeping Madison and kisses her on the cheek. He heads out to the beach and puts his head down. Jade watches him cover his eyes. It took everything out of her not to go and comfort him. He shakes his head and returns to the party. Logan walks to Jade, trying to hide his face, breezing past her.

"Almost that time."

Jade turns to look at him while he hurries back to the cabana.

"Yes, it is."

She whispered painfully to herself, noticing the red eyes on him in that split second. It was 11:57 when Logan woke Madison up for her to get ready for midnight. A boat was out at sea with fireworks ready to blow up the sky.

"God, I can't imagine being in a more perfect place for New Year's, but here." Tonya gets pumped up for midnight.

"No shit, girl. So, I know we don't swing on that side, but do you want to kiss at midnight."

"You must be pretty wasted. I'm going to surprise Cortez."

"Whoa, is there something brewing between..."

Tonya stops Jade, "No, but you know how much I loved Prince, Lord rest his soul."

Jade looks around to see every couple preparing for their New Year's kiss. She sees Logan across the way while counting down with twenty seconds to go. He squats down for the girls to kiss him on each cheek. Midnight struck, fireworks going off, celebrations everywhere, couples kissing. After the girls kiss their daddy, they run off to see the fireworks on the beach. Like Logan said twelve minutes ago, "Almost that time." It was a new year, a new beginning. Jade struts straight toward Logan and stands face-to-face with him.

"Happy New Year, Logan." Jade softly told him. A slight grin hit Logan's face.

"Happy New Year, Jade."

Without a second thought, she pulls Logan's face in and kisses him. In an instant, his past and his heartache evaporated. Their kiss felt perfect, and they enjoyed every millisecond of bliss.

Time didn't exist. Neither one of them could tell if it lasted three seconds or three minutes. Neither one of them wanted to pull away. They slowly did at the same time.

Clinton yells for everyone to head to the beach. Jade slips off her red pumps and walks onto the sand. Logan hadn't left her sight as she walked onto the surface. She turns around to glance at him and smiles. An intoxicated Cortez wraps his arms around Logan.

"Are you ready to say a Happy New Year to your mom and dad?"

"Yeah, I am." A huge smile blew up on his face, feeling born again.

"Look at that smile on you. How was kissing the nanny?"

"I'm not saying a word." He softly says while shaking his head.

Cortez knew if he said that, then it was truly unique. They both head to the beach with their arms around each other. They watch the last of the fireworks go off. Traditionally, you sing "Auld Lang Syne" on New Year's, but not in the Brodie household when Jack Brodie met Katie Mitchell at U2's first Seattle show in 1983. Everybody lined up facing the ocean as the DJ started "New Year's Day," the annual Brodie tradition. Logan sees Jade get her phone to look up the lyrics.

He looked into the ocean with a huge smile and started singing along with everybody. It was Logan and the Crew's way of telling them, "Happy New Year, and we miss you."

CHAPTER 11

THEY PAY TAXES, DON'T THEY?

Regret, sadness, happiness and joy played a fine round of Tug of War in Logan's head as he tossed and turned all night long. That was until that image of Jade kissing him in just that oversized gray sweater and red pumps overtook everything in him. He could still taste her sweet breath every time he licked his lips.

"Dammit!!!!" Logan yells, throwing the comforters off of him in frustration.

It was five a.m. when Logan jumped out of bed. He had been tossing and turning for hours, finally giving up on any sleep chance because that kiss was stuck in his head. He put on a Metallica baseball tee and cargo shorts before snatching his phone from his end table. Logan went downstairs and grabbed a large blanket from the linen closet and headed for the beach, hoping to have any opportunity to clear his head.

After laying down his blanket, Logan starts playing music from a random playlist on his phone while he looks out at the ocean. It was a windy morning with a touch of humidity. Lightning struck out on the horizon with a slight glow from the sun starting to rise. He sat there thinking about past years on the island with his parents and Renee. Looking around, he saw visions of his younger self-building sand castles with his mom, fishing with his dad, and jet skiing with Clinton. "Sit Next to Me" by Foster the People came on when, all of a sudden, Logan looked out into the distance. His breath was taken from him when he saw his older self holding Renee's hand along the shore.

He slowly stood up when the pit of his stomach tightened, watching the ghost of his first marriage. A hallucination? An out-of-body experience? Whatever you wanted to call it. Logan was watching himself lift his wife in the air, slowly bringing her down to kiss her. The stabbing pain in his heart grew more potent as it hardly went away. Three years felt like three days. He closed his eyes, trying to visualize her face as much as possible. Suddenly, he heard a voice muffled through the music he was listening to. He felt a touch on his back and was startled back into reality, scaring him to death. He yells and turns to see Jade. She puts her hand over her mouth.

"I'm so sorry. Are you alright?" Jade yells.

"No, no, I'm sorry. I was daydreaming."

"Daydreaming? You were gone. I called your name like three times." Logan covered his face, getting back to reality. Jade knew he was having another episode like the night before. "Do you want some company?" she asked, hoping he would say yes.

"Yeah, actually, that would be great." Jade sits down, stretched out, crossing her legs with her back arched. "Let me turn off my phone."

"Not yet. I love this song." She stops him.

Jade sat down with Logan while "Next to Me" played, looking at the ocean together. Her perfect blonde hair flew along the gust of wind. He pretends to look out at the ocean when he can't concentrate and resist seeing from the corner of his eye Jade's short white mini skirt with a "Pulp Fiction" shirt cut off from the neck showing her bare right shoulder, just like how she wore that sweater last night.

"So, what are you doing up so early?" She asks.

"Sleep is something I don't do well. I'm lucky to get five hours a night. I also wanted to enjoy this sight before we go home to rain, rain, and more rain. What about you?"

"The crashing of the waves. I've missed that sound so much. The smell, the feel of the sand, it just reminds me of home."

"Where are you from?"

"L.A." She gives Logan a confused look with a slight chuckle. "You don't know a thing about me, do you?"

Logan stammered since he never took a look at her resume. He knew at least she was a genius at beer pong.

"No, Clinton does all the hiring, and I just sign the paychecks. L.A., huh?"

"Well, I was born in Bellflower and raised in Santa Monica. One of the only great things of my childhood was waking up before sunrise, grabbing my board, and surfing before school. Then it was onto Cal State Fullerton." She pounds her heart with her fist and lifts it in the air. "GO, TITANS!!!! Graduated there and lived in Vegas for a few years before I came to Seattle."

"What was in Vegas?"

"Topaz, one of the top ten best gentlemen's clubs according to Men's Journal. I was the head bartender and occasional stripper." She says, clearing her throat and saying under her breath.

"You were a stripper???" He asked, pretending he didn't know already.

"It was just a couple of times to fill in for a friend."

"Well, how was it?"

Jade looks at Logan with a surprised reaction to his response and smiles.

"IT WAS FUCKIN AWESOME!!!!!! I've skydived, bungee jumped, and gone on the Eiffel Tower. Both the French one and the Vegas one. Stripping blew all three away. You know why?" Logan shook his head. "Empowerment. All my life, I've been told, "Jade, you can't do this" or "You can't do that," and I say, "Watch this," and I did it. Also, I made $2,000 both times. Now bartending, that's what we call in Vegas, REAL MONEY!!!"

"Nice."

"So, let me ask this. You don't care that your girls' nanny was once upon a time a stripper?"

Jade raised her eyebrow, waiting for his response. Logan thought back about yesterday with the guys on his balcony. She was good at taking care of the kids, and they loved her. Most importantly, it didn't matter to him what she used to do.

"No. No, I don't. How many of those other strippers legitimately are there so they can go to law or med school?"

"I would say at least 80% of them. The other 20% just had major league daddy issues."

"Well, there you go. No, I truly don't care if you stripped. You pay taxes like everyone else, right?"

"Like a true patriot." She salutes as she giggles. "You're for real." Logan nods. "I was wondering if you would be weirded out about that."

"Was stripping on the resume?" He asks when Jade slaps her forehead.

"I may have left that out."

They both laugh as they both feel the chemistry growing. No head games, no teasing. Just a real conversation. Something they both wanted.

"What about you? Have you lived in Seattle your whole life?"

"Yup. Seattle-born, Seattle-bred, more than likely be Seattle dead. I went to Washington U, got my Master's in business, and took over Horizon after my dad passed. I refused to be that billionaire brat and just be given the business. I worked in the mailroom. I was a coffee boy and a secretary. I learned everything in and out and busted my ass for it. I think I'm doing a good job with it."

"Hey, it hasn't folded, and we're here in Barbados, so obviously, you're doing a good job. Your mom and dad taught you well, especially with compassion for others."

"They taught me that the second I disrespect that dollar, it will kill you. I use my money to give my Crew a great salary and share my life with them." He looks at Jade directly in her eyes. "Especially you. You're taking care of my children. They are so in love with you." Jade gasps.

"Oh my God, those girls, they are amazing. I love them so much. I can't get over how smart they are."

"Well, they got their mother's brains, beauty, and daddy's...." He pretends to think hard. "God, what the hell do they have of mine?"

"Your caring heart. You said you didn't want to be a billionaire brat; neither do they. For six and three, they are level-headed and down to earth. That came from Daddy."

"I guess. I just want them to be happy, and I've felt I haven't done that for a long time."

"Why is that?"

"I work too much. Sometimes, I sleep at the office because I just won't stop and feel guilty. I always tell them that time is more important than money, but I feel like a hypocrite when I'm away from them."

"You're the CEO of a company. Doesn't that come with the territory?"

"Yes, but the fact is, being a single dad, running a company, and just trying to keep going, I still worry I'm failing."

Last night, Jade glanced at what everyone warned her about with Logan. She saw a man beating himself up emotionally because he was drowning in his past. Yet, Jade also saw someone who wanted a fresh start. She puts her hand on his shoulder.

"Hey, I just want you to know you're a great dad and, most importantly, a great person."

The simplest touch from her made Logan heal mentally. That was her power because Logan was taking what she said to heart. He's been told countless times what a great father and person he was, but he always shrugged it off.

"Thanks, I appreciate that."

"Well, I'm glad we had this talk. I'll leave you alone." Jade tries to get up, but Logan instantly reaches for her arm, lightly holding it.

"Hey, you don't have to go. This is fun."

He could say it was the closest thing to begging her not to leave. Jade felt like she got struck by lightning. His touch pulsated through her entire body. Jade shrugs her shoulders.

"OK." Jade sits back down. "Alright, I have one more "Elephant in the room" question I have?"

"Go for it."

"My wardrobe. Do you have any reservations?"

An average person would say, "Don't wear that in front of my kids." Except she looked so hot in anything she wore, Logan didn't have it in him to tell her what to do. Besides, looking at her smooth, tan legs, he would feel like a complete imbecile to say anything.

"No. It's your style. Mine are shirts, jeans, and sneakers. Just, I beg of you. If the girls want to dress like you in short shorts and heels, tell them to wait until they're eighteen or until I'm dead."

"Done, I promise. A billionaire who doesn't worry about appearance. You are so interesting."

"I just never understood the uniform thing!!!! Neither did my parents. Even when they threw parties in the backyard, The Crew would just wear slacks and a nice top, and that's it while everyone was wearing Prada or Gucci. They just didn't care. We all feel everyone should do as they want. Just do your job. That's all I ask. If your uniform is cut-off shorts or yoga pants, so be it. I'm just understanding."

"Oh, someone has noticed." She grins sinfully.

"How could I not? I'm a heterosexual male, and you're beautiful."

Jade noticed he said beautiful, not attractive. She smelled the blood in the water, and she couldn't control herself anymore.

"Since we're getting to know each other, how long have you been wearing that cologne? Tom Ford, is it? Seriously, you cake it on you."

"I've been wearing it since college. It's my go-to stuff." He tells Jade, not clicking in his head, that she's flirting. She stares deep into him.

"Hmm, it's sexy as hell. I got a delicious whiff of it after beer pong." Now, it hit him. He started to sense this conversation going in a different direction. "Speaking of that, Madison spilled the beans and said I was mad at you after our game, and the spank heard around the world."

Logan cleared his throat as it tightened up with nervousness.

"I was in the moment, and you got me toasted. I felt bad, but I texted you and tried talking to you about it, and all I was getting was the cold shoulder. I thought we were messing with each other."

"Ok, first off. I wasn't mad. Number two, I had to avoid you."

"Why?"

"Ohh, how can I put this lightly? When you spanked me, it took everything out of me not to shove my tongue down your throat." Logan's face went bloodshot red instantly, and the mass exodus of any clear thought was gone. "Then I wanted to pull your shorts down and ride you UP AND DOWN!!!" She says, gritting her teeth. Logan initially figured Jade was stepping it up with the head games. That went away quickly when he looked at Jade, as she no longer had a casual demeanor. It quickly turned into a revelation of lust. He was convinced that this was another hallucination. "Here, I'll demonstrate."

Jade quickly mounts on top of Logan, ravaging him with her intensity. She curls her tongue down Logan's mouth, feeling his heat and tightening her hips against his waist so he couldn't move. She pulls away and looks at him with insane passion. Logan's mind was all over the place with every erotic thought of Jade until he realized this was no hallucination. This was as real as it gets. Jade starts nibbling on Logan's neck.

"Also, on Christmas Eve, when we hugged, I felt it brushing against me." She grabs a fistful of Logan's erection before unbuckling his belt. Logan panics as a moment of insecurity hits him. Well, it's more like denial.

"Jade, wait. You are my kids' nann…" Jade gave him a glare that said, "Don't even bother fighting it." Ironically, he told himself the same thing. "Forget it. I'll shut up."

"Yeah. Listen to the red one with the pitchfork on your left shoulder."

Logan grabs her head and presses his lips onto hers. After a few seconds, she unbuttoned his pants and pulled them down. Logan's mind went from 0 to 200 MPH. Not wearing panties, Jade inhales deeply when she feels every inch of him. He was as large as she dreamed, starting to pant when she swayed once with her hips; she saw a look of panic on Logan's face. Eleven seconds was all it took for Logan to lose control of himself.

"Wait, no." Logan sharply inhaled as he released immediately. A combination of frustration and humiliation filled him. "SHIT!!!!!!! SHIT!!!" He hit the sand, upset with himself. Jade softly cuddled his cheek to calm him down.

"Hey, hey, take it easy, Logan." She flashes her angelic smile to him. "When was the last time you had sex?"

Logan is still embarrassed, covering his face. "Almost four years. I couldn't help it. You're so stunning."

"OH, MY GOD!!! Give yourself a break. I mean…" Jade stops when she tries to get off of him but notices he is still rock hard. "You're still up?"

"Kind of."

Jade screamed in her head, "Kind of!!!!!" She tried to rationalize with herself that she was sitting on top of a lead pipe, and he wasn't fully hard. Jade whispers.

"Wonderful."

Jade quickly sits up and continues to ride him cowgirl style, putting her hands on his chest while circling her hips into him. He grabs both sides of Jade's skirt, pulling her deeper in him as she grinds her wet through the motion. He looks Jade straight in the eyes with her fiery desire. Her mouth was wide open, gasping for air from every thrust—his hands caressed Jade's silky thighs. The humidity of the Barbados night starts to make Jade sweat. She kept licking her lips as the sweat came down.

"Jade, that is so hot. It's driving me nuts."

"What, this?" She slowly licks the top of her lips.

"Oh damn." He sits himself up while lifting her so she can adjust herself. Her legs were wrapped around him. Her feet dug into the sand as he pulled her tight, perfect ass into him. Moaning deeper, the faster they were going while Jade felt the mother of all orgasms building.

Logan devours her soft, wet mouth while whimpering harder with every stroke. She lifts her head when Logan kisses her neck, sucking the salt from her sweat. Jade could not believe this was happening. She yanks her shirt off her neck. Logan couldn't breathe, looking at Jade's beautiful, round breasts. They were perfect. She was perfect, he thought to himself. He slowly grabs her back, pulling her in closer. He starts to smear his soft lips onto her chest.

"Suck on them, Logan. Suck on them hard." She commanded.

Logan started gripping her left one with his lip. Jade gasps from the intensity while grinding his groin harder. Jade felt it coming. She ravishes her mouth into his as she orgasms, grabbing a fist full of his shirt and groaning into his mouth. Her body shook as he held her, feeling each contraction pulsate. He gasped as he stared at the sunrise coming up. The only thought he had on his mind was that this was the most beautiful feeling since holding his daughters for the first time. He pulls away to look at her, wiping sweat from her face. Jade can feel his heart pounding out of his chest. Her legs still wrapped around Logan, not wanting to let him go. There was only one thing she could say to him.

"Happy fuckin New Year."

"Yeah, so far, so good."

Jade slowly detaches from Logan. He gets up and hikes his shorts up. He gives Jade his hand and helps her up. She hikes her skirt down while he brushes the sand off of her.

"God, you're too sweet."

"The least I can do."

There was a long pause between them when they matched, neither knowing what to say.

"Well, goodnight."

"Good morning, actually."

"Ahh, good point." She points to the sunrise.

Jade had a different approach. Once she starts to walk back to the mansion. Logan turns to look out into the ocean, overcome by the acceleration of what happened. He couldn't remember the last time he did something so impulsive. All of a sudden, a thought hits Logan hard. In the heat of the moment, he went utterly skin-to-skin with Jade. His mouth fell, and panic filled him. He quickly turns around and yells out.

"Jade!!!!"

"I'm on Mirena, Logan!!!" Jade quickly yells back with a grin, knowing that question was coming.

"OK, thank you!!!" He said, feeling a thousand pounds fall off his back, knowing she was on an IUD.

"Later!!!"

As Jade returned to the house, Logan turned his attention back to the sunrise. He just experienced a sensation new to him. He had the most fantastic sex on the beach with his daughter's nanny.

That's when regret slapped him across the face. He pulls his hair back, cringing at what he just did.

Once Jade got to the mansion, she grabbed a water bottle into the kitchen. She takes a big gulp and falls back on the closed refrigerator door, replaying what she did on that beach. She covered her mouth in disbelief, starting to giggle. Jade took pride in her self-control. Her philosophy was if you want the pussy, you have to get into the brain. Logan was the first man she met who took over her brain, her body, and her soul at the same time effortlessly. She headed upstairs to her room, still trying to catch her breath, unable to shake the massive smile off her face. She checks on Tonya to see if she is still sleeping. Deep down, Jade was dying to tell her. She goes to her bedroom and lays on her bed, looking out the window and watching the sun beam against the water. She closes her eyes, unable to get his scent, touch, or taste away from her train of thought. She grabbed her phone and took a picture of the sunrise with her feet crossed. She immediately sent it to Facebook and Instagram with the caption, "Been up 24hrs.

Best New Year's Eve and, so far, Best New Year's Day, and it's only been six hours old!!!! I need sleep before going home. XOXO!!!" She then put her phone on her nightstand and laid her head on her pillow, looking up at the ceiling. Not an ounce of guilt or regret went through her. She told Logan that stripping was no longer her life's most tremendous adrenaline rush. What she did on that beach with Logan took over that spot.

CHAPTER 12

SHOCK AND AWE

Coming back from Barbados, things were rather strange. Neither Logan nor Jade mentioned that morning on New Year's Day to each other. In all honesty, Logan would avoid Jade as much as possible, much like what she did to him in Barbados. He would have Cortez take him to work earlier, always be on his phone, mostly talking to nobody on the other end, and only talk to Jade about the kids when he got home, barely giving her any eye contact. Jade wasn't a fool, though. She knew about the possibility of Logan feeling weird since she was his first sexual encounter after Renee, but after two weeks back in Seattle, she had just about enough. She wanted to talk about that morning whether he liked it or not.

The night before Logan's business trip to Montreal, he was in his game room after putting the kids to bed. He was in the middle of an "NBA Jam" game when a disembodied voice on his ear pods warned him that his battery was low. He yanks them out of his ear, aggravated that they weren't charged. He noticed music playing outside. He walked out to see that it was coming from Jade's poolhouse. He started walking towards it when he saw her window open. She was dancing and lip-syncing to Johnny Cash's "Cocaine Blues." Logan walked closer, captivated by her body moving to the Man in Black. The only thing on his mind for two weeks was that morning, but he was battling a demon he had been fighting for a long time. Not the ability to move on from Renee but the right to move on. Logan was frozen while watching her dance until the sprinklers came on.

"Shit!!!" He says when he gets sprayed in the face.

Suddenly, the motion detectors near the guest house come on. Lights blare down on Logan. He hears the music stop and the porch lights coming on. "Hey, who's out there?" She yells out, standing over the threshold of her front door.

"Jade, it's Logan!!!" He comes out of the shadows.

"Logan, what the hell?"

"I'm so sorry, I heard the music and…"

Jade interrupts. "Oh God, was it too loud? I can turn it down."

"No, no, it's fine. I love Johnny Cash."

"As well you should; the man IS God."

Logan smiles until he gets a closer look at Jade's shirt. It was a purple tee with Marilyn Monroe covered in tattoos, wearing an L.A. Lakers jersey. There are two things Logan Brodie wasn't crazy about. Racism and war, but being a Sonics fan, he hates one thing: the Los Angeles Lakers.

"A Lakers fan, seriously???" He asked Jade with a sense of disappointment.

"L.A. born, L.A. breed, and I'm a Laker girl until I'm dead."

Logan can barely concentrate. He had to constantly force himself from looking Jade up and down. This L.A. girl went to a tanning salon at least twice a week. The length of her shirt was barely covering her little white boy shorts. She noticed his gaze, knowing how terrible he was at hiding it. His arms flailed like he was landing a jumbo jet, and his cheeks were red. "Game on!!!" She thought to herself, and she was going to be relentless. Jade lifted her left arm and leaned against the doorway, hiking her shirt higher, showing her perfectly toned stomach.

"So, what time is your flight?" She asks sensually, even though she is trying to contain the laughter that was building while watching him squirm. Jade could see where his brain was going. Logan raised his eyebrows in confusion since his mind was stuck on her bare navel.

"Flight??? Montreal, YES!!! Umm, six a.m. I told the girls I won't be here when they wake up."

"Do you have an alarm set?"

"I do at four. So, I better get to bed. Sooo…"

"Well then, Au reVoir!!!!" Jade smiles seductively.

"That's right. I got to get used to that French talk." He chuckles as he walks away.

The tide shifted with Jade in an instant. It was humorous at first, but she was so turned on watching this built, good-looking man have so much difficulty making heads or tails on what to say next. Glancing at her a half a second too long, a slight stutter every time they talked. It was adorable to Jade. Logan looks back and waves. She waves back, giggling, watching him brush back his hair, obviously flustered and tensed. Jade was relieved he could finally say more than two words to her, but she would ensure they talked about New Year's before he left in the morning. He looked at the dark, overcast sky, feeling his parents' disappointment. Not that he had a thing for the nanny, but he had a thing for a Lakers fan.

It was past four a.m. when Logan was in a deep, relaxed sleep. Something that was a novelty for him, but for the first time in months, he was having the best sleep ever. His inner alarm clock normally woke him up a couple of minutes before his phone did, but this time, he was awakened by something else. His eyes started to creep open until they suddenly popped. There was a sensation he never felt before. He looks up and sees blonde hair slowly moving up and down, hearing a deep, slow moan. She noticed he was up and detached herself from him.

"Good Morning!!!!" Jade then continued to inhale his thickness into her soft, wet mouth. Logan couldn't even hold a thought in his head. He grabbed both handfuls of his seamless silk sheets, begging to control himself. Even though Logan was having a moment of exhilaration, he hadn't felt before, and loving every second of it. He just needed to ask her one question that couldn't wait.

"Jade, what the hell are you doing?" He asks while it takes a struggle to get the words out.

"Well, I'm multitasking. I'm making sure you're de-stressed for your trip. I'm breaking the ice from Barbados, and the way your eyes were all over my body in front of my pool house, I just had to give you the greatest wake-up call of all time. So, if you don't mind."

Jade continued to scramble his brain, keeping her seductive, hazel eyes on his. Logan's body was tingling when he felt his dam breaking.

"Jade, Jade. I'm about to explode."

Jade stops immediately, looking at Logan. "Really? Oh, thanks for the warning."

She gives Logan an evil, sweltering grin. His mind was the other thing she was about to blow.

Her carnality, feverishly, was turned up to the highest level. Her moans grew louder while Logan's eyes went up like a window shade, not believing his sight. He couldn't sit still from her intensity. He had to tame himself to not lift his leg or move his body from the force of Jade. He couldn't keep his eyes open when he felt his climax approaching.

"Jade!!! I can't. I can't."

Logan's face went almost maroon, trying not to scream as he released. When he was able to catch his breath, he looked up at Jade, and with her seductress smile, she lifted her head up, and her throat came down. She moaned like she just took a bite of the finest creme brulee. "SHE DID NOT JUST DO THAT!!!" He thought to himself while he looked up at the ceiling, trying to get an idea about Jade. He asked himself, "What won't this girl do? She's so raw and mysterious but, at the same, so caring and sweet. Her presence alone made you fall in love with her. What's stopping you, Logan?" Except, he was lying to himself. Denial was his go-to move, and it's been his primary move since Renee died. Jade climbs off of him and starts to walk out of the bedroom without saying a word.

"Wait!!!" Logan yells, sitting up. Jade stops and slowly turns to look at Logan. He was so lost in confusion at what was in her mind. "What's going on here? I mean, what are we doing, you and I? I need to know."

Jade slowly walks back to his bed. She slowly crawls towards him like a seductive cat, giving him a searing look that goes through his entire soul. He knew he was in over his head with this girl. Jade closed in on Logan's lips; he could smell her sweet breath.

"I'm just having fun with you. My eyes noticed that rod you were packing last night. Also, I lied. I purposely had the Man in Black draw you to me. Most importantly, don't think…" She brushes her fingertip against his forehead, making little circles. "I'm not stuck in that beautiful head of yours. So, why don't we just cut the" Jade air quotes, "Let's avoid each other and not talk about Barbados" bullshit because it's just really silly, Logan. Just think about what you felt and saw a minute ago while stuck in whatever lame, snoozefest meeting you're in and just repeat to yourself." Jade leans to his ear and whispers. "She swallowed, and she loved it." Logan could not respond. More and more, he felt clueless and naive being around her.

Jade immediately changes her scorching tone to little Miss Perky. "Now that you're up. Let's get a move on. Your flight leaves in two hours, and it's snowy and freezing cold in Montreal right now. So, up and at em, tiger."

Jade pats his knee while climbing off of him and heads towards the door. She turns to look at Logan and raises her eyebrows before closing the door. Logan falls back into the pillow, covering his face. Suddenly, he started to chuckle.

"That's it. I'm in the Twilight Zone."

A half-hour later, Logan was dressed, pulling his suitcase into the kitchen. He sees Jade sipping her coffee and scrolling through Facebook on the island with her black silk panties sticking out from under her shirt. He shakes his head, realizing Jade was right. She will be the only thing in his head for the next four days. She turns around and hands him a coffee to go.

"Hey, I made you a quad shot espresso, or I like to call "Jade's rocket up the ass." Cream and sugar, right?"

"How did you know?" Logan smiles.

"Tony told me how you like your coffee before he went on vacation."

"Thanks." His phone dings to see a text from Cortez.

Cortez text: "You ready? I'm out front."

"Well, I'll see you in a few days." He grabs his suitcase and starts walking towards the front door.

"Have fun. Bring me back something French." She quotes the neighbor kid from "Home Alone."

Logan suddenly stops. Jade told him she would be stuck in his head for four days. He wanted to make sure he returned the favor. He drops his suitcase and walks towards her. Logan turns Jade around and lifts her onto the cool countertop of the island by her waist. Exactly how he did in her imagination. Logan proceeds to devour her mouth hard. Her tongue slowly danced inside his firm mouth as her hands went under his shirt and smoothed them along his solid back. Her bare feet slowly brushed against his thigh. They pull apart from each other even though neither wants to stop. Both their hearts were pumping hard and rapidly.

Logan looks at Jade, who has an astonished look on her face. He lifts her down off the island.

"First, I wanted to leave you something French. See ya!!!"

He grabs his bag and espresso and starts whistling "O' Canada" while walking out the door. Jade's mind was spinning out of control then, and her libido was on maximum overdrive. She gets a glass from the cupboard, fills it with cold water from the refrigerator, and promptly splashes it in her face. She exhales, shaking her head.

"WOW!!!" She whispers, getting a cloth to dry the floors. Outside, Cortez sees a huge grin on Logan's face while he struts into the limo.

"Hey, what's up with you?" Logan looks at Cortez and bursts into maniacal laughter. "Man, you're going crazy."

Logan pauses for a second and laughs uncontrollably again. Cortez starts to think his boss is a wasted drunk. Logan enters the limo and lays his head back, thinking back at the past hour. It was like a perfect dream. This mysterious, unpredictable, beautiful manipulator sneaks into his room and gives him the most incredible blow job. Logan goes through another laughing fit while he visualizes Jade's shocked look after he kisses her. He thought of what she had said earlier. It was silly trying to avoid each other. What was even sillier was avoiding his feelings for her.

Logan looked out the window at the far distance of the skyline of Seattle. He wondered what made Jade want to move to the Pacific Northwest. Was it just for Tonya? Or was it for something else, like destiny?

CHAPTER 13

HAVE A COSMO

For four days, Logan was stuck in life-draining meeting after meeting. Except Jade gave him something to get through them. Her special wake-up call was engraved in his mind. He got texts from Jade about the kids' schoolwork and a rundown of their day. She would send him cute selfies of her and the girls folding laundry with Rosa and Angie, cooking with Tony with all four wearing backward baseball caps, and playing "Mario Kart" with Cortez with all of them wearing headsets. One night, Logan was at a business dinner with Paul McInnes and Maurice Mullet, two of Canada's largest and wealthiest logistics CEOs. The waiter came around and collected their drink order.

"Gentlemen, can I start you off with some drinks?" The waiter asks.

"I'll have a screwdriver." Paul orders.

"Highball for me." Maurice requests with his thick French accent.

Logan was undecided, looking at the drink menu when he saw Cosmopolitan. He suddenly bursts into laughter. Paul and Maurice look at each other, perplexed, wondering what the hell has got into Logan. He tries to contain himself.

"I'm sorry, I'm sorry. I'll have a Cosmopolitan." He hysterically laughs again while people from other tables give Logan vacant looks as he tries to compose himself.

"Since when did you drink Cosmos, Logan?" Maurice asks

"Oh, someone got me into them."

After five minutes of business talk, the waiter returned with their drinks. When he put down Logan's Cosmo, he grabbed his phone and took a picture to send to Jade while Paul and Maurice were talking about expansion plans involving Horizon going into Canada.

Logan text: "You were right. Since you beat me, you got me drinking these."

Jade texted a minute later: "I told you I would, bitch!!!! LOL!!!!"

Logan laughs again, slapping the table. Paul and Maurice start to smile, finding it humorous to see this side of Logan, especially since this is the first time seeing him since Renee's funeral.

"Logan, is everything alright?" Maurice chuckles, asking him.

"Yes. I apologize, fellas. Continue, please."

"You seem distracted. Have you met someone?" Paul asks with a curious smile.

"No, why?" Logan's eyes perked up, wondering how they could tell.

"You just look like someone who got laid for the first time. I've never seen you laugh this much, and you're glowing."

Logan didn't realize how much he was showing. After all, he had the most mind-bending sex he'd ever experienced. He even noticed that he hadn't talked to Renee in weeks.

"Guys, can we shut off the business talk for a few minutes and be human?" Both Paul and Maurice nod in agreement. "Why are the decisions we make worth millions and people's livelihoods on the line so much easier than the ones we make personally? Is there a force that stops you from being happy when it's right in front of you?"

Paul and Maurice were in their mid-fifties. They could tell this young man was subliminally asking for help to move on.

"Logan, I'm into my fourth marriage. I've let business ruin them all." Also, the other hidden girlfriends, Logan thought to himself. "I'm old-fashioned. That's why I admire you and your dad. You two changed the way to run a business like Horizon. You're not cutthroats, and you two don't have the "It's not personal, it's business" attitude when we all know it's always personal, and you always put family first. Here's the kicker: You should not ask that question at thirty-five because you are too young."

"Logan, we should be asking you that because we're in the senior stage of our lives. Very quickly, tell me your biggest fear in life?"

Logan knew right away and cringed thinking about it. "I would have to say outliving my children," Logan answers while Maurice points at him.

"Right there, Logan. That was not a hard personal choice, and it took you no time to think about it. Just like in business, it has to be quick, and it has to be done. Yet, you will always fight yourself. We always do."

Logan took a drink of his Cosmo. He put it down and just gazed at it for a minute. He thought about what Jade had done to him in just a short time. It was almost midnight when they got done with dinner.

"Can we give you a lift back to your hotel, Logan?"

Since Renee's death, Logan's business trips have only consisted of going to meetings and returning to the hotel, not taking in the scenery or exploring the different cities—especially beautiful ones like Montreal.

"Thanks, Paul, but I'm going to take a walk." He shakes Paul's hand.

"Logan, I hope you find what you're looking for because, like I said, you're too young and good of a man."

Logan smiles, taking in Paul's compliment as he shakes Maurice's hand.

"Thanks, fellas, for everything. I'll call you next week on when to start expanding."

"Absolutely. We want to work with you. Have a good night. Enjoy Montreal."

"Goodnight, guys."

Logan closes the limo door as they drive off. Logan puts on his gloves and ski hat as snow lightly falls into the night. Logan looked at his phone to see that the famous Maisonneuve Monument was just two miles away. While walking the two miles, he reflected on the apparent change Jade made him feel. He was so envious of her fearless attitude and free spirit. The fact she didn't give a damn about what others thought and did everything her own way. He loved watching her fire for life going into his children. Something in his head was starting to open up. He let his worst critic stop him from moving on, himself. As the snow fell harder, he sat on a bench before the Maisonneuve Monument. He sees a couple taking a selfie and kissing each other. Logan went to the couple.

"Can I take your picture?" Logan makes a picture notion with his fingers to the couple.

"Oh, merci." The boyfriend thanks Logan while he hands him his phone. He lifts his girlfriend, wrapping her legs around him. They kiss as Logan snaps away.

"One more, face-to-face." Logan directs the couple. They smile together, putting their cheeks together. Logan snaps some more. "Fantastique." Logan hands back the phone to the boyfriend.

"Merci beaucoup!!!" The girlfriend thanks Logan.

"Goodnight," Logan says.

He returned to the bench; he looked at the couple one last time, seeing them so in love. He wanted that back in his life more than anything. Except fear and guilt were his roadblocks. He closed his eyes and lifted his head, letting the light snowfall hit his face. He then realized Jade had texted him during dinner. It was the girls saying goodnight.

Jade pointed her phone to the girls. "Ok, go!!!"

McKenna & Madison simultaneously said goodnight in French. "Bonne nuit, Daddy!!!!"

Logan laughed as his precious daughters wished him good-night. Jade turned the phone around to herself.

"Bonne nuit, Logan," Jade tells him in a sultry tone.

She then gives him a sexy smile, flashing her beautiful whites before ending the video. He played the video again and paused it right when Jade smiled. A surge of warmth went through him. She had the most angelic smile. From her smile to her sense of humor to the way she kissed. He couldn't resist; he looked at the time to see it was ten minutes past midnight, hoping she was still awake since it was after nine in Seattle. Logan thought about the count-less selfies Jade took of herself, so he got out his phone and took a selfie with Notre Dame Basilica in the background. A historic two-hundred-year-old church. He looked at the "Send to" button and Jade's name.

Logan texts: "Look where I'm at."

He looked at his phone, sounding pathetic inside, saying, "Please text, please text."

Jade texts: "Oh my God!!! How beautiful. You suck!!! I'm so jealous."

Logan looked at her text. It just wasn't the same. He was des-perate to hear her voice.

Logan texts: "Are you busy?"

Jade text: "No, I'm just hot and wet thinking about you." Logan's mouth fell while he read that. A couple of seconds later, she texts again. "I'm in the Jacuzzi." Sending him a winking emoji.

Logan imagines what bikini she had on. He sees the app on his phone hooked to every security camera around the mansion. One of them was pointed directly to the pool. He was about to press the app and pulled his finger back, bringing that idea to a screeching halt.

Logan says, "Stop. You're not a creep." Instead, he texts her.

Logan text: "Can we talk?"

A few seconds later, Jade calls him. His heart suddenly pumps rapidly, forgetting immediately what he wants to talk to her about. He takes a deep breath and presses the answer button.

"Hey," Logan says, hearing the jacuzzi jets in the background and wishing he was there.

"Hey, yourself. Are you just digging the Montreal scene?"

"I am, but I'm freezing to death sitting on this bench."

Jade lays back, relaxing in the hot, foamy water while one of the jets blasts on her back. "Well,

I'm not. Isn't it midnight over there?

"It is. I just didn't feel like going to bed. How are the kids doing?" He asks.

"Awesome, as usual. McKenna got an A on her math test. I can't believe they're teaching kids fractions in the first grade."

"Seriously, I didn't do fractions until the fourth grade."

"No shit. Madison is turning into a little Bob Ross. She's a really good painter."

"I know. She's got her mother's gift." Logan closed his eyes, visualizing how Madison held her brush like her mother. Something was different in Logan, which he even noticed. He wasn't spiraling into misery thinking of Renee. He watches the young French couple he took pictures of walking away holding hands, imagining how it would feel to hold Jade's hand. "Hey, just out of curiosity. How did you sneak into my room?" He asks while Jade snickers.

"You gave me the security code, goober." Logan shakes his head, realizing what a dumb question that was. "Boy, you should have seen your face when you woke up." Jade laughs aloud while Logan starts to feel warm, thinking of that morning as the snow hits harder.

"Well, gee, how else am I supposed to react?"

"Well, that's what you get for avoiding me." She says while a smile crosses her lips.

Logan rolls his eyes. "Wait a minute. You were avoiding me first in Barbados."

"Apples and oranges. I was avoiding you because I couldn't control my urges. You were avoiding me because you were hiding from a conversation we needed to have. So, I win in that department."

"Ok, you're right. I'm just not used to this. It's been a long time, and I'm just trying to figure you out."

Her smile widened, knowing he couldn't control himself. The thing was, she couldn't either. Jade closed her eyes, imagining being face-to-face with him.

"Well, what have you figured out so far?" She asks.

"Absolutely nothing. You are just a five-foot question mark."

"Well, riddle me that, Batman."

Jade saw firsthand in Barbados what he's been battling inside. She could tell he was lost and confused because his life went into a tale spin the second he saw her. What he needed to do was take a breath and enjoy the moment.

"Logan, you don't need to figure me out. You can ask me anything. We had a good start on that beach. Also, a better finish."

Logan couldn't even count the times he replayed that interaction in his head. It was the most incredible feeling he had in so long. That was until he kissed Jade before he left. He could feel her hands all over his back again. The scent of her Coco Chanel perfume was rooted in his head.

"That's true. As you said, we're just having fun. Aren't you?"

Jade suddenly got warmer down there, feeling Logan inside of her.

"Immensely." Jade visualized Logan all by himself on that bench when she remembered a conversation she had with Tony about Logan's business trips, which only resulted in work and staying in his hotel. Suddenly an image popped in her head back from her sophomore year in college. She took a course in art history and there was a particular statue that was housed at the Montreal Museum of Arts.

"Hey, I've always wanted to see Montreal. Can you do me a favor if you have any free time there?"

"I'm done with work and waiting to fly out late tomorrow night. I will be back in Seattle at eleven tomorrow night. Why?"

She quickly sits up and dries off her hands with a towel, grabbing her phone to quickly Google the Montreal Museum of Fine Arts and goes through their website. She finds a sculpture of a winged man with a hollow chest with Medusa-like hair covering his face. It was the perfect symbol for Logan. The mask he was wearing and the emptiness he had inside.

"There's a statue at the Museum of Fine Arts in their Sculpture Gardens called "The Eye," and it's so drop-dead beautiful. If you don't mind, can you take a picture of it and send it to me?" Logan can hear the glee in Jade's voice. He couldn't resist.

"I can do that."

"YES!!! You're awesome. This naked body is roasting, so I'm heading to Sleepyville. Have a good night, Logan." She says quickly, hanging up.

"Goodnight." Logan stutters, surprised at that sudden turn in their conversation.

He gets up from the bench and brushes the snow off of him. The sound of Jade's voice put him on a natural high. He started to walk back to his hotel with an extra bounce in his step and his head up with just the thought of Jade in his mind. It took him about thirty steps to realize what she just said. "NAKED BODY!!!" He stops to grab his phone, looks at the security app again, and opens it. On the app was a menu of all sixteen cameras on the compound. He saw the pool camera. Still, he could not press it. He grimaces at the thought of her beautiful body soaking wet, letting out a painful groan for not going through with it. Once he composed himself, he did press the camera and pointed right at McKenna and Madison's bedroom. He sees his princesses sleeping softly in their beds. Logan kisses his phone twice, hoping his girls know how much their daddy misses them.

The next day, Logan did precisely what Jade asked. He took an Uber to the Montreal Museum of Fine Arts. Logan never cared for museums. The last one he went to was when he was nine, to the Art Institute of Chicago, known to most as "The Ferris Bueller Museum." He intended to take a picture of "The Eye" and get out of there. Once he entered the museum, he immediately became engrossed with the atmosphere. Before he went to the Sculpture Gardens, he took in a lecture on graphic arts and photography, took a tour of Quebec and Canadian contemporary art, and went through an exhibit of the Royal Canadian Monarchy. Four hours later, he stood right before "The Eye." The only thing he could think about was how happy Jade would be. Jade was at a Hobby Lobby picking up supplies for a project McKenna was doing for school when she got a text from Logan. She sees Logan in front of "The Eye" with a huge smile and arms stretched towards it.

Logan text: "Ta-da!!!"

Jade covers her mouth, bursting into laughter at the sight of him. He looked so happy and so adorable. She kept her gaze right on his glowing smile and bright eyes. She was so proud and also so turned on at the fact he did that for her.

Jade text: "You are too sweet. Thank you."

Logan text: "It was my pleasure. See you when I get home."

Jade then looked at the sculpture in the picture. "Man, that thing is strange."

Jade thought since Logan saw the beauty of Montreal at night, try the daytime. To her, Logan was that boy at the edge of the diving board, afraid to jump into the pool, while she was the girl sneaking behind him and pushing him in. She pushed Logan back into living the moment and taking a picture of a strange statue.

CHAPTER 14

SHOOTING BULLETS

An exhausted Logan pulls his rolling suitcase inside the front door, letting out a relieved sigh of being happy to be home. The mansion is pitch black except for some flashing lights and the voice of Sandra Bullock coming from the movie theater. He walks in to see "Minions" playing on the big screen. He heads to the couch in the middle of the theater to see McKenna, Madison, and Jade snuggled together, fast asleep. Logan smiles and heads to the linen closet to get a down comforter to cover all three up. Logan returns and spreads the comforter on top of them. After he turns off the projector, he leans to kiss his daughters on the top of their foreheads. He was about to head out when he saw Jade's beautiful face. He couldn't resist; he leaned down and softly kissed Jade's forehead. He grinned, looking down at all three girls before exiting the theater. Before heading out the door, Jade lets out a sudden, loud buzzsaw-like snore. Logan holds his mouth, covering his laughter as he leaves.

The following day, Logan walks into the kitchen holding a bag to see Jade making breakfast for the girls since Tony was on vacation. She wore a Coyote Ugly tank top, exposing her toned belly, and tight black jeggings lip-synching to Kylie Minogue's "Can't

Get You Out of My Head." The ultimate irony is that Jade was the only thing in his head. Logan can't help but teeter towards insanity at the sight of her. He exhales profoundly, trying to compose himself before walking into the kitchen.

"Good morning, angels," Logan says.

"Daddy!!!" The girls run to hug Logan.

"Good morning, Charlie."

"No, Jade, Daddy's name is Logan. Not Charlie."

Logan & Jade start giggling at their "Charlie's Angels" inside joke.

"Did you get us anything?" McKenna begs.

"Seriously, you would ask me that? Of course, I did."

He pulls two teddy bears dressed as mounties holding the Canadian flag out of the bag. They both hugged them.

"I love him. Thank you, Daddy!!!" Madison says, holding her teddy bear tight.

Jade clears her throat as her way of saying, "Um, what did you get me?"

"Oh, Jade, there's lozenges in the medicine cabinet right up there." He says sarcastically.

Jade smirks, rubbing her temple with her middle finger. Logan snickers. She goes inside the pantry to get the syrup, shuddering at the sight of Logan. A picture of him could only go so far, but when she saw him up close and could smell his musk, that was a different story. She quickly snaps back into reality. Jade walks out of the pantry with the syrup and puts it on the table.

"I did get you something." He tells her.

"Really? Ohh, Merci. Then I won't have to throw this out." Jade hands him a plate of French toast.

"God, you're incredible."

"Well, duh."

Logan smiles as he sits down with his daughters, discussing his trip. Jade grins, watching Logan with the girls, thinking how much they missed him. After her conversation with him the other night, she instantly noticed a surge in his spirit. She couldn't help but take a couple more stares at him because the girls weren't the only ones who missed him. Logan worked at home when he finished around noon, getting caught up with work emails. He goes to Jade's guest-house, holding a small gift bag. He rings the bell.

Jade opens the door with a sinister look and squinted eyes. "Is that my present???"

Logan smiles and hands her the gift bag. She jumps up and down, being silly. She opens it and pulls out a miniature Montreal Canadiens Zamboni. She gasps.

"This is so adorable. How did you know I love hockey?"

"Wait, you love hockey?" He asked, astonished.

"Hell yeah. I was an ice girl for the Vegas Golden Knights. You know, the ones in those leather jumpsuits who skate around shoveling ice during intermission." Logan's brain was screaming, visualizing Jade in tight leather. "Thank you so much."

"No problem," Logan says before heading back to the house when Jade stops him.

"Hey, I was wondering, are you busy today?"

"I worked from home catching up on emails, but now I'm done. Whatcha got in mind?"

"You wanna get out of here? Go get a beer?" Logan raises his index finger.

"I know the perfect place."

"Sweetness!!! Let me get my sandals."

Logan stretched out his arms in amazement. What's with this girl and the cold? It's 40 degrees and misting, he thought to himself. Once Jade put on her gold Steve Maddens, Logan warmed up as Jade's perfect body approached him.

"Aren't you freezing? You're wearing cut-off shorts, a crop top, and sandals? I don't get it."

"First off, the good Lord blessed me with an outstanding immune system and this killer body, so old man winter can suck it."

"I swear, you L.A. people."

Jade suddenly stops and puts her hands on her hips.

"Uh, what do you mean by "You L.A. people?" Jade playfully snaps back, giving Logan air quotes.

"I'm just saying. You guys have a reputation."

"Oh, so true. I wish my fellow Los Angelenos had that cheery and uplifting spirit like your fellow Seattletopians."

"Touche," Logan says as she mic-dropped him.

They enter the mansion, and Jade notices they walked past the garage.

"Did you forget something? I thought we were heading out."

"Just follow me."

Jade felt skeptical as she walked towards a wing of the house she had never seen before. Logan opens two giant doors, and Jade's eyes are exposed to rays of neon lights from Logan's game room. It is a wonderland filled with over a hundred classic arcade games, a pool table, an air hockey table, a jukebox, and a full-size bar stocked with various beers. Jade gives Logan a marvelous stare.

"Soooo, when did you buy heaven?"

"Pretty much when my Dad knew his inner child wasn't going away in his mid-thirties. So, what can I get you?" He says, standing behind the bar.

"Hmmm, something cool and something Mexican."

Logan hands her a Corona as he opens a Guinness.

"Cheers, Bellflower."

"Cheers, Seattle."

They both swig their beers, making solid eye contact.

"So, what do you think?" Logan asks. Jade looks around, still amazed.

"It's absolutely breathtaking." She marvels while taking a swig of her Corona.

Logan walks around the bar to sit next to Jade. She looks at his ultra-thin black hoodie, which shows off his ripped arms. She screams in her head, I've never felt so jealous of a shirt in my life. I want to wear this man so badly. Jade was living in torture during his Montreal trip. She was putting up a lot of mileage on her vibrator every day he was gone. After a few seconds of awkward silence, Logan, out of nowhere, started shooting out bullet questions.

"What's your favorite movie?

"Pretty Woman, you?

"Braveheart. First celebrity crush?"

"Dwayne Johnson, you?"

"Sandra Bullock. First concert?"

"'N Sync, Rose Bowl, 2000. Pink opened. Go!!!"

"U2, Kingdome, 1988. Metallica opened. Hero?"

"Marilyn Monroe." She gives him a chin lift.

"Ken Griffey Jr."

After three hours, eight beers, three shots of Jameson, a best-of-seven series of air hockey, which Logan won four to two and a pizza from Pizzeria Pulcinella, they continued to learn every little detail about each other. Jade hands Logan a Blue Moon as she grabs a Shock Top.

"Favorite Marvel hero. By the way, Iron Man is disqualified because you're as rich as Tony Stark."

"Deadpool." Jade lets out a gasp.

"ME TOO!!! Common shot!!!" Jade and Logan return to the bar and take another shot of Jameson whenever they find something in common. "Favorite show?"

"Mystery Science Theater 3000." Jade tilts her head, not familiar with the title. "It's that show where this guy has to watch shitty movies."

"Ohh, wait, wait!!!" Jade stops Logan, snapping her fingers. "Is that one with the two robots, and they do commentary throughout?" Logan nods his head. "Oh, that's a good one, but I got to go with "It's Always Sunny in Philadelphia." I know I said Johnny Cash is God, but Charlie Day is vice God." They laugh themselves silly again. Jade stares at Logan as he's still laughing. She wonders how much he knows her already. "OK, how many tattoos do I have? You've seen me in a bikini, as I clearly noticed you were looking in Barbados, so you should know this?"

Logan closes his eyes, trying to concentrate and keep his balance simultaneously. "Three, right?"

She flashes a four with her hand.

"Wait a minute, time out. Rose on the right ankle, angel wings on your back, clover on the left side of your ribs." Jade turns around and pulls her hair up to show him a tattoo of a Ferris wheel on the lower part of her neck. He thought that was a strange choice for a tattoo. "A Ferris wheel?"

"Yeah, it's the one from Santa Monica pier. It's sentimental."

Logan sees Jade's eyes trail off and her tone lower. He senses it may be a sentimental but a sore subject. She lets out a lopsided smile that he catches.

"You have such a cute smile." He says, taking a drink of his beer.

"Ahhh. It's because of my cute cocksuckers mouth."

Logan shoots beer out of his nose and coughs. Jade pats his back as she laughs. Once Logan composes himself, they both laugh uncontrollably.

"Were you born with a filter?"

"Language!!!!! That's the only F-word I have never said. Seriously, you never thought about getting inked."

"No, I never got around to it."

Logan lied. If he had one giant fear other than spiders, it was needles. Jade looked him up and down like an empty canvas.

"Take your shirt off." She ordered with a look of desire.

"Wait, what?" Logan asked.

"Hey, the Sistine Chapel had a dull, white ceiling before Michaelangelo jazzed it up, so I need to see your dull, white ceiling." She tells him. Although she knew very well there was nothing dull underneath that shirt. Logan grinned and nodded like she made a valid point. He took his shirt off, and Jade instantly became sober. She put on a straightforward face, looking at his ripped abs while keeping the screams from the inside.

She made a couple of laps around him while he could feel her eyes burn into him. She stops in front of him with a lustful gaze. She takes a big gulp of her beer before putting it on the bar. She walks up to his hulking body, looking into his pacific blue eyes. She gently strokes her hand onto his ripped left bicep, guiding it across his shoulder with the tip of her index finger.

"This one, I see a Celtic Cross. Mixed with green, white, and orange for your heritage."

She goes behind him and swipes her long fingernails from his neck to his middle back. At that point, he couldn't hide the goose-bumps. Not that it mattered because they were as big as the ones on Jade's body. He takes a deep breath fighting the urge to lift her from her feet, placing her on his pool table, and fucking her rough right then and there. "This one, a skull. Something big, badass, and very hot."

Jade's heart was pounding, fighting the same urge. She was thinking of getting it from behind on the air hockey table. She comes back to face him. She squinted and put her finger on her lips, thinking of the last tattoo. She then gives him an intimate glance. "What to do with that chest?" Jade takes her hand and smooths across his pecks to his broad shoulders while looking into his eyes.

"What do we put here?" Jade asks. She didn't have any more ideas. It was just an excuse to touch Logan's rock-hard chest. "This one's a tough one." Suddenly, "California Love" by Tupac and Dr. Dre play on Jade's phone, her alarm for her to pick up the girls. "We'll get back to that topic later, but it's time to get the girls." Logan was in agony after hearing Jade's phone go off. "We've got a problem, though. I'm pretty toasted. Oh wait, don't you get them on Fridays."

"Yeah, but I can't drive either," Logan says, slurring his words. Then they had the same thought at the same time.

"CORTEZ!!!" They yell together.

"OK, here's the plan. We go get the girls, and we take them out."

"Wait, we? As in me too?"

"If you're cool with that." He grins and nods.

"Beyond cool. Where are you taking us girls and Cortez?"

"Bullwinkle's."

Jade looked at Logan with a weird look.

"As in Bullwinkle J. Moose and Rocky the flying squirrel?"

"Yup. If you think this is heaven, wait until you check this place out. Miniature golf, go-karts, bumper boats, batting cages, bowling." Logan sees Jade bite her lip and close her eyes as she moans. "Jade, are you OK?"

"Yes, I just had a run-in-the-mill orgasm from you describing this place." She playfully moans while Logan cracks up laughing.

"Well, let's get going."

They start to walk out of Logan's playland when she snaps her finger.

"Oh, wait. I never thanked you for the Zamboni." Logan shakes his head.

"It was nothing."

"No, that was a sweet gesture, and I thank you."

Jade goes on her tiptoes and gives Logan a quick, innocent peck on the cheek. "Also, thank you for tucking me and the girls in last night." She pulled Logan down and swept her tongue into his mouth, tasting the mixture of beer and whiskey yet still getting a hint of Jade's sweet taste on his breath. He grips her hips, pulling her closer, feeling her soft pink lips onto his. His hands then went down to the edge of where her cut-off shorts ended and her bare leg started. Jade moaned when she felt his hand touch her thigh. They slowly pull apart, opening their eyes.

"Do I get to see you after the girls go to bed?" He playfully asks. Jade thinks, looking up at the ceiling.

"Let's just say, if you get me enough tickets for a giant stuffed animal, you can sneak into my room, and you can stuff me." She raises her eyebrows before separating herself from his arms. She goes to get her Steve Madden's and walks out of the game room. There was nothing he could do but watch her with complete fascination—the degree of this girl who had him under a spell. He stood by the doorway, watching the back of her walk barefoot with the straps of her sandals between her fingers. He waited intensely, hoping she would turn and give him that side glance that cut like a razor's edge. He didn't have to wait long. She turned and smiled, which went through Logan like a surge of electricity. Jade had absolute power over him.

Cortez chaperoned Logan and Jade to get the girls from school and head to Bullwinkle's. The five spent the next three hours riding go-carts, hitting baseballs in the batting cages, and winning stuffed animals, including a four-foot stuffed Tweety Bird for a certain five-foot blonde. They all sit together eating pizza. Logan and Jade would listen to the girls' day at school, periodically giving each other quick glances at each other.

"OK, girls, don't overeat. We've got laser tag next." He suggests sounding like a little boy their age.

"God, you've got more energy than them." Jade looks at Logan in amazement.

"I've been coming here for years; this place transforms me back to when I was six."

Jade tilts her head, melting over Logan, showing his inner child. Cortez noticed the way they were interacting. He noticed his best friend was following the advice he gave him in Barbados.

"So, what did you do today, Logan?" Cortez asks. Logan wondered what to say, but he knew Cortez would see right through him. Rosa, Angie, and Tony also texted him what they had done already.

"Just got caught up with work at home and…" Jade interrupts.

"And he gave me a tour of the house. Showing me Renee's artwork, looking at family pictures, and playing Barbie in the girl's room."

"Hey!!!!!" McKenna yells out.

"Well, you were at school. I got work done, and we were bored."

Logan and Jade crack up, giggling while whispering in each other's ears. The girls look at each other like they're crazy, while Cortez just grins. He knew they were drinking most of the day, but he could tell that it wasn't just booze doing the talking for the both of them.

"Hey, girls. Why don't we go back to the arcade? I'm not leaving this place until I beat you two at Skee-Ball."

"Ok. Come on, McKenna." Madison jumps out of her seat.

"I'll keep them busy. You two have fun."

The girls take Cortez's giant hands and drag him back to the arcade area as Logan and Jade stare at each other, smiling.

"Hey, now that the coast is clear, I brought something." She pulls out a flask full of rum.

"Oh, you're very naughty."

"Keep that under your hat, Santa," Jade demands while spiking Logan's Pepsi.

"Did your parents take you to places like this?"

It was the first time the parents' subject was brought up with Logan. Jade started to squirm in her stool at the thought of her parents. She needed some help first.

"Hold on, if we're going to talk about my parents. I need a lot more rum." Jade pours more rum into her soda when Logan stops her.

"Whoa, whoa. We'll drop it. I don't want you to be uncomfortable." He says, not wanting her to go down an ugly road down memory lane.

"No, it's cool. Now and then. That was when I didn't act up during kids' church on Wednesday nights. We couldn't do it on Fridays because there was Bible study with their church friends, and I was forced to hang with their kids with a gun to my head. Our little group was supposed to talk about God in our room. Yeah, that's what I will do on a Friday night. Steve and Robin were born at the wrong time. The Salem Witch Trials would have been Mardi Gras for them being the whacked-out zealots they were." Her demeanor changed, and Logan sensed her troubled past. "I had a list of people we were not allowed to talk to. Kids whose parents were gay, atheists, or parents who drank made the blacklist."

"Well, that just screams Christian Fellowship."

"Nailed it!!!" Jade burst out, slapping the table. She laughed hard, yet Logan saw she was masking the pain like he did. "I just loved being told that God sees right through you. You are an abundance of sin, Jade. I see it in your eyes. The devil is all over you." Jade rolls her eyes and scoffs. "Is he, Mom? Whoa, that slap I got across the face was worth it. I didn't cry or give her any emotion. After that slap, I was a brick wall to them, and they knew it. To tell you what my mom was like, have you ever read "Carrie" by Stephen King?"

"I saw the movie."

"Yeah, Carrie White's mother? That was my mommy." She says sarcastically.

"How old were you?"

"Thirteen. That's when puberty hit, and I turned into a transformer." She points to her breasts. "These two went from A's to C's within the year. My ass blew up three times its size. I grew to 5'3 and stayed there. A troublemaker was brewing inside, and they knew it. At that point, I said, "No more bullshit!!!" I refused to go to church with them. The Pacific Ocean was my church. I taught myself how to surf, and I felt closer to God there and felt His love than any Sunday at "His house of judgment, I mean worship."

"So you don't blame God for your upbringing?"

"No!!!" She says sternly. "We're tight as always. Blaming Him for how bad life turned out for anyone is the easy way out. It's not His fault my parents were weak-minded and stupid." She sighs, stirring her Rum and Pepsi. "They were the anti-Jack and Katie. They were the yang to your parent's ying." She takes a deep breath, staring into space while Logan just looks at her, wanting to hold her in his arms. "You know, Logan. It is a profound statement when your parents say that I was an accident, which I was reminded of time and time again."

Logan watched Jade's vulnerability, talking about her upbringing for the first time. He felt violently ill inside, thinking of who would hurt her. Let alone her parents. He reached across the table, gently squeezing Jade's forearm tighter.

"I am so deeply sorry."

The rush from his touch went through Jade. She grabs her cup and raises it. "Don't be. Here's to a beautiful Friday. I'm here, and I'm still standing. I'm stronger than ever; I'm a nanny to two of the most adorable princesses on planet Earth; I'm here at this magical kick-ass place with them, Biggie Small's long lost twin, and I'm sitting next to their wonderful father slash my boss. I'm still Jade." She says proudly as the lights dim in the showroom and the curtain rises for the Rocky & Bullwinkle animatronics stage show was about to start.

"To a great Friday." Logan raises his cup.

They hit their cups together as the show started. Logan could not keep his eyes off Jade. She turned to watch the show. Suddenly, Logan felt Jade's leg accidentally brushing against his. He looks under the table and sees her legs crossed; her foot is inches from his leg. He gently grabs her leg and places it on his thigh. A relaxing grin goes on her face as she continues to watch the show. Logan slowly took off her sandal and started to brush his fingers back and forth slowly across her ankle. Jade closed her eyes and swallowed hard. She shuddered as she couldn't focus on anything but his touch. Logan then turned his head to watch the show as he stroked his fingers onto her, hoping to remove any discomfort from her troubled past. She turns her head to glance at him.

Jade slowly gets out of her stool and walks around the table to sit beside him, not taking her eyes off him. She sits down and gets as close as possible to feel his warmth. She stares at the stage, watching and laughing at Rocky & Bullwinkle's act. Suddenly, she took his hand, put it under the table, and placed it on her soft, sensual thighs. He stroked his hand across them back and forth. Like Jade said, it was a beautiful Friday.

They spent the day bonding and connecting, igniting something between them throughout the day. Yet, in just a few minutes alone in that showroom, the oxytocin between them turned into a raging inferno. Logan didn't feel alone in his pain; more than life itself, he wanted to take it away from her. He took it all away from her with the gentle swipes with his fingers across her legs and that glancing beam from his eyes, just in time for laser tag.

CHAPTER 15

No Twinkle,
Twinkle Little Star

Around 1:30 a.m. Logan was woken by a blood-curdling scream coming from the girls' room. Logan bolts out of bed and heads to their room.

"HELP!!!!! NO!!!!!!! STRANGER!!!!" Madison screams.

"MADISON!!!! MCKENNA!!!" He yells out, running across the hall. Logan opens the door and sees Madison having a nightmare. Logan pats her chest, trying to wake her up. "Madison, you're having a bad dream."

Madison, still incoherent, sits up. "Daddy, I want Jade."

"But, sweetie. She's asleep. Daddy is right here."

"Please, Daddy, I want Jade. Please." Madison starts to cry. "I need Jade."

"Okay, Okay, sweetheart. Don't cry; I'll get her. I'll be right back." Logan starts to run out while McKenna gets out of bed and consoles her sister while he gets Jade. He feels guilty about waking her in the middle of the night but knows Madison would cry all night. He goes to the pool house and knocks on her door.

"Jade!!!" He rings the bell. "Jade!!! It's Logan!!!"

Her porch light comes on, and she opens her door. She was squinting her eyes and having wild bedhead wearing just a Vegas Golden Knights hockey jersey with Murphy #94 on it and a pair of white lace panties just peaking out.

"Logan, what's going on?" Jade asks, half asleep and yawning. Logan pauses, looking her up and down at her one-size-too-big jersey with just her voluptuous legs on display.

"Umm... Uhhhh." His head was so non-existent he couldn't remember why he came over. "Madison!!! She had a bad dream and wants you to comfort her." Hearing that woke Jade up more.

"Oh, poor Mads. Ok. Give me one second."

Jade runs back to her bedroom, putting on a pair of workout pants. She closes the door and starts walking back to the mansion with Logan.

"Thank you so much for this. I'm so sorry to wake you."

"What are you apologizing for? Of course."

"She was screaming, "Stranger!!! Stranger!!!" He tells her when it hits Jade why she might be having nightmares about strangers.

"I've been teaching them about self-defense and what to do when a stranger approaches. She's probably freaked out."

Logan stopped immediately, standing frozen. Guilt went through Logan hard, realizing he never taught them not to talk to strangers. They were both primary targets, especially since their father was a public figure. He pulls his hair back.

"Oh my God, I'm such a lousy father. I never taught them what to do when...." Jade stops him by grabbing his arm like he did to her at Bullwinkle's.

"Stop. You're a wonderful dad. Always know that. Just know that nothing will ever happen to them on my watch. I will happily do the time in jail with a huge smile if someone ever tried anything with them."

Logan knew Jade enough that even standing at five foot three, she would destroy anyone who would harm his children.

"God, you're an amazing nanny. You've never taken care of children before?"

"It doesn't matter. It's instinct, and I'm good because I give a shit. They mean everything to me; losing a mother their age is devastating."

"I know. After Renee died, McKenna had nightmares every day about me dying." Jade closes her eyes, shaking her head.

"Christ. I just want to hold them and make them feel safe always."

Logan smiled, hearing that as they entered the girls' room. McKenna was in bed with Madison, consoling her sister. Madison's face lights up when she sees her.

"Hey girls, did you have a bad dream, Maddi?"

"Yes, can you sleep with us, Jade???" She begs.

"Of course, sweetheart. Let me get in the middle of you two." Both girls slept in queen-sized beds, so there was plenty of room for the three of them. Jade looks at Logan. "OK, you get back to bed. You've got work in the morning."

"Are you sure?" He asks, even though he knows the three would be alright.

"We're good now. I've got this. Nighty night." She shoos Logan away.

He starts to close the door when Jade softly starts singing to Madison. "California" by Lenny Kravitz. Logan had a confused look on his face when he first heard it. He was expecting a standard lullaby, but with Jade, you get the unexpected. Another thing he didn't expect was the beautiful singing voice she had. It sounded like a cross between Carrie Underwood and Whitney Houston. Logan started to question what Jade couldn't do more and more. He shut the door to his room, climbing back into bed, relieved that he wasn't the only one they needed. He wakes up around 5:30 a.m., immediately checks on the girls, and sees all three cuddled together asleep. McKenna and Madison slept on Jade's side, her arms protecting them both. He closes his eyes and says a simple "Thank you" to a crucifix hanging in the hallway before gently closing his door.

Later, at the office, Logan and Sasha were finishing up having lunch together. Sasha has a mouth full of Chinese Lo Mein. "Don't forget you got a FaceTime meeting with the San Francisco district at two and the Environmental Protection Agency at three.

"Again with the E.P.A.?" He says, rolling his eyes. "I just had a meeting with them last week. Tell them I can only give them twenty minutes. I'm falling asleep just thinking about talking to them."

"Done," Sasha responds

"So, since Rick is coming over for the UFC fight Saturday night, what are you up to?"

"I was going to go out to that nightclub Rogue with Bridget since Tony was coming over too. I considered inviting Jade, but I wasn't sure what you thought."

Logan's eyes perked up. He wanted Jade and Sasha to bond more. "That would be great. Why would you think I would have a problem with that?"

"I just want to make sure." Sasha liked Jade more and more, but she still wanted to probe her to make sure. It was her overprotective side for Logan. "Since she taught me those twerking moves, I want to use them at Rogue."

"Oh, I know." Logan thinks back about Barbados.

"How did you know?" She asks, giving him a questionable look. Logan realizes what he said.

"Uh, Jade told me. She also told me she was going to teach the girls. Of course, she was kidding. I swear to God, she better be kidding."

"I'm so impressed with how she interacts with the kids."

"I can't get over it." He says, taking a bite of his egg rolls. "She takes them to museums, the aquarium, and the zoo after school. Because of Jade, McKenna is reading at a third-grade level."

"At six years old?" She's amazed.

"I know!!! Oh, I gotta tell you what happened this morning. Madison had a nightmare, and she wanted Jade to console her."

Sasha was worried Logan wasn't going to take it well. "How did you feel about that?"

Logan had an overjoyed look. "God's honest truth. I felt a giant weight fall off my back. I saw her take control. Madison was relaxed in bed with her, and then she sang her a lullaby. Take a guess what she sang to her."

"I don't know, "Itsy, Bitsy Spider?" Sasha asked, baffled.

"No. Very softly, she sang "California" by Lenny Kravitz."

"Seriously?" She looks out into space. "That is so different and cool.

Logan has an excited expression. "I know!!! No "Twinkle, Twinkle Little Star" or "You are my Sunshine," but she sang Lenny Kravitz. I can't get over how non-traditional she is." Sasha can see his eyes jumping around just talking about her.

"Just like you." She grins. Logan deflects her statement.

"Yeah. I mean, we do have the same line of thinking. Why do everything everybody else does? I swear, the chemistry of those three is so strong when they're together."

He takes a big bite of his orange chicken as Sasha sees the same enchanted look on him when he first meets Renee.

"Just like you two." She says, leaning back and folding her arms.

Logan gives Sasha a confused look with a mouth full of chicken. "What do you mean?" Sasha raises her arms in frustration, yelling at him.

"Oh, for Christ's sake, Logan!!! This is the first woman you have talked to since Renee died, and your face glows every time you bring her up. Don't deny it. I know all about the game room and Bullwinkle's." Logan realized his home was turning into high school with all the gossip. "I've known you for fifteen years; don't think of me as an idiot. I see it in you and haven't seen that part of you in a long time."

Logan sits back in his chair, taking in everything Sasha says.

"OK!!! I like her!!!! Happy now!!!"

"Finally!!!!" She slaps her hand on his desk.

Logan has a huge grin on his face. "I can't stop thinking about her, Sasha. My heart is tap dancing every time I'm around her. I got some clarity, maybe some closure, when I was in Montreal." He sighs deeply, rubbing his chin. "I just don't care if she's my kids' nanny. I don't care if she was a stripper. I just don't care to sit on the sidelines anymore." Sasha closed her eyes in relief. She was so happy to see this side of him.

"Well, listen, I'll call her later today and set up a girls' night with Bridget. Also, I'll invite Tonya, so there's no third wheel."

"Thanks, Sasha. Seriously, no shit, thanks."

"Of course. I know we'll have a good time. By her Instagram pictures, it will be epic because that girl is crazy fun."

Logan took a few seconds to compute until he realized what Sasha said. His eyes go wide.

"Wait, she's on Instagram?"

"Oh yeah. We just started following each other last month. My God, she's led a fun life."

"Really?"

"Sasha exits and closes the office door. Logan rolls his eyes and puts his head down on his desk.

"Oh God, Instagram." He yells to himself.

Logan didn't believe in social media. He didn't think it was real life. He never had Twitter or a Facebook account, but he did have an Instagram account he shared with Renee. It only had 39 posts, and the last thing he posted was a picture of him and Renee in Italy. He last looked at his Instagram account when she died. It never even crossed his mind to look for Jade on social media. The temptation to look at her Instagram builds with every second and every heartbeat.

"No!!! Logan!!! No!!!" He tries to talk himself out of looking, but his knee starts twitching. He looks at his phone but tries to keep his eyes off it. Ten seconds later, he grabbed it. "Son of a bitch."

He opened his Instagram app and typed up Jade Murphy while biting his lip, and there she was. SoCalJgirl94. He sees her small cover picture and puts his hands over his hair.

"Please let her account be private. Please be private; please be private." Logan repeats while closing his eyes. He opened his eyes, and it wasn't private. "Dammit!!!" He looks away, knowing that there's no way of fighting it. He looks at the tops of her account and notices she has 962 posts and 44,376 followers. He closes his eyes again while his thumb scrolls to the middle. He opens his eyes, and his train of thought immediately leaves the station. The only thought in his head was this stunning freak of nature was all over for social media to see. He covers his mouth, shaking his head.

One image of Jade was hotter than the next after the next. He skims through her time in Vegas. One picture of her at the Palms sitting with her legs crossed, wearing a navy plunge sequin mini dress barely covering her breasts with those heels with the straps wrapping around her ankles with the caption "I am the she in shenanigans." Logan started sweating for twenty seconds just at the sight of her legs. Another one at the pool at Caesar's wearing a black string bikini with a cowboy hat, holding a drink with the caption, "Alcohol doesn't solve problems, but neither does milk, so bring on the tequila." Logan chuckles at her sense of humor. He then went through Jade's random videos of herself dancing to music and modeling new outfits until HE FOUND IT!!!

"Holy shit!!!"

It was like he opened the arc of the Covenant, except Logan's face didn't melt off. It was glued to a video of Jade skating around in her black jumpsuit during intermission at a Vegas Golden

Knights game. It was made of leather, and her chest was opened up. He hit his breaking point as his sexual urge was in Mount St. Helens mode. He puts his phone down and walks away from his desk, raising his hands. He takes a few steps when it hits him. He didn't look at her most recent posts. Realizing she took a lot of pictures with the kids. He runs back to his desk and scrolls up to the top of her account.

"Please, there's none of the kids, right?" He mutters to himself.

He goes through the four months since she started working for him and exhales in relief that there were no posts of the girls but many in Barbados. Her first was a selfie in that snakeskin bikini that will forever be sketched in his brain.

"I was called away on an emergency trip to Barbados. I need more emergencies like this in my life." Logan laughs again at her caption. He then thinks of New Year's and scrolls to see pics with the Crew in her "Flashdance" outfit. The one that caught his eye was a picture of her beautiful feet lying in bed and the sun rising in the background of her balcony. It was taken minutes after they had sex. The caption read, "Been up 24 hrs. Best New Year's Eve and so far best New Year's Day ever, and it's only been six hours old!!" Logan drops his phone before finishing the quote.

"Best New Year's morning ever? Because of me? It has to. I was that good?" Logan chuckles, and it turns into maniacal laughter when his pride skyrockets at the thought of how good he is to Jade. A huge smile comes on his face. A minute later, he thought of that morning before he left for Montreal. Waking up to see Jade's blonde hair going up and down on him, the taste of her mouth in the kitchen right before leaving. His heart was pumping like a Texas oil rig, and he was ramped up. HE WAS DONE!!!! He picks up his phone, takes it to the bathroom, scrolls through a random post from her college days, and finds one at a Halloween party where Jade and Tonya are dressed as Baby and Scary Spice. Logan widens the picture to cut Tonya out, where it's just Jade. He starts the shower and begins to disrobe, just implanting that picture in his head. He gets naked and jumps into the shower. Logan starts gently stroking himself, fantasizing about Jade performing "Say You'll Be There" to him.

Logan shakes his head as the hot water pours down, pulling on himself faster and harder. He couldn't help but think about pulling those tiny shorts with the Union Jack on her booty off Jade. It took about six strokes until he yelled out while being released. Letting the hot water hit his head, he looked to see if he still had a hard-on. He quickly turns the water cold; his body suddenly feels acupunctured by a thousand needles. It did nothing. He was still hard and not even close to being done.

He gets out of the shower and quickly goes to his phone again, scrolling randomly again. He watches a video of her skydiving with the caption, "For all the ones who take life seriously, you need to cut that shit out." Logan was turned on more than ever. Jade wasn't just a hot girl in a hot outfit; she was everything. The way she lived her life, he was so envious of her. He scrolled again to see a sweet picture of Jade hugging a little boy with Down Syndrome with the caption, "The only man in my life who's never broken my heart." His erection fell along with his heart at the thought of someone hurting Jade. He knew about her situation with her parents, but what other relationships did she have?

"Who could possibly hurt you?" Logan says to her picture. He just couldn't unravel the thought. Sure, she was independent and strong-willed, but that smile, that body, that sense of humor, that heart. Suddenly, a knock on the door shook him back to reality.

"Logan, don't forget E.P.A.," Sasha reminds him.

"I know. I just wanted a shower. You know them and cleanliness." He answers.

"Alrighty."

Logan turns the screen off his phone and starts to get dried off, heading to his loft. He goes to his closet, grabbing a white polo shirt, a pair of jeans, and a pair of Air Jordans. He sits on the bed when he turns around, realizing he hasn't slept since Jade started. He quickly gets dressed and heads out of the loft. He looks at the bed one last time, thinking about how he's cried and slept on it. With the phone in his hand, he turns the screen back on, and Jade's radiant smile hits his eyes. Her chocolate eyes fueled his focus. She shuts the light off and closes the door. Seeing Jade flash her smile put his mood on a new level, so much so that he decided to give the E.P.A. an extra ten minutes.

CHAPTER 16

GOING ROGUE

Jade, Sasha, Bridget, and Tonya are preparing for a girls' night at Rogue, one of Seattle's hottest nightclubs. Meanwhile, Logan is having a guys' night watching the UFC pay-per-view with Clinton, Tony, and Rick in the theater. The girls lip sync to Patti Labelle's "Lady Marmalade" as they get ready in Jade's guesthouse. Tonya comes out in a sequin navy tube dress and black heels.

"I don't know, am I overdoing it with this."

"No way, you are so hot. If we were lesbians, I'd eat you up." Jade answers.

"Ahhhh!!!! You just made my day."

Bridget puts cream blush on her cheeks while Sasha puts on blood-red lipstick.

"I swear, Tony better not get shit-faced tonight because I expect to get banged tonight," Bridget demands.

"It will be taken care of, Bridget!!!" Jade grabs her phone to text Clinton.

Jade texts: "Don't let Tony get wasted. Bridget wants to get laid tonight."

Clinton texts Jade: "No sweat, I'll watch over him."

Jade text: "You're a gem in God's Eyes."

Sasha, wearing an off-the-shoulder white romper with white four-inch sandals, admires herself in the mirror, thinking back to her modeling days.

"I can't wait to see Rick's face when he sees this. The last time I wore this, I modeled it in Milan."

Jade wolf whistles and speaks like a male chauvinist from the '60s. "Look at the stems you got there, doll." She smacks Sasha in the ass.

Sasha smiles, looking at Jade like a crazy person. She looks her up and down, wearing a satin silver plunge top that barely covers her breasts, a black micro-leather mini skirt, and black leather over-the-knee boots. "Forget about me. Look at you."

"I know. I kind of wanted to go low-key and conservative tonight." The three girls snicker. "All right, my fellow beautiful ladies. Jade is ready for her Seattle nightlife debut. Let's go to the theater and make the guys forget about the Octagon."

"Since I crammed my body into this little thing, I expect a hard boner poking out of Tony's pants," Bridget exclaims, sporting a leopard mini dress and four-inch black stilettos.

The guys are watching one of the undercard fights in the movie theater.

"C'MON!!! Get out of it!!!!" Clinton yells at the big screen.

"He's got his arm tucked under him. He's going to tap out." Logan tells him.

"NO WAY!!! There are twenty seconds left. Rick, can you throw me another beer?" Tony asks

Rick pulls a can of beer out of the cooler and tosses it to Tony. "Incoming."

"Hey, Jade warned me to tell you to take it easy with the beer. Your wife wants to get laid." Clinton warns Tony.

"Got it."

The buzzer goes off as round one ends.

"I've got fifty bucks on Martinez knocking out Alexander within the first thirty seconds," Clinton yells.

"No way, they'll go the distance," Rick replies.

"I'll take that action, Clinton," Logan says when the girls enter the theater.

"OK, boys. Start your drooling." Sasha says.

The guys look at the girls. They all get out of their seats, giving them a standing ovation. Logan was smiling and clapping until he saw Jade. He went utterly frozen, and his heart sped as fast as his Shelby. Her outfit locked Logan's eyes on this mass of beauty. A chill went down his spine when she turned. Everything went slowly to him, watching her long, curly strawberry blonde hair swaying, showing off her angel wings. Her back was bare, but a tiny black tie held her top together. Her large chandelier earrings whipped along with her flowing hair. The only direction she didn't turn was to Logan's, but she felt the power of his gaze.

"Well, babe?" Sasha asks Rick, who closes his eyes, shaking his head, admiring his beautiful wife.

"My God, you're stunning. You got the mace in your purse, right?"

"Always," Sasha answers, then kisses him.

"You be good, Tony. How much is he in the hole, Clinton?" Bridget asks Clinton.

"He owes me a hundred, but the night is young," Clinton answers.

"I'll be good, baby." Tony kisses his wife tenderly.

"What do you think, Uncle?" Tonya asks as she spins.

"You're killing me, honey. I'm not seeing an eight-year-old little girl on my shoulders anymore. Just a beautiful young lady." Clinton kisses his niece on the forehead as the girls say, "Awwww."

"Alright, let's get going," Jade yells out.

The girls leave the theater. Jade was the last to leave when she finally turned to Logan.

"Hey Logan, you can return to blinking again, you silly goose."

Logan is still frozen and overwhelmed at the sight of her. He had a sad look, wishing she wouldn't leave, especially when he had the horrific thought of all the flock of single vultures who'd swarm down and try to devour her. He had to look down because she was so beautiful. It was tearing him apart. She took one last look at him before walking out of the theater and seeing his pained face through the door frame. Her beaming smile changed, feeling remorseful immediately. The pit of her stomach went tight as she walked towards the front door. Before walking out, she paused to turn around, facing the theater. She had that same somber look that Logan had because she wanted to be with him, too.

"Let's get crazy, Jade!!!" Tonya screams at Jade while Sasha and Bridget scream out, getting pumped. Jade shakes it off. She was ready for her girl's night. Ten minutes after the girls left the theater, Clinton checked on Logan, who periodically kept looking out at the exit.

"Son, are you alright?" Clinton asked, knowing full well Jade was on his mind.

"Yeah, why?" Logan tries to concentrate.

"Oh, nothing. You look like Nicholson after he got lobotomized at the end of "Cuckoo's Nest.""

"No, I'm good."

"Great, I don't want to smother you with a pillow. Let's watch some blood splatter." Logan smirked while he tried to watch the pay-per-view, but only two things were on his mind. That leather mini and, most of all, that radiant smile on her face.

Cortez drives the girls to Rogue. Once they arrive, he opens the door and helps them out of the limo. Tonya gives Cortez a flirtatious wink, which makes him smile shyly.

"Alright, Cortez, we'll see you later," Sasha tells Cortez.

"Not so fast, Sasha. I will be with you girls throughout the night—Bossman's orders.

"Oh my God, we have a bodyguard," Bridget yells. Her face goes grim when she sees the line going on forever. "Holy shit, we'll never get in."

"Oh, girls, I wouldn't worry. Right, Cortez?" Jade knew how the nightclub scene worked. She knew what to do. Cortez nods.

"You know it, shorty. Ladies, lock your arms together and start walking before me." He orders the girls.

They see the long line to get into Rogue, but then the doorman sees a massive 6'6 270, pound black bodyguard with a bald head towering over four gorgeous women showing off their bodies locking arms together, which meant a lot of money would be spent. The doorman points to them and signals them to the front. They breeze through the line, hearing rumblings from people waiting an hour. The doorman waits until they reach the front and pulls the rope for them. Before entering, Cortez slips the doorman a hundred into his jacket pocket, to which the doorman returns him with a gentle nod.

They walk through a long tunnel with neon lights guiding the way. Once they get inside, they look around and see the packed place. Jade felt at home, hearing the music's bass pounding into her body while the multi-colored strobe lights entered her eyes. A huge grin grows, feeling her mojo building. Immediately, the men were on high alert with the four of them. At least two of them can flash their wedding rings at them like it was repellent.

"OK, what's first? Dance or drink." Sasha yells out as her voice is very faint.

"I say we dance first to get our bodies going," Bridget suggests. Jade stares at the DJ booth.

"Ladies, excuse me. I know the perfect song to start this night for us." Jade strutted to the DJ booth and typed on her phone to give to the DJ since it was too loud to speak.

Jade text: "Hi there, sweetie, see this face." The DJ looks at Jade, who flashes him with her pearly whites. "Get used to it.

Could you be a peach and play "Kings and Queens" by Ava Max next, and these two Benny Franklins are yours?"

The DJ looks at Jade and whips out $200 folded between her fingers. He texts: "You got it, enchantress."

The DJ hands back her phone as she slips him a $200 and a wink. The DJ stops the song that is playing immediately and starts "Kings and Queens." Once the music begins, Jade turns around and starts mouthing the words to the girls. She beckons them to come dance with her. After a half hour, the girls take a break, go to the bar, and start pounding down the tequila.

"All right, ladies, toast time!!!! Tonya announces. They raise their shots. "Here's to the four hottest women in this joint."

"TESTIFY, sister Tonya!!! Down it, girls." Jade yells out.

They shoot their tequila and then go back to the dance floor. One guy after another tries to cut in with the girls. Jade starts dancing with two tall guys who look like they just came out of a GQ magazine. She was just giving them the satisfaction of dancing with her because Logan's look was the only thing on her mind before they left. An hour later, they get a table by the bar and order a round of Sex on the Beaches and more shots of Patron. Jade takes out her phone.

"Girls, SELFIE TIME!!!" The four of them squeeze together and kiss the camera.

"Post that and make everybody jealous of us," Bridget tells Jade.

"Consider it done." Before Jade posts the picture to Facebook, she sees the text bubble. It was from Logan twenty minutes ago.

Logan text: "Sorry I was a little tongue-tied before you left, but I just really wanted to say how beautiful you look tonight. Have a great time tonight with the girls."

Jade just stared at her phone for the next minute. She could not grasp how sweet one guy could be. Right then, it was killing her inside not being with him. That afternoon in his game room and Bullwinkle's with the kids was one of her best days in a long time.

She thought about how she opened up about her parents and how he just listened. Logan had no idea how Jade's pain went away just from his touch.

"Jade, are you OK?" Bridget asked, noticing how distracted she was. Jade quickly looked up from her phone and stared at the three of them. She couldn't hold it in anymore, especially when she looked at Tonya.

"Yeah, umm. I don't know if I'm catching something, or if these boots are killing me, or the fact I had sex with Logan in Barbados and needed it to get it off my chest and tell someone. OK, now I feel better. Let's get more shots."

Jade tries to signal for a waitress while taking a massive swig from her Sex on the Beach, looking away from the other three stoned faces in shock.

"BEG PARDON???" Tonya screams out at Jade.

Jade swallows hard, wondering what the girls would say with their flabbergasted glances.

"I had sex with Logan in Barbados, and I should feel guilty and bad about it, but I don't," Jade says before the girls start shooting her with questions.

"Are you two still having sex?" Sasha shot first.

"Is he good?" Then Bridget. Tonya was stuck.

"Dammit!!! They took both my questions." Jade points to Sasha.

"Okay, question one, we had sex New Year's morning in Barbados one time. Oh and I did go down on him that morning before he went to Montreal."

"OH, MY GOD!!!! Sasha screams in shock, grabbing her temple. Jade turns to Bridget.

"Question two." Jade inhales deeply. "HOLY FUCKING SHIT!!! He was extraordinary. It was easily the greatest sex I ever had." Jade looks out into space, reminiscing about that New Year's morning. "I swear, the way he touched me, he had the softest lips

I ever felt, and God granted him with those beautiful blue eyes to put on a man. The first time I met him, I was gone." She reminisces about their first encounter while the girls look at each other, completely shell-shocked. Sasha had that one question locked and loaded she had for Jade. She had no choice but to shoot.

"Jade, I like you, but I must ask this because Logan is very special to me. He helped me get through a really bad time in my life. He's not just my boss, but he's like a brother to me. Please tell me you're not…"

Jade stops Sasha with a severe tone. "Sash, I know where you're going with this, and I swear on a stack of Bibles. I am not a gold-digging whore trying to slime herself into his good fortune. Logan is the most seductive man I've ever met. I don't mean in the sexual vibe, even though he gives that too." She tells the girls while Sasha gives Jade a puzzled look.

"I have known Logan since college, and he cannot flirt. What is his seduction?" Sasha asks.

"It's the little things like watching him get down on his knees playing Skeeball with Madison, giving the pizza delivery guy a $200 tip on a $25 bill, being Santa, and interacting with those sick kids. That gets me so hot for him. He did something to me no man has ever done before. He made me let my guard down. I love screwing with his head, but he hits me right back. I felt desperate for the first time when the last seconds of New Year's Eve came around. During those last ten seconds of the year, I knew I had to end it with his connection. I took that chance, and when our lips locked. I was done. Then, when I saw him on that beach that morning, I had to." She says while picking up her glass of Sex on the Beach.

"So, your first time was on the beach," Tonya asks, pointing at her glass. Jade then looks out at her drink.

"Wow, that's some hardcore irony."

"OK, OK!!! Then what happened when you came home?" Bridget asks frantically dying to know more.

"Honest to God, I didn't know where it would go when we returned to Seattle. It was initially awkward because we were waiting on who would make the next move. He had been ducking me, so I said, OK, I'll make the move. I snuck into his bedroom the morning he went to Montreal and gave him "Jade's special alarm clock." The girls gave her a confused look. "I sucked him off so he would wake up."

"WHAT???" Bridget yells. Sasha covers her ears, putting her head on the table, visualizing the man who's been like a brother getting blown.

"JESUS!!! I can't listen to this!!!!" Sasha cries out.

Tonya looks at Jade, knowing that she would never randomly have sex with anyone. She looked into her best friend's eyes, seeing a sparkle in her she had never seen before. Her mouth collapses.

"OH MY GOD!!!! YOU'RE IN LOVE WITH HIM!!!!!!"

Sasha's head bounces up from the table, and Bridget's eyes widen. Jade tried to look at Tonya like she was crazy trying to deny it but Tonya knew Jade too well and she didn't want to deny her heart. A tiny grin snuck on her face and she gave the girls a slight nod. Logan was that needle in a haystack to her. She had been in bad relationships before and was dedicated to being completely careful.

"T, the way he looked at me in that theater before we left, it wasn't lust but desire. He wasn't looking at me like he wanted to spread my legs and hammer me like these pricks do. He looked at me like he wanted to hold me and not let go. Take a look at this." Jade hands over her phone and shows the girls Logan's text. All three melt seeing his sincerity. Jade points to her phone. "That's his seduction. I know what he's gone through, and the last thing I ever want to do is hurt him, but I don't see a billionaire. I don't see someone on the cover of Forbes. I see someone who wants to escape that hell he's in. He doesn't deserve to be in it." Like that, any insecurities Sasha had about Jade were obliterated by the deep compassion in her voice. "I'm having so much fun with you girls, but I wish he was here with me."

"Oh God, I would pay to see him here," Bridget says.

"Wait, he's never gone out clubbing?" Jade wondered.

"No, because of Renee. She had agoraphobia in the worst way. They never went out anywhere. Concerts, ball games. She would have to be on heavy medication if they traveled because of her anxiety. The mansion was her safe haven, and Logan just accepted it so she could feel comfortable. That's how much he was devoted to her." Sasha gives Jade a rundown of Renee's struggles.

Jade's heart ripped for Logan, realizing he probably didn't get to experience many things because of his wife's fears, not faulting Renee because it was an illness. Since Jade got him out of his hotel suite during his Montreal trip, she was determined to have him experience a real Friday night with a smoking hot lady.

"I can get him here," Jade says, determined.

"Seriously???" Tonya tilts her head.

"Can you guys get an Uber and go to Ora without me?"

"Sure but I got to see him here first." Sasha demands.

Jade grabs her phone and dials Logan. "Say no more." Logan picks up on the first ring. She speaks to him like she was drunk out of her mind, slurring and stretching her words. "Hey Logan, I need a huuuuge favor. I really, really need you to pick me up."

"What? Where's Cortez?" Logan asks with a worried tone in his voice.

"Oh, he took the girls to another club, except I wanted to stay here, but now I need youuuu to pick me up."

"Jade, how drunk are you?" He asks, hearing her drunken voice.

"Like a Kennedy on St. Patrick's Day. Also, I am bombarded with these Neanderthals who don't know the meaning of no is." She pulls the phone away and yells out. "HEY BUDDY!!! FOR

THE LAST TIME, GET YOUR HAND OFF MY ASS!!!" The girls collapse onto each other in laughter. Logan wasn't laughing, though. His eyes widen, and his jaw tightens as jealousy hits him quickly.

"Stay there!!! I'm on my way!!!" Logan rapidly says and hangs up.

"Awesomeness." She hangs up and throws her phone onto the table with accomplishment. "There, get me a fuckin Oscar!!!" The girls scream and applaud. Jade bows to the girls. "Damn, I need celebratory alcohol. PRONTO!!!!"

Logan goes into panic mode, worried about Jade being alone where any guy would take advantage of her.

"Are the girls alright?" Rick asks.

Logan tries to dial Cortez: "They're fine, but they're at another club, except Jade stayed at Rogue." Logan tries to dial Cortez, which goes right to voicemail. "SHIT!!!" He yells out.

Rick and Tony looked at each other, wondering what was going on. That was until Tony got a text from Bridget.

Bridget texts: "Hey baby, Jade is tricking Logan into going out with her. Just play along."

"I'm sure she's fine. Jade is a tough broad." Clinton tries to calm Logan down.

"Where is my wallet?" Logan runs out of the theater, looking for his wallet. Tony shows Clinton the text from Bridget. Clinton smiles as he reads it. "Now, where are my damn keys!!! He yells out in frustration from the living room. He comes back into the theater.

"Son, relax. Your keys are in the kitchen. Your wallet is right here." Clinton hands him his wallet. "Now, just calm down and go get her." Logan nods when Clinton makes his point.

"You're right. I'll be cool." Logan leaves the theater and heads out the front door. Clinton looks at Tony and Rick.

"Are we together on this, fellas?" He asks them when they hear the tires of the Shelby screeching from the driveway. The three of them haul it to the front door. Tony opens it to a cloud of smoke from Logan's burning rubber. They look down at the bottom of the hill to see Logan barely passing the main gate while hearing the engine screaming in the distance. The guys look at each other once more, having the same thought.

"Oh yeah, he's got it bad for the nanny," Tony says. "Fifty bucks. He gets pulled over before he gets to Rogue." He adds

"No, a hundred within five miles." Rick chimes in.

Clinton smiled slightly at the thought of Logan driving like a bat out of hell to rescue Jade. He nods at the thought of him finally forward for once, not just standing still. He pulls a wad of bills out of his pocket and lifts it over his head.

"I'll bet everything I've gotten from the three of you tonight that says he'll get the girl home unscathed." Tony and Rick looked at each other, shaking their heads, not wanting to take that gamble. Meanwhile, Logan arrived at Rogue twenty minutes later. He gets out his phone and quickly texts Jade.

Logan texts: "Hey, I'm here."

Jade texts: "Be there in two shakes."

Logan finally settles down, knowing Jade is alright. He exits his Shelby and starts walking toward the club when he notices his limo parked.

"What the hell?" Logan says to himself.

"Logan!!!!" Jade yells out, coming out of the club. She goes to the doorman and whispers in his ear. He nods, pulling the rope for her. She walks towards Logan, swaying and having difficulty keeping her balance, snorting in drunken laughter while still playing along to her Academy Award-worthy performance. Logan couldn't believe the sight of her. She was nothing short of a fantasy. He badly wanted to take this fantasy girl home where she was safe. She stumbles into his arms, laughing uncontrollably. "Whoopsie!!!"

"Uh, you ready to go?" Logan asks. She pokes his hard chest.

"Oh, you misunderstood me. I told you I wanted you to pick me up." She lowers her head and stares him up with those fierce eyes. "You gotta buy me a drink to do that first." Jade's voice changes from drunken lush to vivacious femme fatale. Logan's throat tightened and went utterly numb by her wicked stare. "That's right. You're going clubbing on a Friday night and about to do shots with a smokin' hot piece of ass that the majority of the guys here who aren't gay have been eyeballing. Also, and most importantly," Jade steps closer to Logan in a severe tone. Brushing her finger onto his forearm. "I missed you."

Logan's heart thumps, knowing she felt the same way as he did. He gently takes her hand. "I missed you too. You look stunning."

Jade glances at his ultra-casual attire. Her body was filling up with heat, looking at his white tee, hugging against his tight chest. "You're handsome. By the way, do you have any cash?" Logan pulls out a money clip.

"Yeah, I think $900."

Jade snatches the clip out of his hands. "That should do. Now, let's go. You're about to enter Jade World." She drags him towards the line.

"Wait, look how I'm dressed. I'm just wearing a white shirt, jeans and a pair of Pumas. They won't let me in." Logan warns Jade. They walk past the line, and the doorman opens the rope for them. Jade slips $200 into his front coat pocket and seals it with a kiss on his cheek. "Well, that $200 said that your attire is fine, and I'll repeat, you look handsome. Now, C'mon. I've got this."

Jade stretches out her hand for Logan. He takes her hand and opens the door. Fatboy Slim's "Rockafeller Skank '' blasts in the club. They walk down the long hallway. Jade has a prideful grin as she takes Logan's hand towards the club. She is taking him on a journey into unfamiliar territory. She looks over her left shoulder, catching Logan focused on her tight, shiny leather skirt. She turns her head back forward and suddenly stops, putting her right palm out for the head of Logan's erection running into it. Logan gives her an embarrassed grin with a slight shrug. She turns her head forward and mouths, "OH MY GOD!!!" in shock at the size of him. She was dying to smother him with her body but kept it together. Her objective was to deflower the nightclub virgin. They get to the main room when Logan sees Cortez and the girls. He acknowledges Cortez with his arms stretched out with a "What's going on?" gesture. Cortez gestures back, waving his hands, and points to Jade to say, "Blame her." Logan looks around, soaking in the scene. A huge smile hits his face. A feeling of lost time was hitting him fast. Jade was boarding him with a wide variety of everything new in his life. The effect that this girl was having on him was boggling his mind.

"Well, I'll be damned. I can't believe what I'm seeing. Hey boss!!!!!" Sasha hugs Logan.

"I know, I know." Logan chuckles as he sees Jade talking to Tonya and Bridget.

"Look, do me a huge favor. Please have a good time. She won't stop talking about you."

"Seriously?"

"Yeah, I like her a lot. I'm taking Bridget and Tonya to Ora. I'll see ya Monday." She kisses

Logan on the cheek. "I'm so proud of you."

"Thanks."

Jade kisses the girls goodbye and then pulls Logan to the bar.

"C'mon, fella." They walk to the bar. She pulls $200 from Logan's clip and flashes it to the bartender. "Patron Silver, two glasses, and leave the bottle." Logan's eyes bugged out.

"Whoa, we're going to go through an entire bottle of Patron."

"Sure. I'm not a lush, I'm a pro." Jade says pouring the first shot before handing it to Logan. "Here's to life's little surprises. Yours is five foot three and turning you into Mr. Saturday Night."

They clink glasses together and down their shot. Logan exhales deeply as it burns his throat.

"Why do we drink this again?" Logan asks

"Because it gets me wet."

"Well, you got me there." Jade pours another shot for the both of them and raises her glass.

"Here's to… I don't know, socks. Just down it." They laugh when they take another shot. Cortez walks in between them.

"Logan, hand over the keys, man." Logan hands Cortez the keys to the Shelby. "I've got someone to watch over her tonight. Keep drinking." He walks back to his post, where he can watch them both.

"He's gifted at switching from driver to bodyguard so fast."

"That's why he's the only one of the Crew who gets six figures for double duty."

"Well, I thought that morning in Barbados and that "Wake up call" would give me a bonus. I'll have to…" She says seductively as she strokes his leg to his non-stop erection, "suck up to you harder." Logan grabs the bottle of Patron and the shot glass but starts chugging the bottle. Jade bursts into laughter. She marveled at his face. He was having the time of his life.

"Can I ask you something?" He asks while he scopes out at the club. "Have you ever had moments of regret?" Jade burst into hysterical laughter.

"What do you mean by "Moments"? Many times, but that can't consume me, then I can't live. Logan, I am the most flawed, the most stubborn, and the biggest pain in the ass you will ever meet in your life, and I accept that. I take full responsibility for the things I do and all my hang-ups, but the key is to keep going because I know I will mess up again. Why? I'm Jade."

"I wish I had your attitude," Logan responds.

"You always can. It's never too late. I know you've lost yourself, and it's a process—one day at a time," Jade tells him while seeing his eyes wander to reflect.

"I've had the same recurring dream. I'm standing on a beach, and there's a tsunami right in front of me, but it just grows and grows, and then it just sits there. It doesn't crash on top of me and wash me away. It just freezes."

"I know what it means." Jade nods. Logan waits for her to answer.

"WELL???"

"When the time is right, I'll tell you."

Logan raises his arms and slumps on the back of the stool: "I swear, do you just enjoy messing with my head?"

"It's good to have a hobby." Jade bats her eyes and grins wide. "You see, slugger. That's why I'm here. I'm corrupting you to enjoy life again. I'm not just the caretaker for your children, but I'm your firestarter. So I have the gasoline and the match." She picks up the bottle of Patron and the shot glass. Jade fills up his shot and hands it to Logan. "Let's light this shit up."

"You're going to get me in a lot of trouble, aren't you?" He takes the glass while Jade leans as close as possible to Logan. Their lips are almost touching.

"You need trouble in your life." Logan's body almost pulsates from the mixture of her perfume and sweet breath. "Shake That" by Eminem comes on. Jade caught her ear. She had been waiting for the perfect song for Saturday Night Logan. "Now, give me your hand and dance with me."

Once on the dance floor, Jade saw that Logan had never gone clubbing or danced. He was so stiff but was enjoying every second of it. Jade couldn't stop looking. It was like looking at a plane crash. Her face was stoned in disbelief.

"What?" He asks, seeing her jarred expression.

"Oh wow, you're not joking, are you?" Logan's expression changed, fearing he was embarrassing Jade. She giggles and reaches for his hand, clenching it tight. A rush went through his soul, holding another woman's hand for so long. He didn't know if he could let her go.

"It's okay. I took dance throughout high school and was CSF's cheerleading squad captain." She pounds her heart and raises her fist in the air. "GO, TITANS!!! I'll make you good."

She started dancing with him like a pro and slowly swiveled her hips into him, twerking to the music. Logan slowly takes a step back to watch her dance alone. It was yet another thing she could do effortlessly. Logan was captivated by her moves as she flowed her sexuality into him. Her smokey eyes were sharp as daggers. She could feel his wanting more and more. Jade reaches for Logan's hand and pulls him to the DJ booth. Jade texts the DJ and slips him another $200. After reading her text, the DJ nods, and Jade seals another deal with another kiss on the cheek. She grabs Logan to the dance floor.

"Alright, everyone. I need you all to clear the floor. It's my boy Hugh's birthday, and his girl Jade wants the floor to themselves." The crowd applauds.

"Birthday?" He questions Jade.

"Oh, you'll think it was."

"And Hugh?"

"Your alias. Hugh Jackman, Wolverine. Logan. I thought you were a Marvel fan!!!"

Logan smiles, liking himself linked to Wolverine. Jade takes Logan onto the dance floor, surrounded by patrons ready to watch his "birthday" dance.

"Seriously, are you sure you want to do this? You've seen me dance." Logan tries to talk Jade out of this, not wanting to embarrass her.

"Yes, I have, and it is a sad and tragic spectacle, but don't worry, you don't have to do anything. Remember, it's your birthday." Jade assures him.

Logan had clarity after Jade said it was his birthday. He felt born again, being lost in a new life.

Yet, he found security knowing he had a hand to help him guide it. Savage Garden's "I Want You" starts playing. Jade starts slowly shaking her hips onto Logan's crotch. He sees the moves she learned as a stripper in Vegas. She turns her back from him, takes his hand, and caresses her torso. She notices Logan's stiffness brushing against her ass. Jade reaches from behind and guides his hand across the front of her mini. She closed her eyes while brushing his fingers along the seams of his panties that were hiding behind tight leather. She inhales his cologne, licking her lips.

Logan noticed smartphone recordings and pictures being taken. Any ordinary billionaire would be hiding his face or making a run for it. Logan didn't have a care in the world. Jade was giving him something he never experienced: an overpowering passion. When she turned to face him. Her hungry stare was locked on him. Once the song ended, they stood there and looked at each other as the crowd cheered. Everyone returned to the dance floor when the next song started, but Logan and Jade stood frozen. The mind games, the second-guessing, and the wonder ended right there. Logan would soon discover that Jade was the tsunami, and she was about to wipe him out. She grabs the front of Logan's pants.

"BATHROOM!!! RIGHT NOW!!!" Jade yells in Logan's ear.

From the shock, Logan couldn't compress what Jade said. She takes his hand and walks towards Cortez. She grabs her phone and rapidly texts to show Cortez. He nods with a huge grin. Jade suddenly had a concerned look on her face.

"Oh baby, your eyes!!! It's swollen. It had to be the Vodka you're allergic to. Don't worry. I got the syringe." Logan looks at Jade, confused. "I guess I'll have to do everything since you can't speak clearly or have taken an improv class!!!!" Jade gets frustrated Logan isn't playing along until he finally figures it out.

"Oh, I get it!!!" He starts to mumble. "My tongue is swelling, Jade."

"Oh no, and you're going to need that tongue, too. CORTEZ!!!" Cortez leads Logan and Jade to the men's room. Jade yells past the line of patrons waiting in line.

"Excuse me, my man is having an allergic reaction. Please, life or death here."

"Jade, I need my shot. I'm losing my sight here. It's getting blurry here." Logan waves his hand back and forth, pretending he's going blind.

Jade gets past the door and yells out. "Don't worry, baby. Drop your pants so I can inject you." She looks at the people waiting in line. "Thank you, and we'd appreciate all your prayers from you right now!!!"

Jade slams the door and locks it behind her while Cortez stays up front, blocking it. Jade covers her mouth to cover up her laughter. She turns to look at Logan leaning in front of the sink with his arms crossed, looking at this beautiful mystery woman. He was convinced she was just a fantasy. There was no way she could be real. Jade could feel his hunger going through her soul with his eyes. She knew exactly what to do. She put her hands on her hips and tilted her head.

"Are you ready for this?" She asks Logan.

Not even a second after she asked, he sprung off that sink towards her, crushing his mouth against hers and slamming Jade against the wall. He wanted to devour her body the same way she devoured his mind. Both their tongues danced together while she dug her fingers into his hair. She breathes deep in and out while Logan starts kissing Jade's neck. She pushes him off her, grabs his shirt, and takes him to the front of the sink. He stands right behind her, looking at each other from the reflection. She places his hand on her left breast, gently stroking it while spreading her legs apart when he lifts her skirt and rips her soaked black thong in two. Wasting no time, he unbuckles his belt and pulls his jeans down as he slides into her backside, thrusting into Jade hard. He leans to kiss Jade on her bare back, brushing his hands up and down her smooth legs. She sees him through the mirror, focusing on her ass.

"Look at me while you fuck me. I want to see those eyes on me." Jade tells his reflection.

"You're so beautiful," Logan says, watching himself insert into Jade, thrusting her harder.

"You're so handsome." Jade gasps.

His hips slam into Jade as she moans louder and louder. She digs her nails into his bare thigh. Logan bites his lip, grimacing through the pain as he holds it in. Something happened to Logan when the sting went through him. Jade turned something on in his head because Logan gripped her hip bone and pounded on her with all his force and speed.

"Oh, fuck yeah!!! Bring it!!!" She yells, gritting her teeth. Badly wanting Logan's mouth, Jade pulls her head back to kiss. He pushes his pelvis into her more when he pulls her breasts out of her top, squeezing them tight while they kiss. He reluctantly forces himself from her mouth. He quickly pulls out and turns her around to lift her onto the sink. Both of them take just one second to catch their breath. One second was all they could spare. She pulls him into her, wrapping her legs tight around his torso. Feeling their volcanic needs together, Jade sees a new side of Logan. She smiles, seeing the monster she created.

"You're perfect." He tells her.

Those two words turned something on in Jade. She searched the world for years, biding her time and using every precaution. Jade was looking right at the man she was falling in love with. She pulls Logan into her, slipping his full depth, smothering her mouth against his. He thrusts deep while she clenches harder. Logan was trying to prolong her release as much as possible. Even the zipper from Jade's boot scraping against his upper thigh turned him on.

"I can't get enough of you. You're doing something to me I can't control." Her muscles tensed when she noticed he couldn't control it anymore. "Keep your eyes on me when you fill me."

Logan lets go into Jade while his intensity locks into her eyes. He collapses his head on her shoulders. She undertook her arms, holding him tighter while he looked at himself in the mirror. "What is this girl doing to me?" He thought to himself. He leans and softly kisses her forehead.

"Don't move," Logan whispers.

He soaks some paper towels and starts cleaning her up. Jade smiles, watching Logan take care of her. After helping her off the sink, Jade puts herself together, adjusting her skirt. He sees that tight, shiny ass and Logan just can't resist. He smacks her ass as hard as he can. Smacked leather echoed through the hollowed bathroom, mixed with the music playing in the club. Jade flinched as she didn't see it coming. A grin hits her face.

"I just couldn't resist." He grins.

"Thanks for the Barbados flashback." Jade looks down and picks up her torn-up panties. She chuckles, looking at Logan. "Damn, that was hot." Jade crumbles them up and tosses them in the trash. They can hear a commotion behind the door as the line is restless.

"C'mon already!!!" A random guy yells out.

"We better bail Cortez out," Logan suggests.

"Wait." Jade brushes her fingers across his face. "I can't stop looking at you." Logan takes her hand and kisses her wrist. "OK, let's go. Remember, bad Vodka." Jade reminds him.

"Got it, let's go."

They leave the bathroom as Logan clutches his heart, pretending to come out of his phony allergy attack.

"Baby, you saved my life. She's a hero, everyone." Logan gasps from the bathroom and yells out to the people in line.

"GUILTY!!!!" Jade raises her hand.

They see a massive line of people waiting. Some looked pissed, so Cortez started handing out $20 bills to the people in line.

"Next drink is on them," Cortez says to everybody waiting.

Logan and Jade walk back, unable to control their laughter, thinking about what they got away with. They get back to the bar and sit.

"What do you want to do? I'm up for anything." Logan asks.

"Anything? Do you want to crash girls' night and go to Ora?"

"Are you nuts? Hell yes, let's go!!!" Logan says enthusiastically.

"Oh my God, you are so precious. Let's go."

Jade takes Logan's hand as they start heading out until "She's Fresh" by Kool and the Gang comes on. Logan slowly walks, listening to the lyrics, which grinds him to a stop.

"What's up?"

"Hold on. We can't leave just yet. This song is all about you. One more dance."

Jade smiles as Logan takes her hand and guides her back to the dance floor. Logan took over after a few shots of Tequila, an R-rated dance from Jade, and a hot encounter in the men's room. Even though he was feeling loose, he was still a terrible dancer. Jade had to step back and admire, unable to stop smiling and watching Logan loving life. She took out her phone and snapped pictures. He gave her a John Travolta pose from "Saturday Night Fever." Jade slaps herself on the leg while laughing hysterically.

"OK, dorkwad. Now, take a selfie with me. The girls will want evidence you're coming."

Jade turns the phone into selfie mode. They scrunch their faces together and snap away. They start to review the selfies they just took.

"Number six." They call out together, picking the best one to send.

"I'll be right back. I gotta make a call."

"Alright, I'll be over here shaking my groove thing."

"Yeah, show them how not to do it," Jade says sarcastically. She goes outside to the smoking area to call Sasha.

"Hey, I'm coming to Ora and bringing a plus one."

"Seriously??? I can't believe it." Sasha says with excitement in her voice.

"I know. I'm so proud of him. Take a look at this." Jade texts the selfie to Sasha.

"You two look so adorable together," Sasha says when she pauses for a couple of seconds.

"Listen, Jade, I'm really glad we talked. I'm sorry if I had any kind of doubts about you."

"Hey, no worries, hottie. You're just playing big sister." Jade continues watching Logan dancing terribly with a massive smile on her face. "God, I can't tell if he's dancing or having an epileptic episode." Sasha sighs.

"No, that's his dancing. I'll see you soon, friend."

"See ya in a few, beautiful." She hangs up and heads back to the dance floor, unable to stop smiling at Logan with this new burst of energy he had. "Are you ready??" Logan nods. "Okay, but you need to cool off, rookie. Ora is just ten minutes away."

"I will." Jade yelps as Logan scoops her up and carries her out of Rogue.

"What the hell are you doing?" She yells out.

"Showing these guys how a beautiful woman should be treated."

Jade could not believe how Logan kept outdoing himself effort-lessly like he had found the magic drug of being the perfect guy and taking two doses of it. She noticed couples staring them down. So badly she wanted to scream, "That's right, bitches!!! My man is carrying me to HIS limo with HIS bodyguard leading the way, and later, I'm going to ride HIS cock!!!" They come out of Rogue, passing the doorman.

"Cortez, give him another $200. He's doing a great job."

Jade and Logan laugh as Cortez pulls out his money clip and hands the doorman another $200. They get to the limo, and the both of them can't help but gaze at each other.

"Are you going to put me down?"

"I'm planning on it. I just can't stop looking at you."

After a few seconds, Logan gently puts Jade to the ground. She was about to open the door when Logan stopped her from pulling the handle. He shakes his head and opens the door for her, taking her hand as she enters. He shuts the door. Logan goes to the other side. Before entering, Cortez blocks the other door.

"I'm proud of you, brother." A lump grows in Logan's throat. He took it to heart because Logan was proud of himself for once, too. Cortez opens the door, and they fist bump before Logan gets in. Once inside, Logan sees Jade with her legs crossed and her wicked smile waiting for him. Logan knew exactly what to do. He gets on one knee on the floor. Jade gives him a strange look until he starts unzipping her boots.

"Uh, what are you doing?" She asks. Logan pulls her boots off, and without saying a word, he massages her feet. Jade rolled her eyes, gasping, feeling the sensation that was going on the balls of her feet. "MOTHERFUCKER!!! You've got to be kidding me!!!"

"You said Ora was ten minutes away. We need these beautiful things relaxed because you are killing me in these boots." Logan's big thumbs go hard into the arch of Jade's foot. She groans hard and fast, covering her eyes and collapsing into heaven. "Does that feel good?"

That one question ignited a lust inferno. She uncovers her eyes and looks down at a handsome gentleman in charge of a Fortune 500 company kneeling on the floor of his own limousine, massaging her feet. Her nostrils flared, letting out a hungry growl. She pounced out of her seat and attacked Logan on the floor, pressing her mouth against his. Her wet tongue swirled down his throat, grabbing a fistful of his bulge and craving it to be in her again. Logan started squeezing her bare ass cheeks under her skirt, remembering her panties were long gone. Jade pulls away from his mouth, gasping for air as she kisses Logan's neck. "Please tell me you're not a government-sponsored android who's been programmed as a prototype designed to be the most perfect man ever."

"I'm not saying that I am or I'm not, but I'd have to kill you if I give my answer," Logan replied.

"Never mind, I like a mystery." She whines, continuing to kiss Logan hard. She sits up, straddling Logan's hips while trying to remove his belt with an angry grunt, not keeping her intensely filled eyes off Logan.

"Cortez, do me a favor. Take the long route to Ora. The boss-man and I are going to check out the shocks on this limo." She yells out while Logan lays his head back in surrender with a giant smile.

"You got it, Shorty!!!" Cortez grins wide. He raises the partition before Jade reaches back and unties her top. He puts on his earpods, blasting some Beyonce to drown out any screams. He starts chuckling at the thought of what's happening to his best friend behind him. "Enjoy the ride, my man."

CHAPTER 17

PLAY BALL!!!

Another April means another season of Seattle Mariners baseball. In the Brodie household, Mariners opening day ranked right up there with Christmas and Easter as a religious holiday. Logan would take the Crew and their families to his suite at T-Mobile Park every year. Traditionally, he would leave the office right at three on the dot to come home and pick everybody up. He told Jade to pick up the kids an hour early so they could be ready by the time he got home. Logan arrives home completely stoked until he notices the limousine isn't in the driveway. "Maybe Cortez is getting it washed," Logan says to himself. He started dancing, getting excited the same way every year since childhood. Especially since the Mariners swept the Angels in Anaheim to start the season 3-0, they're home in Seattle, optimistic about the season.

Logan shouts when he walks into the mansion. "LET'S GO, M'S!!! LET'S GO, M'S!!! LET'S GO, M'S!!! THE TRIDENT DROPS TONIGHT!!!" He chants, which usually gets everybody going, but he gets silence. "Hello!!!" He shouts again but gets nothing but his hollowed echo. "Clinton??? Kids??? Jade???"

"In the kitchen, Logan!!!!!" Jade yells out casually.

"Are you alone?" He asks.

"Yeah, everybody is on their way to the stadium." Logan grabs a stack of mail and goes through it while walking towards the kitchen. "The girls wanted to see the Mariners do batting practice, and Clinton said Edgar Martinez would be in your suite tonight."

"Why didn't you go?" He walks into the kitchen to see Jade leaning on the kitchen island, wearing a customized Mariners jersey with Murphy #94 on her back.

"Oh, I thought we could go together. After we pregame." Jade turns around with her jersey unbuttoned, barely covering her breasts with light blue denim daisy dukes and a pair of black booties. She hikes herself up on the island, slowly crossing her baby oil lathered glistening legs.

"Oh, sweet mother of God." He says, flinging his mail over his shoulder, astonished at the sight of her. He was admiring her like she was a Rembrandt painting. Jade slowly beckons to him with her index finger and infectious smile. Without hesitancy, he sprints to the island, which prompts a giggle from Jade at Logan's eagerness. She then scanned his body, wearing a tight Mariners raglan shirt that did not hide his muscular tone. It was three and a half hours until the first pitch, but in Jade's mind, it was three and a half hours of Logan's free range in an empty palace.

"Good Lord, tiger. Someone likes what he sees." Jade uncrosses her legs and spreads them while Logan comes in closer. She wraps her arms around his neck, tangling her fingers in his hair. Shivers go down his spine when she takes the tip of her long nails and brushes his neck.

"Cortez told me you were a pitcher for your high school team."

"As a matter of fact, yes, I was."

"Perfect." Jade's eyebrows perked up. She softly takes Logan's hand to her bare breast as he gently rubs it. He closes his eyes, enthralled by such a beautiful feeling, praying he wasn't dreaming. He opens his eyes to her intoxicating look. "You can show me your slider." Jade curls her tongue into Logan's mouth, tucking her hand into his jeans.

"Play ball!!!" She says quickly, getting off the island and unbuckling his belt with one hand while grabbing the back of his neck, kissing Logan hard, sucking down on his bottom lip while he pulls his jeans down his legs. Her excitement got hotter with every heartbeat while keeping eye contact with his gaze. He suddenly turns her around, bending her over on the island. He slowly unbuttons her shorts, pulling them down to her ankles, noticing she wasn't bothering with her panties. He exhales, looking at her perfectly toned ass. He kicks Jade's legs apart and inserts himself from behind.

Logan lets out a harrowing moan. "How do you keep doing this to me?"

"Because you are way too easy, too hot, and I want that monstrosity you call a cock in me all the time. So, I take full advantage and…" Logan stops her from saying another word by rocking into Jade harder as she grunts, feeling every inch of Logan. "FUCKING, YES!!!" She slams her hands against the island, gritting her teeth.

"Hey, we've got four hours." Logan says, gripping Jade's hips, slowly thrusting into him.

"Oh, that's all? Ok, no time for foreplay."

Logan uses his frame to wrap his right arm around Jade's stomach and thrusts into her thigh, lifting her slightly. Jade screams.

"Logan, that feels so good. Keep doing that."

Logan couldn't help but look down and see her boots left on. He starts slamming into her harder, which sends ripples through her body. Her screams grew louder through the mansion. He gives her one last hard thrust when he releases. They both collapse on the island. He stares at her exposed Ferris wheel tattoo on the back of her neck. He plants a gentle kiss on it. Goosebumps immediately surge through her skin. Jade turns and gives Logan her evil eyes.

"End of the top half of the first. Logan One, Jade up to bat."

Jade yanks her shorts from her ankle and quickly takes off the jersey. Being completely naked except for her boots, Jade tries to take them off when Logan immediately stops her.

"NO!!!! Don't you dare take those off." He demands. She grins, peeling off another layer of the kinky side.

"You're one of those "Keep the heels on" kind of guys." Logan smiles wide and nods. "STOP BEING SO SEXY!!!" Jade takes his Mariners tee off and gasps at his six-pack abs. "and don't stop working out." She growls, wiping her tongue from his belly up to his chest.

"Come with me."

Jade takes Logan's hand and takes him to his office. He sits in his chair as she hops on his desk, grabs a pair of his reading glasses off the table, and puts them on.

"Since Sasha is out sick, I'll be your temp for the day and brought you your lunch." Jade spreads her legs onto the arms of his chair. "Bon Appetit."

He exhales deeply, giving Jade a voracious look when he rolls his chair closer, burying his face into her. She lifts her legs and places them on his neck, pulling Logan's head down deeper. He starts to kiss her inner thigh. Jade arches her back and lifts her head, looking up at the tall ceiling, feeling the burning ecstasy, trying to talk herself down. She lets out a relaxing sigh when Logan darts his tongue into her. He changes gears from fast to slow many times, making her screams louder. When Logan hits her sweet spot, she grips the table's edge as tight as possible. She grinds her body when Logan puts his hands underneath Jade's. She grabs a random piece of paper and squeezes it as the pressure of her orgasm impulses.

"Oh God!!! Oh God, Logan!!!" She screams while she squeezes her breasts. She brushes back her hair, holding the crumbled paper. "I hope this wasn't important."

"I could care less right now."

Logan sits back in his chair when Jade sits at the edge of the desk, slowly crossing her legs, and making Logan go insane.

"I think you and I need to chat in the pit." He lifts her off the desk and carries her out of the office with just one arm.

"Why? Have I been bad??? I swear, I can be badder."

Jade starts sucking on Logan's neck, inhaling his cologne. He carries her to the conversation pit and sits on one of the armless chairs as she straddles on top of him. She softly yelps out quickly a "FUCK" when he plants her body down onto him. He grips Jade's waist, slowly pulling her down, and their bodies ease together perfectly. They talk a little while she ground at a fever pitch.

"What do you want to talk about?" She sways her body.

"I want to know what's off-limits to you?" He softly speaks, pulling her into him. Without missing a beat, Jade stops to look at Logan seriously.

"Threesomes. Total deal breakers." Jade sternly blurts out. Logan groans loudly as his body falls back to the chair. She stops thrusting and looks at him mysteriously, not knowing if he has come yet or is disappointed. "Is there a problem with that?"

"No, that was relief!!!!" He pulls Jade's hips harder as she gyrates into him faster. "I don't believe in them either. One, it's cheating. Two, I'm not sharing you. Third, you have to balance time between both girls." Jade lightly backhand slaps Logan's chest with wide eyes.

"THANK YOU!!!!!! Then, one girl will feel bad and insecure, asking herself, "Why is he focused on her more?" Men never get that!!!"

"Exactly!! Besides, you're enough. I mean, you're like three women in one anyway."

Jade smiles as she wraps her legs around the chair tighter, licking her lips. "You know how to make a girl feel wanted, Romeo."

Jade's momentum matches Logan's the faster they go. Her breasts were so succulent and breathtaking that he started to suck her tips. She starts to shiver, loving the sensation of his mouth on her, especially when he bites them. One thing she loved more than anything was his stamina. Logan was in fantastic shape but didn't look winded at all. He slows down and stops mid-way just to look at her luminous face. Jade's heart pumped harder; knowing what he was doing, he stopped even though it was killing her. She kisses him softly, stroking the back of his hair when she adjusts to grab the back of the chair to get every microscopic inch of him. Gripping the chair, she thrust slowly, feeling her heat grow on his lap. Jade's knees trembled the faster she thrust.

Jade closes her eyes: "Don't slow down!!! Whatever you do!!!!" She takes a sharp breath as Logan's hands grip tighter around her hips. Once she got to her rhythm, he put his strong hands all over her back. He starts to massage her back while driving into her. "SERIOUSLY!!! You're giving me a back massage while we fuck?"

"Yeah, I can multitask too."

Jade devours her lips against Logan's with so much intensity. Logan pulls her ass with one deep thrust and doesn't let go. He holds it as he quivers. Jade hangs onto the top of the chair and arches her back while lifting her head, screaming. Logan lays his head on her chest while he goes off in her. She was feeling complete and utter elation, sharing their own paradise. Each time was more intense than the last, and they knew it. She asks, gasping.

"OK, your turn. What's off limits for you?"

Logan tries to catch his breath. "It's not off-limits but something that doesn't get me off and don't think less of me."

"OK, shoot?"

"I'm not big on lingerie."

"WHAT???" Jade asks, shocked by his answer.

"Wait, water break?" Jade nods as Logan lifts her, carrying Jade to the kitchen with her legs still wrapped around his hips and her arms around her neck.

"I can't believe what I'm hearing. You don't like lingerie." Logan shakes his head.

"Nope. Not my thing. I never got it."

"Seriously, I have never heard of a man not liking lingerie. Garters, baby dolls, they do nothing?"

"I'll be specific. If you wore a tiny silk robe or one of my dress shirts, I'd go ballistic in a good way."

"Note to self: find one of his dress shirts, take a selfie, and send it." She says to herself before going back to him. "WOW!!! Well, what gets you off?" He puts Jade's naked body down on the island as he goes into the refrigerator. He was about to grab two bottles of water when Jade spotted a six-pack of Heineken. "Whoa, time out. Beer me."

Logan grabs the longnecks, opens them with his strong hands, and hands Jade hers. "To the Mariners."

"Mariners!!!" She toasts before clinking bottles, and both take a big gulp. Logan faces Jade, leaning his body towards the island. She wraps her arms around Logan's neck with a beer in her hand. She leans the cold bottle on his neck, cooling off his heat.

"Going back to get me off, I swear, you somehow tapped into my brain and took everything that turns me on, and you wear it. You are the greatest dresser I've ever met."

"We know heels and boots make your sundial hit at noon. Mini dresses, mini skirts, daisy dukes, yoga pants, and leather." She listens while he rolls his eyes.

"Leather isn't even clothes. They're a torture device. What you wore at Rogue, my God. I wanted to ram my head into a wall." She takes a drink.

"What irony, you rammed your head through my wall." Logan spits out his beer, laughing hysterically. "SPIT TAKE!!!!! Good one, Jade. OK, my turn. NO S&M." He shrugs his shoulders.

"No prob….. Whoa, wait, is tying you up, OK?" He questions while Jade waves her hands.

"Oh, that's perfectly fine. Ties, rope, and handcuffs are encouraged, but I mean no whips, floggers, chains, or none of that ball gag bullshit!!! No choking me until I pass out because when it comes to sex, I'm very anti-dying, and you have to swear you don't have one of those secret

Fifty Shades bonus rooms because if I find one, I'm out of here!!!" She takes a swig of her beer.

"I swear I don't. My parents did, but it became a gym after they died." Beer sputters out of Jade's nose, and laughs uncontrollably. "MY FIRST NOSER!!! GO ME!!!!" Logan pumps his fists yelling proudly.

They lean their heads together, laughing hysterically together. They both look up, locking their eyes. The connection was so powerful. Science had no explanation for how any chemistry could be more potent.

"Were you going to wear your jersey, Daisy Dukes, and those boots to the game?" Jade tilts her head.

"Awwww, you're even adorable when you ask me the most idiotic questions. Of course, I was. Number one, I look good, and number two, I would love to see you watching me instead of the game for three hours. Truth be told, I wasn't a real big baseball fan. I go for the nachos, the beer, and the sunshine." Logan gives her a weird look while Jade remembers where she was at. "Oh yeah, I moved to Seattle. Well, at least there's the nachos and beer."

"I'll make you a Mariners fan. Rosa and Angie have their White Sox and Tony has his Mets."

Jade slowly pulls Logan into her, kissing him softly. "You could persuade me to be a Mariner's fan." Jade softly kisses his bare chest as Logan puts his hands under her ass. Jade whispers. "You just gotta persuade me hard." Logan stares Jade down, looking at her tight little body. He was not able to get enough of her.

"Batter up." He states.

She takes a swig of her beer and shares it into his mouth while shoving her tongue down his throat. He penetrates while she pulls Logan's ass into her, gripping it tight.

"Just think, this is the second island you've had me on this year. Oh my God!!!" Jade says as her body quakes.

"Good point," Logan winces from the pleasure. Suddenly, his phone, which was sitting next to Jade, went off. He reaches for it while Jade keeps thrusting.

Jade gasps hard. "Don't answer it, please. Keep going."

Logan looks down to see Clinton's face on the screen and the time. "SHIT!!!, It's six o'clock!!!"

"Ok, we'll make this one a quickie. I know, easier said than done." Jade smacks Logan's bare ass pushing him deeper into her. Jade moans loudly while he grabs his phone. "Wait, Logan, we'll call him back. The score is tied!!!!!"

Logan tries to sush Jade, but she screams louder. Logan pulls one of the drawers and finds a dish rag, putting it into Jade's mouth. He presses the speaker button.

"Hey, on my way. Traffic was a mess; I got tied up and couldn't find my glove. Pick any excuse." Jade laughs while the towel is still in her mouth. Clinton lets out a strong sigh on the other line.

"You forgot to turn off the security cameras in the house."

Logan and Jade freeze instantly while staring at each other in horror. Both their faces flush in a split second.

"Yeah, I've seen too much of you two on my phone." They both slowly turn to see the camera literally pointed right at them. "Hey there!!!" Jade does a small wave. "I told Rosa and Angie to give the kitchen a good sterilization tomorrow, and there will be a huge bonus on their check next month. You don't object, do you, Logan?"

"No." He nods while Jade gives a thumbs up in agreement with the camera. She pulls the towel out of her mouth.

"After you put that towel in the laundry Jade, both of you get dressed, get your asses over here, and hang with the girls, your crew, and support your M's. Got it."

"We're coming," Jade responds. Clinton sighs again.

"Of all the choice of words, seriously, Jade?" Clinton hangs up.

After a couple of seconds, they couldn't hold their laughter. He helps her down from the island and kisses her softly. They gather their clothes and get dressed. Jade puts Logan's Mariners cap backward on him.

"God, you're hot." Jade barely gets the words out. Those three words locked Logan into her eyes. He starts to button her Mariners jersey himself, wholly bewildered at what this woman has done to him. Jade smiled, looking up, knowing what was in his mind.

"I know what you're wondering. "Where have you been all my life, Jade?"

"Does this girl ever stop?"

"Is she an angel sent from heaven?"

"Almost verbatim." He smirks. Jade walks closer to Logan. She wraps her arms around his waist with her eyes softened to his.

"Think of me as your restart button, Logan. Just enjoy this and stop asking questions. It's called being spontaneous." Logan tries to come into a kiss when Jade snatches the keys to the Shelby off the island. "I almost climaxed when Clinton called, which counts as a run, so I won five to four."

Logan has a confused look as Jade heads toward the garage. Finally, it clicked in his head what she was doing. He runs right after her.

"Whoa!!! Wait just a second, Jade!!! You gotta realize something." Before he could utter the words, "Nobody drives this car but me." Jade quickly turned around, whipping her silky blonde hair around, and flashed her angelic, brown eyes at him. A shock wave hit him, and he was under her spell. He had a different choice of words now. "Just remember to jump the clutch and shift into 3rd gear when you hit the highway."

"And 2nd gear when going down a slope. I'll take care of your bitch, now come on." She climbs into the driver's seat while Logan looks without a care in the world that she will drive his beloved Mustang. Jade would become the third person other than Logan and his father to drive it. Hell, Jack didn't even let Katie drive it. He gets into the passenger seat while she looks into the mirror. She notices with her peripheral Logan's eyes stuck on her. "You can't stop looking, can you?"

"How can I not? You're just so beautiful." Logan says, knowing how powerless he was to her.

"Don't blame you in the slightest." She gives him a smug grin. She turns the key, and the sound of the raw power of the Shelby's V8 engine goes through Jade's body. "Oh, the score is now six to four." Logan chuckles while she puts Logan's RayBans on and turns on the radio. Lenny Kravitz's "Are You Going My Way" comes on.

"Hold it," Logan says hungrily, grabbing a fistful of her jersey and pulling her into him, kissing Jade hard as she gently brushes her hand across his cheek, sucking on his tongue. It took everything to peel themselves off each other. Logan slowly pulled himself off of Jade's mouth. Logan grinned. "I had to." Jade moaned inwardly.

"I understand completely, but save it because there's a post-game show later tonight." Logan leans back in his seat, covering his eyes at the thought of what will happen later. Jade speeds out of the garage, tires screeching, and descending the hill. She pushes the gate button to open and hauls it to T-Mobile Park. Ironically, the Mariners beat the Astros six to four that night.

CHAPTER 18

MAY 5TH

Logan and Jade kept each other on the down low in front of the kids for over a month. After they went to bed, it was a different story. From watching movies together, they partnered up for game nights with the Crew and their spouses to practicing yoga and deep meditation. Life, though, was a board game we all played. What would you do if you landed on a space that said to go back ten spaces? May 5th was the day. It was the three-year anniversary of Renee Theresa Brodie succumbing to Ovarian cancer. For the past two years, Logan would take this day off and stay locked in his room to watch their wedding video, look at old pictures, and try to talk to her all day. That morning, The Crew was downstairs at the breakfast table. Tony made chicken and waffles for everybody.

"OK, you girls done?" Jade asked the girls, who both nodded in agreement. "Cool, get your backpacks. We've got ten minutes. The girls try to run upstairs when Jade stops them. "Whoa!!!! Back up. What do we say to Tony?"

"Thank you, Tony." They say together.

"My pleasure, angels." Tony sees them go upstairs, waiting until they're out of sight. "So, what do you think, you guys?"

"How did he seem to you last night, Jade?" Clinton asks.

"He was fine. After putting the girls down, we had a bottle of wine in the pit and just talked about movies, McKenna's dance recital, and watched a little hockey in the theater. That was until ten when we went to bed."

"He didn't have any signs of dread or sadness?" Rosa asks.

"None whatsoever. Seriously, he's never considered seeing a shrink or visiting a widows group?"

"No way. We've tried many times, but he refuses. I don't know if it's his pride or what. He's gone through this with no medication, no nothing."

The Crew expected a dreary, reclusive Logan they'd seen for the past three years. This time, he walks into the kitchen in a white dress shirt, black blazer, and jeans, ready for the day.

"Good morning, soldiers???" The Crew hides their surprise. Angie wolf whistles to him.

"Hey bro, I made a Straight Outta Compton breakfast," Tony informs Logan.

"Ohh, I wonder who suggested that. L.A. woman." Logan jokes, looking right at Jade.

"Hey, I get homesick every now and then. Lay off."

"Oooh la, la. Little extra fancy today." Rosa checks out Logan.

"Yeah, I'm going to San Francisco for the day, but I should be back by dinner." Tony hands him a cup of coffee. "So, what are we talking about?"

The Crew looks at each other, trying to come up with a topic out of thin air. Jade quickly responds:

"McKenna's recital at school in a couple of weeks, and we're thinking of a dance she can do."

"We were talking about making costumes for them and which song to use," Rosa adds. Luckily, Cortez walks in so they can cut the charade.

"Hey, we better go, Logan. Mapquest says traffic to Sea-Tac is up to 45 mins, and your flight leaves in an hour." Logan looks at his watch.

"Cutting it close. Ok, you guys take it easy." He slightly winks at Jade before going upstairs to kiss the girls goodbye. The Crew looked at each other, confused.

"Anybody got a clue?" Tony asks Clinton and the girls.

"Ummm, beats the hell out of me," Angie says, shrugging her shoulders just as confused.

"Crew, maybe he's mourning on his own, and he's still able to keep going," Clinton states while the four of them slowly turn to look at Jade. She sees everyone's gaze on her.

"Yes, what???" She asks

"C'mon, Jade. We all know it's because of you." Rosa adds.

"Seriously, you guys are sleeping together and…" Jade cuts off Tony.

"Whoa, slow down, Ant. Grant it, I'm fucking him blind, but we're not sleeping together. We're not going that far because of the kids."

Clinton knew deep down what Jade's intentions were, but he wanted to make sure it came out of her mouth.

"Jade, just answer me this, please. Is there more to you two than just sex?"

She couldn't speak for Logan, but as for her, it was so much more. Jade was taking small steps with him knowing how fragile Logan was. Especially with this day. "We're getting to know each other, but I'm letting things happen on his terms."

"Is that fair for you?" Clinton asks while Jade gets aggravated.

"I'm a big girl, Clinton. I can deal with it. I've gone through enough shit myself, but I didn't have a spouse die on me."

"Guys, I've never seen him so energetic, so lively. Look at him on opening day." Rosa states while Clinton's eyes go right to Jade. She grins while she takes a sip of her coffee. "He's going clubbing, sneaking out of work to go on your after-school field trips with the kids. For Christ's sake, he's practicing yoga. I don't want to jinx anything."

"Rosa, he's on a high right now. Getting laid again, experiencing new things he never got to do, but he's been battling depression in the worst way, and when you add unresolved grief to the mix, it will always sneak behind you out of nowhere." She looked at her watch and saw it was time to take the girls to school. "C'mon, girls!!! We've got to bolt!!! She calls them from the intercom. "Just keep an eye on him. I'll see you guys later. Thanks for breakfast, Ant." Jade pats Tony's back as she leaves.

"No problem."

The Crew watches Jade and the girls walk out the door. They ponder what Jade said. Clinton wags his finger, looking out of the kitchen.

"That girl is in love with our boy." He says while Angie nods.

"Oh, big time. She's right, though. We have got to keep a close eye on him."

Logan walks out of his conference room ending a meeting with his board members. He stops at Sasha's desk waiting to hear what was next on the day's agenda. As he headed back to his office, he reached Sasha's desk.

"So, how'd it go?" She asks him

"I don't know. One guy said something, another one chimed in, and it was just white noise." Sasha giggles while she looks at her day planner.

"Don't forget. You've got a meeting with the packing rep after lunch." Logan had a confused look on his face.

"I thought that was next week. My mind has been all over the place. What day is it?"

He turns her day planner around and sees that it was May 8th. Logan goes pale white when everything sinks in. He forgot Renee's anniversary.

"Wait. Wait. No. Oh fuck no!!!! No, no, no!!!'

"Logan? What's wrong?" She asks him, filled with worry.

Logan runs into his office and slams the door. He runs to his desk, trying to catch his breath. He checked his phone, looking at the date while his hands shook. The rage and the guilt were building with every second. Logan starts to pace frantically back and forth. Sweat pours down his hair when his body goes completely numb. Everything went black in his mind. Flashbacks of Renee were hitting him one by one like a boxer catching him on the ropes. Their first time meeting, their first time making love, their wedding, her funeral. He started to scream.

"Oh God, no!!!!!! No!!!!" He grabs his head, squeezing it. "No, Renee, I didn't forget!!! I didn't forget!!!" He looks at his calendar on his day planner in complete denial. "NO!!!! I DIDN'T FUCKING FORGET!!!!!!" He turns his head and places it against the window. Both fists clenched, and his eyes closed, pounding on the glass. "The girls. The girls miss you. They miss you. They miss you so much." He pounds on the window harder, screaming. "THEY MISS YOU!!!!!!!! THEY MISS THEIR MOTHER!!!!! They don't have a mother, GODDAMMIT!!!!!!!!" Logan wipes his papers across the desk. Sasha runs into his office.

"LOGAN, What's wrong??? Please talk to me." Logan turns to look at his scared assistant but is entirely incoherent as he falls into a dark portal of madness.

"No, this did not happen. No." He repeatedly shakes his head, pointing at Sasha. "IT CAN'T HAPPEN!!!! This cannot fucking happen. I don't deserve any of this. I don't deserve anything. I deserve to be in pain. I deserve to suffer as much as she did."

"What, Logan? What are you talking about?" Sasha asks in a frantic voice while she starts to cry.

Logan walks to his bathroom, slams the door, and locks it. His hands trembled uncontrollably. He goes to the faucet to splash water on his face. Logan looked up at the mirror, and his guilt was then overtaken by pure hatred.

"FUCK YOU!!!!!!!!!!!" Logan punches the mirror with three stiff jabs. Blood quickly poured out of his right hand. The mirror completely shattered except for a few pieces, including a piece stuck in his knuckle. He looks for whatever piece has a reflection. "You worthless piece of shit!!! How could you forget her, goddamn you!!!!!!!"

Sasha knocked on the door, crying and pleading for him. "LOGAN!!! PLEASE!!! Open the door. Please talk to me!!!"

"That was your daughters' mother!!!!!" He starts to sob uncontrollably, putting his hands over his head. Blood pours down his face and hair. He screams until his voice is hoarse. "THEY'RE NEVER GOING TO SEE HER AGAIN!!! McKenna, Madison. I'm so sorry. Renee. I'm so sorry!!! I'm so sorry!!! I am nothing!!!!" He looks at many small reflections of himself from the small pieces. "God, I hate you. I hate you so fucking much!!!!"

Sasha slaps on the door. "Logan, for Christ's sake. Open the door!!! Please!!!" He couldn't hear her. Logan was in a dark realm of reality. There was no hope, faith, or love for himself.

"WHY AM I ALIVE?????? WHY?????" Logan can barely breathe. He whispers. "Why? Why Logan?"

From the corner of his eye, he glances at a large shard of glass. He stares at it for over a minute. He then picks it up with his right hand, panting and shaking. He then looked at his left wrist. He took a shard towards it when an image of Jade standing alone on a beach flashed in his head for a millisecond. He quickly drops it and starts to hyperventilate. Desperate to catch his breath, he sits in front of his glass shower door. All of a sudden, he breathes normally in an instant.

Sasha hears nothing for over a minute, pounding on the door. She then runs to her desk and grabs her phone to call Jade, who was at the grocery store with Cortez stocking up for the week.

"Hey, Shorty, can I ask you something?" He asks her while Jade sees an old lady walking by with a cart.

"Yes, Cortez, my tits are real, and no, you can't feel them for no less than $50." She embarrasses him as the old lady's eyes go wide. Cortez covers his face while Jade laughs, smacking Cortez on the shoulder. "I just couldn't resist. What's up?"

"I was wondering if Tonya…" She interrupts him, covering her mouth.

"Oh my jumping Jesus, you love Tonya. I knew it." He shakes his head, trying to stop her. "Can I plan the wedding? Wait, I'm going to be the maid of honor. I can't plan it. When's the big day? Throw me a bone here." She playfully grabs his arm. Cortez puts his head down, trying not to giggle. Her phone begins to ring. She sees it's Sasha.

"Say no more, big guy. I'll pass her a note at gym class," Jade answers her phone. "You've got Jade, hotness!!" :

"Jade!!! I need your help!!! Please!!! Logan is flipping the fuck out, and I don't know what to do. I am scared to death." Jade freezes, grabbing Cortez's arm while hearing Sasha's panic-stricken voice.

"Whoa, what's going on? What's happening?" Jade demands to know.

"I don't know!!! He's been talking to himself, screaming and talking about Renee!!! Then I heard glass shatter, and he locked himself in the bathroom. I don't know what to do." She desperately tells her. Jade feels sick to her stomach as she closes her eyes and softly says.

"Oh, Christ. We'll be right there." She hangs up. Cortez has fear in his eyes.

"WHAT???"

"Renee. It hit him." Jade says, filled with fear.

"Let's go!!!" Cortez commanded. He and Jade ran out of the store, leaving their cart behind, and jumped into the Escalade, heading to Brodie Tower. It took them ten minutes to get there, but it seemed like forever for Jade. Cortez weaved through traffic, hoping no cops would stop them. They screech right to the front. "Head for the left elevator!!! It's Logan's personal one!!" Cortez commands. "Got it!!!" Jade swings the passenger and pushes the revolving door hard, flying through the front lobby. Jade, wearing four-inch boots with spiked heels, was running in them like a pair of Nike's. She runs past the main security checkpoint in front of the elevators. A vast, bald security guard named Robby stands in front of Jade while she repeatedly presses the up button to Logan's private elevator.

"Whoa, what do you need, ma'am?" Robby asks.

"I need to see Logan Brodie right now. It's an emergency." Jade tells him with her voice filled with panic.

"You cannot just go up there. You need to be on the meeting list."

"You don't get it. I need to see him. I swear to God. It could be life or death."

"Not without being on this list.

The rage escalated inside Jade, fearing the worst for Logan. Robby looked intimidating, standing at 6'8, weighing 267 lbs, and was covered in tattoos. She looked up to him, not the least intimidated. She may have been 5'3, but her wrath made her nine feet tall.

"Listen to me, you little bitch!!!! You better let me up there right now, or I will kick you in the balls so FUCKING hard that I'll be the Seahawks' new place kicker by tomorrow morning!!!!" She yells throughout the lobby. Everybody there was at a standstill. Robby's eyebrows shot up. He swallowed hard, not knowing what to do, when Cortez finally caught up, yelling across the lobby.

"ROBBY, ROBBY!!! LET HER GO UP!!! LET HER GO!!! LET HER GO!!!"

"Cortez?" Robby asks for assurance.

"We've gotta get up there, now." Cortez gasps when the elevator chimes. Jade and Cortez run in. He presses for the 76th floor as it goes up. Cortez leans onto the elevator, sucking in the air. Every second felt like an eternity.

"Why didn't we say anything?" Cortez says, filled with regret.

"Because we were all hoping he had moved on. MOTHERFUCKER, come on!!!" Jade kicks the door, angry at the slow-moving elevator.

Jade was angry at herself. She wanted Logan to confront his pain with her since she didn't know the whole story, but from what she heard from everybody, he was doing better than he'd ever been, and she didn't want to ruin it.

Once she reaches the 76th floor, Jade and Cortez fly out of the elevator and see Sasha.

"JADE!!!! THANK GOD!!!" Sasha relieves. Jade doesn't stop running.

"WHERE IS HE?" Jade shouts.

"His private bathroom."

They both open his office and run to his bathroom. Jade tries to open the locked door. She starts to knock.

"LOGAN!!!! OPEN UP!!!" She yells out, getting no response. "I want to see you. I know you're hurting and want to take it away." She still gets no response. Cortez finally reaches the office.

"Logan!!! Brother!!! Talk to us."

Jade remembered running past an abstract brass statue by Logan's desk. She runs straight for it. It weighed over forty pounds, but she picked it up with her adrenaline at full force like it weighed four ounces. She heads back to his bathroom with the statue in hand. Cortez is still trying to get Logan to talk, but Jade is done trying to talk.

"Move it!!!!" She yells out, carrying the statue.

Cortez and Sasha move back while Jade slams the bass of the statue against the door handle. A chunk of the door breaks. She throws the statue down, and Cortez kicks the door with all his strength. The door flies open, and Sasha lets out a hard gasp, covering her mouth as the three of them look in horror to see Logan with a blank stare, slumped down on the floor against his shower door, looking straight at his bathroom sink, breathing slowly. A mixture of blood and sweat covered his face. Broken glass and blood were scattered everywhere, his right hand covered in crimson.

"Sash, call his doctor. Tell him to get up here!!!" Cortez orders.

"On it!!!" She runs to her desk to get her phone.

Jade takes very small steps toward Logan so she doesn't startle him. She knew he was in a state of shock with his zombie-like glance. Cortez is in the background calling Clinton about the situation. Not taking his eyes off him, Jade sits right next to him. Streaks of blood were in his hair and his clothes. His face looked pale and clammy, and he was still breathing slowly. He turns his head to see Jade's beautiful face. A stabbing pain went through her heart, seeing the defeated look on his face. Logan slowly slumped down and put his head on her lap. She begins to stroke his face softly.

"I'm here, baby. I swear to Christ Himself. I am not leaving your side." She assures him.

Logan didn't acknowledge her, but he felt peace feeling her touch. A half-hour later, Dr. Woods, Logan's primary doctor since he was six years old, came in and stitched up Logan's busted hand. Clinton arrives soon after. His heart breaks to see his disheveled godson in Jade's lap as she strokes his hair. Sasha cleans up the broken glass and blood from the bathroom. She peaks at Jade, who hasn't left his sight. Sasha bites her lip from crying again.

"How is he, Doc?" Clinton asks.

"I'm shocked he didn't fracture it, but I stitched him up. I'm very worried about his mental state. This breakdown was intense. He's not in there, Clinton." Dr. Woods informs him. Clinton closes his eyes and sighs.

"Son of a bitch."

"Here. Give this to him." Dr. Woods hands Clinton a couple of Ambien tablets. "He badly needs to sleep. I know this time of year is a struggle, and I've begged him to rest. Since he's in this state, this is a good opportunity. This could only get worse, fellas. He has PTSD. Something has got to be done with him."

Clinton extends his hands to shake. "Thanks, Mike, thanks for everything."

"No problem. I'll be in touch."

Cortez and Clinton look at Logan slumped in Jade's lap as Sasha sees Dr. Woods out. They were consumed with guilt for not confronting him about Renee's anniversary earlier.

"You go ahead and take her home," Clinton whispers to Cortez, making him chuckle.

"Good luck, brother. She ain't going anywhere." He whispers back.

"I'm just worried this will scare her off," Clinton says. Cortez points to the bathroom.

"Jade is a fucking pitbull. She threatened to kick Robby's ass, and she would have."

Cortez and Clinton head back to the bathroom. They watch Jade continuing to pet Logan's hair, looking down at him, making sure he felt safe.

"OK, Jade. We got to clean him up. You go ahead and go with Cortez, and I'll…"

"No." Jade softly interrupts while continuing to look down at Logan. He sees his blood stains on her jeans.

"Jade, you've got blood all over you. I will…"

"No." She softly interrupts him again. Clinton sighs.

"Jade. He's my godson. I've got…" Jade interrupts as her eyes turn into laser beams at Clinton.

"Clinton, I need you to look deep in my eyes. Do you think I'm going to be swayed for one fucking second? I am not leaving his side. I will take care of him!" She shouts when her eyes go back down to Logan. Clinton felt a rush of knowing how committed Jade was to Logan.

"OK. I'll call Maggie and we'll stay in Logan's room and watch over the girls. We'll tell them daddy had to go to Tacoma on an emergency trip, and he needed you to assist him since Auntie Sasha was sick."

"Thank you," Jade whispers.

"Rosa and Angie will swing by and bring you some clothes before they head home." Jade nods. "Are you sure you got this?" He reaffirms.

"Absolutely. Take care of the girls while I take care of their father. Thank everybody for me, OK."

Clinton bends down to kiss Jade on the top of her head. "Call me anytime."

Jade nods to him. Once Clinton, Cortez, and Sasha leave, Jade takes over.

"Alright, Iron Mike, you need to shower and get cleaned up."

Logan sits up and looks at Jade with a blank stare. His head was still in a constant daze. The only thing he could concentrate on was her face. She tries to get him up as much as possible, even with her tiny frame. Once they're up, Jade looks into his eyes, feeling his emotional suffering, unable to stop his self-loathing for himself. She unbuttons his bloody shirt and stares at his bare chest for a few seconds. She puts her head on his chest and closes her eyes, hearing his heartbeat racing.

"Please hold me." Jade whispers. Logan slowly embraces Jade and wraps his arms around her. "I'll get you through this—one step at a time. Just think of beautiful things. The girls playing, a sunset, me in a tiny dress with high heels." She giggles. "We'll get back to this position, but let's get you in that shower for now."

Jade turned on the shower and looked down at the floor, making sure there was no more broken glass around before she took his shoes off. Jade kneels and takes his pants off. Steam starts filling up the bathroom.

"Alright, cutes, c'mon. I need you to take this. You need sleep in the worst way." She hands him the Ambien and bottled water, taking it without a problem. "Atta, boy."

She guides a naked Logan into the shower. He puts his head down, letting the multiple showerheads hit his head with the warm water pouring down on him. He watches the blood trickle down the drain coming off of him. He started to tremble, feeling hopeless, feeling like a complete failure to everybody around him. He just wanted it to end. Suddenly, he feels a pair of hands covered in body wash rubbing his back. His head perked up, his heart pumped, and a rapture of light went through him.

He slowly turned around to see a naked Jade before him. A feeling of sweet surrender while Jade took care of him. She smooths her vanilla-scented, soapy, healing hands over his chest and stomach. She looks down and sees his thickness almost brushing against her. In her head, she screamed, "Now's not the time, now's not the time." She squirts shampoo into her hands and gets on her tiptoes to reach his head. Logan bows his head for her to lather him up. Little spreads of blood and shampoo combined were in Jade's hands. She lets out an exhale, rinsing off her hands. When his body swayed, he turned around for the water to rinse his hair. The Ambien was kicking in.

"Whoa, whoa. Hold on. Hold on." She quickly turns off the water. "Alright, handsome. Let's get you ready for bed." Jade helps him out of the shower before he collapses. She grabs a towel and dries him off before putting him in an ultra-soft white bathrobe. "My God, you'll be sleeping in a cloud. Oh wait, so will I." Jade whips out her own robe and snorts, trying to get Logan to smile. A crooked smile hit his face. "I needed to see that out of you."

Logan takes his left hand and caresses Jade's cheek. She closes her eyes, takes his hand, and kisses it.

"C'mon, let's lie down, baby." Logan's eyes get heavier. He lays down on his bed with Jade lying next to him. Both their heads hit the pillow at the same time. "Look at me." Logan struggles to keep his eyes open. "Take a look at this face and dream about it tonight. When you wake up, this face will be right here."

Logan smiled, feeling relaxed and relieved she wouldn't leave his side. She watches him as he closes his eyes, brushing her hand across his cheek. The first night with McKenna and Madison, she sang them to sleep. It was the first time Jade sang anything in over eight years.

Focused on Logan's face while he slept, she swallowed hard when she softly started to sing "I'll Stand by You" by The Pretenders. Jade slowly grabbed his hand and kissed it tight while she sang. She poured her heart and soul into him through her singing. Once the song ended, she repeated what Clinton had asked her three days ago.

"Is it just sex?" She sneered. "Look what you made me do, Logan. You made me sing to you." Jade leaned to his ear and finally said something she thought she would never say to another man again. Whispering tenderly. "Logan Brodie, I love you."

CHAPTER 19

IN TREATMENT

It had been over three years since Logan slept more than five hours a night. Last night, he slept for fourteen. He woke up around ten a.m., and like Jade said, she was the first thing he saw when he woke up. He felt indescribable passion and belonging to another when he saw her beautiful face.

"Good morning, gorgeous. Well, to be technical, good late morning."

"Hi." He says with a groggy whisper. "I had a real shitty day yesterday."

"That's the rumor I heard. It's alright. We get those days every now and then. Here's the deal, though. You get to stay in bed, in your robe, with me.

Logan felt relaxed when he gasped in panic, "God, the girls!!!"

"Hey, they're fine. Everything has been taken care of. Look at me. You will do something different that you haven't done in God knows how long. You're going to relax and think of yourself for once."

"Oh God, what did I do yesterday?"

"Do you even remember anything from yesterday?"

Logan shook his head. One thing he remembered most was being on her lap and not wanting to leave it, feeling that soft hand brushing on him. He felt so safe and sound.

"My hand hurts like hell."

"Yeah, they're replacing the mirror today. What the hell were you thinking?"

"I wasn't. I entered a dark hole and couldn't get out. All I could see was the dark. I never felt such hatred, and it was all towards myself." Logan gets out of bed and walks to the window to look at the city. Jade sits herself up on the bed. "This doesn't seem real. I'm supposed to enjoy all this, and I can't." He lays his head against his forearm on the glass, looking down the 933 feet. Feeling as small as the cars on the ground. "Three years, Jade, and nothing. I can't let her rest in peace because I keep losing myself. My daughters deserve a strong father, and I can't do it. I am barely hanging on here. It doesn't make any sense." He grits his teeth in anger. The self-loathing fills him again.

"It doesn't have to make sense, Logan. That's the reality of it all." Logan turns around to look at her. "You're still grieving, and you may never stop. The bottom line is you are not alone, though. The girls, the Crew, Sasha, Rick, and your trump card." She points to herself. "Except you've buried every emotion inside you, but guess what? Mt. St. Helens blew up in that bathroom yesterday. Well, I'm telling you right now, no more bullshit. You don't want to go to therapy. You don't have a choice because I'm not going anywhere."

Jade folds her arms, blazing her eyes at Logan. She would do something everyone was afraid to do: shoot Logan straight, and there was no holding her back. She was determined to end it all: the flashbacks, the hauntings, the denial. In front of her was a man who deserved joy and to live life to the fullest, yet he was letting an invisible force put a stranglehold on him.

"You're staying in this loft, and you're going to tell me the whole, straight story, and you're going to learn to stop blaming yourself. We get to kill two birds with one stone here. You get to let it out to the hottest shrink you'll ever meet, and I finally get to put my psychology degree to good use."

"You have a degree in Psychology?" Logan crinkles his brow. Jade slumps her shoulders.

"You still haven't seen my resume?" Jade waves her arms. "Forget it; let's start. How long has it been since you took over Horizon after your dad died?"

"Going on seven years." He states.

"Ok, so at twenty-nine. You took over a multi-billion dollar company. That's a lot on your plate already. What was the best advice he gave you?" Logan sits down.

"Something my grandfather told him. He who dies with the most toys STILL DIES. I was seven years old, and we were in the jet about to land, coming home from one of his business trips. I was looking out the window at Puget Sound with the sun about to set when he sneaked beside me and said," Mimicking Jack. "Son, enjoy this. This kingdom is going to be yours. Don't feel guilty about what you have. We've worked hard for this, and you get to enjoy this privilege that God gave us the strength to build upon. Embrace it, drink it in. Here's the catch, pal. The second you disrespect that dollar, IT WILL EAT YOU ALIVE. The second you do not put 100% into your job, family, or life, you have lost your status as a man. The second you don't take the chance to help others, you have lost your status as a human being. They say money can't buy you happiness. That's nonsense. It's up to you, son. Helping people, there's no happier feeling in the world; no matter how dark of a place we live in, you can throw light at it. The people who work with us are our everything. You treat them like fine crystals."

"One day." Logan's lips start quivering. He quickly gets out of his chair and heads toward the window. "I'm going to be gone, pal, and you will be the king of Seattle." Jade gets out of bed and walks toward Logan, standing right behind him. "Find a good wife, have children, and take over my reign. I miss my dad an awful lot, Jade." He says, putting his face down.

"I know. He sounds so amazing." She says softly, putting her arms around his waist and her head against his back. "Your mother, too." Logan turned to look at Jade.

"Oh, Christ almighty, my mom. You would have loved her. She had your moxy and spunk—the heart she also had. Before Rosa & Angie came to us, there was Tina. She was from Jamaica and had only started working for us for two weeks. One day, Mom saw her talking to her father on the phone, balling her eyes out in their bathroom while cleaning. Her mother had a heart attack and was almost near death. Tina saw my mom walk in and panicked, thinking she was in trouble. Without hesitation, she told her, "Tell him you're on your way." She called Sea-Tac and told them to prepare the jet for Ocho Rios. "Take as long as you need, sweetheart. Please be with your mother," she said. When she saw somebody in need, Katie Brodie was Johnny-on-the-spot."

"I noticed those knitted berets with the Jamaican colors and the dreadlocks in M&M's room. Was that from Tina?" She asks while Logan just smiles, thinking about his mother.

"Yeah. Her mom fully recovered and moved back a couple of years later. Tina had a daughter thirteen years ago and named her Katie. That was my parents. They took any opportunity to change someone's life. Race, orientation, nationality. It didn't matter to them. That's the true definition of a rich person."

Jade was engrossed in hearing the stories of his parents. Her phone goes off to see it's Sasha. She answers.

"Hey, girl."

"I bet you're starving."

"Dear God, yes!! This guy has some granola bars and water in his loft." She gives Logan a wink, which makes his stomach flutter.

"I'll get a pizza for you." Sasha was reluctant to ask because she was traumatized by what

Logan did. "Ummm, how's he doing?"

"Progress. I'm working on him." Jade smiles at Logan, except Logan isn't smiling. His sorrow was getting to him hard. He felt like such a failure as a son, a father, and a boss to his Crew, who have stood by him for so long.

"It'll be here in twenty minutes," Sasha tells Jade.

"God, I love you. Thanks, girl." Jade hangs up while Logan walks to an end table near his sofa with a picture of McKenna and Madison. He picks it up, swiping his fingers across their little faces. He could feel Jade approaching. Logan inhales, holding his breath and looking deep at his daughters.

"Am I weak, Jade?" He painfully asked.

"No!!!" She immediately answers. She darts towards him and gets in his face. "I'll tell you why. You're doing it. You're getting a hold of your emotions and spilling your guts. You're searching your soul to release yourself. It doesn't matter if it took three years or three weeks. The point is it's happening. Logan, depression is a disease. No matter how you slice it. Anyone who says it's a state of mind should have they're fucking face caved in. You must realize," she grabs his side, "You're still here. You are one tough son of a bitch just doing that. Trying to raise your kids and keeping this company going. Now, we'll play shrink here, so grab some couch." Logan sighs, wondering how far Jade would go with her therapy session. She pulls out a chair and sits, placing her feet on the couch. She puts her hands behind her head while Logan just looks at her. Sensing his stubbornness, she rolls her eyes, lifts her feet, and, with all her might, pushes him back on the couch.

"Tell me about Renee." She tells him. Logan looks at her like she's the one who went crazy.

"Seriously? You want to know about my wife?" Jade says without hesitation.

"Yes. Everything. The day you met, the day you got married, the day the girls were born." She pauses. "The day she died." Logan swallows and shuts. "C'mon, fella, you've gone this far, and you're doing good. Keep going."

Logan knew Jade would keep pushing and be relentless. He puts the kids' picture back on the end table, taking a deep breath and pulling his hair back.

"I met her Junior year at Washington U. She majored in Art but took a business class in case she wanted to open an art gallery. She was born in Dublin and moved to the States when she was eight. She sat three chairs to the left of me. She looked at me, and she smiled. Boom!!!! I was in. I didn't go nuts with women in my life. I dated a couple of times, but I never slept around. Renee though. She was tall, with green eyes and brown hair, and my God, that slight accent was beautiful. She wore a black tank top, white capris, and black flats. That first day after class, she approached me and said, "Your eyes look like the Atlantic. They're so beautiful."

"I thought more of the Pacific, but I digress." Jade lightens the mood, which brings a smile to Logan's face.

"I was so clueless about what to say next. I just thought of the first thing that popped into my head. "I know a great bar." I winced after saying that. She said, "Yeah, I don't do bars. She said to get a six-pack of Guinness, and I'll meet you on the hood of my car in an hour. That was it. No contest." Logan looks away to contemplate. "We talked for hours. About life, our future, and her Agoraphobia, now understand why she didn't go to the bar. We dated for a year, and I was ready to jump in. After graduation, we married in Ireland. Her dream was to get married right next to the Cliffs of Moher. She wore a silk, slim white dress, and you needed a plastic surgeon to get the smile off her face. Our parents and the Crew were the only ones there. It was small, but my God, it was majestic. I remember my dad saying to me, looking at the Atlantic, "Son, the reign will be coming now that you have your wife." Logan's lips quiver again, choking up his words. A single tear rolls down his cheek. "Two months later, he was a guest speaker for a business conference in Phoenix, and right before he was about to make his speech, he had a heart attack backstage."

"Oh, God." She whispers, covering her mouth.

"He died before the ambulance got there." Logan inhales deeply. "I lost my hero. That killed my mother. She moved into the guesthouse because she couldn't bear sleeping in their bedroom anymore. She was so lively and vibrant, and that woman always glowed on her face. After Dad died, that glow was gone. She was so unrecognizable, yet Renee was determined to get that glow back on her. They didn't have the typical in-law relationship. They were mother and daughter. Renee would be with her every day. She taught my mom how to paint. Every morning, they had tea together and talked about Jack. Sure enough, Renee brought my mom back. That glow returned. One Sunday, we were in the theater ready to watch the Seahawks and let me tell you something: next to my dad, the other love of Katie's life was the Seahawks. It was a late afternoon game, and my mom wanted to nap. A half-hour before game time, we tried calling her, no response. So Renee went to the poolhouse, and she was still in bed. Renee checks on her, but... Logan pauses, trying to let the words out. His voice cracked with his lips shaking. "They said it was a brain aneurysm. She was gone too."

Jade shakes her head, closing her eyes in horror: "Oh, Logan. How long was it after..."

Logan stops her from finishing. "Three months."

"Mother of God." Jade covered her mouth, barely getting the words out. Logan closed his eyes when a tear escaped, shaking his head. I never got to say goodbye to either one of them. Then there was Renee. She was such a gentle soul, but she was so fragile. I had no idea how bad it was going to be. She could never leave the house. Her anxiety was out of control, and she wanted no part of the outside world past those front gates. She painted every day.

Her favorite spot was on that dock. One warm summer day, I went sailing with Clinton and Tony and looked at her. She was wearing a white sundress. She looked up and smiled at me, blowing me a kiss. She learned to cook from Tony, sew from Rosa & Angie, do an excellent fade away jump shot from Clinton, and how to steal a car and pick up hookers from Cortez playing "Grand Theft Auto" Jade laughs.

"Being the great husband you were, you loved seeing that, right." Logan nodded.

"I was happy she felt safe and protected, but something was missing. I'm not going to lie. If I wanted to see a ball game, I would go with the guys but not my wife. A few days after our fourth anniversary, McKenna was born. I fell in love with her as fast as her mother. I held her in my arms and said, "Hello beautiful," and she peed all over me." Jade and Logan burst into laughter. "After McKenna turned two, I noticed Renee wasn't eating much and losing weight fast. She always kept herself in shape, but something was off. Come to find out; she was pregnant with Madison. Through those nine months, we had no idea. Ovarian cancer." Logan broke down, not being able to hold back the tears. "Oh my God, Jade. It was lottery odds for a woman in her 30s to get it. Renee refused to get chemo because she was so afraid for Madison. The pain and suffering she went through with Madison, but goddammit, she was such a tough Irish girl. She gave birth to her, but Renee was pretty much gone. Pencil thin, completely frail, and disheveled." He perks his head up to look at Jade. "She didn't have the strength even to hold her baby daughter. One month. That's all she had with Madison. May fifth came. I looked at her, and she said…" The tears started coming down, and he fell back onto the back of the couch, unable to get the words out.

"C'mon, Logan. What did she say?"

"She said, "I can't do it anymore, Logan. I can't hold my daughters. I'm so sorry." Renee slowly put her hands on my face and said, "I'm so sorry I was a disappointment as a wife." She then started flatlining, and I was screaming for her. It was such a knife to the heart. I wanted to know why she would say that. The doctors scrambled in. It took Cortez, Tony, and Clinton to hold me back, and the doctors shook their heads. Those were her final words to me, Jade. Why? WHY?" He screams and sobs. "Why, Jade, would she say that to me? No, I love you!!!! No, I'll miss you!!! No, please take care of our children!!! Why the fuck would she say that to me? Those were her last fucking words!!!!! GODDAMMIT!!!!"

Jade jumps out of her chair and kneels in front of Logan. She pulls his head to lock his eyes to hers.

"LOGAN!!!!! Look at me! Look at me!" She yells. Logan couldn't even look at her as the tears uncontrollably came down. "She was dying. She was probably on a ton of painkillers, suffering, scared, and knowing her last minutes on this earth were coming and that she wouldn't be there for her daughters to grow up. She felt that she wasn't a great wife because she couldn't control her fear and the fact she was leaving you with two daughters to raise. The guilt was destroying her. She wasn't in the right state of mind. She loved you so much, Logan. You have got to know that." She stands up and pulls Logan's head onto her waist while he continued sobbing. Jade closes her eyes while patting the back of his head.

"It's so unfair. It's so fucking unfair, Jade. I never got to say goodbye to any of them." He sobs harder. Jade is holding Logan tight and gently kissing the top of his head.

"I know. I know. I'm so sorry." She consoles him as her heart aches so badly for Logan. She always knew he would always have a love for Renee. She was the mother of his children. He would be in love with their memories together. The thing was, Jade knew there was something in Logan that was craving to get out. He always wanted to move on, but his resentment toward himself always trapped him.

"You know what I felt like. I felt like Superman after his father died. He said, "All the things I can do, all those powers, and I couldn't even save him." All the money in the world wasn't going to save her." Jade pulls Logan's head away to look at her.

"I'm so sorry you would think that. You got hit with multiple tragedies in such a short span. You are like Superman, though. Like his daddy told him before he died," Jade pokes at Logan's chest like Jonathan Kent did to his son, Clark. "YOU ARE HERE FOR A REASON!!! Right now, your depression and your grief is your Kryptonite. Fortunately, your Lois Lane is right here. I'm so sorry you have been through this, but it's been too long. You're too much of a wonderful man to be in this much pain. I know you're trying to show a brave front to everybody, but it isn't working. Everybody knows you're dying inside, and it's killing them. You need to look at what's in front of you. You've got a hand to hold now, a shoulder to cry on, and someone to ease you back into this life because you're still here. Everyone's seen the difference and is so happy because you are now. Do you know how rare of a person you are? One day you'll look in the mirror and not beat the shit out of it but see Logan Brodie. Not the billionaire but the good man he is. It will make you proud one day, and all of this will be forgotten. I promise you. It will be hard, but I'll be right here with you. Life is way too short to be at war with yourself. You know you're not the enemy. No, your money didn't save her because it's not supposed to. Your money has saved so many others, though." Jade wipes his tears away with her thumb while he is finally feeling peace inside himself. There was a knock on the door.

"That's got to be, Sash. We need to get some food in you, babe. I'll be back." Jade tightens her robe. It was Sasha with pizza and a six-pack of Blue Moon.

"Holy shit, you are a goddess, and you brought six little friends," Jade says, kissing Sasha's forehead. Sasha walks in, not looking at Logan.

"It was the least I could do for you. Let me know if you need anything else. OK." Sasha hugs Jade and leaves the loft, still unable to look at Logan. He could feel her tension brewing. The guilt quickly was eating inside Logan.

"Sasha, wait!!!" He runs to meet her in the middle of his office. "I'm so sorry that I scared you. I just… I just lost it and…"

Sasha puts her head down, covering her mouth, and starts to sob. She runs into Logan's arms.

"You scared me, Logan. I thought you were going to hurt yourself."

It then hit Logan. He remembered that shard of glass from the mirror and reached for it. Logan pulls Sasha away to look at her face.

"I'll get better. I promise. I'm not going to hide anymore." He says while Sasha wipes her tears away.

"I know you will." She turns to look at Jade standing in the middle of the threshold. "You've got her now." Jade smiles at Sasha. "You just let her care for you because you need her." Sasha kisses Logan's forehead as she walks back to her desk. Logan walks back to the loft with that shard of glass in his mind.

"God bless that woman. I am starving. I thought after we eat, we…" Logan interrupts her.

"She was right."

"Come again?"

Logan sits at the edge of the bed, barely able to get the words out of his mouth.

"I…I wanted to hurt myself. There was a piece of the mirror on the sink."

Jade went utterly numb, immediately knowing what Logan was thinking. She crosses her arms while looking up at the ceiling. The rage was building inside of her. She was incensed that Logan would think of killing himself.

"No. Please don't say it, Logan. Please don't say what I think you're going to say." She turned around, not being able to look at him.

"I saw that piece for a few seconds. I grabbed it and then looked at my right wrist."

Jade closes her eyes and lifts her head. She lets out a small moan when she opens her eyes. She was officially in a zone where the white rage takes over, and she's a runaway train. She walks towards Logan and straddles over his lap. Her eyes were dead-locked on his with her heart shivering.

"You would have been the worst thief I've ever heard of. You would have stolen from your family, the world, the worst is you would have stolen from Logan Brodie and nobody steals from Logan Brodie. He's someone who's given so much who deserves so much more." Jade quickly takes Logan's hand and tugs off the right side of her robe, placing his hand on her right breast. "He deserves that." She guides his hand and gently caresses her face. "He deserves that." She then put his palm against her heart. Logan could feel the rapid pulsate against her skin. "He definitely deserves that. Your daughters, your crew, your Seattle..." Jade pauses. "Yours truly deserve Logan Brodie." Logan slowly puts his head down, exhaling deep. Taking in deep breaths.

"What prevented you from ending it?" She asks. Logan slowly raises his head to look at her.

"You. You stopped me. You just popped into my head for a split second. In that split second, I could feel you: your intensity, your passion. I could smell and taste you. Then, when I saw your face, I felt alive again." Tears come down Logan's face. "Every time I'm with you, everything is just perfect." He looks at her with the most pained stare on his face. "I've been so tired for so long, Jade. I've never been more awake until you came along."

Jade kisses Logan with so much force and power. Her mouth intensified on every inch of his mouth., Logan grabs her waist tight, not wanting to let go of her. She finally forced herself from his lips. They both hold each other tight, not wanting to let go of each other. More than anything, Jade wanted to climb on top of Logan and take the pain out of him. Except, she knew how fragile he was. She thought of the next best thing. Jade places her forehead, panting against his.

"OK, I think we made a breakthrough. Let's call it a day, shall we?"

"Sounds good." He says, exasperated, mentally drained.

"Let's just eat pizza, drink beer, watch nothing but funny movies, and not get out of these robes?"

"You can take yours off. I'm okay with that." He jokes as Jade playfully hits him and hugs him.

"This therapy session wasn't free, you know. Now, you have to pay." Logan gives her a little grin when he sees her face. "Service me. Get me a few slices and a beer, stream me some Hulu, and put on "It's Alway Sunny," and let's laugh our asses off."

"Done."

Throughout the day, Logan and Jade lay in bed and watched many episodes of "It's Always Sunny in Philadelphia,"

"Young Frankenstein," and the forgotten classic "Top Secret." They did what Jade said. They laughed and held each other and stayed in their robes. Logan occasionally kept looking at Jade as she laughed uncontrollably during "Top Secret" since she never saw it. He could not stop smiling every time she burst into tears from laughter. They get out of their robes when they "FaceTime" the girls, not adding suspicion to them. Jade puts on one of Logan's sweaters while he puts on an old Nirvana shirt, telling them about their "emergency trip to Tacoma" and how Jade was a great assistant to Daddy since Auntie Sasha was sick. They told them about their day at school and how Uncle Clinton and Auntie Maggie took them for ice cream after school. Jade held Logan's hand, knowing how difficult it would be for him to talk to them. She knew the guilt would hit him hard, thinking of leaving this world for them to lose a father. He starts to choke up, seeing their beautiful faces on the TV.

"We'll see you tomorrow. You two be good for Clinton and Maggie." The girls wave.

"Bye, Daddy, bye, Jade!!!"

Logan has a tear forming, and his voice cracks deep. "Daddy loves his M&M's." Jade grips his hand tight as a tear trickles down his cheek.

"We love you too, Daddy," McKenna yells.

The girls disconnect the call, and Logan fights his tears as Jade holds him tight. Never in his life did he feel so low. Suicide continuously trickled into his thoughts, but he never considered doing it. That edge never came so close as yesterday did. Jade knew exactly what was on his mind.

"You didn't go through with it. Just remember that, Logan."

He sniffs, exhaling hard while wiping a single tear. He looks and nods to Jade, caressing her face. He thought of the power this woman had on him. For so long, he slammed any door to anyone who tried to help him grieve. Jade broke that door down with a brass statue. Around eight, Logan was watching a Mariners/Yankees game when he noticed Jade passed out with her head pillowed on Logan's chest with her leg across his pelvis. At that point, he couldn't focus on the game. He couldn't stop looking at Jade's beautiful, smooth leg draped on him like that with nothing but his sweater, which was giant on her. Seven years later, Logan could not think of anything but a world of despair and pain from losing his parents. For four years, he couldn't have imagined being with another woman that wasn't Renee.

Six months ago, a tiny, beautiful, wise-cracking blonde from L.A. turned the tide. He repeated the question Jade asked him at Rogue. "Are you ready for this?" The truth of the matter is that he was ready. Jade was his teacher, giving him not just a different life but a new one, and Logan craved it more and more. Renee was nothing like Jade. She was conservative and proper, always wanting to make love in the most gentle sense and always be in the bedroom. With Jade, it was always a game of "Let's top this." She opened a portal into Logan's desires. Something new was forming in him. While she slept, she moaned while grinding her leg up and down onto his groin. Logan watched his hard on grow from his sweatpants. That wasn't the only thing that was growing. The obsession and desire for her body were overtaking him. He grinned when he felt his inner beast released. Jade would need her rest because she would meet his own personal Mr. Hyde, Mr. Brodie.

CHAPTER 20

THE ARRIVAL

Water is essential to life. Even in our dreams. Jade dreamt of walking towards the shore of the ocean where a man stood alone, looking up at a behemoth-sized tidal wave standing frozen. She slowly walked behind him, giving him a gentle touch on his back. Logan jerked his head to look at Jade. His face was overtaken with fear, while Jade had a calm expression with that beaming smile of hers. Jade takes Logan's hand when suddenly Johnny Cash's "Hurt" starts playing. The fear on Logan's face started to fade away when the wave started to move towards them. They held each other with ease as the wave was about to crash on top of them when Jade woke up to find herself alone in bed.

"Logan!!!" She says with fright in her voice. All of a sudden, she hears "Hurt" is playing outside the loft, not knowing he was listening to it on a continuous loop for over two hours. She heads out of the loft to find Logan sitting in his chair in his sweatpants, looking out the window and watching the drizzle come down the Seattle night. Jade's head was racing frantically because the last time he had that blank stare, he was sitting on the bathroom floor in a vegetative state. Logan didn't move a muscle for three minutes and forty seconds during one of Johnny Cash's most haunting songs. Her stomach was in a giant knot, dying to know what he was thinking. She took very slow steps towards his desk, feeling the coldness of his tile floor beneath her bare feet. When the song ends, Jade has her regular perky tone.

"Hey you, why aren't you in bed? You should be sleeping." Logan doesn't even acknowledge her. He looks down at his phone to make sure the loop stops. Jade sighs, looking down, and talks to him in a severe tone. "Look, I know yesterday took a lot out of you, and you let out so much. The thing is, Logan..."

"Move in." He cuts her off, still looking out the window. Jade's head jerks up from the floor in shock, not knowing if she heard him right.

"Wait. What?" She screams out, blown away.

"I said move in."

Jade, as usual, is trying to lighten the mood. "Umm, you mean to move in closer to you or...

"GODDAMMIT, JADE!!! You know what I mean!!!" Logan snaps, not being in the mood.

She swallows, hearing his harsh tone for the first time. The tension was so thick in his gigantic office. Logan turns back to look out at the city lights again. The fire in Logan grows higher with every pump from his heart. He could hear it thumping harder the closer she came to him. She walks around the table and stands right in front of him. He looks down at her feet, going up to her thigh, when she caresses her fingers across his face.

"Is that what you truly want? What is in that head of yours?"

Logan leans closer, looking at her body furiously, his sweater coming down to her upper thigh. The lust erupted faster, looking down at her long, smooth legs. He looks up at her, seeing the sweater completely off her right shoulder. Jade noticed his eyes were not of a soft, warm man but the eyes of a hunter incarnated by her. Greed was something Logan never worried about. He never needed more money or power to stroke his ego and to feel superior. Mr. Brodie, though, was filled with greed, and it was, for one thing, HER!!! He grabs her thigh and slowly puts his hand under the sweater. Jade lets out a sharp gasp.

"Does that answer your question?" He answers in a graveled, snarky voice. Jade didn't know what to think. Who was this person?

"Pretty much." She softly whimpers.

She looks at Logan's sexually unhinged expression. It was cold, and it shook her core. He lifts her by the waist and plants her hard on his desk. She looks at him while digging into his sweatpants to feel that bulging pleasure she craves. She yanks his pants down to see it right in front of her, looking at it like she found water in the middle of crossing the Mojave desert. Logan's mouth attacks Jade's, spreading her body across the smooth, cool marble, taking in her perfect nude body on display. He looks down at this living fantasy splayed across his desk. Overcome by her beauty, he just couldn't wait. He slips his thickness inside of her with one deep thrust.

"OH, SHIT!!!" She screams, slapping his desk while rasping hard. He lifts her legs, putting her feet around his neck. Logan grabbed the neckline of his sweater and ripped it in half. "OH MY GOD!!!" Jade yelled out while her mind was far gone by sure elation while he groped her breasts softly, gyrating his hips while Jade bent up her legs and placed her feet against his hard chest. Her eyes closed, feeling the rush from the magnitude of his lust through him. That was until she heard his voice.

"Open your eyes, now." He gravely orders her. She opens her eyes to a man possessed with absolute power. "You are to keep your eyes on me while I fuck your soul out of you." The sexually naive Logan was nowhere to be found. Before, Logan was the one with the kingdom and all the power, but the one thing he wanted to rule was her naked body, which was on top of a desk where he met with mayors, governors, and fellow billionaires. Jade screams while pounding her right fist onto the desk. Her essence melted, watching Logan conquer her body as it rippled with his drive, when suddenly, with his own evil grin, Logan pulled out of Jade.

"Oh no, don't you dare tease me, damn you. Give me everything. Right fucking now!!!" She demanded.

Jade had never craved something so much in her life. Feeling the pulse inside of her, she was dying for his sex. She wanted it even more when she grabbed his quivering bicep. Logan inserts just a little at a time.

"The day we met, what did you think when you opened your eyes and saw me for the first time?"

Jade moans uncontrollably, swallowing to clear her voice. "You were the hottest man I've ever seen. I wanted you more and more each day. Our kiss on New Year's, a part of me died." Logan gives her more. She closes her eyes, groaning louder. "What we did on that beach was a life changer." Like a boost of Nitro, Logan leaned and pulled Jade up. "Give me that mouth." Jade pulls Logan's face hard while driving her pelvis into him, gripping his thick, enormous neck. She feels his force coming. A jolt goes through her entire body when Logan ravenously pounds into her. Jade lets go of Logan's neck and gripped her legs and thighs like a fortress. He looked down at her as he could feel his climax coming, pausing momentarily before giving her one last deep push. He lets out a deep, loud grunt while Jade lays back down on the desk while he hovers over her. He looked at the one who performed the impossible by opening his soul. She covers her eyes as she breathes in deeply.

"Oh, my God. Oh my God. I'm going to sleep well." Jade says in a low, raspy voice. Logan pulls himself off of her with a bright smile and playfully says.

"Oh, we're done?" His face and tone quickly go serious. "Not quite yet."

Jade's eyes widen when Logan pulls her arms and lifts Jade off the desk, pressing her body against his.

"Oh, shit!!!!!!!!" She whimpers.

Logan carries her and slams Jade against the window in front of the wet Seattle night. She looks at his salacious stare, knowing she brought him to her sonic world that he was not ever leaving. She reaches down, feeling his heat, pulling it into her. He starts rocking her up and down into him, not being able to process that this man took over her.

"DON'T YOU DARE STOP FUCKING ME!!!!" Jade screamed. Logan was demanding, raw, and unapologetic to her body. She knew the revelation that he enjoyed a little pain and pressed her dominant lips onto Logan's as hard as she could. Slanting her head to kiss him deeper, she dug her nails hard into his back as Logan grunted in pain. "I'm not hurting you, am I, baby?"

Logan looks at Jade with so much predatory energy. "No."

"Well, we're just going to have to work on that." Jade thrusts harder when she scratches her nails across his back, leaving deep marks. Logan stops and yells out the pain.

"GOD!!!!!" he smacks the window, looking at Jade angrily. "Much better," Jade licks her lips. "After I'm through with you, you'll hobble to your first meeting." Jade's intensity hits an all-time high, sucking on his earlobes and then going after his neck, leaving massive purple marks all over him.

"Son of a bitch!!!!" Logan growls, embracing the pain mixed with pleasure, now banging his fist against the window. "FUCK!!!!"

"Try explaining these to the board tomorrow."

"I'll tell them that I received the mark of the beast."

"Why, you!!!!!" She aggressively kisses him, fighting her tongue against his. Logan suddenly pauses again. Jade is not even close to being done.

"What are you doing??? Logan, you can't just stop. I WANT MORE!!!"

Logan shushes her when he slowly puts her down. Still, he did not avert his eyes from hers. Jade looked confused. He grabs her waist and quickly spins her around. Taking her arms and putting them high on the glass, Logan hovers his hot body over Jade's from behind.

"Keep them up there. I want the overnight maintenance crew from the next building to see who I'm nailing." Jade lets out a deep exhale with a relentless grin,

"What have I done?"

"You woke someone up." Logan whispers in her ear. Jade closes her eyes and breathes in, not knowing what to expect next. She gasps again when Logan gives her tiny, gentle kisses down her bare back. He gets on his knees and kisses her firm, smooth ass. He stops to admire them.

"Logan, I swear. I want it, NOW!!!" She begs and moans. Except, he's hypnotized by the most beautiful ass on a woman.

"One second, I'm just admiring this work of art God made."

"Take two seconds and then OWN IT!!!"

Logan sticks out his tongue and gives her one long lick up from the bottom of her back to the top of her neck. The goosebumps explode onto Jade as her body shakes. She slaps the window.

"You're killing me!!!!"

Both their hunger was uncontrollable. She lifts her head as Logan softly kisses the back of her neck. He looks down and tries to plunge into her when she stops him.

"No, Logan, lower." She softly says, biting her lips. Her palms turned into fists high on the glass, lowering her body and sticking her ass straight out. She looks at him over her right shoulder and whispers passionately. "I want you to feel how bad I am."

Logan knew what he was about to do was considered raw, taboo, and completely sinful. Everything Jade craved for. No way he was going to question her. He was going to give Jade what she wanted. Her eyes closed, her body leaned back, her head looked up, and her mouth fell. Jade took a deep inhale when she felt him enter.

"Ohhhhh, yeah!!" She let out deep satisfaction into her paradise with just one thrust. Jade was already forcing herself not to let herself go. Logan was gentle and took it slow, waiting for the green light. He knew she was not going to take this slow. Immediately, Jade was dying for more as she pounded on the window, bending down lower. Jade gasped louder as Logan's speed increased. "Fuck this little whore, baby!!!!" Logan leaned towards her ear.

"Who are you?" He says in a menacing voice.

Jade turns her head over her shoulder and slowly says. "Fuck YOUR little whore!!!" She gives him a quick lick of the top of her lip like the viper she was. Green light, GO!!! Logan was then put into a madness of sexual depth he never felt before. He grabs a fistful of Jade's blonde hair, twists it in a ponytail with his right hand, and pulls it. Jade yelps when he propels rapidly.

"C'mon, baby!!! C'mon!!!" She commands.

Logan lets go of her hair and grabs her breasts while sucking her neck. Jade's head was in a tailspin as she went through multiple orgasms, craving more. The synergy between them was unstoppable. She pulls the back of his neck and starts deep-tonguing Logan's mouth, taking in every ounce of euphoria while passing through one rapid orgasm after another. Logan puts his left hand against the window while his right is around Jade's waist, feeling his release coming. The momentum picks up while Jade's body pulsates harder when Logan yells out while letting himself go. Jade collapses against the window while Logan collapses behind her, breathing heavily on her sweaty blonde hair. She looked at herself from the window's reflection, watching Logan hover over her. She watches him lean toward her neck and plant the softest kiss on her Ferris wheel tattoo. She trembles at the slightest touch of his lips.

"Don't move. I'm going to get you some water," he tells her before going to the mini fridge by his desk. Jade continues to catch her breath, and her voice is ultimately horse.

"OK, I'll just be right here." She watches his naked backside go to his desk. She couldn't believe she had let Logan conquer her. Even more shocking was how much she loved it. Logan comes back with a bottle and hands it to her. "Who are you, and what have you done to Logan?" She asks before taking a sip.

"Hey, you created this monster." He chuckles. An exhausted Jade turns around and collapses her limp body onto Logan, wrapping her arms around his neck.

"Oh well, shame on me then. Oh my God, your neck." Jade looks at the enormous purple hickeys on Logan and starts to laugh, covering her mouth.

"You mean my trophies." He says proudly. He feels more proud when he looks down. "Oh my goodness, look at that." Jade looked down and saw Logan was still primed and ready to go. Her mouth drops.

"No!!! Fucking!!! Way!!!" She looks up at him. "I don't know what's harder, your desk or this gift God blessed you with."

"Well, he's warmed up. Let's really have sex." He gives Jade a devilish grin as she does and lifts a frazzled Jade into his bathroom. She whines, overcome with exhaustion.

"No, seriously, Logan. You win, you win. You're a sex machine, but can we end this with a handshake and a job well done and go to bed? Please!!! I'm so tired."

Logan passes the newly assembled mirror. He stares at the man he lost respect for, who he wanted to hurt and kill. This time, there wasn't any hatred for himself but the amazement of the beautiful woman he held pressed against his body. Jade holds him tighter as she can feel everything he is thinking. Jade stares at the mirror along with him.

"Do you see what I see?" She asked while he couldn't answer with a lump in his throat. "A beautiful man." Jade nuzzles her mouth on his neck, giving him soft kisses "with a beautiful soul," She softly kisses the other side "with a really beautiful woman."

He turns to look at Jade and kisses her. "You're going to get along with him again."

"I'll try. I promise." He says when he turns to his reflection again before turning his sights on her.

"Except, he sees the most beautiful girl he's ever seen. Who's also incredibly filthy."

"Oh, dear Christ, no." She moans from exhaustion, not knowing how much this man can stretch her. Logan gently puts her down and turns on his shower.

"Relax. It's my turn to clean you." He says with sincerity in his voice. He reaches out his hand and takes her into the shower. Jade moans, feeling the warm water hit her naked flesh, melting from the relaxation of two faucets hitting her front and back. Logan goes behind her, smoothing her backside with vanilla sugar body wash and using extra strength to massage her simultaneously. She groaned, feeling the heaven Logan was sending her. The thing was, in the back of her mind. Jade was wondering if Logan was serious about his proposal.

"Logan, you do realize this is not a one-and-done thing. Depression, grief, it's a lifelong struggle. I know you're going to have your good days and bad days. Are you sure you want me to move in with you three? I mean…"

"Jade, look at me." He takes his soap-filled fingers and softly takes her hand to face him. "I just lied to my daughters that you were assisting me in Tacoma. I don't want to hide us from the girls anymore. I don't want to sneak into the pool house and then leave you. I want you to be in my bed like you did tonight with your head on my chest, so I know you're with me the next morning. I know I'll have bad days, but you're right there with me as long as I know." Logan brushes Jade's wet hair, slicking it back with his fingers. "I need to see this beautiful face as much as I humanly can because I know this beautiful face is my remedy."

"Well, you twisted my arm; I guess I'll move in." She says sarcastically, wrapping her arms around Logan's waist and kissing him softly. He grabs more body wash and starts rubbing up Jade's chest. He was lost in Jade's brown eyes, looking at the woman who made him finally open up.

"Thank you." Jade shook her head and grinned. She rested her head on his chest as he held her with the water coming down on them.

"Don't thank me. I had to take care of my man. Can I ask you something?"

"Of course."

Jade separates herself and looks at Logan. "When I called you to pick me up from Rogue, and I told you that guys were trying to pick me up, was that jealousy, or were you trying to protect me?"

"Both. Here's the deal, I know you'll be checked out, get double takes…"

"Eyefucked." She adds.

"Exactly. To me, that's fine. I can't stop that. Now, if someone tries to touch you or say anything inappropriate, I'll…"

"You'll do nothing." She demands. Logan gives her a confused look. "I know how to take care of myself. If push comes to shove, Cortez will take care of it. I loathe and will not tolerate jealousy because there's no need for it. You are Seattle royalty and have so much respect in this town. I will not allow you to get your hands dirty. You have the easiest job when we go out. That is to trust me, stare at me, lust over me, and know you get all of me. Alright?"

"Okay. What happens if I get checked out?"

"Oh, then there will be blood on my hands." He says while he gives her a "seriously?" glance. "Hey, you're the billionaire with a heart of gold and a little naive. You are beyond rare. Don't get me wrong, I trust you completely, but" Jade touches his heart. "This is mine." She guides her hand from his chest to his erection. "This is definitely mine, and the only way they'll get near it is when they smell my breath."

Logan knew well enough that Jade was an unstoppable entity on her own. She could destroy everything in her path if anything got in her way. Yet simultaneously, she was a supernova who brightened every room she entered. Her beauty, heart, and passion for life absorbed like a sponge to everybody she was around. She was an angel who just happened to have horns, too.

"How are you this amazing?" He asks. She shrugs.

"I don't know, I'd just fuckin roll with it if I were you." Logan laughs as Jade grabs her arms around Logan's torso. "I know I can count on you never to break my heart. I do count on you," Jade said, brushing his hand along her entrance, "to break me."

Logan could see Jade wasn't done with him. Their bodies crash together, slamming against the shower wall, kissing each other in a deep frenzy. She nibbled on his neck when she paused to whisper in his ear.

"You're my man."

Logan stared deep into that shower wall, hearing those three powerful words. His heart was pounding out of his chest, and he felt a sense of freedom. He felt something go away in him that had gripped him for so long. Logan finally felt closure.

"You're my girl." He closes his eyes with a prideful grin on his face.

"Take your girl to bed. I can't seem to walk." She demands.

Logan turns off the water, lifts Jade back up, and carries her back to his loft. Their soaking-wet bodies collapse onto the bed. He started sucking the water off her left breast. Jade brushes her foot back and forth across his ass. He looks up at her as he starts sucking her right nipple.

"Lay against the headboard." She orders.

Logan lays down on his back. Jade straddles on top of him, leaning towards him, putting his arms behind his neck. Jade positions herself closer to the headboard and hovers over Logan's face. He exhaled gently, knowing what she had in mind. Logan started a long stroke of his tongue on her. Jade began to make quick gasps when he started to hum. She thrusts her hips into his mouth, gripping the top of the headboard as hard as she could, especially when he started french kissing her inside. She started screaming when he rolled his tongue around her. "FUCK!!! FUCK!!! My man is a genius!!!!" She screams out, shuttering, and looking down, she sees him looking up at her while grinding against his stubble. Jade's heart pumps faster at the realization that she will sleep with this man every day and not have to hide or separate from him. She felt her orgasm coming on fast. Logan softly puts his hands on her ass cheeks and pushes her closer. She bites her lip, pounding onto the headboard, spreading her thighs wider. She thrusts deep, feeling the tip of his tongue flutter. With her eyes shut, Jade screams in a sexy, husky voice as she climaxes. Jade pulled the headboard so hard she could hear a crack.

"LOGAN!!!"

Feeling the rush of pride hearing his name screamed out through his loft. Jade continues to grip the headboard as her body shivers from the high of her last orgasm. It takes a while for her to catch her breath. Jade exhales, coming back from nirvana. She smiles as she climbs off him and covers them with a comforter. She lays her head onto his chest, taking his arm to put it around her. Jade giggles excitedly at the notion that this would be the new normal feeling for her. Logan could sense she was thinking.

"I'll see you in the morning."

Jade couldn't help but smile wide. She closed her eyes and fell into a slumber on his chest. Around seven a.m., Jade woke up and noticed Logan not in bed again. She tries to get out of bed but can barely walk, completely sore from the waist down. Jade takes a couple of baby steps with the heels of her feet, groaning from the pain when Logan returns to the loft from the bathroom, completely clean-shaven, wearing a gray, fitted Christan Dior suit, hugging his built frame. Jade took one look, and her foundation was shot entirely. Her heart raced; the lust compounded her to no end. She'd been dying to see Logan in a suit, but like they say, be careful what you wish for.

"OH, C'MON!!!!" She says as she lifts her head and her arms in the air.

"Well?" He asks, wrapping a tie around his neck. Jade sighs deeply with a whiny voice.

"Mouthwatering." She falls back into the bed, spreading her legs and points between her legs. "GET BACK IN HERE, NOW!!!!"

Logan climbs on top of her and kisses Jade. "I wish, but I've got a meeting in twenty minutes."

She whines louder as he climbs off of her. "Hey, before our shower, what did you call me?"

Jade sits up, trying to remember what she said, and then it hits her. She rolled her eyes, remembering the term. "I called you a sex machine."

"Hmmm," Logan grabs his phone and plays James Brown's "Sex Machine." Logan starts dancing in front of Jade, proud of his new nickname. Jade starts laughing hysterically, unable to contain herself watching his horrible dancing.

"Please stop, STOP!!! Logan, I'm about to piss myself and also show some respect to the Godfather of Soul. May he rest in peace," She begs him while doing the sign of the cross. Logan smiles wide.

"Sorry, my ego couldn't help it." Jade sees Logan having difficulty putting on his tie.

"Come here. I'll give you a hand." Jade gets on her knees while Logan sits on the bed. She can barely contain herself looking at Logan's suit. "God, you look so yummy. When was the last time you wore a suit?"

"The funeral." He says in a sorrowful tone. Jade stops to look at Logan's eyes as her heart sinks. She strokes her hand gently across his face.

"Are you alright?" She asked, concerned. Logan looks back at her and nods.

"Yah, yah I'm OK, really. It's just that McKenna loved that hamster." He tries to hold his laughter while Jade is incensed. Her eyes lit up with rage.

"YOU PRICK!!!" She smacks him repeatedly on his chest.

"Like you wouldn't have said it if the role was reversed?" He hits Jade back with the truth.

"Ooooh, good point." She growls under her breath. Jade finishes tightening his tie. "There you go, sexy."

"Well, I've got to do CEO stuff for a couple of hours, then we'll get you moved into OUR room. Jade squeals, jumping on the bed when he refers to it as their room. "Then we'll get the kids together and tell them about us."

"Us. Wow!!!" She sighs. Logan brushes the hair out of her face.

"I know; I can't stop saying it either." Logan gives her a long kiss. "I'll be back in a few hours."

"Go get 'em, Wolverine." Jade smacks his tight ass as he leaves. She watches Logan head out of the office. She leans against the door frame, filled with pride for her man. This was the beginning for Logan to one day get over something he swore he'd never get over. Logan leaves his office to confront Sasha. She's shocked to see him in a suit.

"Wow, ready to show them who's boss." Sasha was impressed.

"Let's do it. Listen, clear my schedule after eleven. I got someone moving in today." Sasha's mouth falls.

"You mean Jade is…"

"That's right." He interrupts with a glowing face. "The little Bellflower blonde finally slapped some sense into me last night. It's going to get a lot better here." Logan assures her. He grabs her hands. "I love you, Sasha. Thanks for having my back for all of these years. I'm so sorry again for…"

Sasha interrupts as she hugs Logan tight. "STOP!!! Look forward, not backwards."

"I will. My therapist taught me that. Luckily, I can pay her in sex." Logan grins while Sasha closes her eyes.

"Oh, good Lord, what has she done to you?" Logan bursts into laughter.

"Get out of here." Logan walks off to his boardroom. Sasha smiles at the pride she has in her boss and good friend. "He's back, folks!!!!"

Logan pumps his right fist in the air as he walks by. Once he makes the corner, he sees his boardroom filled with new empowerment and purpose. He enters, seeing his board members already sitting.

"Good morning!!!" Logan says with enthusiasm and authority.

CHAPTER 21

THE NEW ROOMIE

Logan and Jade returned to the mansion after his board meeting and catching up with clients. The tightness in his stomach grew more potent once they got closer to the house. Logan was nerve-wracked when confronting the crew, knowing what they knew about the previous days, especially Clinton. Once they reached the driveway, Logan turned off the Shelby but still gripped the steering wheel.

"Are you alright?" She grabs his thigh.

"I've put all of them through hell, Jade. I just can't imagine how disappointed they are with me." Logan says with a heavy heart.

"You know, you're right. Especially what heartless assholes they are. Seriously, Logan? These guys?" Jade points to the mansion. He looks at her when she grabs his hand and loosens his grip on the steering wheel. "They're your family. They've never given up on you, and they never will." Jade takes Logan's hand and softly kisses it. "It's going to be alright."

They get out of the Shelby, and Jade walks a few steps in front of Logan, who is still reluctant to go into the house. She reaches out her hand.

"C'mon. Just like Rogue, I'll lead you the way. Look at my ass if you need to." Logan chuckles.

"Well, it may not help, but I'll do it anyway."

Logan takes Jade's hand, and they enter the house.

"Hey, I'm home, and I brought someone with me," Jade yells out to the house.

Angie and Rosa come downstairs from the kids' room, and Tony and Cortez are from the kitchen. Logan looks at all of them, still gripping Jade's hand. There was still no sign of Clinton.

"Hey, guys." He swallows hard. Stammering and choking up his words. "Umm, I'm really sorry if I…"

Without any hesitation, Angie walks toward Logan to hug him tight. Rosa followed her sister soon after. Tony comes from behind, hugging his back. Cortez comes and smothers all of them with his enormous body. Jade smiles, watching in amazement at their overwhelming love for their boss, seeing this one big family together. Clinton then exits Logan's office, locking his eyes with his godson. Everyone separates from Logan. They stare at each other for what seems like forever. A single tear falls down Clinton's face when he pulls Logan into him, starting to weep. The rest all get together for a group hug, except Jade watches in the background so they can have their moment. Clinton, though, would not allow that.

"What are you doing over there, girl? Get over here." Clinton tells her.

Jade walks and joins in together. Logan looks around at all of them. He is smothered with love and support. He felt the world's weight fall off his back, knowing these people would be with him now and forever. After having lunch with the Crew, Logan showed Jade her new room. Whenever they got together to have sex, it was always in the pool house. Besides that night when she snuck into his room before he went to Montreal, Jade had never seen his bedroom. Logan opens the two giant doors, and immediately, Jade soaks it in, doing a slow turnaround when the motorized black-out curtains suddenly rise with the view of the Seattle skyline in the far distance. Jade covers her mouth.

"Wait until you see the closet." Logan extends his hand. Her eyes explode, and she takes his hand, jumping up and down and giggling like a little girl. They walk into the empty closet that goes on forever. Jade gasps when she sees a rack that could fit 400 pairs of shoes.

"Oh my God, I'm going to fill this bastard up."

"We will. This closet has been empty for too long."

"Why is it empty? Where are your clothes?"

"Jade, my closet is across the way." Jade closes her eyes and grabs her heart.

"Hold on. Let's try to get a grip here. Are you trying to tell me that this is just MY closet?" Logan nods.

"What I have now in the poolhouse won't even make a dent here."

"We're going to fix that. Come with me, there's more." They leave the closet and walk down a vast hallway. We've got our own gym, sauna, and over here... the master bathroom."

They both walk in and suddenly, Jade lets out a deafening scream. She sees a giant whirlpool tub in the middle of the bathroom. A replica of the one from "Scarface."

"Logan, is that Tony Montana's tub?" She points with her mouth open. Logan grins.

"It sure is. "Scarface" was my dad's favorite movie. It took a lot of persuading my mom to build this. She caved in and said, "OK, but NO CARPET!!!!" Hence the marble tile." Jade rapidly starts to disrobe.

"Could I love your parents more?" Jade gets naked and jumps into the tub. Logan turns on the jets, and Jade rests in relaxing heavenly ecstasy.

"Awwww, you know those run-of-the-mill orgasms I get. I think I just had three in one." Logan shakes his head, loving every second of her happiness. Jade just looks around, trying to comprehend that this is happening to her.

"This can't be real. You are not real. How did this happen????" Logan squats down.

"What brought you here? Was it just Tonya?"

"I missed Tonya and… I just don't know. Something just pulled me out here. Fate, the universe, God. I knew I would say goodbye to that wonderful California sunshine and say hello to gray and rain, but I have loved every second since I moved here. Then, all of you came into my life. I still can't believe this is happening to me. I can't believe I'm with you."

"Do you know how many times I've asked the same thing about you? I've asked myself, "What's the catch on this girl?" Still in his suit, Logan climbs into the tub, emitting another ear-piercing shriek from Jade.

"Logan!!!!!! What are you doing? That's a Christian Dior!!!"

"Does she know what she does to me?" He grabs her and holds her against him. She shakes her head.

"The fashion gods are so pissed at you right now."

"Does she have a clue how agonizing it is when she's not near me?" Jade looks into his eyes, caressing Logan's face.

"You need to ask yourself, "How fast can I get this suit off so she can ride me like I'm racing the Preakness?" Jade shoves her mouth into his when suddenly "California Love" plays in her jeans pocket. "Nooooooo." She moans.

"C'mon, beautiful. Let's get the girls and tell them about Daddy's new roommate." Jade smiles and lifts her eyebrows. Logan holds Jade tight when a thought hits him. "Now that you've moved in, we've got to be very careful around them." Jade rolls her eyes.

"I know, my cursing, my wardrobe, my innuendo." He gives her a crazy look.

"No!!! I don't care about that, with our sex life. Privacy is going to be a novelty now with you around. They're going to be glued to us."

"You're right. We must be crafty and lock this bedroom up like Fort Knox. They're not going to block us!!!!" Jade yells.

"NO, THEY WON'T!!!" He yells back, high-fiving each other.

"Now, let's get those angels. I miss them so much." Jade says with sad eyes.

"Me too. Let's go."

After getting dried up, Cortez drives Logan and Jade to the girls' school. Every day when they head to the office, Logan and Cortez have a guy's conversation topic like "What Would You Rather Do?" or "Who belongs on the Mt. Rushmore of rappers or NBA legends." This time, Logan and Cortez discuss which movies they cried over. Jade had a disgusted look on her face when she heard their conversation. She understood the notion of crying through life, but over movies was way over the top.

"I've got a good one. When Brooks was on the outside, and later hung himself in "Shawshank." Cortez nods.

"That was brutal, but I can top that in two words. "Sophie's Choice"

"OH, MY GOD!!!" Logan exhales.

Jade looks at both of them like they're the biggest tools in the world.

"God, do you two share the same brand of tampons, too? Yikes!!!" Logan looks at Jade like she's crazy.

"Are you serious? What movie have you cried over?"

"None." Jade scoffs.

"Not even "The Green Mile" when John Coffey gets electrocuted," Cortez asks.

"Nope."

"Ok, when Drago kills Apollo in "Rocky IV," Logan adds.

"Nah."

"Ok, here's the ultimate. The first six minutes of "Up"?" Jade acts sympathetic.

"Oh, that was sad…. NO!!!!!"

"You're fucked up, Shorty." Cortez shoots at Jade.

"Seriously," Logan agrees.

"Piss off, you dicks. I don't cry."

Logan looks at her, astonished. "Wait, you've never cried before?"

"No, but I'm starting to wonder who's got the pussy in this car. Me or you two." Logan shakes his head, looking at Jade.

"Oh my good, good God. You are insane." Logan shakes his head.

"Ah, excuse me. You just jumped into a jacuzzi in a $1,500 suit, and you're calling me insane? Yeah, a valiant effort, though." Jade says sarcastically. Cortez pulls in front of the girls' school.

"Okay, we're here. Can you turn that knob of yours from R to PG, Miss "I don't cry because I'm a robot," Murphy?"

"Alright, before I do." Jade flips off Logan and turns the invisible censorship knob on the back of her neck. "Let's get the girls, you two stinkers. Gosh darn to heck, I've had just enough of your bunk." Jade exits the limo and slams the door. Logan and Cortez burst into laughter together.

"Cortez, you're a stinker." Logan collapses on the floor, rolling from laughter, and tears roll down Cortez's cheek. Logan opens the door when Cortez adds.

"Don't take any of her bunk, Logan." They cannot escape from busting a gut when Logan gets out to catch up to Jade. She yells and smacks Logan.

"No, don't you touch me. Get away from me!!!" Logan picks her up and carries her over his shoulder. Jade lets out a scream. "Put me down right now!!! I swear to…" Jade pauses when her face gets up close and really personal to the back of Logan's jeans.

"God, you've got a sweet a..." Logan stops her before "Ass" can hit her lips.

"Jade!!!! PG!!!! Young children are present!!!"

"Apple!!! Sweet round apple. I swear that's all I was going to say. We are in Washington, you know."

The girls spot their daddy and Jade with a confused look, wondering why their daddy is carrying their nanny around.

"Daddy??? Jade???" They yell out.

Logan puts Jade down while the girls run towards them. "Hey, angels, how was school?" He asks while hugging them both.

"Good," Madison answers.

"Listen, girls, your daddy and I have something to tell you." Jade grabs Logan's hand and holds it in front of the girls. The girls' mouths open wide in delight.

"Also, Jade is going to move in with us," Logan adds.

"Does that mean you're boyfriend and girlfriend?" McKenna asks, barely able to control her excitement. They lock their eyes into each other's gaze. Both their hearts skip beating when Logan tells them.

"That's right, baby, she's my girlfriend."

Jade didn't see any fear in Logan's eyes when he said it while the girls started screaming and jumping up and down. His eyes were genuine. Filled with hope with that feeling of their souls connecting. All of a sudden, Madison starts to cry. Jade kneels down to console her.

"Maddi, what's wrong?" Jade asks worriedly.

"I'm so happy." She buries her face into Jade's chest. She kisses the top of Madison's head and holds her tight. McKenna then starts to cry.

"Daddy, does that mean you're not sad anymore?" She asked, filled with hope to finally see her father happy. Logan's stomach started to turn. No matter how much he tried to hide his sadness from the girls, they knew their daddy was suffering. He kneels to McKenna.

"Honey, you have no idea how happy I am now. You girls mean everything to me." He wipes a tear from McKenna's face. His heart shattered for what he's put them through. He hugs his daughters tight, promising never to let them down. "Now, C'mon, let's go home." Logan watches the girls run to the limo.

"You do realize they weren't fooled for a second, right? They're too smart, Logan." She turns to look at him. "Look at me." Logan then turns to look at Jade. "You're done hiding." They both turn to see the girls hug Cortez. "Now you have three smart, strong-willed gals in your house. Do you think you can handle us?"

"Well…" Logan tries to respond, but Jade immediately stops him by chuckling.

"Wow, that is so precious. You thought you had a say." Jade laughs and pats his chest. "MY BOYFRIEND IS GOING TO BE SO WHIPPED!!!!" She yells while walking away from him.

"Your what???" Logan yells back. A huge smile goes on Jade's face.

"My boyfriend. Want to hear it again??? "MY BOYFRIEND!!!" She screams out enthusiastically in front of children, parents, and teachers.

"You're my girlfriend." He says. Jade puts her finger under her earlobe for him to repeat it. "JADE NICOLE MURPHY IS MY GIRLFRIEND!!!!" He screams.

"TAKE YOUR GIRLS HOME!!!! LOGAN JOSHUA BRODIE!!! BOYFRIEND TO JADE NICOLE MURPHY!!!!" Logan walks up to a laughing Jade and gently kisses her. The girls lower down their window with their heads sticking out and sing.

"Jade and Daddy sitting in a tree K-I-S-S-I-N-G!!!!"

They walk towards the limo when Jade starts to whisper her version. "Jade and Logan later in the spa F-U-C….." Logan cuts her off.

"We're still in a school zone." Jade laughs out loud while grabbing her neck.

"Gee willikers, Logan. The knob got turned somehow. It passed PG-13 and R and went right to NC-17. Golly goose, this silly little doohickey is a pain in my derriere."

They both burst into laughter, heading back to the car. Later that night, after dinner, Logan took Jade and the girls into the theater to see "Brave." McKenna and Madison fell asleep a third into the movie. They both carried each girl upstairs into bed, laying both girls down and covering them up. Right when they try to creep out, McKenna wakes up.

"Jade, can you sing to me?" She pleads.

Logan and Jade wince together, thinking they were going to be free.

"I'll wait up for you," Logan tells Jade.

"Thanks, baby." She kisses him before he leaves. Jade sits at the edge of McKenna's bed, tucking her in while clutching her Princess Merida doll. She looks into the beautiful blue eyes that came from her father.

"Jade, can I ask you something?"

"Of course, sweetheart." She whispers.

"Why do you only sing to us?"

Jade slightly smirks, hiding the gut punch she was feeling being asked. For years, she's deflected the conversation or used every excuse in the book why she doesn't sing in front of people. The connection Jade had with the girls, lying to them, was impossible.

"Sweetie, it's because I get a little scared singing in front of people." McKenna's eyes grew wide, thinking she was fearless of anything. "You get scared, Jade?"

"Now and then." Jade smiles, turning to look at Madison sleeping in her bed. She looks back at McKenna, swiping a lock of her brown hair out of her face. "Except for you two. You and your sister are the only ones I want to sing to. That's the power you girls have on me."

"I love it when you sing to us." She whispers.

"I love it too. Now let's get some sleep, you beautiful thing."

She closed her eyes when Jade stared at her Princess Merida doll that she clutched tightly under her arm. She knew exactly what to sing. Softly, she started singing "Daughter" by Pearl Jam. It was a song about a mother who abused her daughter because she had learning disabilities, thinking she was being disobedient. Jade never left eye contact with the doll while thinking of her mother. After the song ended, she looked at McKenna's sweet face, vowing that no one would ever harm her or her sister. She gets off the bed and slowly closes the door, taking a hard swallow, feeling the pain from the dark memories from childhood hitting her. She exhales, going across the hall to her brand-new bedroom with the man of her dreams just behind it. Jade walks through the massive door to see Logan on the balcony looking out at the lake, waiting for his new roommate, almost certainly wanting to christen Jade into it. He comes inside, wanting every piece of her clothing around her ankles.

"Our first night together." He tells her while the guilt was hitting Jade hard about disappointing him because for once, sex with Logan was not on her mind.

"Yeah, um. I feel like a horrible girlfriend saying this, but I'm exhausted from today, and last night you turned me into a Stretch Armstrong doll down there. Do you think it'll be okay if we hop into the tub with a bottle of wine and you just hold me?" It pained Jade so much to ask him that, but Logan's eyes glistened at her not having a care in the world.

"We'll do anything you want." He says, not showing an inkling of disappointment.

Jade runs into his arms, burying her head in his lower chest. Logan sighed in happiness, having Jade to hold and comfort, not knowing that she was screaming inside. Not letting him suspect a thing, she springs off his chest.

"Okay, you get the wine, and I will be waiting for that naked body and those huge thumbs massaging my neck."

"I thought we weren't having sex." He looked at her, puzzled.

"I can still look at you like a piece of meat. Hello, you do have the body for it."

"Point taken. I'll be right back."

He kisses Jade on the forehead before he heads downstairs. For the first time, she's by herself in the massive master bedroom she was going to share with Logan. Unfortunately, the trauma from her own past consumed her. Much like Logan, Jade never sought help or went to a therapist. It wasn't because of others' judgment or looking weak. It was the fact she'd done everything on her own from this point. One sense of therapy she always counted on was the power of music. To Jade, the key to figuring out life's mysteries was by song. She takes her phone out of her back pocket and goes to her playlist, connecting with the bedroom's speakers. One in particular on the list talked to her about all the people who let her down in life. "It's a Shame" by Monie Love while she sits on the edge of the bed, wrapping her arms around her knees, holding them tight.

She was zoned into her own personal therapy session. Jade knew the past had a way of coming back to haunt you, but sometimes, she needed a reminder of who she was. She closed her eyes and started mouthing the words while she was sucked into her hellacious childhood, past relationships, and struggles growing up. A liar, a disappointment, a letdown. Those were some of the choice words she heard, but it was usually by one person. Once the song ended, she exited her zone, looking around at her bedroom. Yes, her bedroom. A slight, crooked grin grew, knowing where she's at now. She nodded and said with complete awakening, doing a 360 around the room.

"You're Jade FUCKIN Murphy. This is yours and not theirs. They can't hurt you anymore. Always remember. Their hate is your happiness." She repeats to herself like a mantra. Jade starts to disrobe while heading to the bathroom. Logan soon after walks in with a bottle of Cabernet and two flutes. He sees the trail of clothes splayed on the floor towards the bathroom. He sees Jade with her hair up and shooting him that vampirish look, with her breasts barely covered with bubbles. Before Logan could ask, Jade stopped him. "I got a second wind. So get in here and fuck that out of me." Logan was doing backflips in his mind, relieved they were getting to christen the tub, along with the sauna, the gym, and the balcony.

CHAPTER 22

CALL ME MR. BRODIE

L ogan was lost in a daydream, remembering when he was sixteen, fishing with his father and Clinton out in Barbados— sharing a twelve-pack of Corona. Not technically sharing, Jack got to have five to Logan's one as long as his mother didn't find out.

"Hey guys, let me ask you something," Clinton asked.

"Go for it," Jack told him.

"You're granted one superpower. What would it be?"

"Too easy, teleportation. Just think about it. Get here from Seattle in less than a second. I'll take that. Also, imagine how high Horizon's stock would fly if we found a way for our freighters to teleport. What about you, Clinton?" Jack asks him back.

"Mine's easy, too. Most would say fly like Superman and Ironman, but if I could, freeze time. God, just imagining having all the time in the world. No doubt about it. It's worth more than money. What would you pick, son?" His father wondered. Logan took a sip of his only bottle of Corona.

"I want the ability to read a woman's mind like Mel Gibson did in "What Women Want." You can easily be the man of her dreams without even trying.

Jack and Clinton turn their heads to look at Logan and then at each other.

"Shit, that's a good one," Jack says.

"Jack, this kid is going to be a hopeless romantic," Clinton adds. "Whoever snatches you,

Logan, she will never let you go. I bet you already have a proposal in mind." Logan turns to Clinton, "Yup, I want to propose to my girlfriend at the Seahawks new stadium."

Jack looks at his son with wonder. "Why do you want to do it at Qwest Field, son?"

Suddenly, Sasha's voice snaps him back to reality.

"Logan!!! Emergency conference with Denver. Trains aren't moving." She panics.

Logan throws his pen down in disgust. Unfortunately, there is a downside to being a CEO. Sure, it can be glamorous, and the perks that come with it are extraordinary. The money and the travel, but the problem was time. A month had passed since Jade moved into the mansion, except times have been hard at Horizon. He's had to cancel dates with Jade, miss the girls' dance recitals, and, the worst, spend nights in his loft again, pulling in eighteen-hour days. He hated not being home with the kids, but it was much worse without Jade. He was stuck in emergency meetings all day for the third consecutive Friday night. Around midnight, Logan gets a text from Jade.

Jade's text: "I am so sorry you had to break our date. Don't worry. I finished it for you." Jade sends Logan a video of her pleasuring herself, yelling his name. "I miss you so much."

Logan winces in emotional pain and adds physical pain by banging his head on the desk. He desperately needed to call Jade. He leaves the board room and dials her, answering it on the second ring in the most seductive tone.

"Hi, you've got Jade. For $3.99 a minute, I'll tell you about your most erotic fantasies. Make sure you get your parent's permission." Logan snickers out loud.

"Oh my God, I didn't think anything could cheer me up until I heard that. I miss you too. I am sorry I had to cancel again."

"Well, you're the boss. Can't you cut loose and be the boss of me? I got my hair French braided, and since we're almost halfway to Christmas, I thought you could practice being Santa early and pull my reins." Logan closes his eyes in disgust.

"Aww, Jade, you're killing me. I'm having so much trouble all over. Deliveries are not getting done, strikes are on the rise, and unions are screwing me over. To top all that off, I've got to go to Boston the week before my birthday, and I got to spend the night here again."

"SERIOUSLY??? Logan, that's the third time this week, and when you don't sleep there, you don't get home until after M&M are already in bed? What the hell is going on over there?" She wonders. Logan raises his voice.

"I don't have a clue!!! Nobody can get their shit together with anything, and I've got to make sure I'm here early in the morning to fix the previous day's problem. Jade, I swear I will make this up to you. I promise." Logan says with guilt in his voice.

"Stop!!! Stop!!!, I know you're stressed out, and I don't want to add more for you. I want you to hold me, be with me, and be IN ME!!!!"

Logan sighs heavily: "Jade, you have no clue..." Logan then gets interrupted by one of the board members.

"Logan, you've got a conference call with Roger in Dallas. We've got trucks lined up with nowhere to go." Thomas, board member #2, states. Logan grinds his teeth in frustration.

"Be right there!!! Jade, I gotta go. I'll see ya real soon. OK."

"Listen to me. Relax. I'm proud of you, baby, but I will send you some pictures so you can whack your bag before you go to bed tonight." Jade calms him down. "Just hang in there, OK. I love you."

She repeated it. Yet Logan has been hesitant. He kept screaming in his head, Say it!!! Say it!!! I love you!!! "Thanks, beautiful, goodnight."

He hangs up the phone, reaching his boiling point. With the combination of missing Jade, his kids, and work getting out of control, the last thing he wanted was to feel held back by his emotions. He noticed a text he hadn't seen earlier. It was a video of Jade and the girls at Pike Place fish market yelling "We miss you, Daddy!!!" while a large salmon flew over their heads. He closed his eyes and entered a world of rage. "GOD!!!!!!!!" He yells.

The guilt officially took full possession. He was surprised his clothes weren't tearing and turning green. He walked into the madness that was his boardroom. Before he walked in, he asked himself one simple question: What Would Jade Do? Logan enters the boardroom with pandemonium going on. Board members are talking to executives around the country on their phones when Sasha rushes to Logan with her eyes glued to her tablet.

"OK, here's the situation. The trucks are all out of order."

Logan looks straight at his board members and tells Sasha in a deep, gravel voice. "Go home."

"Wait, what?" Sasha asks.

"I said go home." He turns to look at her, knowing she's never seen this side of him. "You've worked too much. You leave this to me. Turn off the iPad, and I'll see you tomorrow."

Sasha wasn't going to argue. She simply exited the boardroom. Even though she was battling exhaustion, she planted her ear against the door. Her curiosity got the most out of her, wondering what Logan would do next. The commotion continues when Logan goes to a cart full of bottled water. He casually opens a bottle and takes a small swig. He puts the water down, aggressively picks up the cart, and throws it across the room, smashing it against the wall. The boardroom goes church quiet, looking at Logan.

"Get Dallas on Zoom right FUCKING NOW!!!!!" He snaps. All his board members looked at each other, stunned seeing this side of him.

"Whoa, whoa, Logan, let's calm down," Steven said, who was in charge of the Mid-South territory. Logan squeezed the bridge of his nose.

"Steve, I beg of you. Not one word. I truly, truly beg you." His board members went dead silent and frozen. "WHY DON'T I HAVE DALLAS ON MY SCREEN???" He screams.

"I don't know how to set this up. Where is Sasha?" One of the board members messes with the remote to find which input to use FaceTime.

"I sent her home!!! She's done enough for the night. She doesn't make the fucking money you make, Andrew, so with the half-million salary you get, you can figure it out." Logan snarls.

They scrambled to set up the Zoom meeting while Logan could feel the rage building. One of the executives in charge of the Dallas offices comes on screen. Logan stared at his desk while feeling his insides burn.

"Logan? How are you?" The executive from Dallas asks. Logan has a smug look on his face.

"Roger, I'm great. I'm in my board room after midnight on yet another FUCKING FRIDAY NIGHT instead of being home with my family!!! How are you, Roger? Most of all, how do you feel being moments away from being punted out of my company?" Everybody looked at each other, seeing this dark side of Logan. Roger swallowed hard, taking in all of Logan's wrath.

"Look, Logan, we're trying to fix the situation. Orders are being dropped, or they're getting switched around." He stammers.

"Okay, find out who in tech is responsible for that and fire them. Wow, you really needed me for that. Next problem?" He says sarcastically. Roger swallows hard.

"The unions aren't cooperating with the trucking companies and..." Logan interrupts.

"Breach of contract, have them try to sue me and get rid of them. We've got many other unions who've got a hard-on for Horizon who would love to join us. NEXT!!!" There was a pause. "C'MON, Roger!!!!!!!! Let's go!!!!!!!" He claps his hands. "Keep them fucking coming!!!!"

"We've been having problems with the government with regulations and dealing with forced layoffs with many drivers."

"Wait!!! Wait!!! Who's laying off the drivers? Why are you telling me this?" Logan looks at his board members. "Guys, what is this bullshit? They are our heart and soul!!! We are not losing ONE FUCKIN DRIVER!!! NOT ONE, ROGER!!!" Logan turns around to see his board members about to explode. He starts to walk around the table. "Do I have everybody's attention now? I know what you're thinking. "I've never seen Logan this upset. I've never heard him curse or fire anybody." Well, you saw three historical firsts today. Speaking of three. Three words I will repeat: NOT!!! ONE!!! DRIVER!!! Roger, I would spread that word like a virus because you don't want me in Texas any time soon."

"Yes, Logan."

"You've been downgraded. It's Mr. Brodie to you." Logan grabs the remote, shuts off the monitor, and throws the remote across the boardroom table. He takes a deep breath, gets his phone, and looks at a selfie Jade sent him earlier of her in a blue top, and black pumps she would have worn on their date. It calms him down rapidly. He sits in his chair and turns his back on his board members. "I'm sorry you had to see this side of me, but at the same time, you HAVE to see this side of me. For the past month, I've been practically living here in this building, trying to fix problems that didn't need me to fix. For three years, I would have happily spent every waking moment being here and avoided reality, but I can't do that to my children anymore, and they're missing me. I have missed too much of their lives. I've missed too much of my life. I truly hate being this guy. The yelling and firing are not me, but if I'm being held back from family, may Christ have mercy on you because I WON'T!!! Now, I'm going to quickly go home, kiss my daughters, and come right back here before the sun rises, and I swear, this will be fixed. Now, goodnight." All eight board members get up, feeling hit in the head with a baseball bat. Logan contemplates what he has said and done, but failing his grandfather's company is not an option. Neither was being away from home either.

After three hours of phone calls to offices from Charlotte, Nashville, and San Diego, Logan finally got to take a break to look at the other pictures Jade sent of her in that blue top and mini skirt sitting in front of the mirror with her legs crossed. Logan bolts out of his chair and heads to the elevator down to the garage. Logan's heart pumps fast, and his urge to get home to Jade goes stronger by the second. He gets into the Shelby and jets out of the garage. The V-6 engine echoes through the late Seattle night. He calls Jade.

"Hey, baby." She says in a groggy voice. She can hear the Shelby's engine screaming while he speaks to her with authority.

"You've got twenty minutes to get up, get smoking hot, which should only take you two seconds, and I want that blue top and black mini on you. Plus, I want those "fuck-me" heels on your feet!!!

"Oh, OK. I thought you were spending the night in the loft." She says, tongue-tied, hearing his forceful voice.

"Not til I'm done with you. I'm fed up, pissed off, and ready to tear some ass, and I will start with yours first." Jade's mouth falls in shock, and her body trembles at thinking of what he would do to her. Her heart rises, dying to hear more. "I've had a hard fucking month, Jade, but let me tell you something, YOU are about to have a harder fucking night!!! Mr. Brodie is coming home for you."

Logan hangs up and throws the phone onto the passenger seat. He tightens the wheel and guns it into second gear.

Jade was utterly flabbergasted. She imagined the storm going through that door once he got home. Her hormones and libido swelled through her at the sound of Logan's hunger for her through his demanding voice. She shrieks, kicking her feet in the air, knowing her man is coming home to her and she is about to get pulverized. She quickly turns on Selena Gomez's "Come and Get It" while springing out of bed. Jade dances and lip-syncs while she goes into her bathroom to freshen up, getting ready for Mr. Brodie to come home.

CHAPTER 23

MY GIRLS DON'T WEAR
PURPLE AND GOLD

The following day, Jade woke up with a smile on her face—that is, until she tried to get out of bed.

"Ow, ow, ow," Jade yells out, trying to get up but then collapses back on her pillows. Her body was paralyzed from soreness from the waist down. "That son of a bitch ripped my uterus in two."

She sees the bedsheets torn up and huge, long scratches on the headboard. Jade picks up one of her heels on the side of the bed and lines the heels to the scratches. Jade shakes her head, staring at the shoe. "My boyfriend is a crazy man."

Jade gasps when she sees a rose and a note on Logan's pillow.

"No, he's not. My boyfriend is amazing." She says to herself.

Logan's note: "Hey, beautiful angel. I'll be home around seven and make sure this is the last Saturday I work. They don't want Mr. Brodie around. I know you like him, though." Jade nods in agreement. "I've missed you all so much, Logan. P.S. Don't worry about the sheets and headboard. Totally worth it."

Jade giggles when the girls knock on the door.

"Morning, Jade!!!" They run into the bedroom. Jade quickly jumps back into bed and covers up her naked body.

"Morning, M&M." Madison sees the scratches and the sheet torn up.

"What happened to the bed?" McKenna asks. Jade tries desperately to come up with an explanation.

"Oh, um. Earthquake!!!! I don't like them, so I grabbed tight to the sheets."

"We were taught to go by a doorway during earthquake drills," Madison says.

"Yeah, I was frozen in fear." She says quickly before changing the subject as fast as possible.

"Anyway, go to your room and let me get dressed. I'll be right there."

"Okay." They run back to their room. Jade collapses back on her pillow, missing her man so much, relieved she got a small taste of him. After getting dressed, she heads to the girls' room.

"Alright, ladies, let's get this beautiful…" She opens the curtains to see it's raining. "Gray, dreary Saturday morning going, shall we? Oh my God, I forgot, I bought you girls these new outfits that you girls will love." She heads towards their closet. There was a picture of Logan and Renee holding a newborn McKenna hanging by on the wall. Jade notices Renee's face covered up with a cut-up Post-it note.

"Girls, why is your mommy's face covered up in this picture?" McKenna was silent with a pained look on her face, looking down. "McKenna, honey, it's alright." Jade kneels to the girl's level. McKenna was hesitant to tell her.

"Because I didn't want you mad seeing her since you're my daddy's girlfriend now." She nervously spoke. Feeling the wind knocked out of her, Jade says in a very soft tone.

"McKenna Anne Brodie," Jade cups McKenna's chin and stares into her watery eyes. "That's your mommy. I never, ever want you to forget her. She loves you so much." Tears start to fall on McKenna's cheeks.

"Jade, why did Jesus take our mommy away?" Jade felt like someone took a sledgehammer to her heart. She turns to see Madison's little lips quivering as she puts her head down to the floor. Jade wiped the tears from McKenna's face, desperate to take the emotional pain away from the girls.

"Because He needed her help. So he made her an angel. To watch over you two, your daddy, the Crew, but mostly to watch over me to ensure I do a good job taking care of you girls. I know it's unfair that she's not here, but you'll see her again one day. I promise." McKenna starts to sob when she wraps her arms around Jade's neck.

"I wish you were our mommy." The wind was knocked out of Jade, holding McKenna tight. She was feeling the warm little tears on her shoulders. Jade holds her tight while stretching out her other arm.

"Come here, Maddi." Madison walks over and pulls her into her arms, holding them both. Jade's breath escaped her chest, and the heartache was unbearable for her. More and more, she was figuring out why she moved to Seattle. This family was her reason. Like an angel brought down from heaven to hover her wings to heal their pain.

"You two are so smart and so strong. I hope you both know how proud your mommy must be of you two." Jade pulls the girls away to face them. "I could never replace her, but always know I will always be here for you. Now, let's go downstairs, and I'm making waffles." She impersonates Donkey from "Shrek," which has the girls giggling. "First, Mac, we're going to fix this picture." Jade opens the back of the frame and peels the Post-it note off her mother's face. "Now, kiss your mommy." McKenna and Madison kiss the picture and hand it to Jade to hang it back up. "Perfect." The girls take her hand and stare at the picture together. Jade was never interested in being a mother, but she remembered what Tonya said: "You will fall in love with these girls." Never in her wildest dreams did she imagine they would be everything to her. They were no longer part of a job but a part of her life. The girls go downstairs and have breakfast together, chatting primarily about boys.

"Tell me, Mac, are there any cute boys you like in your class?"

"Ewww, no. They're gross. Except for Tyler. I like him." McKenna says

"Is Tyler cute?" Jade questions, which makes McKenna blush. "I promise I won't say a word. You promise, Mads?"

"I promise." She says, putting some more waffles in her mouth.

"See, it's just us girls here. Believe me. Your father does not need to know. He's got enough to worry about. Like me."

"I'm glad you're my daddy's girlfriend."

"Me too, sweetheart."

"Do you love our daddy?" Madison asks.

"What????" Jade gives them a puzzled look, not knowing how to tell them.

"Yes, you do," McKenna tells her. Jade squints her eyes.

"How can you possibly tell?"

"Because you're so happy when you're with him, and you can't stop looking at him." McKenna smiles, telling Jade.

"Okay, Okay. Your inquisition finally broke me." Jade's face brightens. "I do. I love your daddy so much, girls. I've loved him for a long time." The girls smile big. "I've wanted to tell you two for a long time. Just don't mention it to your daddy, please."

"Why?" Madison asks.

"Well, I've told him, and he hasn't said it yet." Jade knew Logan loved her, but she was dying to hear it from his mouth. "Do you think your daddy loves me?"

"Uh, yeah." McKenna gives Jade a crazy look.

"He stopped talking to Mommy long ago," Madison added. Jade knew the stories of the conversations Logan had with Renee.

She felt heartbroken that the girls caught their father talking to their dead mother. She knew it was an uphill climb for not just him but for the girls. A buzz goes off on the intercom. An Amazon driver was at the front gate.

*Hello?"

"Hi, I've got a package for Jade Murphy." He says through the intercom. Jade smiles and opens the gate for the driver.

"What is it, Jade?" Madison asks with intrigue.

"Oh, I got something for you girls, and it's an early birthday present for your daddy. Oh, he's got a surprise in store for him tonight." She laughs in an evil, diabolical way. "First thing, we got a project to work on.

That night in his loft, when Logan slept for hours, Jade thought about the different traditions Logan did. She thought May 5th would not be a day of sadness again. The girls color a little picture of themselves and their mommy on light blue paper. Jade looks at it in awe.

"Oh, my God. Masterpiece, ladies. Masterpiece. This will make your daddy so happy. First, though, we'll play with your daddy when he gets home. Now, let's get dressed for tonight."

"Won't he be mad if we wear this?" McKenna asks. Jade gives McKenna her patent angelic smile.

"You leave him to me because why girls?" McKenna and Madison say simultaneously.

"Because boys will always bend to us, girls."

"You two are wise, and your teacher is pleased." Jade bows her head to them.

Tonight was game one of the NBA Finals between Jade's beloved L.A. Lakers against the Miami Heat. Knowing Logan's intense loathing for the Lakers, she was ready to see how much he loved her. Logan got home around eight, closed the front door, and released a massive sigh from working fifteen hours on a Saturday. He badly just wanted to collapse into bed from exhaustion and stress. That was until he heard a sudden cheer coming from the theater. Logan was so consumed with work he forgot the playoffs were going on. He sees the Crew, Jade, and the girls watching the game. To Logan's horror, he sees Jade and his daughters turn with beautiful smiles, wearing Lakers gear. He grabbed his chest, seeing McKenna wearing a gold shirt that said "Got rings?" with every year they won a championship. Madison was sporting a white Kobe Bryant jersey covered in rhinestones. He looks at Jade, who has a glowing smile on her face, which is the most sinister.

"What have you done? What the hell are my daughters wearing?" Clinton squints his eyes and points at Logan, asking Cortez.

"Who does Logan remind me of?" Sasha thinks when it hits her, snapping her fingers.

"Ooh, ooh. Mia Farrow at the end of "Rosemary's Baby" when she realizes she's got Satan's baby."

"YES!!!" Clinton and Cortez yell together, busting a gut. The only one who wasn't laughing was Logan. He looks at Jade with disdain, who keeps her beautiful smile locked on.

"I bought them Laker gear for the finals." Jade hugs them both tight while sitting on her lap in Logan's lounge chair. "Don't they look beautiful in purple & championship gold?" Logan closes his eyes.

"I can't look at this. Christ, it's too late. I can still see it with my eyes closed."

"C'mon Logan, even though it's the Lakers, they look adorable," Rosa states.

"Thank you, Rosa." Jade agrees.

"Jade, this is a Sonics household." Logan lays it on thick even though the Seattle Supersonics moved to Oklahoma City back in 2007.

"Oh?" She looks at the girls. "You see, girls, once upon a time, before you were born, your daddy had a basketball team here in Seattle. Then they moved away, and he still hasn't moved. The END!!!"

"OH SHUT UP, JADE !!!!" Clinton yells while everyone boo and starts throwing food at Jade. Cortez throws a handful of mini pretzels at her.

"You suck, Jade!!! Those were our Sonics, and it still hurts!!!"

"That was so low." Logan angrily looks at Jade. She has the girls move onto the couch, whispering between their ears.

"Watch this boy bend, girls." She turns to Logan. "C'mon, baby. Just accept it. Your three girls are Laker fans."

"Look at it this way, Logan, at least it's not Portland," Tony says.

"Amen!!!!!!!!" Everyone yells in agreement.

Logan couldn't take it anymore. He will pay Jade back for this, but then she gets out of Logan's recliner and approaches him. Right then, his mind is hypnotized by the fact that she is dressed as one of the "Laker Girls." She was sporting a purple Laker's tube top, gold boy shorts, and white Reeboks. Suddenly, he didn't mind the Lakers so much anymore. Jade lowers her head with her eyes sensually shooting at Logan.

"But baby, doesn't it matter how much I love them." She takes his hands. "I mean, seriously, look at your daughters." Logan looks at them, and he gets suckered in. They looked adorable together. "Then, look at me." Logan looked Jade up and down. He was officially done for—the power this woman had. The Crew watches Logan bend to the knee of Jade's power.

Maggie whispers to Rosa and Angie. "God, she's good."

"I'd rather watch this game more than the one on the screen." Angie whispers back.

"I warmed your seat for you, handsome," Jade says in her alluring voice that she can make any man submit in defeat, taking him to his chair. He sits down feeling relaxed until Jade slowly glides her body on his lap. He closes his eyes when a hardness forms in his pants. "Best seat in the house, huh?" Jade whispers in his ear.

"Indeed," Logan says, shuddering.

Jade gets a bowl of popcorn and starts feeding Logan as he watches his girls cheering. Jade notices Logan doesn't have a beer.

"Hey, Ant!!! My hard-working man here needs a beer." Tony tosses Jade a can and hands it to Logan in a soft, sultry tone. "Here you go, my man." She then kisses his cheek.

As usual, Logan was drugged by Jade's seduction. As he kept going back and forth from the game to her smooth, tanned, crossed legs, she was ready to give him the knockout punch: her smile. He shook his head in surrender while opening his beer and taking a big chug. "Alright, go, Lakers!!!" Jade kisses his cheek again in delight. Logan then quickly turned to look at her with a stern look. "But the second we get the Sonics back in Seattle, all bets are off!!!!"

"No problem!!! We will be a house divided." She looks deep into his eyes, caressing his cheek. "I've missed you so much." Jade looks around and notices everybody is not paying attention to the game but to them. They all smiled and comforted, knowing how happy this blonde ball of fire had made him. "We've all missed you."

McKenna and Madison jump off the couch and climb on his La-Z-Boy, hugging their father. He was covered with his three women. Logan looks around the theater, seeing the most important people in his life all together in the theater, watching him proudly. He raised his beer to them. They returned the favor and raised theirs to him. Jade looks down at Logan and kisses him. She then lays her head on his shoulder. He stayed in that position throughout the game. After the game ended, which the Lakers won by fourteen, Jade told everybody to go to the dock for part two of her surprise.

"What's going on?" Logan asks while Jade takes his hand.

"I knew seeing your daughters becoming Laker fans before your eyes was surprising enough, but I got something else for you to see tonight." Everyone gathers at the dock, waiting for Logan and Jade. He sees everybody surrounded by a brown box.

"Ok, guys, thanks for coming over and watching my boys kick some Miami ass, but that isn't the main reason why I invited you tonight. I know we're a month late, but tonight is a perfect night to do this since the rain finally stopped." She turns to Logan. "You told me this was Renee's favorite painting spot, so I thought this was the perfect place to do this."

Logan was baffled when Jade opened the box and pulled out a beautiful blue sky lantern with a picture written in crayon. The picture has the girls holding their mother's hand, with Renee wearing a yellow halo. His heart collapsed to the ground. Clinton, Cortez, and Tony hold the lantern up while Jade pulls out a zippo and lit the candle. They release it into the night sky. It was the most majestic sight as it slowly climbed toward the heavens. Jade goes to Logan, wrapping her arms around him.

"You didn't miss this; it just got delayed. I'll never let you and the kids forget this day again from now on." Logan lets out a slight chuckle. It was just so silly to him. How did something so difficult to do become so easy? Especially at the lengths this woman's heart could go.

"I love you, Jade." Logan choked on his words while a single tear ran down his cheek.

Jade's heart pulsated when those three words finally came out. She always knew he did, but when you hear it for the first time, nothing prepares you for that shock to your system. She turns around to look at his glazed, watery blue eyes. She smiles, holding Logan tight.

"I sure hope so because sky lanterns are illegal in Washington, and I'm committing a possible felony for you." Logan chuckles as she wipes away his tears. "From now on, you won't be locked in your room and drinking yourself into oblivion. You won't be punching mirrors anymore. Every May 5th, we will be on this dock together, lighting up for Renee."

Jade kisses Logan when both girls walk up to them. Logan picks up McKenna, and Jade picks up Madison. They walk towards the rest of the Crew, with all of them looking up with tears of their own. Clinton puts his arms around Logan's neck.

"She's pretty amazing, isn't she?" Clinton asks. Logan looks down at Jade.

"You hired a good one. She's a keeper."

The three of them chuckle together as they look up in the sky.

"Hey, that lantern was eco-friendly, right?" Clinton asks Jade.

"Please, I may have committed a felony, but I am fully committed to Mother Earth," Jade responds.

"That's my girl," Logan says, kissing her head.

CHAPTER 24

NEW INK

Ironically, Jade was reading an article in Cosmopolitan about the best luxury gifts for men. Logan was about to turn thirty-four, and Jade was lost on what to get him. Seriously, what do you get someone who can get anything he wants? Logan was in Boston for the next five days, and she was desperate to come up with something. Jade & Tonya were upstairs in the girl's bedroom playing beauty parlor. Madison was giving Jade a make-believe pedicure when she slammed shut the Cosmo and threw it across the room in frustration. From tech gadgets to portable charcoal grills to chain bracelets, nothing seemed appealing to her.

"OK, you three!!! I NEED HELP!!!!!! I have no idea what to get your father for his birthday."

"I know what to get him. How about a tie?" McKenna answers while she pretends to paint Jade's toes.

"I'll leave the tie for you girls. I gotta get him something special since this is his first birthday together. On the pros and cons of dating a billionaire, this is the ultimate con." Tonya quickly takes the cucumbers out of her eyes to give Jade the stink eye.

"Oh yeah, I'm bleeding for you." McKenna shows Tonya two different toy nail polishes. "Hmmm, I'll go with white."

"I know, get daddy flowers," Madison says when she looks at Jade's rose tattoo on her ankle while applying phony red polish on her toes.

"Well, sweetie, girls don't typically give boys...." Jade stops mid-sentence, looking at her rose tattoo when it hits her. "Oh my God, I got it!!!!! I love you, Maddi!!!" Jade bends down to kiss Madison's cheek.

"What do ya got?" Tonya wonders. Jade subconsciously tells Tonya to look at her bare ankle.

Tonya grabs her phone to write a text so the girls don't see.

Tonya text: "New ink??? For Logan???" Jade nods with a smile. "Can you heal by next week???"

Jade takes the phone and texts: "Oh yeah, the longest for me is usually a week, so I'll cut it close."

Tonya text: "Are you sure about this because isn't it the kiss of death getting a tattoo for your boyfriend?"

Jade text: "You know I don't buy into that bullshit." Tonya looks at her best friend for a while with a slight grin. "What???" Jade yells at Tonya.

Tonya texts: "Is Jade "Marriage is for suckers" Murphy changing her mind?"

Being so heavily independent, Jade never believed in marriage. That was until Logan and the kids were the game-changers. Jade looked at the girls pretending to paint Tonya's toes when she started reminiscing about the past six months. She thought about Logan and all his breakthroughs moving on from Renee. He even joined an online chat group for widows trying to cope with grief.

"WELL????" Tonya excitedly asks.

Jade text: "MAYBE. I just didn't see all of this coming, and you know it." Tonya looks shocked on her face while Jade keeps typing. "Look at them. I fell in love the second I met these two. Then, their father. He's the most caring, the most loving...She makes sure the girls didn't see what she was about to type, "and in bed, he's on nonstop porn mode." Tonya rolls her eyes as Jade laughs.

"For God's sake, you couldn't be serious for more than ten seconds," Tonya says as Jade snickers.

"Hey, I gave you ten and you're welcome." She laughs.

"Ok, here's the deal: you've got to get this done pronto. He'll be back from Boston in four days."

"I know. I'll have to hide it for a few days. You know, not see me… She grabs Tonya's phone and types "Naked."

"Any idea what and where?"

"Not what yet, but where? I'm thinking of a tramp stamp."

"What's a tramp stamp?" Madison asks.

Jade and Tonya nervously look at each other, figuring out what to say to the girls.

"Ummm. Well, you know Lady and the Tramp. Jade will give your daddy a stamp of Tramp on his hand." Tonya desperately tries to pull any idea out of thin air while Jade nods in agreement.

"I want a tramp stamp," McKenna yells out.

"Ok. Blow on our nails so they can dry," Jade tells McKenna. Tonya looks at Jade.

"We gotta find you a filter for that mouth."

"Yeah, good luck on that."

Tonya and Jade just smile at the girls. The next day, Jade goes to "Inked Up." It is a dingy-looking place near Chinatown, but Jade thinks the darker the place is, the better the artist since she already has four tattoos. The bell rings when she walks in. A tall, bald-headed artist named Max, completely covered in ink goes to her.

"Hi, can I help you?" Max asks.

"Maybe I'm just trying to understand what I want; thanks."

"Well, let me know if you need anything. Just ask for Max. Your name?"

"Jade and will do." She watches him head to the back when she notices his neck. "Wait, Max, can I see your neck?" Max had a

Bible verse tattoo on his neck. "There is no fear in love… 1 Peter 4:8". She knew right then what she wanted. "How long does a tramp stamp quote take, and how much?"

"35 to 45 minutes and $150."

"Done!!!"

"Right this way." They both walk to his station. "Go ahead and hop onto the bed."

Jade lies on her stomach and lowers her black mini down just enough to show a little crack. Max sits on his stool, puts on latex gloves, and prepares his equipment.

"Alright, Jade, tramp stamp, huh? For your boyfriend, girl-friend, husband, or wife?"

"Boyfriend." Max takes a swig of water. "I want him to have something to remind him when he's fucking me from behind." Max spits out his water and bursts into laughter. Jade grins. "Oooh, another home run there, Jade." Max grabs his tattoo machine when she turns to look at him. Jade was never superstitious, but a moment of doubt hit her. She started thinking that what Tonya said the day before about getting a tattoo of your boyfriend was the kiss of death. "Listen, can I ask you something serious?"

"You're going to have to. You cannot make me laugh that hard while I'm inking you." Max warns her, preparing his ink gun.

"Ok, fair enough. Is this the right thing to do? I've always heard that getting inked for your partner before marriage is bad luck. What do you think?"

Max has had this question thrown at him many times. He puts down his ink gun and rolls his stool to look into Jade's eyes. "Do you mind if I talk to you straight forward between the eyes?" Jade nods. "My pussy resume went on forever. I fucked around for years because I was Mr. Anti-commitment. That tattoo you saw on my neck was my very first one. I met her at a Slipknot concert ten years ago. Everything just quit on me. The lust, the conquest, just dis-appeared because of her. I needed that woman forever. Ten years later, we're still married with a son. Remember that verse's two most important words, "No fear." I wanted this on my neck to tell people who walk behind me while holding Deidre's hand that I'm not afraid anymore."

Jade smiles at Max for putting her mind at ease. She lays back on her stomach. "Zap away, Maxwell."

"Wait, what kind of quote do you want?" He asks.

"Something that describes Logan and I. Also, just like your neck, I want people to see it behind me." She smiles, thinking of the most perfect quote.

Three days later, Jade is in her bathroom, still admiring her new tattoo. She is excited and nervous simultaneously, knowing Logan is coming home in just a few hours but trying to find ways not to see her naked until his birthday. Clinton knocks on the bedroom door.

"Jade???"

"Bathroom, Clinton, and I'm decent."

Clinton enters and sees Jade in Logan's college hoodie and sweatpants, which are giant on her. It even covered up her bare feet.

"Well, I'll be damned; you can dress casually."

"Don't remind me. I feel dirty wearing this." Clinton chuckles when he hands Jade a jar of tattoo balm.

"Here, try this on. Maggie and I got matching tattoos in Mexico two years ago, and this stuff was perfect." Jade looks at the jar.

"Awesome. Thanks." She opens the jar. "Do you want to do me the honors? Rosa and Angie went toy shopping with M&M for the warehouse, so I need someone to put it on."

"Alright." Clinton smiles, looking at the quote. He takes a couple of fingers full of the ointment and starts tapping it onto her skin.

"Ohh, that's nice," Jade says seductively.

"Ok. I'm out of here. Goodbye." Jade giggles while grabbing Clinton.

"You get back here. I'm messing with you." Clinton contin-ues moisturizing Jade's back. She notices his nod from the mirror, admiring it. "So, do you think he'll love it?"

"That quote fits you both perfectly." Clinton agrees. Jade looked deep into the mirror at Clinton's reflection.

"You knew right away, didn't you?"

"About what, sweetie?" Clinton asks.

"Logan and I. Did you know we would go this far right away?"

"Not quite." He finishes applying the ointment on her tattoo and heads to the sink to wash his hands. "It was Opening Day; before you ask, it wasn't before the game. Christ, I'll never get that image out of my head." Jade snickers. "It was during the game." Clinton dries his hands and leans against the sink, being face to face with Jade. "Logan hasn't missed a Mariners home opener in twenty-two years, and that boy was never late for one until you came along. I don't think he paid an ounce of attention to that game. I watched him like a hawk; he could only look at you. When you were with the girls, taking selfies with all of us. The last thing on Logan's mind was baseball that night. Seeing you both on that bathroom floor in his office put me over the top with you two when you held him in his darkest state. Do you remember when you stayed with us Christmas night, you walked past that guest room?"

"Yeah. It looked like a nursery for a baby boy. I thought you two didn't have children."

"We don't, but at one point, Maggie and I had a son. We decked that room out, and I was so excited because I always wanted a son. A couple of weeks before Maggie was due, she slipped in the kitchen and fell on her stomach, and we lost him."

Jade gasps, covering her mouth. "Oh, my God!!! Clinton, I'm so sorry!!!" He painfully exhales, reminiscing like it was yesterday.

"For two weeks straight, Maggie would lay on my lap, and I just held her. Stroking her blonde head like you did with Logan in that bathroom." Clinton starts to choke up. He grabs Jade's shoulders and stares down deep into her eyes. "For years, Jade, I have feared losing another son. That was until you came along. When you told me you would care for him in that bathroom, I stopped being afraid." Jade sees a tear come down Clinton's cheek. She pulls Clinton in and holds him tight.

"God, it just hit me what a dwarf I am surrounded by all you giants." Clinton bursts into laughter, knowing Jade can brighten up any dark situation. Jade looks up at his face, wiping his tears away. "You've all cried enough for him. It's going to stop because you're staring at his guardian angel. Every time he goes down, I will make damn sure he's lifted right back up."

Clinton smiles down at Jade, gazing into her eyes. He pulls her into him again and hugs her tight. "I thank God every day you've come into our lives."

Jade smiles, closing her eyes: "That makes two of us, big daddy." Jade then realized she couldn't remember the last time her father held her like Clinton did. He started to loosen up on her. "Wait, can you just hang on to me a little longer?" Knowing the situation with Jade's parents, the closest thing he had to a child was Tonya. Clinton was happy to hold her like a daughter.

"As long as you want, sweetheart." He whispers.

Jade and Clinton closed their eyes as they held each other tighter, feeling the bond they never got to have.

Around 8:30, Logan was home from Boston to a dark home. He dropped his bag when Jade yelled out.

"Baby! I'm in the kitchen!!!"

Memories of Opening Day enter Logan's head. He starts skipping towards the kitchen, hoping to see Jade in nothing but heels. However, he sees her barefoot, her hair in a bun, wearing his purple Washington U hoodie and sweatpants. It wasn't leather, a little skirt, or heels, but she looked just as gorgeous. He loved the fact she was wearing his clothes. What he loved was to get them off of her.

"Hey, you," Logan says with glee.

Logan walked towards Jade and kissed her passionately. She knew what he wanted, and it was killing her, but she didn't want to take any chances of him seeing her tattoo. Logan kisses her neck. Jade realizes her plan of dressing down isn't working. Especially with the animalistic look he was giving her, so she pulled up Plan B.

"I missed you so much. Upstairs, NOW!!!! Or right here on the island will work, too." Jade pushes Logan away.

"Well, there's a little problem, sport. Alabama is here." Logan looked confused. "That's what I call my time of the month."

Logan started to deflate everywhere, especially down there. "Ohh, alright. Do you just want to go to bed?" Jade pretends to get emotional and upset by biting her lip.

"Bed? Oh, I see, so you just got back from Beantown, expecting to get some Jade action, but you can't because the Crimson Tide is attacking me. Now, suddenly, you want to get some sleep. No, "Let's watch a movie together, Jade," or "Sweetheart, let me rub your feet because you feel bloated and repulsive, which I AM BY THE WAY!!!!!" Jade screeches out when Logan panics, watching her unravel, feeling like a complete jerk.

"Jade, Jade!!! I'm so sorry. I didn't mean anything like that. Come here." He pulls her in for a hug. She sucks in her lip, trying to hold her laughter while enjoying screwing with him. "I missed you so much." Logan then stroked his hand, where the tattoo was still very tender. She takes in a deep breath, holding in the sting, and silently mouths, "FUCK!!!!"

"I missed you too," she says, barely able to utter the words. She exhales as the sting starts to fade.

CHAPTER 25

IT'S LOGAN'S BIRTHDAY; WHAT DID HE GET YOU?

Logan had a huge smile while sleeping soundly on the morning of his birthday when suddenly, he was awakened by a very familiar feeling and sight. That blonde hair repeatedly bobbed, giving him his "birthday wake-up call." Jade notices his warm stare on him. She pulled her mouth off of him and gave her man her patent glow. "Happy birthday, sweetie." She continues to give the greatest start to any man's birthday. Logan melts in relaxation, feeling Jade's warm gullet.

"SHIT!!!" He tightens his voice and slams his eyes shut, feeling the beautiful heaven Jade was giving him, but what he wanted deep down was just to hold his woman. "Jade, I'm going to say the stupidest thing I will say now and for the rest of my life. Please stop and get over here." Jade looks at him like he's gone insane.

"You want to cuddle? What makes you think I'm that kind of girl?" Jade shrugs her shoulders. "It is your birthday, though."

Jade gets off of Logan and lies in his arms. He starts to smooth Jade's back when he brushes his hand where the tattoo is. Jade smiles, feeling the anticipation of him seeing it for the first time. All of a sudden, Logan pinched Jade's ass.

"Ahhhh, Logan!"

"Good, you're still real." Jade giggles.

"I'm as real as my tits are, baby."

After showering, Jade gets dressed and heads downstairs when she hears Skee Lo's "I Wish" in the kitchen. She sees Logan and Tony making breakfast for the Crew and the kids. Jade couldn't help but laugh watching Logan's horrible dancing and lip-syncing with Tony. Clinton starts recording them dancing on his phone.

"What are you doing, Clinton?" Angie asks.

"I'm making a YouTube page and titling it "White People Embarrassing Themselves." Clinton answers, which got laughter going through the entire kitchen.

Logan quickly spots Jade. She sees him in a red dress shirt, tight jeans, and black high tops. Jade went from laughing at Logan to wanting to rip that shirt off and trouncing him. He sees her and starts dancing in front of her.

"Guys, this ain't Rogue. There are children present." Cortez pleads while trying to cover the kids' eyes. They both raise their eyebrows and grin, thinking back to that night.

"Hey, homeboy, I need to talk to you for a second. I've got a problem." Jade takes Logan to the garage, who's immediately concerned.

"What's wrong?" He asks worriedly.

Jade pulls Logan and crashes her lips into his. She untucks his shirt and strokes her hands across his back. A few seconds later, Logan's phone started ringing from his back pocket. Jade grabs it, sees it's Sasha, and answers it.

"Hello, this is Logan's phone. He's about to fuck his girlfriend hard, so please leave a message, beep!!!"

Logan snatches the phone as Jade starts to suck his neck. "Hey Sasha, what's up?"

"First of all, happy birthday. Second, eww. Third, did you forget your interview with Maria Betellimo on Fox Business is in two hours, and then you've got three more meetings piled up after that?" Sasha goes through his agenda.

"Oh God, don't remind me. I'll be there in an hour." Logan hangs up.

"Whoa, what is this I'm hearing? My baby is going to be on Fox Business. Why didn't you tell me?"

"I just didn't think about it. I could care less about being on T.V. I'm doing it for Horizon. Especially since I dug it out of a hole this month, the stock is flying, and I finalized the expansion for Canada and Europe."

"Don't take this badly, but I love what a dullard you are when it comes to your fame."

Jade didn't know that he felt the same way about his birthday. Especially this one, and he was going to show her. After breakfast, Logan asks Jade, Angie, and Rosa to meet in the bedroom. The three gathered, sitting on the edge of the bed.

"What's this all about, Logan?" Rosa asks. Logan whips out his American Express Centurion Card. One of the most challenging credit cards to receive.

"I'm giving you all the day off. You three are going to take this and get facials, massages, and most of all", he walks towards Jade's closet, "I want this filled." He hands the card to Rosa, who does the sign of the cross, staring at the Holy Grail of credit cards. She hands it to Angie.

"Oh, mi Dios misericordioso!!!" Translation: "Oh my gracious God!!!" She says.

"I want you girls to splurge on yourselves and…" Jade interrupts and raises her hand. "Ohhh, Ohhh, Ohhh…"

"Yes, Jade."

"Can I invite Tonya and Sasha?" She pleads.

"Tonya, yes. Sasha, no. I need her today, so pick her up something nice. Before you ask, there is no limit you can spend, so go nuts."

Rosa and Angie jump off the bed and hug Logan tight.

"Thank you so much, Logan. Happy birthday." Angie screams.

"Of course." The three of them look at Jade, who is glued to the credit card. "What's up, Jade?"

Jade shakes her head. "It's your birthday, and you're spoiling us with shopping, massages, and facials. I just can't comprehend you."

"It's my gift to myself. I want to spoil the people I love for my birthday."

Jade could not grasp how modest one person could be. She felt Logan deserved more than just a tattoo. Even though threesomes were a dealbreaker, Jade knew Logan had to meet "the other girl."

Madison & McKenna run into the bedroom.

"Dad, we're going to be late for school," McKenna warns Logan.

"Okay." He turns to Jade. "Have fun, babe." Logan and the girls kiss Jade, Rosa, and Angie goodbye.

"Bye, guys. Have a good day." Jade yells out.

Logan and the girls head down the stairs when he gets a notification on his phone that there is a Mariners/Royals afternoon game. He gets an idea when he sees Clinton, Cortez, and Tony together waiting by the door.

"You guys ready?" Clinton asks.

"Actually, I was wondering, do you guys want to take the girls to the Mariners game and use my suite?"

The three of them look at each other in shock.

"Hell yeah. The girls are ditching school?" Cortez asks.

"Yeah. They should be off for the summer anyway if it wasn't for those snow days. Girls, I declare your school year is over!!!"

"Really, Daddy? Can we go to the game?" McKenna asks, filled with excitement.

"Yes, angel, it's my birthday, and I want my family to enjoy themselves today. On the other hand,

I have to go to work and be on TV, so kiss Daddy. I'll see you, girls, later today."

"Bye, Daddy. Happy Birthday."

"I love you, birthday boy!!!" Madison says.

Logan kisses and hugs both girls.

"Thanks, son." Clinton hugs his godson. "How do you feel this year?"

"It's been a long time since I looked forward to this day. I'm so pumped up right now."

"Does a certain short, blonde-haired L.A. girl who's banging you royally have anything to do with that?" Tony asks while Clinton rolls his eyes, not expecting less from him

"There's an instinct possibility that she has something to do with it," Logan answers.

As Logan heads to the front door, Jade, Angie, and Rosa head down the stairs.

"Alright, guys. Enjoy today. I know I will."

Everybody except Jade says "Happy Birthday" as she seductively mouths it. Logan blows her a kiss as he leaves. He stops after he opens the door. At that moment, he realized what he wanted for his birthday: the world to see his happiness. He slams the door and turns to look at his family.

"You know, I want to take a selfie with my family and post it."

Everybody looked at each other, surprised. Logan was embracing social media.

"Seriously? You haven't been on Facebook in years." Tony says.

"I know, but I'm adjusting." He says, staring directly at Jade. "C'mon guys, get together." Logan didn't want to brag about his wealth or share his political opinions. He wanted to show off his loved ones and those who stood by him through his worst times. Right now, they were standing by him at his best. The Crew, Madison, and McKenna, cram with Jade far from Logan. "Jade, what are you doing over there?" He asks.

"I didn't know where you wanted me." Jade wondered, unsure if he wanted everyone to know about their relationship.

"No, you're right next to me." Jade smiles as she walks towards Logan. She stands next to them while they are all squeezed together. "Okay, all together. 1,2,3" Click. Everybody leaves, but Logan pulls Jade's shirt back to him. "You're not going anywhere. Cortez, can you take this?" Logan hands Cortez his phone.

"What are you doing?" She asks worriedly if he knows what he is doing. Logan dips Jade.

"Like I said, I give on my birthday." Logan kisses her as Cortez takes several pics.

"Oh my God, you're crazy," Jade tells him.

"Your fault."

"Will you please get the hell out of here?" Jade orders him.

"One more." Jade rolls her eyes at the fact Logan won't leave. "Come here, girls." Logan squats down as the girls kiss their daddy's cheek. Cortez starts snapping.

"Jade, get in with them," Clinton suggests.

"No, it should be the three of them." She says, still feeling conflicted. That was when she read the sincerity in his eyes.

"Jade, I said, "Come here, girls.""

Logan stands, reaching out his hand. Jade couldn't believe it. He was going public with their relationship. She knew the media would start digging into her life and mostly her past, which she hadn't entirely told Logan about. The thing was, she was so in love with him. Jade grabs Logan's face and kisses him, with the girls covering their eyes as Cortez snaps away.

"Bro, that belongs on your Instagram cover," Cortez says, returning Logan's phone.

"OK, I swear I'm leaving. Have a great day." Logan hurries out the door.

Jade's heart was racing. Everyone is going to find out that she is with billionaire tycoon Logan Brodie. She started to worry that he would regret this. Was he level-headed to say that he has moved on? Jade runs outside to catch him.

"Wait, are you sure you're okay with this? Us, being out there for everyone to see. You're opening Pandora's Box here." Logan brushes a strand of hair away from her face, beaming his spell-bound eyes to her's.

"You're not going to be a hidden figure in my life, Jade. I love you, and I want everyone to know who I'm in love with. Who is this Jade Murphy girl who gave Logan Brodie his resurgence? Who is this girl that makes him feel invincible? Who is this miracle worker who taught him to love again?" Jade swallows hard, knowing how honest he is. "If you're uncomfortable, I won't post..." Jade places her two fingers on his lips.

"No. I'm not. I want people to know I'm with the man who makes me feel so beautiful and loves his girl unconditionally." She points at Mt. Rainier in the distance. "I want to climb to the top of that thing and scream, "I'm in love with Logan Brodie!!!" Except posting it would be much less dangerous, more people would hear it, and I don't want that thing to erupt before I get to use this bad boy." She whips out the AmEx card while Logan cracks up laughing. He leans back on the Mustang, pulls Jade, and consumes her mouth passionately. He slips his hand under her denim mini, feeling her thong. For both their sake, she forces herself away from his mouth. "OK, get out of here, go on TV, and don't embarrass me in front of Maria Betellimo since you insist on telling everybody I'm with you."

"I promise nothing." He states.

He kisses Jade one more time before driving off to work. Once Logan got to the office, he was prepped for his interview with Fox

News Business financial journalist Maria Betellimoto to talk about Horizon and how their stock is at a record high. Logan despised being on TV. Fame and Logan never clicked together, but he knew it was best for business by doing it. He was going through the pictures from the morning. He couldn't stop smiling until that last one with him, Jade, and the girls. It took his breath away because he finally didn't look back and dwell on his past.

The rush of pride went through him because he looked into his future and was excited about it. Suddenly, a Fox producer from New York says in his earpiece.

"Two minutes, Mr. Brodie."

"Thank you. Also, it's Logan, please." He smiles, still looking at his phone.

"I apologize, Logan." The producer corrects herself.

Logan went onto his Instagram page. He stared at the last one he posted with him and Renee standing in front of the Trevi fountain in Rome. He remembered the both of them throwing a coin behind their backs, wishing her cancer would disappear. Before he could let any despair hit him, he took a deep breath and immediately posted the pictures from the morning. With a smile, he shared it and tagged Jade in them with the caption, "I'm back on track. Especially with these guiding lights." It was out there, and it was done. He then got a text from Jade.

Jade texts: "Have fun talking to Maria. I can't wait to be in bed with a T.V. star. Love you!!!"

"One minute, Logan." The producer informs him. Sasha comes toward Logan with a shot glass. "Here's your medicine from Dr. Jose Quervo."

Logan shoots the tequila. "Gracias" barely gets the words out as his mouth is on fire.

"Better?" She asks

"Yeah, my pussy's wet." Logan chuckles. Sasha closes her eyes, knowing exactly where he would get that from.

"Oh God, Jade." She mutters, knowing he is speaking in Jade talk.

Logan continues to laugh when he gets another text from Jade. It was a screenshot of her Facebook cover. Her profile cover was of them with the girls, and her status changed to "In a relationship." An avalanche of emotion hit Logan hard when the producer was counting down until he got in the air. At that second, Logan knew he was having the most fantastic birthday of his life, and it was only nine a.m. Logan looks at Jade before he puts his phone down when he hears Maria Bartiromo's voice.

"Now we are joined by Logan Brodie, CEO of Horizon Logistics. One of the youngest CEOs who just turned 34 today. Thank you for joining us, and happy birthday."

"Thank you, Maria. I'm very happy to be here." Logan says with a genuine beam on his face.

CHAPTER 26

JADE MURPHY: UNLEASHED

Jade, Angie, Rosa, and Tonya celebrated Logan's birthday with massages, facials, and mani-pedis. Before their shopping spree, they head to a rooftop bar overlooking Puget Sound called "The Nest." After an hour and a half and four rounds of cocktails, Jade sat by herself while the rest used the ladies' room. She went through her phone, which blew up throughout the morning with texts, calls, and notifications.

Brandy's voicemail: "You're dating THE Logan Brodie!!!! The billionaire. I hate you so much. Call me later; love you bitch!!!!"

Laura's voicemail: "OH MY GOD!!!! He is so gorgeous, and he's rich. YOU ARE MY HERO!!!! Call me soon."

Athena text: I am so happy for you, Jade. Cody and I miss you so much.

Jade then noticed a voicemail from an unknown number. After a long pause, she hears a voice.

"Hello, Myrtle."

Only one person would ever call Jade by her birth name: her mother. After getting emancipated from her parents, she legally changed her name. Jade's stomach turned from the sound of her voice. She quickly hung up the voicemail and erased it, immediately blocking the phone number. She took a deep breath and downed the last of her martini. She was determined not to let her mother ruin her day, especially on Logan's birthday.

"I just can't let go of my phone. Logan is on Instagram. Do you know how adorable you two are?" Rosa says, coming out of the bathroom.

"Yup. My plan is working. I marry him, kill him in his sleep, fire you all, take over his empire, have myself cloned and form an army of Jades, and THEN!!!!" In a soft tone, staring at Rosa and Angie. "The world." Jade lets out a maniacal laugh. The girls stay silent. Rosa looks at her like a crazy woman while trying to hold her laughter. A few seconds later, Rosa loses it, bursting into tears. Angie and Tonya cover their faces as the tears roll down their cheeks. Jade tries hard to compose herself. "I knew you would break first. I just knew it."

"C'mon Jade, please, no bullshit. How do you feel?" Angie asks. Jade smiles at her.

"To be perfectly honest, I know we're going to have a spotlight on us now and everybody is going to want the skinny of the new dish in his life, but all I know is I'm dating "the kindest, the most wonderful, and beautiful man" Logan Brodie. This craving for him builds up all the time. It's a constant craving."

"That's why you two are made for each other. I mean, what you did for him and the girls to remember Renee. What girlfriends would do that?" Tonya informs her.

"I had to, T. When I saw him that day, covered in blood and looking like the loneliest person alive. Seeing this gentle soul suffering killed me. I wanted to give him something back to him and Renee." The girls give Jade an admired glance. "Normally, I wouldn't ask this, but do you think Renee would approve of me?"

Rosa and Angie stare at each other with a sentimental look. Angie opens up.

"Jade, Renee was one of my best friends, and I know she's up there looking down saying "This girl knows how to do it. Taking care of my children and loving Logan how he should be loved." I know she would approve of you."

Jade's face brightened hearing what Angie said. She never cared about anyone's opinion of her, but Renee was an exception to her. Their waitress, Wendy, comes to the table.

"Is there anything else I can get you, ladies?" She asks.

"I think we're great," Rosa states.

"Absolutely!!!" Jade whips out Logan's card. "Let's shop until this card drops." Jade hands the card to Wendy. "There you are, love."

"Alright, I'll be right back with your check."

Wendy was heading back to the bar, two tables down when a man in a stylish Charles Tyrwhitt suit with slicked black hair yelled for her.

"You. Over here now." He barks at her.

Wendy walks over nervously, looking at his deadpan eyes and two friends wearing similar stylish suits. These were successful businessmen who didn't give a damn about anything or anybody that didn't meet their credentials: wealth, power, entitlement. Of course, a regular waitress was an insect to them.

"How long do I have to wait for another fucking drink? Shit, you're slow." Jade and the girls noticed the commotion going on.

"I'm, I'm so sorry, sir. What can..." Wendy stammers before he cuts her off, sticking his finger out for Wendy to shut up. He arrogantly leers at her.

"First of all, this job must be very difficult for you since you've got that extra weight on you, and I know you've got a learning disability since this glass has been empty for five minutes and hasn't been replaced with a full one. That's usually the universal sign to get me another one. Don't you think, Wendy?" He pulls her name badge, brushing his finger against her right breast.

"Yes, I'll... I'll be right back." Wendy bites her lip in embarrassment and humiliation. She heads back to the bar, trying to hold back her tears. One of her fellow waitresses patted her on the back to console her. Jade locked her eyes on Wendy, absorbing her pain into her, which was gasoline to Jade. She then eyes the man and his buddies laughing their asses off. She knew his type. Women were nothing to him. Just to order around, belittle, wet his dick with and then toss them out like toilet paper. The girls watched in horror, feeling so bad for Wendy.

"What an asshole," Angie says under her breath in anger.

Jade gets out of her seat, lifts her head, and closes her eyes to meditate. A rush of pure rage rises in her like the Phoenix. She lets out a small moan before opening her eyes with a slight grin. Jade power struts towards their table in a leopard button-down blouse, tiny black shorts, and chunky leopard heels. Her hips sway repeatedly to let everyone know this leopard is the predator.

"Jade, what are you doing?" Rosa asks. Tonya immediately whispers, warning her.

"Rosa, Rosa, don't talk to her. You're about to see a man get castrated minus the knife."

Jade was about ten feet away, closing in towards the table. Her grin never left her face, knowing these guys hadn't realized they had opened their portal to hell. Godzilla had his atomic breath. Well, so did Jade. Right before she got to the table, she glanced at Wendy behind the bar, who had tears running down her cheek. She gave her a nod that told her, "I've got this." She leans her arm on the back of the guy's chair.

"Hello." She says flirtatiously.

"Hey, baby." The man looks at Jade with immediate lust.

"Hey, baby? Whoa, is that pickup line for sale because that is an antique?" Jade chuckles. "I know which line was next, and yes, it hurt a lot falling from heaven." Jade chuckles harder and louder for everybody to hear. Rosa and Angie look at Tonya with a questionable glance while Tonya covers her mouth, waiting for the pain that is coming. "Listen, just out of curiosity, when you slimed your way out of your mother's cunt, how long did it take her to turn pro-choice after seeing you for the first time? What five, ten seconds?" Her evil stance was glued to the drunken man's eyes, which were filling up with rage. "Did she also tell you, "Son, you can be anything you want to be? "I think a soulless sack of dog shit wasn't what she had in mind."

The girls and everybody else who overheard were shocked—especially the ladies at the following table. One of them smiled in delight while overhearing.

"Bitch, go…" The man snaps before Jade sticks out her finger precisely like he did to Wendy.

"Hold on there, um, what's your name?" Before he could open his mouth, Jade stopped him. "I'm just kidding. I could give a rat's ass, thimble dick." Jade leans closer to him. "You're successful because I see a Rolex, a gold money clip," Jade sees Wendy with his drink on her tray. "What is he drinking, Wendy?"

"Umm, Macallan on the rocks." She informs Jade nervously.

"Oh, there must be some mistake. Only men drink that." Jade takes the glass of scotch and downs it, exhaling hard from the burn in her throat, slamming the glass down hard on the table. "Where was I? Oh yes, you are a very powerful figure in your own mind, but you know deep down in your black heart that YOU ARE A ZILCH!!!" The man's nostrils flared, giving Jade a smug look.

"Do you know who the hell I…" Jade interrupts again.

"Ahhhhh, how adorable." She looks at her table. "Hey girls, he's trying so hard. Just precious. I'm the bitch who's getting in your face in front of your little buddies who are smart enough not to open their fucking mouths to chime in." Jade looks at the man's friends. "I applaud you on that aspect, boys, but here's a tip, get rid of this shit stain which has a severe case of arrested emotional development and a fixation on trying to act superior to everyone else." Jade looks back at the man. "The fact that you would insult this woman who busts her ass serving you, me, and everybody here for no apparent reason whatsoever but just the fact you feel you can, makes me wish you get into your car and smash head first into a pole, so I can visit you in the hospital and hopefully run into your mother so I can slap the bitch silly and tell her "Out of millions of sperm, this piece of shit had to hit your worthless egg." A long silence echoes throughout while the girls glare in disbelief. The Man gives Jade a death stare.

"If you think I give a damn what you think…" Jade looks at her watch, cutting him off once again.

"Oh wow, I don't have the time or the crayons to help you figure this out since third grade was obviously your senior year, so I'll leave you saying something in Russian." Jade grabs a White Russian from the following table and pours it on the man's head. "Pozzhe mudak!!! Translation: "Later, asshole" Sorry ladies, Wendy, make sure you put that on my tab and give these ladies doubles." The women at the table look at Jade like a superhero.

"Yes, ma'am," Wendy says with so much glee.

Jade struts back to her table. A mixture of anger and satisfaction, without a hint of regret, fills her. She wants to prove a point that if you don't live by "the Golden Rule," Jade Murphy will end you. Angie, Tonya, and Rosa look at Jade with aspiration and pride, calling her their friend.

"I think we should give Wendy a cash tip. She did a good job, don't you think, girls?" Angie looks at Rosa and Tonya with a slight smirk.

"I got it, Jade." Angie pulls a hundred out of her purse.

"Me too." Rosa also pulls a hundred as well.

Tonya stares proudly at Jade, pulling out her hundred. Jade looks at the three one-hundred dollar bills on the table. A feeling of pride hits her, seeing her sisters helping another one in need. She throws her hundred onto the table. Jade gets a pen from her purse and writes on each bill. Wendy comes back with a new check and hands it to Jade.

"Here you are." As Jade grabs the bill, Wendy puts her hand on hers. "Thank you so much for that." She choked on her words. Jade looks back, expressing tenderness and patting Wendy's hand.

"It was my pleasure, beautiful."

Jade looks at Logan's card and starts to sign her name. She wrote "Jade" and paused before she started to write the "M." Curiosity hit her on just what it would like. She took a deep breath when she wrote the cursive "B" and then finished it with "Brodie." Jade's heart raced when she saw the name "Jade Brodie." The only thought in her head was, "I can get used to that."

"Are you girls ready?" Rosa asks while Jade puts the $400 cash in the bill.

"Yeah, let's fill up our closets," Jade replies.

The four of them look back at the drunken man cleaning up as he stares down at Jade. All four promptly flip him off, heading towards the elevators. Wendy goes and gets the bill that was left on the table. Upon opening it, she sees four crisp one hundred dollar bills with a considerable word written on Benjamin Franklin's forehead. "Never. Take. Shit. Again!!!" Wendy smiled as Jade's advice soaked into her. She runs to the elevator before it closes on the girls.

"I won't, Mrs. Brodie!!!! Thank you again!!!" Wendy yells out before the elevator doors close.

Jade's eyes went wide, and her heart thumped hearing that name out loud for the first time. Angie, Rosa, and Tonya slowly look at Jade with a mystified look.

"Mrs. Brodie?" Angie asks, confused. Jade shrugs her shoulders.

"I guess she must have assumed I was married to Logan since we're using his card. Weird, huh?"

After getting out of the elevator, they headed back to the car. Jade gets a ping on her phone. She looks to see a text from Tonya.

Tonya: "You are so full of shit. You did that on purpose."

Jade turns around to see Tonya in front of the elevator with a wide grin on her face. Jade shrugged her shoulders in a "You got me" kind of a way. Tonya walks toward Jade, wrapping her arm around her heading to the car. She felt so proud of her sister, who had faced many obstacles and heartache. She saw her on top of the world in love, something she thought she would never experience again.

Seattle was a different fashion world compared to L.A. and Vegas. Jade went to many different boutiques, none of which caught her style. Normally, she would shop online, but since she was armed with the mother of all credit cards and a green light to spend as much as she wanted, she knew she had to go old school, the Mall. For a half hour, Jade was like a bloodhound trying to find the right place until she found the one that understood her taste, Windsor. She gulped hard, clutching her chest, kneeling to one knee with her hands together.

"Oh heavenly Lord who brought us the stars, the oceans, the Lakers, and tequila. You have shown me the way, and now you have shown me the light." Angie and Rosa try not to laugh as Tonya shakes her head in embarrassment. "I give praise. Amen." She gets off the ground. "Ok, ladies, here we go."

A sales lady named Devin welcomed the girls as they walked in.

"Hello, ladies. Can I help you?" Devin asks the girls.

"Why yes, you can, love." Jade pulls out $200 and hands Devin her phone. "If you can be a blooming rose and connect my phone to your store's stereo, press play on it, and accept that $200, that would be just keen."

"You got it." Devin gives Jade a glowing smile.

Jade puts her head down and folds her hands in front of her waist. The girls wonder why they're waiting and why Jade looks like she's meditating in front of Windsor.

"Uhh, are we going to shop or what?" Angie asks anxiously. Jade quietly sushes her.

"Not just yet, dear Angela. You'll know when." The girls wait twenty seconds when Roy Orbison's "Oh, Pretty Woman" plays throughout the store. They grin and look at each other. "Now, we can shop."

"Lead the way, Vivian," Tonya tells Jade.

"OK, Tonya. You're on dress duty. You know my criteria, trampy. Rosa, shoes. Four inches and skanky. Angie, skirts, and shorts. Micro and slutty."

"We're on it. Wait, where are you going to be?" Angie asks.

"It's Logan's birthday. I'm going after the leather." She tells the girls, raising her eyebrows.

For three hours, the four made a huge dent on Windsor's inventory for that day. They followed Logan's birthday orders and filled up Jade's closet. While Jade took an armful of dresses to the counter, she saw Rosa eyeing a red silky cocktail mini dress. She walks behind her.

"Hey sexy, are you going to get it?" Jade asks.

"Nah!!!

"Why not? You'll look so smoking in it."

"I'm just dreaming. I can't wear this. I'm approaching 45." Jade has a blank look and then shrugs.

"And? Do you know what 45 is? It's after 44 and before 46. That's all. Now, do me a favor and put it on."

"Ok." Rosa goes into the dressing room with the dress. Jade whispers to the girls.

"Angie, Tonya, come here. Devin, you too." All three girls go to Jade. "We need help. A woman in that dressing room gave me that "I'm over 40, and I can't be hot anymore" bullshit excuse, so I need you three to be ready for her to blow us away."

"Oh God, it's because of her husband. Alex likes her dresses conservatively."

"Oh???" Jade puts her hands on her hips and slowly looks at her with sinister intended eyes. Angie knew she opened the wrong door.

"I've said too much, haven't I." Angie covers her mouth, seeing her older sister exit the dressing room. She didn't have to act blown away. "Oh, my God!!!"

All three girls look at Rosa's radiant smile. She knew deep down how beautiful she looked but couldn't get it.

"Ok, we need heels to complete her. STAT!!!"

"Jade!!! Jade!!! Wait." Rosa pleads with her. "There's no way in hell Alex would let me out the front door if I went out in this." Jade walks toward Rosa, taking her hands and locking her eyes onto hers.

"I hope why is because he's fucking you against the front door." Rosa closes her eyes, shaking her head. "If that's not the case, then he's got a major problem because you are stunning in that dress, and you've got a major problem because your husband is an insecure tool. You're going to take that dress off and throw it into your pile, and you will wear that dress on a Saturday night either with him or with me because at least I'll know I'll be with a hot ass bitch while Alex beats himself off that night missing an opportunity to be with you. You didn't protect your little sister and survive the mean streets of Chicago's southside for a man to tell you that you can't wear a dress because you're showing too much leg. One more thing, I NEVER, EVER want you to mention your age in my presence ever again because age doesn't mean shit because you are Rosa Lopez, and Rosa Lopez can do anything she wants whenever she wants. Now, turn around." Rosa and Jade turn to look at each other in the mirror. She holds Rosa's shoulders. "There's one woman you have inspired in this mirror, and she's right behind you. You need to inspire the other one."

That last line hit Rosa hard. Her lips tightened with a golf ball-sized lump in her throat. She turned to look Jade in the face.

"Thank you, Jade." Rosa runs back to the dressing room to change when she spots a white Micro mini and snatches it without thinking twice. "I'll take this too."

Jade turns to see Angie, Tonya, Devin, and other female customers staring at her. She puts her arms behind her back.

"So ladies, the moral is if your man can't handle you wearing something provocative, slinky, or racy because they're preoccupied with another man's thoughts, then they need to look into that tiny dick syndrome they obviously have because the only thought that should be running in their head is finding a secluded place because there's no way I'm getting her home to the bedroom, and I will take the risk getting arrested for public indecency with a huge smile on his face while his woman is riding his cock in the driver's seat. I'm Jade Murphy, and I'm right as usual."

The women in the store started to clap while one was shooting her boyfriend, an evil eye who promptly put his head down. For the next fifteen minutes, the girls were starting to wind down and about to check out when Tonya spotted the dress of dresses.

"J!!!! Get over here, quick!!!!" She yells out—Jade races across the store.

"What do you got for me?" Tonya flashed the dress, which stopped Jade right in her tracks.

"Does this dress look like it would belong to somebody?"

Jade's eyes grew, and had a vision of the future for later that day. Logan's birthday was about to turn historic.

"Is there a place in the mall that sells wigs?" Jade asks Devin

"Yes, over at "Elegance." It's near the front of the mall." She informs Jade, who grins fiendishly. "Thank you so much." She looks at Tonya, who knows that grin all too well. "Can you and Rosa go down there, and you know what I'm looking for? Morticia Adams, Elvira, Nicki Minaj. Long, straight, and black. I want Logan to meet her when he opens his present."

"Got it, c'mon, Rosa. I'll explain it to you on the way over." Tonya takes Rosa's hand as they head to "Elegance."

"Meet who?" Rosa asks Tonya while they walk.

Jade grabs a pair of black suede block heels with rhinestones on the straps and goes to the dressing room. Once she puts everything on, she turns to look at the mirror.

"Oooooh!!!!! Damn!!!!!"

"Hurray, Jade, I'm dying here." Angie was pleading for Jade to hurry. She comes out of the dressing room, which makes Angie gasp. "Oh my God, Jade. It screams YOU."

Jade comes out in a tight, satin black mini dress that only reaches her upper thigh, with the front barely covering her breasts. The rhinestones of her caged heels made her freshly painted red toenails glow brighter. As they looked in the mirror, everything shot into Jade's head. The signature, being called Mrs. Brodie, the family picture with the girls, and her status on Facebook. She went even further. She was in her husband's arms, watching her two little step daughters under the Christmas tree opening presents. Jade then remembered the last thing her mother told her on that hot July day, carrying her duffle bag and walking out of her bedroom for the last time. She headed towards the front door when she spotted her father sitting in the dining room with his hands covering his face. She took one last glance at him and didn't look back. Jade walked out the front door where her mother stood.

"You will always be Godless." Robin snaps at the girl who was formerly her daughter. A sixteen-year-old Jade just smiled and turned to her.

"No, I'm limitless, fearless, relentless, and most importantly, ROBIN!!!! I'm motherless!!!"

She turned her head, putting on her aviators, plugging in her ear pods, and playing "Building a Mystery" by Sarah McLachlan on her iPod while walking out of her parent's life. Jade opened her eyes, coming back from the future and the past. She looked at her attire, checking herself out. She had always dressed provocatively for herself as a rebellious statement. Now, she was doing it because her man loved it.

"Angie, I need to tell someone this. Can you please keep a secret?" She asks while looking at her reflection.

"Of course, tell me anything."

"Remember when I told you about July 8th?" Jade reminds Angie.

"Yes. That's the day of your emancipation from your parents. You called it your "Liberation Day.""

Jade turns to look at Angie with a large lump in her throat. Angie had a hint of concern because Jade never looked so serious. "It's going to be the day I propose to Logan."

Angie burst into laughter, wagging her finger. "Ok, Jade. Not this time." Jade didn't even budge.

Angie froze in shock, barely getting out the words. "Seriously?"

Jade pauses and lets out a deep breath, taking her hands. "I want to marry him, Angie. I can't be more serious when it comes to Logan. I purposely wrote Jade Brodie on that bill at the Nest, and when Wendy called me Mrs. Brodie, it was the most beautiful sound I had ever heard. I am so in love with that man. He's gone this far. I know he will always have a part of Renee, but I feel he is ready to keep going with me. I can't go one day without ensuring he's happy and safe. Please, please don't say a word. Not even to your sister."

Angie is seeing a side of Jade probably no one has ever seen. At the same time, though, she worried so much for Logan. She agreed with Jade that he's gone way and beyond with moving on, but simultaneously, she wondered if this was too fast and Logan would fall back into a world of despair and pain.

"Jade, I…"

"We got it!!!" Rosa and Tonya yell out, returning with a black wig.

"Hallelujah!!!! Devin, you can start ringing us up."

"You got it, Jade!!!" Devin complies.

Jade grabs the wig and scurries back into the dressing room while Angie goes pale white, still trying to comprehend Jade's bombshell. She walks out of the dressing room, transformed into her stripper alter ego, Dani California. The girls look at her like a luminous revelation.

"Hello, Dani!!!!!!!" Tonya says while Dani gives her a luscious wink.

"Logan is going to freak!!!!!"

"No, Rosa, he's going to get whiplash after I'm done with him!!! Can you ladies do me a favor and drop me off at Brodie Tower? I will see if Logan can pencil in one more meeting today."

Jade grabs her phone and dials Sasha. "Hey beautiful, what's up??"

"Overwhelmed with jealousy and sadness because I'm not there spending my boss' money with you girls." Sasha bluntly tells Jade her disappointment.

"Ahhh, but I got you something nice."

"Ok, awesome. What's up?" Sasha perks up.

"When is Logan's last meeting?"

"2:30." Jade checks her phone to see it's 1:45.

"Can you schedule another one for him at the last second? He's got a woman who's eager to meet him."

Sasha smiles, figuring out what Jade had in mind: "Yes, I can. I'll have Rick buy you some time."

"YES!!!! I'll see you soon; love you, girl!!!!" Jade hangs up and turns to look at the mirror, putting on red wine lipstick. Oh, Logan Brodie, you think I'm full of surprises? This one is going to be Biblical."

CHAPTER 27

MISS CALIFORNIA

The girls drive to the front of Brodie Tower to drop off Jade, who just finished applying more eyeliner.

"Girls, this was one of the most epic days ever."

"You think Logan will make this an every birthday tradition?" Tonya asks. "Sweetie, after what I'm going to do to this man, this will be a monthly tradition." The girls laughed, except Angie was still unresponsive.

"Well, time to give Logan his birthday present and rock his world along with his spinal cord. Love you, girls!!!"

"We love you, Jade." Tonya and Rosa scream out.

Jade gets out of the Escalade. She slips on her earbuds and puts on her Michael Kors sunglasses. Right before she heads to the front revolving door, she turns on "Rumor Has It" by Adele from her phone. Dani California was going to start rumors strutting down the lobby of Brodie Tower with a Louis Vitton purse around her left arm and carrying a Nordstrom's bag on her right. Her hips swayed with every step, dressed like a movie star, with her Jimmy Choo heels echoing through the lobby floor. The looks, the double takes, and the glances were endless as she flowed sensually throughout the building. Who was this woman in black? Her head was up, her walk was filled with attitude and flare, and her presence was felt with every look beaming at her. Soaking it all in, knowing the innuendo would spread like a brush fire. She reached the security desk checkpoint before the elevators and ran into a familiar face.

"Hello, ma'am. Do you have an appointment?" Robby asks, not recognizing that this is the same woman ready to cut him down to her size. Jade lowers her glasses, showing her sexy, smokey rebel eyes. He remembers their previous encounter, and a nervous, intimated feeling goes through him. "Oh, hello, Miss Murphy. You, you have clearance to his private elevator over there. Go right ahead." He says stuttering.

Jade smiles as she puts her glasses back on and heads to the elevator without saying a word.

Before she could press the up button, her conscience told her she had unfinished business with Robby. Jade never had a problem with being a bitch. This wasn't that time. Especially after seeing the fear in his gentle eyes. Jade taps pause on her earpod and returns to the security podium, taking off her glasses. She looks up into his feared eyes.

"Robby, I am so deeply sorry about threatening to kick your balls through the uprights. You were just doing your job and you didn't deserve that." She lightly presses his hand. A rush goes through him like she had magical powers. "Please, don't be afraid of me. I'm ninety-five percent angel. That five percent, though, whoa." She whistles. "Fresh start?"

A small nervous smile goes on his face with a slight nod. "Yes, Miss Murphy."

"Call me Jade, and lower your head." She says, putting her glasses back on. With a questionable look, Robby did what she asked. Jade gently gives him a kiss on his bald head before heading to the elevator. A huge smile glows on Robby's face.

"You look lovely today, Jade," Robby says.

"No shit!!!!" She agrees, pressing the button for the top floor. "You're a jewel, Robby."

She unpauses her phone as the song plays on while being shot up straight to the 76th floor. Jade reaches the top floor and struts to Sasha's desk. She sees Jade in amazement.

"Wow!!! Girl, look at you." She tells Jade.

"I have many times today, thank you." She says with her deep, alluring voice, getting into character. "My name is Danielle." California. You may call me Dani, and I don't have an appointment with Logan, and whatever upcoming appointments he has, I would cancel them." Sasha plays along.

"Well, Dani. He had to step out for a few minutes, but you can wait in his office."

"Thank you so much. A token of my appreciation." Before entering Logan's office, Jade drops the Nordstrom bag onto Sasha's desk. She hears Sasha scream, pulling out a Valentino Garavani handbag from the other side of the door.

"Oh, my God!!! It's so beautiful!!!"

Jade quickly opens the door, sticking her head out, breaking character, giddy from Sasha's reaction. "I'm so happy you love it. How much time do I have?"

"Five minutes, ten at most."

"Lovely!!!!" She slams the door. Ten minutes later, after sharing a scotch and a joint with Rick on the roof, Logan heads back to his office. He reaches Sasha's desk.

"Hey, Sash, I've got to make a few calls, and we're done. It's my birthday. I own this place and this company, and I say we get the hell out of here." He says exhaustedly.

"Not so fast. You have another meeting, and she's waiting in your office." Logan was exasperated as he looked up at the ceiling.

"No!!!! Where did this come from? There weren't any meetings after two on the schedule.

"Yeah, I penciled her in at the last second, and before you kill me, you want to take this one." Logan exhales as he brushes his hair in frustration.

"Ok. What's her name?"

"She didn't give a last name but called herself Danielle."

"Alright. Let's get this over with."

"Wait, open your mouth," Sasha commands while Logan gives Sasha a baffled look. He complied anyway while she sprayed Binaca into his mouth to remove the bourbon and pot breath. Logan looks at Sasha, confused, as he opens his office door. He sees a woman with jet black hair from behind with a faux fur coat facing the city, holding a glass with clear liquid and two ice cubes. He notices his bottle of Grey Goose on his desk. "Who is this woman, and why is she drinking my Vodka?" he asks himself.

"Uh, Danielle, is it?"

She slopes her shoulders and the coat falls to the ground, exposing her angel wing tattoo, and quickly whips her black hair around.

"You may call me Dani." She says in a voluptuous, husky voice.

The air was ripped out of his lungs, and he felt utterly paralyzed by the sight of her. She was as beautiful with black hair as she was blonde. He relished every second of observing her beauty. Logan notices his chairs are rearranged.

"Hello, Dani." He can barely utter with the frog in his throat.

He tried to compose himself, but after taking a few steps, he tripped over his feet and caught himself. Dani slowly walks toward him. That dress had a tight grip on his sanity. The dress plunged down to her belly button. God only knows how she didn't flash anybody by every step. The clicking sound of her heels was a deafening crescendo inside Logan's brain, and Dani knew it.

"Don't you just love that sound?" She walks down and notices the bulge in his pants. Dani rubs on his tip with one of her nails. "Apparently, you do." She snickers as she walks around him, putting her hands around Logan's collar. "I heard it was somebody's birthday. Thirty-four, hmm?" Logan couldn't even speak. He just nodded. "What's wrong?" She says in his ear softly. "Pussy got your tongue?" The chills and the goosebumps took over Logan's body as he breathed a collective sigh. "What's on your mind, handsome?"

"Praying that this shortness of blood in my brain is not from a stroke because I can't even remember my name right now." Dani lets out a devilish laugh.

"Oh, darling, the only stroke you'll have are the ones into me. So, sit down, don't touch, keep your mouth shut, and keep your eyes wide open. Trust me; you will be doing a lot of praying because you will say His name a lot when I'm done with you."

If Jade wasn't femme fatale enough, Dani was femme fatale on steroids and Adderall combined. Logan sits down on one of the guest chairs. She leans down, grabbing the neck of the chair with her right arm. Dani had her left hand in a fist. She let loose a pair of handcuffs between her two fingers. Logan swallows, trying to put on the best Poker face, but it's impossible. He knew this woman had a royal flush with every hand.

"Do you know what this is?" She asks, jingling the cuffs with her fingers. Logan slowly shakes his head. "Absolute power." Dani goes behind Logan, grabs both arms behind the chair, and cuffs both hands tight. "Supposedly, there are seven deadly sins, but they forgot the eighth." Dani comes back forward, facing Logan, and whispers. "Me." She puts the key in her bra and then grabs his phone from his desk. She sits on top of the desk, slowly crossing her legs. Logan had an instinctive thought of breaking off the handcuffs. Dani smacks her lips and gives Logan a vampish glance while she finishes scrolling through her playlist.

"Don't just look, listen." She orders him.

"Talking Body" by Tove Lo starts playing in his office. She climbs off his desk and poses with her hands on her hips, which she knew drove Logan psychotic. Dani walks towards him, putting one knee on his hardened crotch while unbuttoning the first two buttons of his dress shirt. He tries to look down, but she lifts his chin so his eyes are directly on hers. She starts to sway her hips into his pelvis as her hands go underneath his shirt, feeling his warm, muscular chest. She gets up to turn around, slowly sitting on his lap in reverse cowgirl position as her ass slowly circles his lap. She looks over her shoulder, giving him an air kiss while grinding deep. Dani takes Logan's hands and guides them across her silky smooth legs, moving her body faster as the song continues. She starts rubbing her own breasts while gyrating her hips into his. Logan fought everything in his power not to show emotion, even though his mind was spellbound. Dani suddenly stands up, turns to face him, and rips his shirt wide open. Buttons fly, and Dani gets back on Logan's lap, thrusting into him harder and harder. She lowers down and licks from his chest to his chin with just the tip of her tongue. She grabs his head, getting as close to him as possible without kissing him when the song ends. Logan's heart is about to burst out of his chest. He breathes deeply over and over.

"That was something." Logan softly tried to catch his breath. Dani's eyes look down to Logan's crotch and notice a wet spot.

"Obviously." Logan closes his eyes in embarrassment while she uncuffs him. "Well, I guess he's done for the day. Happy birthday." She grabs her purse and puts her sunglasses back on. "See ya."

Dani starts to walk towards the office door when Logan quickly gets out of his chair. Logan turns Dani around and surges his lips onto hers. His lust blows up as he lifts her, carrying her into his loft. Dani's tongue rolled inside Logan's mouth as she gasped for every breath. Her body heat intensified, being pressed against his. Logan lowers Dani onto the bed, taking off his sportcoat and torn shirt. He flips her over. Logan yanks her silk thong off of her while she positions herself on her knees. She looks at him over her shoulder with a sizzled stare. Logan pulls her silk thong off. Dani looks at Logan over her shoulder.

"Fuck this little bitch, big dog."

Logan wets his lips as he pushes her dress up. He then saw it. "You keep me loved, I keep you untamed." written in a Sans Serif font. He couldn't believe what he was looking at.

"Wait, you got a tattoo for me?"

"Do you like it?" Jade immediately breaks character to ask. She turns around to face him. "What do I get the man who can get anything he wants."

Logan slumped down, overcome by his birthday present. It would be a constant reminder of the life she's given him. He knew right then that their playtime was over.

"Take the wig off." He whispers. Jade was shocked.

"What? Why? You don't want to fuck Dani?"

"No, I don't want to fuck Dani." He responds immediately. "I want to make love to my Jade."

Logan snatched the breath out of Jade. She took her black wig off, and Logan gently stroked her smooth, blonde hair front to back, drowning into her eyes. He stands her up and promptly unzips her dress as it falls to her heels. Jade sits on the bed and slowly unbuckles his belt and kisses his ripped stomach. Taking one second at a time, Jade slowly took Logan's pants down. She looked at him without lust or want but of pure love and heaven.

Jade pulls herself to the middle of the bed while Logan's body hovers over her. He starts to kiss from her stomach to the center of her bare breasts. Jade shuddered from every tender kiss as her craving was unbearable. The power of desire was boiling over her, wanting him deep inside her. Yet, this time, she embraced time.

"Please, Logan. I want you. Right now." Logan brushes her silky cheek.

Jade gently guides Logan's straining core into her soaked heat. She closes her eyes in beautiful completion. Logan pushed very slowly as he kissed her neck inch by inch. Jade gasped slightly at every soft, tender drive from Logan. She never felt so clear in all the years she practiced yoga and meditation. She was elevated into a different world as her mind and body connected in such a way.

"Are you…?" She interrupts him

"Yes!!! Oh my God, yes!!! Three times. I've never felt this before. I can't even scream." She could hardly get the words out.

"Kiss me the next time it happens again." He says while driving deeper into her.

Jade nods, not being able to speak. A minute later, she felt another orgasm build again. She grabs his face and softly kisses Logan's lips. She lets out a slight whimper as her orgasm builds stronger. Jade closed her eyes tight as she took in every pulsating contraction. One orgasm after another was more powerful than the last. She holds Logan tight as he lays his head next to her neck. The power from the orgasm was so strong a tear came down her face when she opened her eyes. She quickly wipes it away. Logan lifts his head to look at her. "Again, Logan. Again. Please."

Logan smiles, looking at her. He pulls himself back and sits on his knees. He lifts Jade's left leg over his shoulder and slowly pushes hard inside. Her right leg brushes his ribcage with every gyration. Even her spiked heel scraped against his thigh. Logan didn't even notice. Their rhythm was perfectly in sync with every motion as Logan kneeled to kiss Jade in the softest, most sensual way. Something freed inside of Jade. It was a sweet surrender to just pure passion. Logan kisses down his neckline while taking his hand and gently caresses two fingers into her. Jade started shaking, trying to fight the urge to take control, but she forced herself to let go and embrace her man to just love on her. Each gentle stroke as he kissed her softly simultaneously put her in an indescribable world. It was the most beautiful feeling she ever felt.

"Logan, I'm begging you. I can't get enough, please." She asks earnestly.

Logan looks at her angelically. "Never beg Jade. I'm always yours." He lifts her onto his lap, slipping into her as she pushes her hips up and down into him. She was so soft and smooth, her legs wrapped around Logan's toned body as she slowly grinds her pelvis into him. He sat as he let her take control of him, looking at her, enjoying every breathtaking second as her eyes were closed, soaking in every slow thrust. Jade opens her eyes, which are locked into his devotion. She arches her back; Logan kisses her pink nipples as she groans deeper. The air was coming out of them faster, with the sensation building quicker. He pulls her back, sitting up, facing each other.

"We're doing this together. I can feel it." Logan says.

"I can feel it, too. Oh my God. This can't be real."

Jade clutched the back of his head when he pulled in her hard, and he couldn't hold off. What he didn't know was neither did she. He lifts her slightly, cupping her ass and pushing it into him. She shoves her mouth into his lips, sucking his tongue when they both let go of themselves at the same time simultaneously. He collapses his body on top of hers. Both of them experienced a majestic release at the same time. Jade collapsed with Logan's head on her chest, looking at the ceiling. Her past started to flash in her head. She thought about her past lovers. Suddenly, there was something she hadn't felt before. Insecurity and fear started to hit her. Logan was the man of her dreams and the man she wanted to spend her life with, but something was eating her up inside.

"I've never made love before." She revealed. Logan looks at Jade in wonder.

"What do you mean?"

"I've never done it that slow and soft." Jade sits up, trying to wrap her mind around what she just did. Logan broke down a barrier of hers that she thought was unbreakable." I need to confess. I was a little hesitant about telling the world about us."

Logan's face was filled with worry. "I did pressure you. Jade, I'm sorry, I just wanted…"

"No, no, no, no!!! I'm glad you did because I don't want to hide us either. People are going to start digging into me, into my past." Logan grabs Jade's cheek.

"Whatever it is, you can tell me anything." Jade knew that phrase was a toss-up for most people, but she knew Logan was genuine. She took a deep breath.

"Do you know how many men I've been with?"

Logan's eyebrows went up, not knowing how to answer. At the same time, he was afraid to know the answer. "Jade, I don't need to know…"

"Three. Only three." Logan's eyes darted up. "You're shocked, I know." Jade chuckles. "That's right, slutty looking Jade Murphy has only had sex with three men. C'mon, don't deny it. You're surprised."

"I'm not going to lie. I'm a little surprised. You never had a one-night stand when you bartend or stripped?"

"No. Not one time. I have built and saved it for that one man. Also, I do love it rough."

"Yeah, evidently. Not that I'm complaining." Jade chuckles.

"First, there was Tommy Nash. I met him junior year in high school. He was the star defensive end for our school. I lost my virginity to him after homecoming. Suddenly, he dumped me through a text, "I'm done with you." That's all he said. Never spoke to me ever again." Logan's heart ached for Jade. "Second was Eddie Hendricks. I met him sophomore year at CSF. I thought we had a good thing going. That was until I walked in on my fellow captain of our cheerleading squad going down on Eddie in our locker room. Logan went from heartache to his blood boiling. He was ready to hunt down these two pricks and spend the rest of his life making sure their lives were a living hell. "The third guy, though. The charm, as they say. He owns a business, has two beautiful children, and has the same name as Wolverine." Logan smirks. "Do you know what this guy did to me that no other man ever had?"

"What did he do?"

"He gave me hope that I thought I lost forever. He treats me like an angel. He's like a human vibrator. He's the first man I ever moved in with." Jade gets out of bed and heads toward the window, looking at the Seattle skyline. "Logan, I caught Eddie cheating on me the same month you lost Renee." Logan can feel his heart being ripped apart. The fact that she was going through the death of her relationship with Eddie. "The thing is, I refuse to change for any man. I have too much pride in that. It took me so long to find out who I truly am, and I will never lose that because I've gone through too much shit."

She turns to look at Logan. "Tommy and Eddie couldn't handle my strength or spirit because they were the alpha males with the "It's my way or the highway" attitude. So yes, I do get afraid I'll be too much for you sometimes. I know I'm not everyone's cup of tea. I'm a Long Island Iced Tea." Logan gives her a slight chuckle while giving Jade a somber look. "I sometimes worry you'll regret me like Tommy or Eddie or…" Jade pauses to get the words out, "My parents did. Get this straight, Logan: I want you, but I don't need you. I hope you understand that. I've done too much for too long on my own."

She turns back at the window, looking out Elliot Bay, when Logan slowly gets out of bed and walks towards Jade, folding his arms. Standing behind her, she was hoping Logan understood where she came from. Logan knew why she wanted to let everything out. It was all about trust since so many people took it away. Survivor was a moniker she owned and wore like a championship belt.

"Jade, you say the most inappropriate things. You confuse my mansion with the Playboy mansion in how you dress. You have the most carefree attitude I've ever seen. You curse more in one day than Joe Pesci did in "Goodfellas." Most of all, you are a Laker fan." She smirks. "Jade, you have to promise me since I put us out there for everyone to see and for this relationship ever to make it."

Logan unfolds her arms to take her hand and turns to face him. "You have to promise me you won't change a thing. I want you and all of you. I love your inappropriate comments because you're one of the funniest people I've ever met. I love your outfits because," Logan pauses, "Well, I can go on for hours on that one, so we'll skip that. I love your carefree attitude because you're fearless. I love that you're a Laker fan, even though I've despised them my entire life because what's better than a hot girl who loves sports?"

Jade couldn't stop smiling. She strokes his cheek. Logan gently kisses her wrist. "Jade, I've had my past drag me down to hell for so long until you came along and pulled me out of that hell. You gave me a present and a future. I need you way more than you need me. That's why I wanted us out there for everybody to see so they can say, "That's the woman who saved Logan Brodie." I want the world to know that you're not mine, but I'm yours."

Jade slowly shook her head. Logan gave her something nobody ever gave her—a safe haven just to be Jade Murphy.

"I love you, Logan Brodie. I love you so much." She shook in relief. Logan slowly turns her around to face the window and hovers over Jade, wrapping his arms around her small frame. He lowered himself down with his eyes peeking from behind her head. Jade sees their reflection through the window. Chills go through her entire body at what she sees.

"Do you see what I see?" He asks, looking at their reflection. "The king behind his queen looking out at his kingdom. Always know that." He softly says in her ear. "I'll stand here not making a move unless you let me, but know my sword is in my hand." A shiver went through Jade while he smoothed his hands up and down her soft, gentle arms, feeling the comfort she'd been craving.

"Take the queen home. She's got a fashion show to perform tonight for her king." Jade puts her dress back on and turns to Logan. "Can you zip me up?" Logan grabs the zipper but stops at the tattoo.

"Wait, I want to see my present again." Jade smiles as she pulls her dress back down to see her bare back facing Logan. He shakes his head, reading her beautiful quote. He sits on the bed and pulls Jade's waist towards him so he can kiss every word on the tattoo. Goosebumps go all over her as she trembles all over her body. "There's no way you could ever give me something more perfect than this." Jade turns around and strokes Logan's hair.

"I'm so happy you love it, baby. By the way, you know I can't top this. Next year, I'm taking you to Olive Garden." Logan nods in agreement while pulling up his jeans when Jade scopes out his perfectly toned back. "So, when are you getting your first tattoo?" Logan swallows, knowing he has something to confess to her.

"I hate needles, Jade." Logan lets out.

"Oh, my big, brawny man is a pussy." Logan rolls his eyes while Jade consoles him, remembering Max's tattoo. "No fear, baby. No fear. Remember all those tattoo suggestions I had? I thought of a perfect one for your first. My face inked on your entire back." Logan rolls his eyes as he turns off the lights in the loft. "It'll look beautiful, of course, and I'll always have your back."

"Let's go, Jade." He orders her out. They leave the office and see Sasha packing up for the day and filling her new bag.

"Neat purse, Sasha," Logan exclaims. Sasha and Jade look at each other, giving each other a crazy stare that says, "This bag cost $1,500, and all he can say is "Neat purse."

"Where's Dani?" Sasha asks. Jade wraps her arms around her man, grinning and marveling at his eyes.

"Somebody missed his girl." Jade wraps her arms around Logan's waist. "We'll see you tonight for the little birthday boy's party." Jade pinches Logan's cheeks like he was five. Logan then reached around and pinched her ass for good measure.

"We'll see you tonight." Sasha watches them head to his elevator, shaking her head, mesmerized at their chemistry. Before Logan could press the down button, Jade had a vision in her head and quickly stopped Logan from pressing it. The lobby was surrounded by people who got to meet Dani. Now, it was time for them to meet Jade.

"Logan, do you have your ear pods?"

"Of course, they're right here." He taps his coat pocket.

"Put them on and hand over your phone." At this point, Logan was getting the hang of Jade's unpredictability. If she asks you to do any off-the-wall task, you don't bother asking; you just do it. Jade goes to his playlist. She prepares "My Type" by Saint Motel, handing him back the phone. She does the same thing on her phone. "Don't press play until I say so." She hands him a pair of Aviators matching hers. "I got these for you today. Put them on." Jade proceeds to press the down button. Logan gives her a crooked grin before putting on his glasses. They both enter and press the first-floor button. "Look straight, keep your head up, hold my hand, and walk with me like you own the place."

"I DO own the place." He tells her, giving Jade an awkward look. She turns to look at him, lowering her glasses to her nose.

"That was until I walked in." Logan lets out an exasperated sigh, completely turned on with her confidence. "Press play now."

Logan knew precisely how long his own elevator took to reach the lobby from the 76th floor. He saw an opening and took it. Logan pulls Jade into him and hungrily kisses her. Her body felt on fire while she twined her tongue against his, grabbing a fist full of his tight, vigorous ass. He gently swiped his hand against her smooth, silky thighs. The elevator slows down as it descends to the lobby. They quickly pulled each other away and looked forward.

"Now, show off your new gold trophy." Jade grins diabolically before walking out together hand to hand when the doors open. The power couple strutted forward, not before saluting Robby and the other guards at their post. It was Logan's turn to feel the glances and the stares. "That's the girl he posted on Instagram.", "She's beautiful!!!", "Logan looks so happy." Those were some of the lines he caught people mouthing through his sunglasses. His smile beamed on him as the pride flowed through him, holding this enchantress, this definition of beauty's hand, through his building. Jade could feel his energy through her. Feeding into holding the man who gets her, who loved her uncontrollably and unconditionally. They reach the front entrance when Logan turns Jade and dips her, kissing her to show everybody at Brodie Tower he's alive and crazy in love.

CHAPTER 28

2 TIMOTHY 4:7

Logan and Jade had the mansion all to themselves while the girls had a slumber party at Rosa's place. But Logan was lying in bed, finally reviewing Jade's resume with his eyes bugging out of his head.

"You graduated high school with a 4.4 GPA, you got 1570 on your SATs, double Master's degree with honors in Psychology at CSF, and you speak seven languages?"

"Jade says in French: Juste un peu. Translation: Just a tad."

"Wait a second!! You were invited to join Mensa?"

Yeah, but when they invited me, I was heading to Coachella. So you know, priorities."

Logan closes his eyes and shakes his head, knowing only Jade would pass a once-in-a-lifetime opportunity to join a society for geniuses for one of the biggest music festivals in the world.

"Jade, why haven't you gone after your doctorate? It would be such a breeze for you."

"Maybe, one day. After college, I just wanted to mess around, live in Vegas, and work the bar circuit, and I loved every second of it. No regrets whatsoever."

"That's what I love about you. You do whatever you want."

Jade stretches her arms, chuckling. "I got to be me." She goes into the bathroom and closes the door. Logan sits on the bed. "Looking at your S.A.T. scores, I'm a total drooling idiot compared to you."

"Yeah, but look at the bright side. Us geniuses orgasm a lot more." Jade yells through the closed door.

"Yeah, I guess I got that going for me." He says, agreeing with her point. He looks at Jade's resume while he checks his watch for the sixth time. "Mensa, I cannot believe…" Logan stopped when Jade came out of the bathroom completely naked with her arms behind her back. Logan is spellbound by her beautifully toned physique, wanting to devour all of it. He tosses her resume onto his bedside table.

"What are you up to, beautiful?" Logan's demeanor changes immediately when he sees Jade looking nervous, swallowing the lump in her throat. He didn't think that was even possible. She pulls a velvet blue box behind her back and kneels to one knee. Logan goes wholly frozen in shock, stumbling on his words. "Jade, what are you doing?"

Jade reaches out her arms and pulls the top of the box. In it was a Damascus steel Claddagh Irish ring. She exhaled deeply, looking up at Logan and laying her cards on the table. "There's something I need to ask you."

{Flashback: Three Weeks Ago}

"Well, time to give Logan his birthday present and rock his world along with his spinal cord. Love you girls!!!!!"

"We love you, Jade!!!!" They scream when she exits the Escalade.

After Jade closes the Escalade door to give Logan his little birthday show, Angie is about to drive the car but hesitates.

"OH, MY GOD!!! This was so much fun!!!!" Tonya shouts out.

"I know, it was perfect. I'm telling Alex we're going on a date Saturday night, and I'm going to wear my "I dare you not to fuck your wife" dress and…"

"Jade is going to propose to Logan!!!!" Angie yells out, gripping the steering wheel. She quickly turned around to the backseat where Tonya and Rosa were sitting. Angie felt guilty about breaking Jade's promise but worried more about Logan's mental state. Rosa and Tonya look at each other until Tonya closes her eyes and lays her head in the backseat.

"Let me guess, Angie, July 8th?" Tonya lets out.

"Yes!!!"

"God Almighty, Jade!!!!" Tonya says, aggravated, covering her face.

"What if we try to convince her not to," Rosa suggested.

"Not a chance, Rosa. When Jade has an idea, she's a runaway train. Jesus, I never thought she would go through with this." Tonya grabs her temple.

"I promised her I wouldn't tell but she put me in a quandary here," Angie says when a horn honks behind her to move. She starts to drive.

"Wait, let's think about this. Maybe we're worried over nothing. What if Logan is ready to get married?" Rosa tries to be rational.

"Or he may not be ready. We don't know, but this can't blindside him. For Christ's sake, he had a mental breakdown over Renee just a month ago. This could put him over the edge. I just don't know if we should take that risk." Angie says.

"Yes, but honestly, have you ever seen Logan this happy since he met Jade? Look how much she's changed him." Rosa tells her sister.

"And what he's changed in her. Back in the day, Jade would vomit at the thought of marriage. I visualized Jade being best friends with McKenna and Madison, but she's been their mother. She called me the second she met him, and the Jade I knew was gone. After the hell that girl has gone through, I didn't think it was humanly possible." Tonya shakes her head at the change in Jade and how proud she is of her.

Angie and Rosa felt the same about Logan. That the ghost of his marriage would strangle him forever until Tonya's college roommate came along with her magic wand. The three saw the finish line, but monstrous hurdles were coming their way. Rosa looked at her phone to check on the baseball game.

"Well, the M's game ended an hour ago, so everybody should be home. We'll talk to the guys when we get home. We just can't say anything in front of the kids."

"I'll keep them busy and show them the dresses we got at the Disney Store, but they need to know immediately and develop a game plan."

When the girls got home, Angie and Rosa gave Clinton, Cortez, and Tony a rundown of Jade's plan in the kitchen while Tonya kept the kids entertained in their room. The guys exhaled deeply, thinking the same thing the girls thought in the Escalade. This was a game of Russian Roulette. Clinton looks out at the lake, remembering when Renee was sick.

"I've missed this side of Logan so much." Tony says. "Marriage, though? I just don't know." Tony sees Clinton looking out the window with his arms folded at the lake. What do you think, captain?" He asks Clinton. He just shook his head, not being able to find answers himself.

"It's like when Arthur pulled Excalibur out of the stone. He was destined to be the chosen one. We know she is Logan's Excalibur." Cortez stood by the refrigerator with his head down, feeling conflicted along with everyone else.

"What about, Shorty? Her mom and dad treated her like trash. People have judged her entire life because of her personality. That poor girl barely had any support. Jade did everything on her own. Logan is the only guy who's treated her like a queen. You're right,

C." Clinton turns around to face Cortez. "She is the chosen one because this isn't just an act of God. This is an act of Renee.

We can't sit and do nothing if he freaks out."

"What do we do if he has another breakdown?" Tony wonders.

"We'll take care of it. It's Jade I worry about." Angie answers.

The uncertainty was killing everyone. How much could Jade take if he rejects her proposal? Would she leave? They were all thinking the same thing. The ones who would suffer the worst were the children.

"Look, he needs to enjoy his birthday first. He hasn't had a good one in a while. We'll tell him Monday before he goes to Olympia." Clinton tells the Crew, who nod in agreement. When Monday came around, Logan didn't go into the office since he was going to meet with the governor in Olympia. Clinton waited until Jade and Rosa took the kids to go grocery shopping when he knocked on Logan's bedroom door.

"Are you decent, son?" He asks while his stomach is filled with nerves.

"Yeah, come on in," Logan says, splashing some cologne. Clinton sits on the bed, rubbing his hands together. Next to giving up drugs, this was the hardest decision Clinton had to make. The image of seeing him in that bathroom room was plaguing his mind, especially imagining him alone without Jade to hold him.

"We got to talk about Jade," Clinton yells out. Logan comes out of the bedroom with a wondered look.

"What's up?" Angie and Tony dash into Logan's room together, not wanting Clinton to do this alone.

"I think we should be here too."

Logan had a confused look on his face. He never saw his Crew with a more concerned look since they told him they had to rush Renee to the hospital for the last time. He felt like he was in the middle of an intervention.

"Could someone please tell me what the hell is going on? What about Jade?" He asks with a harsh tone.

"Logan, I need you to be ready for this," Clinton warns Logan as his body tenses up. "Jade told Angie that she's planning on proposing to you in three weeks."

Logan rolls his eyes, thinking they're joking since he never heard of a woman proposing marriage to a man. "Guys, I don't have time for your jokes. I've got a meeting with the governor." He heads back to the bathroom, not giving a second thought. The thing was, their silence pulled him back. He walks back to see them not cracking.

"You're not kidding." Logan's words, along with his body, tightened. They all shook their heads. In an instant, his anxiety was climbing to a critical level. Even though he was the happiest he'd ever been, marriage was the furthest on his mind. Pain and fear were hitting him hard. The fear of betraying Renee, the fear of the unknown, and most of all, the fear of losing Jade if he said no.

"What are you thinking, son?"

Logan couldn't even look at them. It was impossible to hold a single thought as a million of them were going through his brain. He pulled his head back in disbelief and didn't know what to do next.

"Logan, please say something," Tony begs, watching his boss and good friend unravel before him. Logan freezes after taking a deep breath with his eyes closed. "Call Sasha; I'm not going to Olympia. I…" Clinton stood while watching Logan zone out as he did in his office bathroom. "I have to go see her. I have to see her. Right now, right now."

He continues to ramble when he immediately leaves his room. The Crew follows close behind, worried about what he would say to Jade.

"Wait a minute, Logan. You have to think this through." Angie tries to reason with him.

"I have, and that's why I need to talk to her. I have to talk to her right now." He grabs the keys to the Shelby.

"Stop, Logan; you've got to realize what you're doing," Angie yells as Logan opens the front door.

"Seriously, bro, it's not fair to Jade to confront her about this," Tony says. Logan stops in the middle of the threshold with the door in his hand. He turns to look at all of them.

"I wasn't talking about Jade!!!" Logan yells before slamming the door.

Clinton, Angie, and Tony are stunned, all having the same thought. They hear tires screech, and the engine roaring from the Mustang can be heard outside. Moments later, Cortez runs into the house, returning from filling up the limo, just missing Logan by seconds. He looks at each of their worried faces.

"Now what?" Cortez asks.

"We have an idea where he's going, and you better tail him," Clinton informs Cortez. Being Logan's bodyguard and best friend for eighteen years, Cortez always had a good read on Logan's next move.

"Renee?" He asks. Clinton nods to Cortez, who immediately bolts out the door and goes after him in the limo. Clinton looks at Tony and Angie.

"When Jade gets home, not a word about this. Ang, text your sister and give her a heads-up. We cannot have her suspect anything." The both of them nodded as Angie texted Rosa. Clinton let out a long sigh, rubbing his bald head in frustration. "Goddammit, Logan!!!!!!"

For over three years, Logan has driven to the front entrance of Calvary Catholic cemetery but never gained the courage to make it past the front gate since the funeral. The feeling of a sinking heart hit him as he sat in the Shelby. He looked at the half dozen roses he bought lying on the passenger seat. They were the twenty-seventh set that sat on his passenger seat, never making it to the gravesite. At this point, he would reverse the Shelby and drive off. This time, though, he turned off the ignition, grabbed the roses, and walked the quarter mile to Renee's gravesite. The nausea was more substantial with each step he took. Logan looked down at the pavement when he started to retch, dropping to one knee and dry heaving as everything in his head was in a haze. His face was going numb, and he was trying to catch his breath, thinking he was having a heart attack. "You're going to see her. You're going to talk to her. You will do this for her." He kept repeating to himself.

When he got composed, he looked up to see the cemetery filled with limos and cars lined up for miles. Hundreds of people in black gathered together to say goodbye to someone beloved.

From a distance, Logan recognized Renee's casket, which was overflowing with roses and lilies. A tear escaped knowing he was a football field away from her. Their relationship flashed stronger in his head the closer he got. The day they met, their graduation, proposing to her on her birthday, standing on the cliffs of Mohr as husband and wife, her father taking a picture of them after McKenna was born, holding her hand when the doctor told her she would only have three months to live, collapsing on her lifeless begging her to know she was the best wife a man could have. The tears started raining when he saw Sandra holding a newborn Madison in her arms, Tony with his head down crying with Bridget, and Rosa and Angie crying in each other's arms. He felt life get sucked out of him when he saw himself approaching the casket carrying a three-year-old McKenna with Clinton and Cortez behind him. She clutched hard around her daddy's neck and buried her head on his shoulders, not baring to look where her mother was lying. He put her down and asked her if she wanted to kiss Mommy. McKenna nodded. She ran towards her mother's casket, quickly kissing it, then back in her daddy's arms, putting her head back on his shoulders, hiding as she wailed. Logan quickly closed his eyes, remembering the echoes of McKenna's cries haunting his head, feeling her warm tears go down his neck. He let out a deep sigh before opening his eyes.

Suddenly, there were no cars, no people, no rose-covered casket. He was all alone again, holding nothing but stems. Logan looked down to see flower petals on the ground, realizing he had accidentally crushed them in half. He picked up the top halves and headed towards a bench in front of her four-foot tombstone with a picture of Renee with a Bible verse from 2 Timothy 4:7: "I have fought the good fight. I have finished the race. I have kept the faith." Born March 14, 1987-Died May 5th, 2017. Logan sits down, trying to get himself to open his mouth.

"Hi," He tries to clear his throat. "Hi, Renee. I know I…" Logan pauses for a couple of seconds, struggling to come up with anything. "I know I haven't been around in a long time. Sorry about the flowers." Logan placed the roses and stems on her tombstone. Once he touched that smooth marble, he completely lost it. The tears flowed down his face again, collapsing right before it. The guilt exploded into him. From not letting go, feeling like a failure to his children, and, most importantly, the fear of losing Jade. His voice muffled as his face was buried in the grass. "I'm a coward, Renee." He looks up, gently stroking the tombstone. "There's no excuse why it took me so long to get here. I'm so sorry. I know you know about Jade. I love her, and she wants to marry me. The pain won't go away, though. I cannot find peace, and it's unfair to Jade. She's amazing. She loves the Crew." Logan starts sobbing, clenching his shaking fists. "She loves our daughters. They're so beautiful, Renee. She loves me, but I don't deserve it. I don't know how to let you go. I'm drowning here, honey."

Logan just couldn't make sense of any of it. He had fallen in love again and could proceed with his life, but that darkness pulled him back to square one. A familiar engine sound got his attention. He sees his limo approaching. Logan gets up quickly, wiping his tears, and sits back on the bench. Cortez gets out and walks behind Logan.

"What are you doing here?" Logan whispers without looking. Cortez walks to sit on the bench next to Logan.

"There was a rumor that your white, stubborn ass finally made it out here, so I had to see it myself. Continue chatting. I won't bother you." Logan was quiet, not knowing what to say to Renee with Cortez there.

"Man, Jade is a hot piece of ass," Cortez says, stopping any train of thought from Logan. He quickly turns to Cortez, incensed.

"SERIOUSLY??? ARE YOU OUT OF YOUR FUCKING MIND???" Logan yells when he realizes what he just said. "Forgive me, Lord, Renee." Logan quickly does the sign of the cross before looking back at Cortez with intense fury. "Why would you say that?"

"I'm just stating a fact. She's hot as hell." He started snickering. "Could you imagine Renee wearing half the shit Jade wears? Her cut-offs, bikinis, and that tiny top she wore at Rogue with the leather mini that made her ass go "BOOM!!!!"" Cortez laughs while Logan looks at him, wondering where his sanity went. "They could not be more opposite of each other. Well, except for a couple of things, I guess." He turns to look at Logan. "They both love you so much. They both love those kids. They both love me and the Crew."

Cortez puts his hand on Logan's shoulder. "I love you, brother, but I'm going to be doing some shooting on you." Cortez takes off his shades and stares right at Logan. "Do you think she's up there saying, "Don't move on, don't be with her, stay miserable in front of our daughters?""

"She's talking to you right in front of you." Logan looks at the Bible verse on the tombstone. A feeling of openness hits Logan. "You haven't finished the race yet. If you lose Jade, you lose the fight. The same Jade who threatened to kick big Robby's ass if he didn't let her see you when you had your little breakdown? Did you know that?"

Logan slowly shook his head. He even gave a light chuckle seeing Jade doing that to Robby. "The same Jade who paid tribute to your late wife, a woman she's never met so all of us can honor her together."

Logan turns his head to his trusted friend. "She did not have to do that. That little blonde girl is obsessed with you and those kids, and I know you are obsessed with her. Call me a liar." Logan nods his head. "We all felt it between you two from the get-go. The bottom line is this. I'm returning the favor when you saved my life in high school. Now I'm saving your life." A tear comes down Cortez's face as his voice cracks. "The day before Renee died, she called one last meeting with the Crew." Cortez cries harder as Logan cries along with him.

"What? What did she say? C'mon." Logan pleads with him. Cortez wipes his tears away.

"She asked for her final wish. For us to help you find some-one—a 180 of her. Renee wanted you to have your memories of what you two had but, simultaneously, live a different life so you can move on and continue the race. It's all set up, Logan. Think about it. Why did Jade move to Seattle? She was drawn to you. God was just setting up the chessboard. Sandy retiring the way she did, and then Clinton met his niece's best friend, who just moved here and needed a job. Now, six months later, you are so close to checkmate. Your parents and Renee are watching, saying, "You're almost there. Keep the faith and finish the race.""

Never in his life did Logan feel so conflicted about his future. Reeling at the fact his late wife wanted his Crew to play match-maker. A few weeks ago, he started practicing yoga with Jade and the kids. He closed his eyes and started doing the meditation tech-niques she had taught him. A cool breeze blew into his face as clarity and a gentle cleanse went through his head as sudden visions of Logan holding hands with Renee on the beach in Barbados. She turned to him, stroking his face while gently letting go of his hand. Renee continued walking without him turning around to look at her husband one last time. Her silky brown hair flew around her, smiling at him. Logan had a confused look, wondering where Renee was going. Before he could ask, Renee stopped him.

"Don't worry." Renee looks over his shoulder and smiles wide. "She's got this."

She smiles at Logan one last time before walking along the beach without him. He turns around to see Jade from far away with her back to him. She slowly turns her head, giving him an angelic smile while her blonde hair whipped from the Caribbean wind. Logan immediately snaps back to reality. It was the same vision that stopped him from killing himself. An abundance of peace came onto him. He takes a couple of deep breaths, collecting himself.

"You OK, man?" Cortez asks.

Logan couldn't even look at Cortez. With a huge smile, he felt ultimate clarity. "Yeah, I am." Logan stood up and walked in front of Renee's tombstone. He placed his hands on the gray marble. "Okay. I got your message." He slowly swipes his fingers across the Bible verse. "The answer was right here all this time." He pulls out his wedding ring from his pocket. "I'll always have you here and in our girls." Cortez stood up and put his arms around Logan's neck. "I know I have angels around me." Both start to tear up, tapping Cortez's hand on his shoulder. "I love you, sweetheart." Logan kisses her tombstone and lays his forehead on it. He separates himself from the tombstone and walks away toward the limo. Cortez lays his head on the tombstone and whispers to Renee.

"I think we got through to him. Rest in peace now, beautiful. We love you." Cortez sees Logan standing behind the limo with his hands in his pocket, reflecting and knowing there is nowhere to go but forward. He looks up at the overcast sky when another strong wind hits his face. Cortez leaned back next to him.

"Serenity is awesome, isn't it?" Cortez asks while Logan gives him an awkward gaze.

"She's got you doing this yoga thing, too?" Cortez laughs.

"What's our next move?" Logan starts nodding his head with a huge grin growing.

"Project Qwest. It's a green light." Cortez quickly whips his head to look at Logan. His mouth slowly falls.

"Motherfucker."

"Exactly. Spread it. Get everyone ready. You know where I'll be."

"It will be done." Logan turns to Renee's gravesite one more time. "She's pretty special, Logan. How many other wives would ask to help pimp out their widowed husbands?"

Logan looks at Cortez, not holding back the laughter. They laugh uncontrollably when they try to embrace a bro hug. They both hit shoulders when Cortez pulls Logan in for a long, brothers-for-life hug. They both think of the long, dark road it's been, but now that road is clear. They both separate from each other, looking at Renee's grave together. "She's one of the greats," Logan tells Cortez.

"So is Jade. Now, let's do this thing. Do you want a ride to the Shelby?"

"Nah. I've got another person to talk to."

Cortez gets into the limo and starts heading off. Logan walks back, looking at the gray sky with hope, optimism, and unadulterated happiness. He takes his phone out of his pocket and remembers his earpods were in the other. He puts them in his ear and presses shuffle on his playlist. "Unforgettable" by Godsmack starts. Logan started lip-synching like Jade while he walked with a cleanse from despair and suffering. A strong gust of wind hit Logan again. He stretched out his arms into the sky like Andy Dufrene did when he escaped from Shawshank Prison because, just like Andy Dufrene, Logan was free. He started running again, looking at the surrounding gravesites, visualizing every soul along with Renee watching over him with pride. Once he got into his car, he looked at himself in the rearview mirror.

Logan pulls the mirror view down to get a complete image of himself. "Like Jade said, we need to get along. Right now, embrace this, drink it in, and enjoy Logan. Do it for all of them. It's time to give them their queen."

Logan started the Shelby and sped off, heading for downtown. He looks at the rearview mirror, looking back at the cemetery entrance gate one last time with immense gratitude for what Renee did for him. He revs up the engine, shifting gears, and speeding, feeling unstoppable. Not just today but from now on.

CHAPTER 29

PROJECT QWEST

Clinton was talking with Ramon, the head gardener, and his team about what needed to be worked on for the week when he got the group text from Cortez.

Cortez group text: "Project Qwest is a go. July 8."

Clinton's body jolted as he read the text. He closes his eyes, sighing deeply in relief and closure. It was happening. It was real. Angie and Tony run outside screaming.

"CLINTON!!! IS THIS TRUE???? Have you talked to Logan???" Angie screams, ecstatic. Clinton tries to calm them both.

"Whoa, whoa. I just got this myself, guys. I have yet to talk to Logan, but when he does, we must ensure Jade is not around.

"We got to stretch this out for four weeks?" Tony asks.

"We're going to have to. Jade cannot suspect a thing." He warns them.

"Oh no, Rosa is with Jade." Angie rolls her eyes, worried her sister will blow her cover.

"Oh Christ, she's probably sobbing buckets by now," Tony predicts.

Jade, Rosa, and the girls were getting groceries when Rosa looked at her phone. She lets out a scream as she covers her mouth.

Her eyes immediately start to tear up. Jade and the girls were two aisles down, running to find her. Jade runs with the girls frantically.

"ROSA!!! Are you okay???" Jade asks. Rosa tries to collect herself and comes up with a lie to Jade.

"Umm... I got a notification on my phone for a special on Cap N Crunch." She says, wiping away a tear.

"Seriously? Oh my God, this is the greatest day of our lives." Jade is sarcastically excited. "I thought meeting Weird Al Yankovic at Knott's Berry Farm was the high point of my life." Jade and the girls jumped up and down as Rosa went from uncontrollable happiness to wanting to slap Jade senselessly. She takes the girls back to the other aisle. "Girls, we need to spread the word to everybody in produce about the glorious news of our treasure. Let's go!!" Jade looks back at Rosa with a silly grin.

"Yeah, wait til what's in store for you. You little shit." Rosa says under her breath.

The text went all the way to Minneapolis. Sandra's son, Chad, yells out for his mom, who is doing the dishes.

"Hey, Mom, your phone is going off."

"Can you check it, baby? My hands are wet." Sandra yells from the kitchen. Chad was puzzled reading the text.

"It says Project Qwest is a go. July 8".

The sound of plates shattering shook Chad as his mother ran from the kitchen to the living room.

"WHAT DID IT SAY???" Sandra screams, overjoyed. Chad gives the phone to his mother. She starts to cry, collapsing to the ground. "MOM!!! What does this mean?

"It means you need to book me a flight to Seattle right now."

Later that day, Logan arrived home. He was having a hard time covering the glow on his face. He sees Clinton and mouths the "Ready?" Clinton nods and gives him a wink. Logan goes into his office, where he goes into the safe. He pulls out his first wedding ring and kisses it before locking it away in his safe. He looks out the window facing Lake Washington and sees Jade and the girls with their legs crossed and eyes closed, practicing meditation together. The flashbacks returned. On the day he came back from Atlanta. That same feeling was still there. Her overpowering beauty sent shock waves of chills through his body, still feeling their first handshake.

All of a sudden, Clinton's hand gently pressed on Logan's shoulder. Logan turned his head and smiled at his godfather, sharing in the moment. Tony wasn't far behind and joined in. Rosa and Angie swooped between them, wrapping their arms around Logan's waist. Logan smiles at the both of them, lowering down to kiss the top of their heads. Last but not least, Cortez goes behind Clinton and Tony, laying his arms between them. Logan closes his eyes, feeling the strength of his family standing with him. Taking it all in, knowing they never gave up on him. They watched Jade and the kids silently, looking at the creation they helped make together.

"Logan, I think you should go out there and meditate with your girls," Rosa suggests motherly. Logan gives a slight nod, not fighting her like the last time.

"Yes, ma'am." Logan breaks away, heading out of the office. The Crew continues to look out at the young man they watch grow up, go to the three most influential women in his life. Jade, McKenna, and Madison were in a deep musing of tranquility when a strong, cool breeze came off the lake. Jade embraced it with a vast smile, lifting her head. She opened her eyes and saw her man squatting right before her like the day they met. A radiance of joy streamed through her as the girls yelled and tackled their father.

Jade says with a gleaming smile. "What are you doing back from Olympia so early?"

"I told the governor I missed my girls." Jade quickly jumps on Logan, wrapping her legs around him and kissing her softly. M&M covers their eyes. After about ten seconds, Logan and Jade wouldn't stop.

"Are you two done?" McKenna asks, grossed out. Logan breaks away from Jade's mouth. "Not yet." Jade giggles as Logan continues kissing her. He looked into Jade's eyes; he knew the next four weeks would be the longest in his life.

"OK, girls, we're not done yet, Daddy c'mon. Get your mind, spirit, and earth into you; let's go."

Logan grabs a yoga mat and sits in between Jade and the girls. He closes his eyes and starts meditating with them. Legs were crossed, palms were up, and head to the sky. Except his concentration was lost in her low-cut sports bra with his peeked right eye, Jade caught him with her peeked left eye.

"Sweetie, focus on one's soul, not my tits." She whispers.

"Sorry." Logan whispers back with a wide grin on his face.

{Present Day}

Logan was silent, seeing a naked Jade proposing marriage to him. He looked uncomfortable and was taking in deep breaths. Logan has been researching acting for beginners on YouTube for the past four weeks.

"Logan, I could never imagine what this year would bring to me. Moving here, Clinton hiring me and meeting you, McKenna, and Madison." Logan couldn't make eye contact with Jade. She knew this was a coin flip, but she loved Logan so much that she was determined to know the answer. "Logan, are you OK? I know you've gone through so much, but I think…" Logan interrupts.

"Jade. I need…" Logan was trying to get the words out, but he kept stuttering and shaking his head. "I need to take care of something." Jade had a concerned look on her face when he headed towards the door. "Please, stay right here. Just give me a minute. Okay."

Logan leaves the bedroom with Jade standing there naked with a dejected look. She sits at the edge of the bed, placing the ring off to the side and her hands over her face.

"What have I done? He's not ready." Suddenly, her head pops up when she hears the familiar sound of the Shelby's engine. "No, no, no, no!!!" She runs out the bedroom door, forgetting that she's completely naked. She runs back to the bathroom and grabs her silk robe. She puts it on, grabs her phone, runs down the stairs, and opens the front door. She sees the gate open with the Shelby speeding off. "LOGAN!!!!!! SHIT!!!!!!!!!!!!! Goddamn it!!!!!" Jade goes back into the house, slamming the front door, screaming. "FUCK!!!!!" She tries to call Logan's phone, which goes straight to voicemail. She hangs up and tries calling Clinton while she runs into the bedroom to change.

"Hey kid. What's up?" Clinton answered.

"Has that fuckin Godson of yours called you yet?" Jade screams out. Clinton pulls the phone away from his ear.

"Whoa, wait a minute. What's going on?" Jade quickly puts on a white top, jeans, and boots, her mind racing as she wonders what had just happened.

"I did something incredibly stupid. I tried proposing marriage to him, thinking he was ready. I poured myself to him. I even got naked for him, and he didn't let me finish asking if he would spend the rest of my life with him, and he ran for the FUCKING HILLS!!!"

Clinton was prepared for the wrath of Jade. So far, she was doing everything he expected her to say. He tries to calm her down.

"Honey, listen. We don't know what's in his head. Where are you?"

Jade sees the Claddagh ring on the bed and stuffs it in her pocket. She runs down the stairs and grabs the keys to the Escalade.

"I'm heading for your place because that's where I assume the asshole is going."

"I'm not at home, though. Maggie and I just went out for dinner."

When in reality, he was in the limo with Cortez driving, holding his phone with Logan on the other line. He was listening the whole time to Jade's outburst.

"Well, I'm going over there anyway because he's probably hiding under your bed, the little chicken shit." She tries to start the engine, but it doesn't turn over. She tries again, and it still doesn't start. She starts hitting the steering wheel. "You've got to be kidding me!!!! The Escalade won't start." She screams bloody murder, not knowing that the anti-theft system was turned on before Cortez left for the night. Jade looked around for the limo, but that was missing too.

"Where did Cortez take the limo? WHY COULDN'T LOGAN BE LIKE ANY SELF-RESPECTED BILLIONAIRE AND OWN FIFTY CARS?" Jade tried to order an Uber, but her app was missing.

Her fury was at a boiling point, and she was seeing spots around her. "MY UBER APP IS GONE!!!! WHAT THE LIVING HELL IS GOING ON!!!!" She screams, not knowing Logan uninstalled it that morning.

Clinton tries calming her down even though finding the lost city of Atlantis would be easier.

"Jade, I will call you an Uber. I will see you at my place."

Jade breathed deeply, trying everything in her power to compose herself. The thing was, she was losing control of herself.

"He loves me, right? Please tell me he loves me because I am so done getting hurt by these guys." Jade started shaking, not able to take the pain. "I'm scared, Dad."

For the first time in his life, Clinton was called "Dad." He looked straight at the road, visualizing holding her in that bathroom and entering into "Father mode."

"Jade Nicole Murphy, you listen to me. That man worships the ground you walk on. You brought him back to us. You!!! You gave those little girls a mother figure. You!!! You are their everything. You!!" Jade sat in the Escalade, compressing Clinton's fatherly words, desperately trying to give Logan the benefit of the doubt. "An Uber is coming in four minutes, and his name is Richie. We'll talk about this later, sweetheart."

"Okay." Jade nods, barely getting the words out.

Clinton hangs up and grabs Cortez's phone with Logan on the line.

"Did you get all that?" Clinton asks.

"Yes, I did. I may not make it alive tonight." Logan said with fear in his voice.

"No. This will be the greatest night of your life. You've been wanting to do this for years. This is your second chance. We'll meet you there." Clinton hangs up on Logan, continuing with the plan. Back at the mansion, Jade collapses her head against the driver's seat. Everything is a blur in her head. She goes to the one person who knows how to solve her problems. She adjusts the rearview mirror, not looking at the strong woman behind it but the strong woman beyond it.

"You walked through hell, and you burned that motherfucker to the ground. Nothing stops you. Nothing. No one will..." Jade stops herself. She tried convincing herself that Logan was on the list of male figures who hurt her. She remembered what Tonya said; Logan was the last of a dying breed. No man loved her more than he did. She gave him a life; he gave her a family. Suddenly, she gets a call from an unknown number.

"Hello?"

"Hi, Jade, I'm Richie; you're Uber driver. I'm behind the gate."

"Hold on. I'll buzz you in."

She swipes her phone to find the app to open the gate. She gets out of the Escalade and waits for the Uber driver. A red Jeep Grand

Cherokee comes up the hill. The driver sported a thick goatee and long hair with glasses.

"Richie?"

"That's right. Come on in."

He says in a deep, low-toned voice. Jade gets in the backseat as Richie drives away from the mansion. "How are you doing tonight?"

Jade in an exasperated tone. "Just trying to figure out why I feel my life is flushing down the toilet." Jade then changes to a perky yet sarcastic tone. "How is your day?"

"Uhh, can't complain. No rain; the Mariners won today. It's a beautiful night."

Jade shook her head, wishing to agree. Clinton and Maggie's house was located two blocks from the campus of Washington U. Jade notices Richie took the wrong highway heading towards downtown.

"Rich, what's with your GPS? We're supposed to take Interstate 5 towards Washington U."

"Uhh, no, Jade. It says to drop you off at Lumen Field." Jade has the most confused look on her face.

"Lumen Field? Where the Seahawks play?"

"Well, to be technical, where the Sounders play right now since it is soccer season." Jade lays back in her seat with her hands across her face, feeling completely confused. She didn't know how much she could take. She tried calling Clinton again, but got no answer. One question after another was shooting in her brain. "What the hell is at Lumen Field? Did she pressure Logan and scare him off? Or is he afraid of losing me?" That last question opened Jade's mind. Was Logan afraid of being a widower again? Or was she fooling herself? Either way, she had to stop making herself go insane. She decided to make small talk with her driver.

"Are you married, Richie?"

"Yup. To a wonderful girl. We're, uh, expecting."

"Congrats."

"Thanks. It took me a long time to finally accept that my wife adores me because she is so out of my league. I just go with the fact I hit the life lottery."

"I'm just not sure about anything right now. I thought I hit the lottery, too. Whenever I think my boyfriend is ready to let go of his past, his past sucks him back."

"I'm sorry to hear that. He'll come around. You're a beautiful woman, and he'd be out of mind not to be with someone like you."

Jade grins. Richie looks at his phone to see how far they have left.

"We're just twenty minutes away." Jade nods, laying back in her seat and looking at the night.

"Do you mind turning on the radio? I need to lay here and search my soul for the next twenty minutes."

"You got it."

Richie looks in the rearview at Jade with a concerned look for her. He turned on his Sirius/XM on the classic rock channel. Alice in Chains' "No Excuses" was playing. Jade changed so much in herself because of Logan. It took her so long to surrender herself to a man. He was indeed the first and only love in her life. She knew her stubbornness was uncontrollable, but her love for him was also uncontrollable. They arrived at the stadium's front entrance.

"OK, Jade. Lumen Field. I miss the old name. Qwest Field had more zing."

Jade gets out, goes to the passenger's side window, and tries to tip him a five. "Thanks,

Rich…." She pauses and notices a familiar face taking off his long hair wig. "RICK!!!!!"

Rick peels off his goatee. "Hi, Jade."

"Rick, what is going on??? Please." She pleads to him for answers. He smiles.

"You know I asked that when Sasha agreed to go out with me. I mean, the supermodel isn't supposed to be with the accountant. I was as confused as you are now, but eventually, I got my answer. The supermodel just fell in love with the accountant. This will all come together. Have a great night."

Rick drives off while Jade is alone, still wondering what this leads to. She starts walking to the front entrance when she realizes what Rick said.

"WAIT!!!!!! EXPECTING ???" She screams out with excitement in her voice. The Jeep's tires screech to a halt. Rick sticks his head out and nods. Jade smiles in shock at the notion that Sasha is pregnant. All of a sudden, she hears a disembodied voice.

"Jade Murphy???"

"Yes," Jade says to complete darkness, standing before the gate and holding the bars tight. A black elderly security guard walking with a hobble emerges from the darkness. He unlocks the gate and opens it for her. He points at the long concourse.

"Right down that way, honey."

"Thank you." She whispers.

She first walked down Lumen Field's hollow, empty halls; her mind fogged with uncertainty. Suddenly, another security guard popped out and pointed in the direction she needed to go. It got unbearable for her. She started to jog lightly. The clicking sound of her boots going through the stadium concourse was getting louder and faster. It went from a jog to an entire run as she passed another guard. Six months of memories were blowing up in her mind. Not only memories but hope because she got a life she didn't expect. A female security guard popped out of the tunnel, showing her the section to the stadium entrance. She entered the stadium's seating area through the tunnel and saw a figure in the middle of the darkened soccer field. The security guard took her down onto the field. A chill went down on her when she stepped onto the grass. The field was still pitch black when she heard a familiar voice.

"Am I that bad of a dancer?"

Jade didn't know what to think when she heard that question. Suddenly, the lights around the stadium came on. The figure got brighter and brighter. She sees Logan standing in the center circle, wearing a gray suit with his hands in his pockets. She slowly walks toward him. She didn't know what to think at that point or what to say. She had so many things she wanted to ask him. "Why did you run?", "Are you capable of moving on?", "Do you want to spend your life with me?", and most importantly, "Can you handle me?" Yet, she could only tell him, "You're horrendous." She says in a whispered tone.

Logan reached out his hand. "Let's try it slow this time."

Jade looks over Logan's shoulder and sees Clinton and Maggie walking hand in hand on the opposite end of the field, walking out of a tunnel and onto the grass. More and more came out. Cortez & Tonya carried both McKenna and Madison. Rosa, Angie, their families, Tony and Bridget, Sasha and Rick, and Sandra with her son and daughter. They all lined up right in front of the goal.

Logan still extended his hand when "Sit Next to Me" by Foster the People came on through the stadium's sound system. It was the same song playing that morning in Barbados on New Year's Day. Jade took Logan's hand and slowly danced right on the center circle. Logan Brodie witnessed many events in this building. The Sounders winning the Major League Soccer Cup, the Seahawks beating the San Francisco 49ers to go to the Super Bowl, spreading a vile of his parents' ashes onto the field during a U2 concert, but this moment was more than we could ever imagine. They danced briskly with the woman he loved in front of his extended family fifty yards away, with God and his parents looking down. Jade Murphy was one to go to the extreme with the world. To show everyone that she was in charge of herself. You either took her, or you didn't. She danced with the man who got her for four minutes and three seconds. Her quirkiness, hunger for life, and, most importantly, her iron will to be herself. Once the song ended, Logan and Jade could only hear the sound of their hearts pounding out of their chests. All of a sudden, Clinton whispers in McKenna and Madison's ears. They started yelling for Jade to get her attention. McKenna and Madison started waving their arms while they ran. "Jade!!!!! Look over here!!!!"

"What is it, girls?" Jade yells out with a confused look.

The girls suddenly stopped with their mouths dropping. It hit Jade the second she saw the girls' expressions. She slowly turned around to see Logan on one knee.

"Oh sweet Jesus!!!" She covers her mouth while tears roll down Logan's face as he holds out a black velvet box with a 8.76 carat oval diamond ring. After taking a deep breath and wiping his tears, Logan finally spoke.

"I know you wanted to ask me something at the house because this day is very important to you, but I needed to ask you something first. I was wondering if I could share this day with you since it's my Liberation Day, too. This is the day I can go on one knee for the last time with no pain, doubt, or fear because Jade Murphy took all of that away from me." Logan started sobbing, barely able to get the words out. "You're my hero, my savior, and my existence."

Jade's demeanor changed. She had a severe look on her face. Logan had never seen a more intense face on her before. He didn't know what to think. "Will you please…"

"Stop!!!" Jade interrupts with a stern tone. She closes her eyes, looking up and taking in a deep sigh. Logan's mouth went completely dry instantly when she opened her eyes, and he could feel the fire coming from them. This was Jade in control. "You just hold it right there because I have something to get off my chest. I had something very important I wanted to ask you an hour ago in our bedroom before you ran and left me hanging alone with the thought of why he's running away." Every member of the Crew tensed up, not knowing what was going to happen next. McKenna and Madison stood watching when they both held each other's hand, filled with worry. Jade sighs and shakes her head. "I guess you underestimate me because you showed me what fear looks like, except I finally dare to say this to your face." Then it happened. Her lips quivered, her voice cracked, and a tear formed before Logan's eyes as it trickled down her cheek. "I need you. I need you, Logan Brodie." Jade turns to look out at the girls and the Crew. "I need them. I need all of them." Jade for the first time started sobbing, trying to control herself as Logan retook her hand and kissed it as tears flowed through him. "I'm not going to lie to myself anymore. I always need you behind me with that sword ready for me. I need to know that you love me no matter what a major pain in the ass I am." Logan chuckles for a second but stops immediately when Jade reaches out in her pocket and pulls out the Claddagh ring she was going to give him. She kneels with him. "Most of all, I need to know if you can share this day and eternity with me." Jade couldn't control the tears. Logan wiped her cheek. He puts his forehead against hers and whispers.

"Take a deep breath, and let's do this on three." She nods. "One, two, three."

"I will." Logan and Jade at the same time.

Their smiles glisten as they slip on each other's rings. Cheering erupts on the other end of the field. Logan picks Jade up. Her legs wrap around Logan's waist, refusing to let go. She would be contemptuous to be in that position forever.

"God, I love you so much," Logan says through tears. Jade looks at Logan with more tears coming down.

"You didn't have to go through this much trouble for me." Logan looks at her with a crazy look.

"What trouble?" Jade hugs him tight as her tears keep falling.

"Oh, baby. I am so riding on that face of yours tonight."

Logan smiles, not expecting less from his future wife's response. He looks deep into her eyes.

"If it looks like an angel and talks like an angel, well then." She kisses him tight, not wanting to let go.

"Also, she has the wings to prove it." Her smile glistens when they turn to the Crew. They signal everyone to greet them. Everyone runs to the Center Circle with smiles and tears on their faces. McKenna and Madison get there first. McKenna jumped into her daddy's arms, and Madison jumped into Jade's. All four held on to each other tight as tears came down their cheeks.

"We have a family again." McKenna cries out.

"Yes, we do, sweetheart." Logan and Jade look out at everybody coming towards them. "Here they come."

They all embrace each other. The guys pile on Logan, hugging him, and the women cry, hugging Jade. One by one, they want to see Jade's ring. Angie and Rosa are nervous about approaching Jade because they are worried she is angry with Angie for breaking her trust.

"Jade, I hope you're not mad at me for…"

"I love you both so much." Jade interrupts, sobbing and shaking. She was too happy to be mad at anyone. Angie and Rosa start sobbing together.

"We love you, Jade!!!!!"

The three cry uncontrollably together. Logan sees Sandra. She raises her eyebrows, looking at him with a look that says, "What did I tell you?" They both hug each other tight.

"Didn't I tell you she was out there?" Sandra tells him.

"You were right all along." He agrees. They both look at Jade, who is showing off her ring to Bridget and Sasha.

"She's beautiful. I'm sure she's a good Christian girl, right?" Logan needed to learn how to respond.

"Oh, you're just going to love her, Sandy."

Tonya screams and jumps up and down with Jade. "I love you, bestie."

"I love you too, sweetie!!!" The girls look around the stadium, awed by the happiness around them. "This isn't a dream, right? This is real, right? Please tell me, T." Tonya grabs her face.

"This is as real as those tears, Jade. You deserve this so much, sweetie." Tonya bursts into tears of joy for Jade as she holds her tight.

Logan stood soaking in the moment. He watched Rosa introduce Sandra to Jade. He laughed when he saw Sandra embrace her with a huge hug, which surprised Jade. Logan turned around and saw Cortez standing alone, just watching for everybody, as always. He gives Logan a slight grin and a nod. Logan walked towards Cortez, hugging him tight.

"Thank you, brother." Logan whispers in his ear.

"No. Thank you for helping me fulfill Renee's last wish." Logan grinned, closing his eyes, mentally thanking Renee. "Now, I have to congratulate your better half."

Logan watches Cortez sneak behind Jade and pick her up, prompting a scream from her. She holds Cortez tight, kissing his forehead. Logan couldn't help but chuckle. At that moment, he knew it was the perfect time to signal the stadium's sound operator again. "Everybody Wants to Rule the World" by Tears for Fears continues throughout the stadium. Logan started walking ten yards away from the Center Circle, turned to sit on the grass, and watched his close-knit family dancing and laughing together. Logan Brodie started pondering the beautiful future right before his eyes. Jade turned to see Logan sitting by himself. She started heading towards her fiance's direction and sat right behind him with her arms around him and her head resting on his shoulder, watching their family together.

"You know I could have killed you for leading me on like you did," Jade tells him.

"Just look at your ring, baby." Jade looks at her giant, glowing diamond ring valued at $478,000.

"Oh yeah, all's forgiven." Jade pulls out her phone to give to Logan. "Are you ready to blow up the world and create devastating envy and jealousy?"

"Beyond ready." He agrees happily.

They kiss with her hand in front of the phone, showing off her ring. Jade then posted it to Instagram with the caption. "That's right!!! I'm marrying Logan Brodie, and you're not." Logan laughs at her caption, loving that she's keeping her promise never to change. Jade turns her body as her head lays on his lap, looking up at his handsome face.

"The tsunami is your new life." Jade reminds him of the recurring dream he told her about at Rogue.

"What?"

"The tsunami represents your resurrected life. Tonight, it just crashed on top of you. Except, you came up to the surface, and you're cleansed swimming in that water." Logan pondered what she described as the dream. He looks up to see his daughters run toward them.

"Oh God, speaking of a tsunami," Logan warns when the girls jump on top of them. Jade lets out a scream, which prompts everybody to turn.

"DOGPILE!!!!!!!!" Cortez yells out.

Everyone runs and starts piling on top of Logan and Jade. Jade then sees Sasha coming and panics.

"SASHA!!!! BE CAREFUL!!! YOU'RE PREGNANT!!!!"

Everybody froze entirely in one place and stared at Rick and Sasha, who looked horrified. Jade cups her mouth, realizing what she said.

"You're what?" Logan says in shock.

Sasha yells at Rick in complete disappointment. "You told???" Rick swallows, knowing his wife will kill him.

"I was into my "Richie" character, Jade was in a bad place, and it slipped out. Why did you make me the Uber Driver? I had to wear a fake wig and mustache and talk in a Barry White voice."

"In your defense, you were convincing. I didn't know it was you." Jade says.

"Whoa!!! Can we focus here?" Logan tries to get back on track to the bombshell.

"We just found out the other day. We were going to tell you all next week, but we just wanted this day to be perfect for both of you. I'm so sorry, guys." Sasha begins to cry, feeling she has over-shadowed Logan and Jade's engagement.

Logan gives Sasha a questionable look and scoffs.

"Are you kidding me? You know this has been my dream. I proposed to my girlfriend on this field with my family, and I just did it. I thought I would never get another chance at this, but the bottom line is, I will be someone's husband again."

Jade leans on Logan's shoulder. "And I'm going to be some-body's wife."

"And you two are going to be somebody's parents. How dare you apologize." Logan reaches down and grabs Jade's hand. "Our family is expanding."

Sasha starts sobbing uncontrollably as she runs and hugs Logan, lifting her off her feet while

Rick goes to hug Jade. Logan whipped out his phone and started recording a live video to Instagram. Everybody gathered quickly and squeezed as one. Logan had Jade and Sasha together with him side by side.

"I'm marrying an angel, my sister here is having a baby, and my family is with me in the Hawks house." Everybody in uni-son screams out, "FLY SEAHAWKS FLY!!!!" while Jade clears her throat, letting out a grunted "GO RAIDERS!!!" Logan's eyes close, dropping his head, shaking it in disappointment while the family rains down boos her way. "She may have a flaw or two, but we love her anyway. Especially her future husband." He gives Jade a soft kiss while still holding out his phone. "I just got to say to you all. The race is never over. Keep running, everybody."

Logan turns off the video and looks down at Jade. For three years, he hardly took any pictures because he didn't feel the desire to record his life. He wanted everyone to know that Logan Brodie finally felt like a rich man. A few minutes later, everyone started heading their way off the field. The girls held Logan and Clinton's hand when Madison turned around to see Jade standing in the center circle, looking up to the sky, silently praying, thanking God for pointing her toward paradise, asking Him to help her not screw up being a wife and stepmother. Suddenly, she felt a tug on the back of her shirt. Jade turns and looks down to see Madison's beautiful, sweet face. She stretches out her hand.

"C'mon, Mommy. Let's go home."

Jade's eyes lit up as tears filled up all over again. She picked Madison up and held her tight as she started to cry uncontrollably again. Logan and Clinton looked on. They waited until Jade, who was blubbering uncontrollably, could catch up.

"She called me "mommy," and I love it." Logan starts chuckling. She smacks him in the chest. "Stop laughing, you jerk. That I love so much and is going to be my husband." She continues crying as Logan and Clinton wrap their arms around Jade, consoling her as they walk off the field with McKenna in his arms.

"Don't worry, Jade. You'll get used to it." Clinton tells her.

"I better because I can't take much more of this crybaby shit."

CHAPTER 30

Seamstress for the Band
{Three Months Later}

On a Tuesday night, Cortez parked the limo before a packed Rogue. Drinks were half-price, and the DJ played "Two for Tuesdays." Cortez goes around to open the limo door for Jade. She takes his hand and emerges in a red silk top with a black high hip side slit skirt and red strappy caged heels. Her blonde hair was tightly curled, and her plumped lips were coated in scarlet; she walked towards the long line with Cortez in front of her. The sounds of "The Bitch is Back" by Elton John from the club grew louder with every step. The people in line parted like Moses to the Red Sea. She didn't look at anybody, and her intimidating smokey eyes were locked directly forward while she walked with a straight purpose. The doorman lifted the rope immediately once she got to it, not letting her stop. Her back arched with her breasts leading the way, taking her strides through the dark hallway with every person turning their heads to her. She cut through the dance floor and headed to the bar, where a tall, built figure became more visible. Everyone at the club followed her as she approached his stranger. Once Jade reached the bar, the stranger lifted his head, feeling her presence. Jade taps him on the back and arches her body with her hands on her hips.

"Would it destroy your precious male ego if I told you that I know how to take care of myself, that I don't need your money, your power, and your masculine energy to fight my wars? I will always be the queen of me? Now, bow down and acknowledge her."

He slowly turns his head to face her. Mr. Brodie instantly gives her a smug look. He removes the straw from his Macallan neat and places it between their shoes, drawing a line in the sand. She just stares at him, standing her ground. He looks down at her and says in the most patronizing, arrogant voice.

"Then why do I smell your need? You need my power when I slam you up and down on my lap like a pogo stick. You need your limbs trembling, your soul shaken, and your limits pushed. I will open your door, earn your trust, and support you because you need that. At the same time, I will smack you in the ass, I will fondle you in public, and my lips are for your lips and between your legs only until I draw my last breath." He fires her down with lust. Jade's nostrils flared, and her heat pulsed through her.

"Oh, you're good!!!" She snarls with fire in her breath. Mr. Brodie turns back to Logan, gently taking her hand and kissing her knuckle like the queen she is.

"Good enough to have Her Majesty's permission for this dance?" He gently asks. "Tiny Dancer" by Elton John starts on. She takes Logan's hand and leads him to the dance floor, stepping over the tiny straw. The patrons at the club part for both of them, leaving the dance floor to Logan and Jade again. They slowly danced together, listening to Sir Elton describe an L.A. lady who was a seamstress for the band. Their eyes danced together along with their bodies. Right before the chorus hit, Logan firmly grabbed her hips and lifted her. Her arms and legs wrapped around Logan, holding him close, locked together face to face.

Once the song ended, they were both thinking the same thing. He walked her out of the club with her body attached and her hungry eyes never leaving his. They come out outside Rogue; Logan places his hands off her hips onto her ass, marking her territory for every guy to see. Jade turns to look, and all the women give Logan a seductive lick up his cheek to say to all the single ladies, "Look what's MINE!!!" They walked towards his Shelby. Logan opens the passenger door for Jade. She slowly gets in, not taking her torrid eyes off of him. Before he closes the door, he takes a few seconds to admire the view. Especially when she crosses her slit leg over to the other side; he closes the door and enters the driver's seat, putting the key into the ignition.

The Shelby's engine rumbles when Jade jumps onto Logan's lap, diving into his mouth, inhaling his taste while undoing his buckle. She pulled his jeans down while adjusting her dress, mounting his groin. Jade heaves herself while grabbing a handful of his neck. A deep rush went through her body from every forceful thrust in such a cramped space. Every window fogged, sweat pouring through the both of them. Logan looks deep into Jade's intense gaze when he slowly stops thrusting. "Why did he stop? Stop teasing me!!!!" She thought, looking at him, who had a playful leer. When somehow, a bolt hit Jade. She quickly lets go of Logan's neck and presses her hands on the roof. She cried out, feeling the hum hitting below her waist. Another shot went through her. She leaned back against the steering wheel, pounding both fists against the roof while another jolt hit. Looking confused, she feels a cramp inside her building. He smiles, just watching her have an orgasm without doing a thing. Her breasts ached, and her body strained. She was so close. Her fists went white and numb from squeezing the blood out. His deviant grin grew more significant when one last rush of her passed through her tightened body. Her eyes slammed shut, and her screams flew out of her lungs. Suddenly, her eyes darted open.

Jade was no longer in the Shelby, and daylight was all around. Her body was melted in a Brooklinen down comforter in the softest Egyptian cotton sheets. All of a sudden, that sensation hit her again. She moaned and started to bite her lip, exhaling in and out. Logan crawls out under the covers to see his fiance's satisfied face.

"Good morning, my beautiful birthday girl."

He crawls back under the covers and continues giving her his birthday alarm clock. She looked joyfully, placing her hands behind her neck and lying relaxed.

"Happy fucking birthday JADE!!!!" She screams out her name and shudders when Logan hits that sweet spot. After a good birthday orgasm, Jade lays alone in bed on a cool, crisp October morning, going through her phone, which was already flooding with texts and notifications wishing her a happy birthday, when Logan and the girls came in carrying a tray with eggs Benedict, toast, coffee and a Mimosa.

"HAPPY BIRTHDAY, MOMMY!!!" McKenna & Madison run to the bed.

"My girls!!!" she kisses both their rosy cheeks. Thank you so much." She looks at the beautifully made eggs Benedict brought up by Logan. "Wow, baby, you did this?" she gleams. "Well, I started, then failed miserably, so Tony bailed me out. I did butter the toast, though." Logan places the tray between Jade's legs, kissing her.

Jade gasps sarcastically. "You were on butter duty. I am so proud of you, Logan." Jade clasps her hands together. "Did Tony let you pull down the little lever on the toaster, too? I mean, that is a big responsibility, you know."

Logan playfully squints his eyes, chuckling at his fiancee as she pulls his head for another kiss.

All four sat in bed while Jade ate her breakfast. She had a busy birthday agenda. After taking the girls to school, she headed to Gas Works Park to meet up with an old friend of hers.

"Jade!!!" Aurora shouts.

Jade was finally putting her degree to good use. She became the new counselor for the children's hospital. It was nice to get some pull since her soon-to-be husband owned the hospital. Of course, she did it for free. Three days a week, she met with kids and their parents, helping them cope with their struggles and guiding them psychologically. Today, it was Aurora's day. She ran and gave Jade a big hug. While hugging Aurora and her mother, she knew she had found her true calling.

Around one, she met up with Tonya, Bridget, and Maggie to find her wedding dress. She tried on seven dresses, but one thing was the same on each. The beautiful future stared back at her every time she stood in front of that mirror. After the last dress, she grabbed her phone to text Logan.

Jade text: "I'm ready to marry you. RIGHT FUCKING NOW!!!!"

Logan text: City hall, Vegas, Paris. You name it. I'll call Captain Jacobs, and we'll do it anywhere today."

Jade visualized Logan's low-key first wedding with Renee in Ireland with just their parents and the crew. Low-key was something Jade wasn't. She looked back at the girls drinking champagne and laughing together while skimming through other dresses. She knew she had to wait. Not just Logan but M&M and the Crew deserved an extravaganza.

Jade text: "No, I'll be a good girl. I can't wait to be a bad girl to you tonight."

Logan text: "I know we're anti-threesomes, but what about you and Dani getting together? I promise to share equal time."

Jade grins while texting him back: "No, I get more time than that black-haired bitch. Unless they invent cloning from here to February, then we'll talk. XOXO"

After a few seconds, Logan sends her kissing emojis. Jade got a case of the giggles that came regularly. Before getting the girls, she stopped at Espresso Vivace for a late afternoon boost.

"Can I get a Vanilla Latte with three shots of Espresso to go?" She orders.

"Can I get a name?" The barista asked.

"Jade." She waits a couple of seconds. "Brodie". She writes the name on the cup.

"That will be $4.60." Jade hands her a twenty when the barista whispers to her. "Are you the one marrying Logan Brodie?" Jade lets out a slight grin and nods. The barista looked around to see if her boss was around. "Please, can I see the ring?" Jade couldn't turn down her new fans. She flashes her ring to the barista, who's mesmerized. "Oh my God, I just love it." She hands her $15.40 in change.

"As well you should." She drops her change into the tip jar along with another fifty for complementing her ring. "Seriously, thank you. Have a blessed day, beautiful."

"Thank you, you too." The barista glows from Jade's generosity.

Jade was getting her shares of the mixed press. She got a "Golddigger," a "Skank," an "Opportunist," along with a "Princess," an "Angel," and an "Inspiration" from social media. She starts the Escalade, looking forward to hearing her new favorite word. "Mom." Once she arrived at the school, she heading towards Madison's preschool class, and saw that Logan had signed her out at one o'clock. She went to Madison's teacher, Miss Mary.

"Hi, Miss Mary. Logan already picked up Madison?"

"Yes, he and McKenna got her. He didn't tell you?"

Jade looked out into space, rolling her tongue against her cheek. What were they cooking up?

"No, he did not. Huh, that's very strange. Thanks, Mary."

"Bye, Jade."

Jade grabs her phone and tries calling Logan, but it goes to voicemail. She starts texting him with a grin on her face.

Jade text: "What shenanigans are you three up to?"

Logan texted back with a devil emoji. Jade imagined what they could plan for her birthday and whether it was possible to top his proposal. Her anticipation grew stronger when she started heading home. She flies out of the Escalade when she sees the limo in the driveway. Her heart was going to explode out of her chest.

"Hello?????"

Clinton walks down the stairs wearing a 2020 World Champion L.A. Lakers shirt. "Hello, sweetheart."

Jade was shocked because that's not what he wore this morning. He kisses Jade on the cheek.

"Hey, umm. Three things. Where are those three, what are they up to, and why are you wearing a Lakers shirt that looks fantastic on you?"

"First, he took a short day and picked them up early, and second, it's a surprise; and third, it's your birthday. Jade turns her head and gives Clinton a suspicious squint.

Rosa and Angie come from behind Jade, wearing Laker caps. "Happy birthday, Jade!!!!" Jade gasped after the girls startled her. She gasped again when she turned around and saw the Lopez sisters, lifelong Chicago Bulls fans wearing Lakers caps.

"Oh my God, thank you. You're all wearing this for me?"

"Of course. St. Patrick's Day, we're all Irish. Cinco de Mayo, we're all Mexican. Today, we're Laker fans." Angie grins.

"Now, if the Bulls play them on your birthday, you're shit out of luck." Rosa informs her.

"That goes the same for my Nets." Tony, a lifelong Brooklyn Nets fan, emerges from the kitchen sporting a Lakers skull cap.

Jade shakes her head. "You guys, did Logan put you all up to this?"

"He may have." Angie smiles. "Oh, while you were gone, an envelope was on your nightstand. Jade's eyes grew suspecting it was from Logan.

"Is it a present? Is it a present?" She screams like one of the girls on Christmas.

Rosa and Angie's eyebrows rose. Jade bolts upstairs to her bedroom, over-excited, making squealing sounds. Sure enough, there was an envelope waiting on her nightstand. She tears the envelope and pulls out five front row/center courtside tickets to tonight's Lakers/Trail Blazers game in Portland. Jade lets out an ear-splitting shriek.

"Turn around, Jade." Cortez tells Jade, who's recording her reaction. She sees him wearing a Magic Johnson jersey with a grin. "Bossman wanted me to record this."

Jade jumps up and down, screaming. She charges Cortez and jumps into his arms, wrapping her body around him.

"Oh, my God!!!" She grabs Cortez's phone, which is still recording, and points it to herself. "Oh, you're getting my ass tonight!!!"

Cortez takes the phone away from Jade, "Ok, I think that's a good place to stop right there." He shuts off the recording. "Happy birthday, Shorty, but we've only got fifteen minutes."

"I need to change. I need to change. All I need is five. All I need is five." She jumps off Cortez and runs to her closet, quickly getting undressed. It only took her ten seconds to figure out what to wear. She found something to show her team spirit and to distract Logan from watching the game. She grabs a studded yellow Laker's tube top, a black blazer, shiny black latex pants, and a pair of purple stiletto pumps. She jets out of the closet and runs onto the bed, pulling her pants with all her might and gritting her teeth. After zipping them up and putting on her pumps, she admires herself in the mirror. She thought about her birthday the year before. She was celebrating it at an IHOP with her Topaz girls after a shift. She remembered blowing out a candle on her New York cheesecake pancakes, wishing to find "Him." Cortez knocks, snapping her back into reality.

"Shorty, you ready?"

"Yeah, c'mon in."

Cortez walks in and checks Jade up and down. His eyes grew. "Damn, Jade!!! Not bad."

Jade sarcastically sounded unsure about her attire. "Yeah, I don't know, Cortez. Do I look good in this? Will this be appropriate for the…" Jade bursts into laughter. "God, I'm a hot, little crack-up.

"Logan is going to go crazy when he sees you." Jade takes her hand and gives herself a good self-spank. The sound of the tight latex goes through the room.

"He's going to be put in a straight jacket when he hears that." Jade chains her arm around Cortez's, and they walk downstairs. About halfway down, she sees the Crew waiting for her at the bottom of the stairs. Tony holds a slice of Baked Alaska with a candle, and Rosa holds one of Jade's large plastic tube glasses from Vegas. Angie had a tiara on a pillow, saying, "26 going on 69". They started singing "Happy Birthday" while she descended the long, curvy stairway.

Her heart was fluttering rapidly, overcome by the love of her fellow Crew members. She shakes her head in disbelief when she blows out her candle.

"Did you make a wish, young lady?" Clinton asks. Jade gazed into his eyes, smiling while shaking her head.

"No point."

"Well, here's a little something for you to pregame on the way to the airport along with this. I hope you love it." Tony presents her with a picturesque Baked Alaska, which took him hours to make. Jade kisses Tony on the cheek, knowing how much hell he went through to make it. make. Rosa then hands Jade a long tube cup.

"I followed your recipe. Forty-nine percent Grey Goose, forty-nine percent Peach Schnapps, and two drops of orange juice." Rosa hands her the tube cup.

"A Fuck on the Beach!!!" Jade takes a big drink. "Phenomenal. My liver is tingling and pleased."

Cortez takes the plate and her drink. "We need to get going, Shorty."

"Okay. Thank you guys so much."

The Crew watches Jade and Cortez head out the front door. She stops right when her hand hits the knob. The first day flashes before her eyes. She couldn't remember the last time she was ever instantly accepted. Behind her were five people who meant everything to her.

"Every time I drive past that gate, I feel like I'm in another realm of reality." She turns to look at them. "I was slinging Vodka bottles to become a mentor to two little girls. Meeting their father who is…." Jade struggles for the perfect word for Logan, but it is damn near impossible. "A wish coming true. Then there's you five. You have done NOTHING!!! NOTHING!!! But open your arms to me, embracing me since day one without asking, "Who is this, and what's her agenda?" Tears rolled down her face. "You gave me a family. You are my family. GODDAMMIT!!! I DON'T KNOW HOW TO STOP CRYING NOW!!!" Clinton chuckles.

"Come here, sweetheart." Jade runs into Clinton's arms, burying her face into him, sobbing. They all got together for another group hug, which was the routine by now.

"I love my fellow Crew." Jade says in a muffled voice while still buried in Clinton. He pulls Jade away from him to face her. He wipes the tears from her like a father.

"Sweetheart, we're your crew now."

It never sunk in for Jade; much stayed the same three months after getting engaged. It was already second nature for her. Rosa holds her shoulders.

"You're the queen of the castle now." Jade looks around. All of them nodding.

"We've been waiting for you, Jade," Tony adds.

"Now get out of here and have a great birthday with your family," Angie tells her. Jade embraces everybody together.

"C'mon, sweetheart, they're waiting for you." Cortez pulls her away from the Crew.

"Okay, okay. I'm going. I swear."

"Go, Lakers!!!" The Crew yells out together. Jade chuckles, raising her glass before closing the door. It took twenty-five minutes to get to the tarmac of Sea-Tac. Jade sees Logan and the girls holding hands, waiting for her in front of the jet. She exited the limo with her cup, which was halfway gone. The girls break from their dad and run to Jade, hugging her tight. His body tremored seeing her game attire.

"My M&M's!!!" She screams out seeing them in matching gold Laker jerseys with "M&M 14 & 17" on them.

"Do you love your present?" McKenna asks while Jade holds her.

"My first Laker game with my family. I love it so much." Jade tells her, elated.

She looks up at Logan, walking towards him. She was relieved Cortez and the girls were close by because if they weren't, she would have shown him her appreciation for her birthday present on that tarmac. She licks her lips, her libido at an all-time high seeing him in a gray Bruno Cucinelli suit. Logan holds a gift bag up for her.

"We made something for you."

Jade couldn't contain her excitement when she saw a new purple Lakers jersey. She turned it around to see Mrs. Brodie #21 on the back. Jade squeals in excitement.

"Oh, my God!!! This is just too much!!! I can't…" Jade went frozen in complete shock when

Logan slipped on a Lakers cap. With her mouth to the ground, she looked at her cup. "I must be really drunk." Logan gives Jade a grimacing, painful look. "Oh my good, good God!!!!!! This is the greatest birthday of my life."

"I'm so happy you love it." Logan gives her a slight smirk. Jade wraps her arms around Logan.

"You feel dirty wearing that, don't you?"

"I want to shower so badly, but seeing your smile, I'll wear it forever."

Jade kisses Logan while the kids get anxious on the jet.

"Can we go now, guys???" Madison begs.

"Yes!!! Let's go!!!"

Jade takes Logan's cap off, puts it on backwards on herself, and hops on Logan's back.

"Take me to the jet, my stud!!!"

"How many giggle juices have you had?"

"Umm, almost one. Have some." Logan sucks on the straw.

"Oooh, a..." Jade interrupts him.

"PG, Logan."

"Futz on the beach."

After a short half-hour flight, a limo awaited them at Portland International to take them to the Moda Center. Jade couldn't contain herself when she got out of the limo. Once inside the arena, Cortez walks ahead, holding both girls' hands. Logan and Jade are right behind them, with Jade clinging onto Logan's arms and giggling nonstop. He notices the endless glances and looks Jade was getting. He never felt so invisible.

"You're not jealous, are you?" Jade reassures Logan.

"Nope." Jade smiled, loving that he had no hint of jealousy. Her dream from earlier in the morning was still fresh on her mind. Jade decided to make another dream come true.

"Good, now grab a handful of latex to show everyone I'm yours."

Logan grinned as he stroked his hand across her smooth latex-covered ass while they walked through the concourse. They go to an elevator with a guard standing before a velvet rope. Logan shows him the tickets, and the guard lets them proceed. Jade was trying so hard to look composed but was screaming her head off on the inside. The elevator goes down underneath the Moda Center, and the five start to walk up the same ramp the players come out of. An usher escorts them to their seats in the middle of center court. Jade looks all around, soaking in the atmosphere.

"Well, birthday girl, what do you think?" Logan asks. Jade gives Logan a heated gaze with her seductive brown eyes like she will rip his clothes off him.

"I hope you heard that telepathically because the kids are around, so we'll need to devise an excuse for why their father is limping in the morning."

Logan plastered a kiddish smile, imagining who would score more points after tonight: the Lakers, the Blazers, or him. After the opening tipoff, Jade and the girls go completely crazy. Especially when Lebron James had the ball. With three minutes left of the first quarter, the scoreboard shows the Kiss Cam capturing Trailblazer fans kissing.

"You know there's no way they'll show us." Jade yells out.

"No sweat, we'll come up with our own. Kids, kiss Cortez." Logan gets out his phone. The girls stands next to Cortez. He leans down, and they kiss both cheeks. Logan starts snapping away while Jade covers her mouth in awe. "Ok, girls, now kiss Mommy." The girls go to Jade and kiss her cheeks. Cortez sneaks in and kisses the top of Jade's head while Logan snaps, smiling ear to ear. "Love it!!! It looks better with purple and ..." Jade raises her eyebrows. "Championship gold." She nods in agreement with his choice of words. Suddenly, the kiss cam on the Moda Center's scoreboard hits directly right on Jade and Logan. Jade is stunned since they're cheering for the visiting team. She kisses Logan while a chorus of boos from the Portland crowd hits them. After they kiss, Jade can't control her excitement. She looked at Logan, knowing he had something to do with that.

"How much, Logan?" She wonders.

"Oh, a lot." He stretches the truth when making a $25,000 donation to the Trailblazers Boys and Girls Club.

Logan could only focus on the game in the third quarter's closing minute. Not just for Jade's wardrobe but watching Jade jump up and down with M&M, fist bumping Cortez, screaming at the refs, and trying so hard from cursing. His heart blew up like fireworks in the sky, watching his woman enjoy her birthday. The horn goes off at the end of the quarter. Jade grabs her cup of beer and takes a chug. She sees Logan looking at her.

"What are you staring at, hotty?" She asks him.

"Perfection. My beautiful fiancee is drinking a beer, watching her boys on her birthday, wearing those pants." He shakes his head, overwhelmed by how hot she looks. "Those two angels sitting there with that teddy bear of theirs," Cortez smirks. "I'm just the richest S.O.B. alive with you four here."

Jade puts her beer under her seat. She stands and takes his hand. Logan stands with her. She loops her arms around his neck.

"Let's show everybody in this arena how rich you are." Jade flutters her eyelashes at Logan.

She kisses Logan in front of everyone. Some random Trailblazers fan two rows back yells at them.

"Hey, Laker fans, get a room!!!!!!!!" Jade quickly turns to the guy. The horns and the tail were forming in her.

"Hey, Blazer fan, look up there!!!!!!" She yells, pointing at the Blazers' only championship banner from 1977. "WIN ANOTHER TITLE!!!! 43 YEARS NOT LONG ENOUGH FOR YOU!!!" That shut the Blazer fan up. "Fucking asshole!!!!" Jade and Logan winced, realizing she had cursed in front of the girls. They both look at the girls, who are giggling. "Sorry girls, Mommy has a potty mouth."

"It's OK. We're used to it." McKenna says.

Cortez laughs as Jade walks toward the girls and kisses both of them and then Cortez on the top of his bald head. The fourth quarter starts. Jade sits down, tucks her arm underneath Logan's arm, and lays her head on his shoulders, closing her eyes and sighing.

"You're right, baby. This is perfection."

Lakers power forward Anthony Davis stands in front of Logan and Jade when he is passed the ball. He shoots and hits a three-pointer.

"Nice shooting, A.D.!!!" Jade screams.

Davis looks at Jade and then gives her a double take while running to the other side of the court. Logan and Cortez immediately sit up in shock.

"Ummm, did I just see Anthony Davis...." Cortez asks in disbelief. Jade interrupts ballistically.

"YES CORTEZ!!! Anthony Davis rubbernecked me!!!" She grabs her heart. "OH, MY GOD!!!! GREATEST BIRTHDAY EVER!!!!!!!" She turns to look at Logan, who has his arms folded and his feet crossed, looking relaxed. She lays her head on his shoulder. "You're still not jealous, right?" He slowly turns to look at Jade with stone-cold eyes and says in a gravel voice.

"I'm richer than A.D.." Jade swallows, hearing Mr. Brodie's voice.

"Uh, Mr. Brodie, he's coming..." Mr. Brodie quickly interrupts and nods.

"Over and over and over." He leans his mouth to her ear. "Wait until what I have in store with your ass." Logan pulls away nonchalantly, returning to watching the game. Jade freezes, thinking of the visual Logan gave her. She grabs an empty cardboard cup holder from under her seat and fans herself while rolling her eyes, looking up at the rafters. Her 26th birthday was the pinnacle of birthdays. Logan kisses her head as they watch the rest of the game locked together. After the game, they headed back to Seattle. Jade's smile never left her, even though the Lakers lost 106 to 101. She snuggled beside Logan, staring down at McKenna and Madison, sleeping on their laps.

"Are you alright?" Logan whispered, concerned.

"I'm fantastic; why?" Jade whispers back.

"Well, the Lakers lost. I was expecting more profanity and stopping at an Occult store to get a voodoo doll for the refs before we get home." A satisfying grin hits Jade's face.

"Not this time. I just sat in Jack Nicholson-type seats watching my Lakers and A.D. rubbernecking me. I did all that with my fiance, stepdaughters, and brother/Biggie Smalls doppelganger. They both look at Cortez, passed out in his seat, snoring. "Then tomorrow morning, I get to see my father, my sisters, and my other brother." Jade brushes the top of McKenna's head, looking down at her. "Nothing in this world could possibly bring me down."

She shakes her head in disbelief at how this turned out for her. Ironically, Logan was thinking the same thing. He couldn't help but gaze at this remarkable force of nature. Not one single day went by that he didn't thank God for her. Jade Murphy showed him what power and strength was. It is just his one shot to live and not take it too seriously. Most importantly, she taught him to bury the hatchet with himself. Jade turned her eyes to that man who showed her that someone out there allowed her to be her unconditionally. She found the treasure she was looking for. She didn't need a compass or a pick ax, just a Toyota Camry. They feel the jet's landing gears come down as they descend back to Seattle. Logan looks out the window.

"Hello, beautiful," Logan says to the Seattle skyline whenever he comes home. Jade sees the lighted-up Seattle skyline, taking a deep breath, thinking back at what Logan's father told him when he was a young boy. His family would be complete with a queen to reign over their Emerald City. She turns to look at her man with a soft smile.

"Before us, our kingdom." She turns to look at the skyline once again. "Let's rule, baby."

"We will, tiny dancer."

Her eyes go wide. For a couple of seconds, Jade thought she was going crazy, wondering why Logan would call her that, especially since what she had dreamt that morning. Yet with the life Jade Murphy has led, she just shrugged her shoulders and just fucking rolled with it.

ABOUT THE AUTHOR

James Sullivan is an emerging author based in Fayetteville, Arkansas, originally from southern California. With a background in retail spanning over two decades, Sullivan found his true calling during the pandemic when he was struck by inspiration for a romantic novel centered around two individuals from contrasting backgrounds. After pouring his heart and soul into the project for nearly four years, Sullivan's debut novel, "Edge of Resurrection," is now available for readers to enjoy. When he's not writing, Sullivan enjoys spending time with his wife and two daughters, who all have a passion for traveling, and is an avid sports and pop culture connoisseur.